ENDORSEMENTS

"Nancy Potter's recounting of the lives of her great-grandparents recreates the bayous of Louisiana and the boardrooms of New York City in such detail that you'll be transported back in time and to places you've never been. Her characters' struggles and successes will inspire you. It was particularly exciting for me to read about these people who lived at Oaklawn Manor as I have for many years. The town of Franklin, Louisiana, has felt indebted to Captain Barbour since the Great Depression when he renovated Oaklawn keeping so many townspeople employed."

–Mrs. Mike (Alice) Foster,
Former First Lady of Louisiana 1996-2006

"*Barbours Cut* is a literary journey that captivates the reader from the onset, weaving a rich tapestry of triumph, emotion, and wit. Following the remarkable rise of Clyde Barbour, this enthralling tale not only entertains but educates, providing valuable insights into seizing opportunities and navigating life's complex paths. The fusion of romance, suspense, and humor breathes life into a rags-to-riches story that resonates with real human experience. Clyde Barbour's wisdom and humanity make him a relatable and inspiring figure. You won't want to put this book down; it's a guide and companion for anyone seeking to flourish in life with grace and intelligence."

–Peggy McColl,
New York Times Bestselling Author

"Nancy Potter draws on a wealth of family history to bring this unique story to life. It is the rags-to-riches story of her great-grandparents' lives around the turn of the 20th century. It reads like historical fiction but then, inserted among the pages, are amazing, vintage photographs of the real characters, reminding the reader that this is a true story. Nancy's wealth of knowledge and attention to detail add much credibility to this remarkable story. I couldn't put it down."

–Willard Howe ,
Author of the International bestseller,
Sticks in the Clouds.

"I was roped into the story from the very first page and didn't want to put it down. *Barbours Cut* has a great combination of rags-to-riches story, suspense, romance, humor, real human emotion, and one of my favorite elements, insight into how someone with a poor background was able to spot one opportunity after another and capitalize on them. Clyde Barbour is a good role model for almost anybody on how to get ahead in the world in an intelligent and humanistic way."

–Mike Rydin,
Former HCSS CEO

"As it takes you down the Mississippi River and then to Texas, Mexico, and New York, *Barbours Cut* is so engrossing and at times so gripping that you completely forget it's a story about real people and their lives. Nancy Potter brings to life people whose voices you can hear and emotions you can feel, she evokes them all so vividly that you feel you're in the room with them."

–Judy O'Beirn,
President, Hasmark Publishing Intr.

Barbours Cut

Beyond the River's Reach

Nancy E. Potter

Published by
Hasmark Publishing International
www.hasmarkpublishing.com

Disclaimer

This work depicts actual events in the life of the author as truthfully as recollection permits of experiences over time and/or can be verified by research. The story is a weaving of fiction with nonfiction wrapped around historical points in time. Occasionally, dialogue consistent with the character or nature of the person speaking has been supplemented or recreated. Some events have been compressed. Persons within are actual individuals, composite characters and fictional characters. The views and opinions expressed in the book are of those of the author and do not necessarily reflect or represent the views and opinions held by individuals whose characters, their heirs, and descendants are portrayed in the book. The author recognizes that their memories of the events described in this book may be different than that of the author.

Permission should be addressed in writing to Nancy E. Potter at nancypotterauthor@gmail.com

Editor: Murray Lewis | Murray@hasmarkpublishing.com
Cover Illustrator: Abul Basit | abdulbasitart@gmail.com
Cover Designer: Anne Karklins | anne@hasmarkpublishing.com
Layout Artist: Amit Dey | amit@hasmarkpublishing.com

ISBN 13: 978-1-77482-205-0
ISBN 10: 1774822059

DEDICATION

I lovingly dedicate this novel to my grandmother, Lilly, who brushed my hair while she told me stories of her life and that of her parents, Clyde and Jennie, who are the protagonists of this novel. It was the kind of oral history that is all too rare these days. If she had not been such a wonderful keeper of things pertaining to our family, I would never have been able to write this novel.

Lilly was always smiling and happy. I can see her sweet face and hear her soft-spoken Southern voice in my mind and remember how gracious, kind, loving, and accepting she was of all people. I wear her engagement ring every day as a reminder of how I should behave to make her proud.

I have used Jergens lotion on my skin my entire life because Lilly taught me that a lady needs to have soft skin. She lent me her hoop skirt, which was three sizes too big, so that I could pretend to be a Southern belle. Most importantly, Lilly showed me how to survive the tumultuous shift from woman of great wealth to woman of none, and how to do it with grace, dignity, and charm.

TABLE OF CONTENTS

ACKNOWLEDGEMENTS

I would first like to express my gratitude to Clyde and Jennie, my great-grandparents, who lived the kind of life that people enjoy reading about and who provided me with the kind of family lore and connection most people can only dream about.

To my two beloved sons, Spencer and Forrest, who hold my heart in their hands. Each of them has and continues to support me in his own way, Forrest doing the daily lifting when the days were difficult and Spencer feigning interest in my writing woes.

To my family who treasures its ancestors with such steadfastness as to have left me with a virtual museum worth of keepsakes that made writing *Barbours Cut* possible. Due to my father's work, my very Southern family lived many places around the world which gave me a deeper understanding and appreciation of the differences in people and how to make that beneficial to my writing. I am forever grateful for the unconditional love I have always received from my four sisters; DeVoe Allen, Susan Adams, Pamela Williams and Julie Treece, as well as Mom and Dad who gave everything they had to help me in all my various endeavors.

I also pay homage to my grandparents, Lilly and Tom, who spent their lives trying, unsuccessfully, to care for Oaklawn Manor, and instilled in us the values of grace, elegance and of being a good person. Their love and guidance have left a lasting, positive impact on my life.

To Mike Rydin, my benefactor and friend, who loved my story so much that he was determined to help me get it out to the world. We share a love of words and history, and he didn't flinch at the mention of Sisyphus! His ideas helped to shape *Barbours Cut* and his ability to deflect the negative is always appreciated. That attitude is a help to me daily. I also greatly admire his desire to help America get back to its basic values.

To Chip Julian, my collaborator, whose hours of dedication to my craft allowed me to make *Barbours Cut* even better! He pulled from me an even deeper layer to the story and put up with the temperamental author who initially negated most every suggestion he had.

To Joe Blackmon who believed in me so much that he made it possible for me to stay at home long enough to write the majority of my book. His spiritual tutelage took me to a higher plane of understanding that I know will benefit me the rest of my life.

To Governor Mike and Alice Foster who have so lovingly taken care of Oaklawn Manor the last 30 years. They took me into their family and into their hearts and made my trips to Franklin possible and fun!

To Peggy McColl, and later Bob Proctor, who taught me a new way of thinking and viewing the world which allowed me to get to this place where my life's dream is being realized; the publishing of *Barbours Cut*!

To Scott Meadows, my tech guru, who patiently helped me daily with computer problems while only occasionally giggling at my ineptitude. And to everyone at Isani Consultants who helped this book come about in many ways.

To all my defenders whose support was unyielding; Roxanne D'Ascenzo, Bridget Yeung, and Loretta Brzoza.

Lastly, but most importantly, to my God whose patience and love is omnipresent as my safety net in this roller coaster of a ride we call life.

PREFACE

This is my great-grandfather's story; it has been a long time in the making, 35 years to be precise. Life simply kept getting in the way. Captain Clyde Arthur Barbour had a 1,000-page life that I struggled to condense down to about 500 pages. I am sure you will find his story extraordinary, as well as inspirational and thought-provoking. He became a significant historical figure in Louisiana and Texas of whom most people have never heard, and I want to give him the acclaim he deserves. That is one of the reasons that I felt compelled to write this novel.

One of the amazing things about Captain Barbour was that he was able to get cooperation from people by being kind and helpful and by offering them opportunities that were wins for everyone involved; he was a businessman who was able to acquire great wealth in a manner that was the opposite of the way a man stereotypically makes it to the top. He was also a great problem solver and was always generous.

Within these pages, you will read about the family lore which I grew up listening to. Clyde was a larger-than-life character whose presence continued to be felt by many long after his soul left his body. As I traveled to Louisiana many times around the year 2000 to do research in the town of Franklin, where he lived for a number of years, everyone I met there of the older generations knew of him and spoke of him fondly, 70 years after his passing. I learned many stories I had never heard which added dimension and depth to his story. Luckily, I was able to record these interviews before all of those people were no longer with us.

My home is a museum to my main characters, Clyde and Jennie, his wife and my great-grandmother. My grandmother was Clyde and Jennie's daughter, Lilly Barbour, who is also a character in this novel. Lilly kept so many family things that it's unimaginable, and I'm the loyal custodian of most of them. Clyde's pince-nez are on my desk; his passports, telegrams, diaries, photos, letters, etc. are in boxes and drawers. A few pieces of furniture from one of their houses have a home with me, as do sterling flatware, china, clothes, and even a few pieces of jewelry. I drew on all of these things heavily in writing this novel.

When the inevitable discouragement set in while I was writing *Barbours Cut*, I would reflect on Clyde and Jennie and draw upon the parts of them that I needed to help encourage me to persevere. I know you'll enjoy these stories that have captivated me my entire life. I am particularly proud to be their great-granddaughter.

Barbour Family Flatboat

CHAPTER 1

THE RUNAWAY

Fall 1894

The moon's light touched her face, telling her it was time. Her eyes had not closed since she'd laid her head on her pillow hours before. She told herself for the hundredth time, *Don't wake Leona. Roll over slowly. Put one foot on the floor and ease out from under the covers.*

Before getting on with her well-thought-out plan, Jennie turned her head to see her sleeping sister. She could smell the acidic scent of her sister's breath. She kissed the tip of Leona's nose and wiped away the tear falling down her own cheek. *She looks so little,* Jennie thought, as she lingered just long enough to ensure that she would remember forever this last moment of sisterly sleeping. Slowly rolling over, she put one foot on the floor and eased out from under the covers.

The moon was shining brightly that night as Jennie tiptoed to the wardrobe. She had hung the black riding habit all the way to the right, well-hidden but easy to retrieve in the dark. Fumbling with the rubber buttons on her nightdress, Jennie silently fussed at her clumsiness while shivering in the cold night air.

Once undressed, she pulled her stockings up with trembling hands. Finding the pocket she had sewn inside her camisole, Jennie felt the money she had placed there. She dressed quickly

1

as her heart pounded so loudly that she feared it would wake the still-sleeping Leona.

Reaching under her bed, Jennie pulled out the small satchel borrowed from Miss Dora and stuffed her nightdress inside. She set the satchel, her boots, and her black hat with the veil next to the door, stopping short when she heard a soft whistle. Jennie stole her way to the window and looked out to see Miss Dora and a Black man waiting in the distance with three horses. Jennie felt she was going to be sick.

What am I doing? How can I leave my family? How can I leave Leona? What's gonna happen to me?

Shaking her head as if to clear the negative thoughts from her mind, Jennie walked around the bed once again and to the door. *I'll be back as soon as things quiet down and Papa has a chance to forgive me.*

"What are you doing, Jennie?" came a soft voice from under the covers.

"Sh-h-h, Leona honey, it's nothing. Go back to sleep."

"But it's the middle of the night. What are you wearing?" Leona whispered as she rubbed her eyes.

"I'm leaving. I can't marry old Mr. Miller; I won't. And Papa can't make me!" Jennie replied in a quiet yet defiant tone.

"But what'll I do? You can't just leave me here all alone with the boys! I need you! Please don't go, Jennie. I beg you!" Leona began sobbing, the noise frightening Jennie.

"Sh-h-h. Now calm down. You know I wouldn't leave you. I'm coming back for you, and we'll be together forever. Remember? I promised Mother I'd always take care of you, and I swear on a stack of Bibles that I will," Jennie whispered, her usual fervor showing through.

"Don't swear, Jennie. You know how much trouble you get into when you swear," Leona pleaded as tears rolled down her cheeks. "Please, you have to take me with you. What if Papa wants *me* to marry some old rich man?"

"You're only 14. I'm 18! This is the third time Papa has tried to marry me off. He's not gonna take no for an answer this time. I'll be back for you before he has a chance to sell you off like he's trying to do to me."

"But where are you going? Who are you going with?" Leona asked between sniffles.

"I can't tell you. You have to be strong, Leona, and be a good girl. And I'll come back for you, I promise! Now please stop crying. I hate it when you cry." Jennie brushed the tears away from her sister's face and stroked her hair. "I love you more than anything," she said and leaned over to kiss Leona on the cheek, pulling her close for a last warm hug.

"I love you, too, Jennie. I'll try to be good, but please don't wait too long to come back for me," Leona begged.

"I won't. And we'll have a grand life together; I promise that, too!"

Walking to the bedroom door and ever so gingerly turning the doorknob, Jennie pulled it open. She picked up her boots and satchel, put on her hat, and smiled at her tearful little sister before turning away to walk barefoot down the hallway. At the top of the stairs, Jennie paused outside her father's bedroom door.

If only Mother was still alive! Jennie felt the familiar pang of loneliness in the depth of her soul as she thought about Mother. *If only…. If only…* she thought.

From much careful scrutiny, Jennie knew all of the wooden steps creaked when you walked on them, but the sixth from the top was the worst. However, if you stepped as close as possible to the right-hand side, it creaked a little bit less.

One, two, three, she counted, descending the stairs. *Four, five, now…all the way to the right…six…*she coached herself.

C-R-E-A-K!

Jennie froze, not daring even to breathe. She heard the familiar sound of Papa turning over in his bed. Jennie's heart seemed to stop. She descended the remaining steps quickly and turned the corner at the bottom, out of sight of any curious eyes.

As she walked across the floor toward the side door, Jennie reached into her satchel and pulled out the letter she had addressed to her father. She kissed it and placed it on the table. As she closed the side door, Jennie rubbed the knob in farewell.

Once outside, Jennie squeezed her cold feet into her riding boots and pulled down the black veil on her hat. It was Miss Dora's Black servant, Zeke, who was waiting with her. He took Jennie's satchel and helped her up onto her horse.

As the trio made their way into the woods, tulip poplars on all sides stood tall and straight as though standing at attention. Looking back at her house in the Kentucky moonlight one last time, Jennie promised herself out loud, as if that gave the statement more validity, "I'll be back soon. I promise!"

Horses had never seemed as noisy as they did that night. Jennie jumped at their every snort. Every hoof tap on a rock was followed by Jennie turning her head to see if they were being followed. She didn't have butterflies in her stomach—instead, giant waves turned over and over deep inside her gut, convincing Jennie she was going to get sick at any moment.

Jennie could not stop the flood of tears down her face and beneath her veil. She pulled a handkerchief from one of her pockets, wiping her tear-stained cheeks over and over. Her thin body shook with grief, mixed with fear.

It's gonna be fine. It's gonna be fine, she kept reassuring herself. *I really don't have a choice.*

They rode on in silence, Zeke leading the way, Jennie in the middle, and Miss Dora at the rear. Jennie could see the saddlebags she had packed at Miss Dora's house on Zeke's horse. They held so little of her life, but there was no room for anything more. *I'll be back soon*, she thought.

Jennie could smell the sweet scent of her horse's sweat and feel its muscles contract beneath her. She patted her mount and thought of her grandmother, Linda Jane Richardson, who had run away on horseback and gotten married. The two young lovers went galloping through the hills of North Carolina on their way to the Cumberland Gap, with Grandmother's servant following along behind. When her father and brothers caught up to the young pair, only to find they had already been married, they turned around in disgust. Soon thereafter, the Gap had been closed due to an Indian uprising. Jennie's grandmother never saw her family again.

Stop thinking about such things, Jennie scolded herself. *It's ridiculous! That was in the old days. Nothing like that is gonna happen to me.* Still, a shudder ran up her spine. Just then a screech owl hollered out its call, frightening the horses and giving Jennie a feeling of foreboding.

After what seemed an eternity, the travelers stopped and dismounted. Jennie was thirsty, and Miss Dora gave her some water. As Jennie pulled back her veil to drink, her friend could see the swollen eyes and wet cheeks of this young woman about to embark reluctantly on a voyage down the Mississippi River.

"I know you must be feeling awful," Miss Dora comforted, "but remember, you have an interesting time ahead of you. Try to learn from this unfortunate situation and use it to return a wiser woman."

"But Leona! I left her crying," Jennie sobbed. "I promised her I'd come back for her!"

"And you will. In the meantime, I will keep an extra eye on her for you and your mother." She wrapped her arms around Jennie and rocked her as a mother would her own child. "Your mama and I were best friends our whole lives. She wanted you to be happy. Now that she's gone, I feel like it's my responsibility to help make her wish for you come true. But remember, no one can know I helped you get away. If they find out, I won't be able to look after Leona. Now let's get going again. It's not much farther. The boat should be waiting for us."

Dora Banks was a plumpish woman of average stature with dark brown wavy hair cut to her shoulders. There was a softness to her facial expression, warm and inviting. Her puffy cheeks always seemed to be holding back a smile that waited to break through. Her dark brown eyes were kind, if sometimes sad.

During The War Between the States, Miss Dora served as a nurse with on-the-job training. She held many a soldier's hand and spoke kindly to them as they passed away. When her fiancé didn't return from the fighting, she'd had enough of grief and separation, vowing never to marry, and she never did.

When Jennie had gone to Miss Dora, in great distress over her intended marriage to Mr. Miller, Miss Dora had devised a plan. "I have some close friends who I think will be more than happy to have you stay with them for a time. They have a trading boat they float down the Ohio and Mississippi Rivers all the way to New Orleans. Then they turn around and get a tow back up to Jeffersonville, Indiana. The entire trip takes them about six months, which should be plenty of time for your father to forget this whole crazy notion of his. They have two nice sons. I'll get in touch with them right away. They should be passing through here soon."

True to her promise, Miss Dora had contacted her friends, the Barbours, who were delighted to have another pair of hands onboard for the trip to New Orleans and back. They would be passing through in about a week.

The chilly autumn night turned into a cool morning with the rising sun. As the town and the river came into view, Jennie's anxiety over leaving her home, and especially Leona, was replaced with dread over what this journey might hold for her.

What if I hate being on the river? What if Mrs. Barbour isn't nice to me? What if her sons are awful? Questions raced through her anxious and fearful mind. *If I hate it, I'll just leave. I'll pack up and find my way home, or no, not back home, but I'll find somewhere to stay.*

At the edge of the town of Hickman, Kentucky, Miss Dora stopped her horse and said to Jennie, "Promise me you'll write your family as soon as you get settled on the boat. And promise me you'll come see all of us again."

"Of course, I will! Hopefully Papa will forgive me, but I want to have a happy life. I can't bear the thought of having to live with some old man!"

The trio rode on through the small town, Jennie's black veil hiding her face from any curious townspeople. The only sound was the quiet stillness of the early morning.

As they approached the Mississippi River, the Barbour's boat came into view. "There's your new home, Jennie," Miss Dora declared.

"Oh, my," was the only answer Jennie could muster.

The wooden trading boat was 100 feet long and 20 feet wide with a flat-topped, single-story cabin. A covered deck with a railing made up the front end of this vessel that Jennie could not fathom being anyone's "home," let alone hers.

A woman was seated on the deck. Next to her, sitting on the railing, was a man holding a fishing pole. As Jennie, Miss Dora, and Zeke neared the boat, the man waved and motioned to them. Both stepped off the boat and walked out to meet the travelers in the early morning dew.

"Jennie Hobbs?" the approaching stranger asked.

"Yes, sir," she replied quietly, tasting the grit from the night's ride between her teeth.

"I'm Jim Barbour. I hope you'll call me Pa. And this is my wife, Annie." He put his arm around his wife's shoulders and smiled up at Jennie, still on her horse. His thick mustache quivered as his close-set eyes enveloped her with kindness. "Let me help you down." Although short in stature, Jim Barbour lifted Jennie up and off her horse with ease.

"You must be exhausted," Annie declared. "And please, call me Ma." As her wide, thin lips pulled up into a soft smile, long dimples appeared on both sides of Ma's face, stretching from the corners of her mouth down to her chin. Her plain, faded dress showed off her rounded figure.

Jennie, happy to have her feet back on the ground, brushed the dirt and dampness from her skirt. Her legs ached and her throat was dry. She didn't know what to say.

"It's awfully nice of you to let me go down the river with you and your family. I don't know anything about boats, but my papa always told me I was a quick learner." Jennie looked around to be sure no one else was nearby, lifted her veil, and smiled at the Barbours.

Jennie had one of those smiles, the kind that makes you want to hold her close and take care of her, no matter the cost. Her young lips looked sweet, soft, and full. Her hazel eyes were big and wide open, begging for approval. The morning light sparkled and danced on the moistness left behind by her hours of tear-letting.

"Zeke," Miss Dora said, "please take Jennie's saddlebags onto the boat."

"Miss Dora, how are you?" Pa asked. "How was your trip?"

"Just as we planned," Miss Dora answered before leaning over to whisper, "It's been hard on the girl."

"No doubt. But don't you worry. We'll take good care of her. My wife has always wanted a daughter, and I must confess, me too! Not to mention, we can always use an extra pair of hands around here." Pa reached the boat first but stopped to allow the women to board. Jennie followed the two older women.

As Jennie walked through the door and into the cabin, her eyes had to adjust to the indoor light. Small windows lined the boat's sides and had wooden shutters but had no glass in them.

Just inside the door, Jennie found herself in a large room lined with counters. On the walls behind the counters were shelves holding all manner of glassware, tinware, and Queensware, cooking utensils, all kinds of household notions, toys, and other novelties. The cabinets and shelves were packed full but were orderly and very clean. Detecting a faint smell of partially cured lumber, Jennie moved with her guides into the next room, which appeared to be for storage, and then walked down a short hallway with a sleeping cabin on each side. From there Jennie saw what appeared to be the galley at the end of the hall, just beyond the sleeping cabins.

"This will be your room," Pa told Jennie, pointing to a door on the left. "It's not much, but it'll give you some privacy, which is hard to come by here." Ma opened the door, and Jennie walked into her new "room."

The cabin was tiny, with a small window on the opposite wall, some shelves, a washstand with drawers, and a bed. "You can hang your dresses on the hooks next to the washstand," Ma pointed out. Taking off her hat, Jennie examined her room and began to cry yet again. *I've got to stop this!* She moaned silently.

"You must think I'm awful to be crying. All of this is just so new to me, and so different. I know this is gonna be a wonderful room for me. Thank you," she managed to say.

"Here, child," Ma said as she handed Jennie a handkerchief. "We understand. Maybe one day you'll love the river like we all do. Now maybe we should give you a chance to rest up. There's some spring water in the pitcher for you to drink. You can use it to wash up if you like but remember, spring water is hard to come by on a boat. Use as little as you can. I don't think you're ready to try drinkin' our river water yet. I'll check on you after a while." Ma put her arms around Jennie's slim shoulders and hugged her.

It was time to say goodbye. The Barbours left the room so Jennie and Miss Dora could make their farewells. Miss Dora hugged Jennie tightly, then grasped her shoulders at arm's length and looked straight into Jennie's eyes.

"You may feel alone here, but remember, God is always with you. And so is your mother's spirit. Both will keep you company and watch over you. The Barbours are fine people. They'll take good care of you. And I'll miss you," she said as her eyes filled with tears. "Write to me soon!" She kissed the young woman goodbye, held her close again for a long moment, and then left.

As Miss Dora closed the door behind her, Jennie collapsed onto her new bed and cried long and hard.

Left Back Row: Clyde Barbour, Unknown Gentleman,
Unknown Gentleman, and James Barbour.
Front Row: William Barbour (Grandpa) and Jim Barbour (Pa). About 1891

CHAPTER 2

THE BAPTISM

As Jennie was making her way to the boat, the two Barbour brothers were settling down on the bank of the river with their cane fishing poles.

"They oughta be good and hungry about now," said James, the younger of the two. He had always wanted to be called Jim like their father, but everyone thought that would be too confusing. James made light work of spearing a worm with his hook, wiping his hand on the side of his dark brown trousers.

"I hope we're luckier than yesterday. I don't want to disappoint Ma again," Clyde answered, as his small, strong hands struggled with his bait. He finally got the bait on his hook, letting out a sigh of relief. He looked around for something to wipe his hands on, finally using the trunk of a nearby tree. He wondered who it was that had decided this was supposed to be fun.

One at a time the boys put their lines into the murky river.

"It's a good thing you don't have to see 'em to catch 'em!" James exclaimed, staring into the water, trying to will a fish to his line.

Earlier, they had made their way down the bank away from their flatboat. The river on both sides was lined with poplar trees. Clyde looked around him at the familiar Mississippi River. The Kentucky golden rods were in bloom in an odd contrast to the leaves falling

11

from the trees. The sky was brushed with pink, which faded to blue as the sun began to warm up the cool dampness left over from the night. The river was moving smoothly and slowly on its way to the Gulf of Mexico, hardly making a sound. Clyde was content; it should be an easy day on the river.

"What do you make of that girl comin' to live with us? What are we gonna do with her? Why is she comin' anyway?" asked James, who, at 15, seemed to Clyde to still be a boy.

Clyde looked at his confused younger brother, whose slicked-back brown hair exposed James' protruding ears. "You're too young to understand. She has a family problem and we're helpin' her out; that's all you need to know. And you'd better behave yourself around her or Pa will skin you alive!" At the age of 19, Clyde considered himself quite well seasoned.

"What do we call her?" the ever-inquisitive James asked.

"I guess we call her by her name, stupid, what do you think? Her name is Jennie."

"Why is she sleepin' in our cabin, and we have to sleep under the counter? Doesn't seem right to me," James sulked.

"That's just the way you treat girls, that's all. You can't have her sleepin' on the floor and us two in the cabin. It just wouldn't be right!"

"Sounds to me like one more person to boss me around. I'm tired of bein' everybody's baby." James sat up straight as he felt a tug on his line. "I've got one! I've got one!" he yelled.

"Calm down, you're scarin' the fish!" Clyde said.

James pulled the pole out of the water and flung it back over his shoulder. When the fish was flapping around in the air, he grabbed the line and pulled it in. "It's a beauty!" he said proudly, holding his slippery catch at arm's length.

"Yes, it is. Now let's see if we can catch a few more so Jennie has a fine dinner with us." Clyde picked up his pole and stuck it down into the ground a few inches so he could grab the book his grandpa, who had graduated from college in Ireland long ago, had lent him. He tried squinting his eyes to compensate for the lack of light.

"You're the only fella I've ever seen who reads a book and fishes at the same time," James remarked as he watched Clyde get comfortable. Although older than James, Clyde had never been fond of fishing or hunting and therefore wasn't very adept at either.

"That makes me smarter than all those other fellas," replied Clyde, not bothering to look up. He took a deep breath, filling his nostrils with the smell of moist earth from the morning dew and settled down on the hard ground to try to read.

A few minutes later, it was Clyde's turn. He was relaxing with one hand on his pole and the other holding his book, *The Adventures of Tom Sawyer*. The first tug was strong. It startled Clyde and he dropped his book. Instantly, Clyde let go of the pole and tried to catch the book before it went into the water.

"What in the world?" cried James as he jumped up and raced over to save Clyde's pole from a swim in the Mississippi, hoping to get the fish as well. He saved the pole and was struggling with the fish. "Clyde, give me a hand!" he yelled.

But Clyde was busy. He lunged after the book to no avail as he heard the sound of a splash. He managed to grab it by one corner and retrieve it. "Jesus!" he gasped as he got himself back onto the bank safely. He turned around in time to see James slipping down the bank and heading for the river. It looked as though he was being pulled by the fish, making Clyde chuckle. He grabbed James, who was still holding onto the fishing pole, and together they wrestled the fish out of the dark water.

"Hallelujah! What a catch!" James yelled. "Now that was fun!"

"Yeah, great fun; my book is soaked. Grandpa is gonna be so mad!" Clyde took the book and carefully removed some of the water with his shirt. He tried to fan it out to start the drying process, but it was too wet, and he was afraid he had hurt the spine. *I'll have to figure it out when I get back to the flatboat.* Books were a rare commodity in their world and meant to be treasured.

Clyde and James spent the rest of the morning ignoring each other as much as possible. After catching five good-sized fish, they decided to head back to their flatboat. James had caught one last fish, but Clyde thought it was too small and made him throw it back.

On the way to the boat, James started talking about "the girl" again. "How long do you think she'll stay with us?" he asked.

"Don't know," his brother answered in a far-off tone.

"I sure hope it's not for long!"

As they approached their floating home, the two brothers saw Ma and Pa sitting on the porch. There was no sign of "the girl."

James ran ahead carrying the bucket with the fish. "Look, Pa, five fish!" he yelled.

"No. I don't believe you. Yesterday you didn't come within throwin' distance of a fish." Pa was smiling as James handed the fish to him to back up his story.

"See?" the younger brother beamed.

"I'm glad," Ma said. "This'll make a fittin' meal for our new family member."

"Family member? What do you mean? Is she gonna stay with us forever?" asked James, suddenly feeling threatened.

"I don't imagine so," Pa answered. "But just the same, I want you to treat her like family as long as she's here. Understand?"

James nodded.

"Do I get a proper answer?" Pa asked.

"Yes, sir. I will."

"Fine, fine," said Pa, dismissing the subject with the wave of his hand.

"So where is she?" Clyde asked.

"Sleepin'. She was upset when she first got here and she's gone to sleep, poor child. We'll let her be," Ma answered. "And James, don't you go askin' her all kinds of questions like you always do. Be polite."

"Yes, ma'am," James said.

"Okay, let's get these fish in the galley and get this boat goin'," Pa ordered.

"First I've got to put this book somewhere to dry out," Clyde told him.

"What happened?" Ma asked.

"It fell in the river when I was fishin," he answered sheepishly.

"Grandpa is gonna have your hide!" Pa exclaimed.

"Not if I can fix it before he comes," Clyde declared as he walked on into the cabin.

"Where's Luke?" Pa looked around and then headed off down the road to town to look for his hired hand.

Luke had made the trip up and down the rivers with the Barbours for years. Luke wasn't sure just how old he was but figured he was about 43. Clyde and James were both fascinated with and horrified by Luke's stories of life as a slave in Louisiana before the War of the Rebellion, as it came to be called up North, or the War for Southern Independence, down South. Once free, Luke had spent many years working on a steamboat before settling in with the Barbours. His stories helped pass the time on those often-lonely trips.

Ma took the fish to the galley to start preparing it for cooking. The two boys scurried around putting away their fishing gear and making sure it was safely stowed. There was still no sign of Jennie.

As soon as Pa and Luke returned, they made ready to shove off.

The Barbours' trading boat was sometimes referred to as a sweeps boat or flatboat and worked much like a rowboat with a rudder on the stern. The flatboat had three sweeps, each operated from the flat top of the cabin. Like long oars, one sweep on either side propelled the vessel, while the rear oar served as a rudder to steer right and left. On both sides of the rooftop was a platform where the oarsmen would walk up and back with one end of the sweep on their shoulder. The elevated platform on the stern was called the lazy board because the boatmen would rest there when not working the sweeps. These flatboats had no other means of propulsion. They depended entirely on the current to send them down the rivers, which were not always kind to their travelers, and because they couldn't travel back up the rivers unless they were towed, they were usually broken up for lumber at the end of their journeys. For that reason, they rarely had names.

Raised on the rivers, Clyde was the steersman, manning the stern's sweep. Luke and Pa manned the other two, while James was responsible for keeping the lines on the flatboat, making sure they didn't slip into the water. The flatboat always faced upstream when docked. James would take in the breast line and then the head line; they used the stern line to swing the boat out into the stream.

"Thanks, mister!" James yelled as he caught the last line.

Pa called out from on top, "To oars!" and then whistled his customary whistle as he, Luke, and Clyde set about getting the flatboat into the middle of the river. Manning the sweeps was often very hard work, as evidenced by the calluses on the trio's shoulders from pushing the sweeps in difficult weather conditions.

A soft breeze blew down the river that day, making the morning's work easy. Once headed downstream, Luke and Pa secured their sweeps and climbed down to the deck.

"Luke, James, sort out that last bunch of rags we just bought and get them baled." Pa was not one for fooling around.

"Yes, sir," Luke answered.

"But Pa, when are you gonna wake that girl?" James asked.

"That girl has a name. It's Jennie, and we're gonna let her be," Pa told him.

"But Pa, she could help us sort these old rags!" James protested, not willing to give up.

"You worry about what you're supposed to be doin' and I'll worry about what Jennie's supposed to be doin'. There'll be plenty for her to do once she gets settled in." Pa was obviously irritated.

"Okay. Okay," James mumbled.

"What did you say?" asked Pa sternly.

"I meant, 'Yes, sir!'" James replied resolutely.

"That's better." Pa left the front room and headed through the deck room to the galley in the back.

"I don't even know that girl and already I don't like her!" James whispered to Luke.

"If I was you, I'd stop all that kind a talkin'. You gonna end up in trouble. 'Sides, maybe she be a nice lady," Luke suggested.

"You sound like my brother."

"Thank you! There's nothin' wrong with soundin' like that smart brother a yours," exclaimed Luke, a smile on his face. "He's teachin' me to read! I never knowed a Negro could read!"

"I could care less about readin'." James sat on the floor, holding his head in his hands.

"Come on, let's get goin'," Luke said, pulling on James' arm to get him up.

The two went back to the deck room where the rags sat in a large heap. They began to sort through them and separate them into piles. Clean rags could get one and a half cents per pound; dirty rags, one cent per pound; and woolen rags, six cents.

"I just don't like that musty smell you get from those dirty rags!" James complained as he sorted.

"Don't even smell it no more," Luke remarked.

To secure the sorted bundles, Luke put two wide pieces of burlap down inside the baler which were long enough to hang halfway down the outside. When the baler was full, James took the ends of the burlap and lapped them on top of each other. Luke then sewed the burlap pieces together on the top.

"Stack 'em up!" Luke cried as he lifted the heavy bale and tossed it into a corner, and then started another bale.

Sitting on top of his world, Clyde enjoyed this time to himself. With the most recent edition of Cramer's *Ohio and Mississippi Navigator* by his side, he felt ready for anything. This was his time, time to think in the peaceful quietness of the Mississippi River.

He saw a steamer approaching, a side-wheel packet. It was the beautiful *Morning Glory*, which belonged to the Louis and Evansville Packet Company. Clyde knew it had been built at Howard Shipyards in the late 1870s in Jeffersonville, Indiana. Pa had worked there for years as a ship's carpenter before venturing out on his flatboat, and he still worked there when they returned home after each trip. The Barbours lived in Jeffersonville when not on the river.

The *Morning Glory* carried freight as well as passengers, who waved to Clyde as they passed on his left. He knew it must be dinnertime, as he could hear the orchestra music from the packet echoing across the river. The passengers were treated to this music at mealtimes, and when the packet was tied up at a landing, the orchestra played for the locals. The townspeople would come out in large numbers to hear the orchestra. It was one of the few entertainments available to people living in the towns along the river. The music brought back fond memories of Clyde's boyhood, carefree with no responsibilities, just sitting on the dock, clapping his hands in rhythm to the music.

One day, Clyde thought, *I'm gonna pilot one of those big packets. I'm gonna start the side-wheels and steer from the pilothouse without havin' to worry about the current takin' me somewhere I don't wanna go.*

He thought about Tom Sawyer. *Now there's somebody I have somethin' in common with. Huckleberry's another story; I never did understand him!*

The Mississippi was a beautiful river at this point. The towns sat on bluffs looking down on the river. Here, the banks were woody and hilly. A kingfisher flew right in front of Clyde's face and startled him. He followed it with his eyes until it became a speck on the horizon.

Jennie woke with a start from her nap, thinking she heard music playing. *I must be dreaming*, she thought until another song began, blaring right through the thin walls and her lone window. *What in the world?* She got up and looked out the window in time to see a side-wheel packet passing by. She smiled from ear to ear, the first smile since leaving home. She even felt herself swaying to the music as the words rang out:

"Beautiful dreamer, wake unto me,
Starlight and dewdrops are waiting for thee..."

Music, in the middle of the day; how wonderful! As she stood at the window, Jennie became aware of the movement of the flatboat. She hadn't noticed they were floating downstream until she looked outside. There was only the slightest sensation of rocking as they made their way along.

Stepping back from the window as the packet made its way upstream, Jennie decided, reluctantly, that she would have to leave the safe confines of her sleeping cabin and meet the rest of the family. She smelled the strong odor of fish cooking and heard the clang of pots and pans in the galley next door. *I need to go out there and help. I have to be helpful.*

Jennie had not changed out of her black riding habit. Her long, thick hair was still held back in a braid. *I need to change,* she decided and took the three dresses she had brought with her out of the saddlebags and hung them on the pegs. After putting on her favorite dress, the blue floral one, Jennie pulled on her white cotton stockings and shoes, and stood poised at her door. *I can do this. I can do this,* she reassured herself. *If I can leave Papa sleeping in his bed, I can go out this door and meet everyone.*

And she did. With a smile on her face, she opened the door, looked around and, turning left, headed into the galley.

Once there, she found Mrs. Barbour busy, with rolled-up sleeves and wearing a tattered, red-and-white-checked apron. Jennie could feel the heat coming from the stove and imagined what it must feel like in the summer.

"Jennie! My, don't you look pretty! Have a rest?" Mrs. Barbour looked up briefly from her cooking to greet the newcomer.

"Yes, ma'am. And I woke up to beautiful music comin' off that packet!"

"What a nice welcome for you. They play music at mealtimes and when they stop at a landing. Now come over here and I'll show you where I keep things so you can set the table for me." Mrs. Barbour walked over to the coarse wooden cupboards with latches on the outside and showed Jennie where to find things. Then she went back to cooking.

"Excuse me, but how many people will be eatin'?" Jennie asked.

"There's Pa, Clyde, James, Luke, and us two. That makes, um, six of us. Set the table for six. Of course, Pa and Clyde have to switch off so somebody is always steerin'. Even so, I always set a place for each of 'em."

The wooden dinner table sat to one side of the small galley, with a bench on each long side, both made of rough, untreated wood. At both ends was a chair, each of a different design. They looked out of place with their polished, smooth surfaces.

"Who are Clyde, James, and Luke?" asked Jennie, setting the table.

"Clyde's my oldest boy and James, he's my baby! But don't call him that unless you want to make him mad!" Mrs. Barbour giggled. "And Luke, he's our hired hand. Been with us for years, just like a member of the family. Used to be a slave."

Jennie was confused. *Luke used to be a slave,* she thought, *which means he's a Negro. So how could he be like one of the family?*

"Mrs. Barbour, he eats with y'all?" she inquired.

"Oh yes, honey. Livin' on a flatboat don't leave you room for worryin' about such things. Besides, I don't know what we'd do without him." Mrs. Barbour turned the fish over in the hot oil. "And you've got to start callin' us Ma and Pa, remember?"

"Yes, ma'am." Jennie stood next to Ma, watching her. "Where did you get the fish?"

"The boys caught these catfish this mornin'. Livin' on the water, we eat a lot of fish." She took a piece of the golden-fried fish out of the oil and placed it on a plate. Jennie watched her coat a piece of raw fish with cornmeal and carefully place it in the hot pan.

"Oh," Jennie said, not excited at the prospect of eating a lot of fish. "We eat mostly beef and pork on the farm. Oh, and venison sometimes."

"Well, I hope you like fish. Hand me another plate, honey. I'd say dinner is ready. Please ring that bell sittin' over on the cupboard and they'll come runnin'!"

Jennie took the pewter hand bell, stepped just outside the galley door, and rang it gently, feeling self-conscious.

"You'll have to do better than that if you want them to hear you!" Ma chuckled.

"Sorry, I'll try again." Jennie rang the bell loudly five or six times, embarrassed for making such a racket.

James and Luke showed up quickly. James introduced himself to Jennie while Luke just hung his head and said, "Ma'am." Pa entered next, only to say he would let Clyde eat first and left to go fetch him. Ma didn't wait for Clyde. She served up three plates and Jennie passed them out.

"Put one at the head of the table for Clyde."

"Jennie's up," Pa told Clyde. "I think it would be nice if you went down and had dinner with everyone. I'll take over up here and you can take over when you're done."

"Okay, Pa," Clyde replied.

He wasn't sure why, but Clyde felt nervous as he walked back to the galley. James, Luke, and Jennie were already seated at the table. Ma was dishing up food from the stove on the opposite side of the room as Clyde walked in and went over to see what she was putting on the plates.

"Smells great, Ma!" he exclaimed. "Must have been some expert fishermen who caught all those fish!" He smiled teasingly.

"I'd say lucky fishermen. From what I understand, they nearly made a mess of the whole mornin'," Ma replied.

Jennie was busy trying to deal with all the fish bones and hadn't noticed Clyde until he walked up behind her to introduce himself. In the dim light of the galley, he saw the back of Jennie's head as she sat facing the opposite direction. *Look at that beautiful hair!* he thought.

"Apple pie?" asked James. "We're even havin' dessert? I thought we only ate dessert on special days?"

"This is a special day, havin' Jennie join us, so don't go gettin' used to the idea!" Ma teased.

"I'm Clyde. It's nice to meet you," he said nervously to the back of her head.

Jennie's head tilted slightly downward, and she turned just enough for Clyde to see her profile. Her nose was straight and dark eyelashes and soft brown eyebrows outlined her big, almond-shaped eyes. Her hair was held back in a braid, showing off her perfectly sized ears and smooth complexion. And although her mouth was small, her lips were full. She was lovely!

"Hello, I'm Jennie. It's nice to meet you, too," she replied shyly, not looking Clyde in the eye but smiling politely.

He wondered about her eyes. *Are they hazel?* He wasn't sure. His thoughts made him blush, and he was thankful she wasn't really looking at him; he wouldn't want to be so obvious. He stood, transfixed and slightly embarrassed, until Ma saved him by saying, "Go sit in Pa's chair at the head of the table." Clyde obeyed, glad to have something to do.

"Jennie's never been on a flatboat before. Can you believe that?" asked James, amazed.

"Well then, we'll have to give her a proper tour of the boat after dinner," Clyde answered, attempting to assert his authority as heir apparent, while desperately trying to keep his eyes off of the newcomer.

"I would like that," Jennie responded quietly, not looking directly at anyone.

The noon meal was rarely this lavish. The fish Clyde and James had caught that morning had been fried to golden perfection. Clyde knew the smell would linger into the late afternoon when he would be hungry again. Ma was known for her good cooking. There were thick biscuits with butter and honey, lima beans with onions, and lots of hot coffee.

Luke, having never become accustomed to eating with the family, sat quietly with his eyes lowered slightly, trying to eat without anyone taking particular notice of his presence.

"How's the pie?" Ma asked.

"No complaints from me," Clyde smiled as he looked in Jennie's direction just in time to catch a glimpse of her turning her eyes away from him. It pleased him to think she had been looking in his direction.

Jennie was surprised at how handsome Clyde was. His face was round but not fat, with thin eyebrows and an ample nose. His ears were perfectly proportioned, and his thin lips rested in a slight smile, making him appear friendly.

"Everything is delicious, Mrs. Barbour," said Jennie as she turned to look at Ma, sitting at the opposite end of the table from Clyde.

"Now remember, it's Ma," she responded.

"Yes, ma'am, Ma," Jennie recited. "And your plates are so pretty!" Jennie looked admiringly at the dish.

"We trade in china and pottery, so we're lucky to have a lot to choose from. Food tastes even better when it's on a beautiful plate!" Ma was pleased that Jennie noticed.

As soon as Clyde had finished his dinner, he excused himself to relieve Pa up on top.

"Dinner was great, Pa! Ma even made apple pie! I'm so full I could take a nap," Clyde confided as he took over, rubbing his stomach.

"Now don't be fallin' asleep. If you get too sleepy, I'll come back up," Pa replied. "How's Jennie?"

"Fine, I guess. She didn't say much." Clyde looked at his father and wondered if he dare say what was on his mind. "Pa?"

"Yes?"

"Well, it's just that, you know, she's, well, awful pretty, don't you think?" Clyde asked.

"Sure is. She's one of the prettiest girls I think I ever saw, except for Ma, of course," Pa responded with a smile on his face.

"You don't have to tell anybody what I just said," Clyde added, a little worried about confiding in his pa.

"It's our secret." Pa patted Clyde on the back and smiled at him before descending to the lower deck.

Clyde pondered his good fortune in having such an attractive "sister" onboard.

When Pa finally returned to eat, James and Luke had already finished and left the room. He ate quietly as the two women talked.

Jennie's insides were turning all around. The grease from the catfish had not agreed with her stomach and just wouldn't go down. *I hope nobody noticed I didn't eat much,* she thought. *And Clyde looking at me just made it worse! I guess it's a compliment.* She wasn't sure how she felt about anything at the moment, except for two things: her stomach was upset, and she was already homesick.

"Can I help you with the dishes?" she asked.

"Yes. Let's do it together this time. Then, you can manage on your own." They cleared the table and cleaned up together.

"That didn't take any time at all with you helpin'!" Ma exclaimed. "But if you're gonna be helpin' around here, I hope you'll do a better job of eatin'." She looked at Jennie sympathetically.

"I'm sorry. It's just I'm not used to eatin' fish and for some reason, it won't go down," Jennie apologized, her eyes downcast.

"Oh now, don't apologize. Give it some time. Your stomach will settle down as soon as the rest of you does. Next time, we'll try puttin' a little vinegar on your fish. You didn't hurt my feelings. I just don't want you walkin' round hungry, that's all."

Ma put the last plate in the cupboard and turned around to face Jennie. "You know, we have somethin' in common. When I was only seven, I lost both my parents at the same time. I was hardly old enough to take care of myself, so my two younger brothers and younger sister had to be separated and raised by other people. All of a sudden, I was an orphan. It was horrible. So, you see, life got a hold of me and shook me real good, like it's doin' you right now. But one day you'll shake off all the hard times and be better off 'cause of it all." She placed her hand on Jennie's back and smiled. Those words were forever etched on Jennie's mind.

"Both of your parents at the same time?"

"Yes."

"How awful! Did it take a long time to stop missin' 'em?" Jennie asked softly.

"To tell you the truth, I still miss 'em. It don't hurt down deep in my stomach anymore, but I still miss 'em." Ma turned around as if to end the conversation.

Pa changed the subject for them. "Jennie, why don't you go up on top and let Clyde show you how the boat works?"

"Yes, sir, but isn't there somethin' else I can do? I want to help." Jennie felt uncertain how to proceed.

"Sure, sure," Pa answered, "but I think you need a look around the boat." He smiled as he wiped his mustache on the back of his hand and got up to leave. "Follow me and I'll show you how to get up top."

Jennie followed Pa to the other end of the flatboat and onto the front deck. At the end of the deck on the starboard side was a ladder up to the roof. Pa climbed up with ease. It took Jennie a minute to figure out how to hold her skirt up and hang onto the ladder at the same time.

"I guess I could end up in the river if I fell," Jennie said out loud, feeling uneasy.

"Just take it slow. You'll get the hang of it soon enough," Pa assured her as he watched her climb. He helped Jennie up the last few rungs, and there she was, standing on top of her new floating home.

"Oh, my!" she exclaimed as she struggled for her bearings. "It feels so strange standin' up here seeing the river go by with nothin' to keep you from fallin' over the edge! Have you ever fallen in?" she asked Pa.

"We've all done it a time or two," Pa laughed as he waved to Clyde who was steering, standing on the lazy board at the other end of the flatboat. "Now Jennie, come over here and let me show you how the sweeps work." He walked with her over to the port side and stood on the long, slightly elevated wooden platform. There was an identical one on the other side. "See this long pole?" He pointed to what looked to Jennie like an oversized fishing pole secured in a metal bracket. One end was rounded, and the other was shaped like an oar. Pa picked it up and swung it so that the oar end was in the water, with the round end extending back over his shoulder. Jennie could see where Pa's shirt was worn at the spot where the sweep rested on his shoulder.

"You use your shoulders and your arms to push the sweep as you walk along the platform, then you lift the end up out of the water and walk back to where you started, put it back into the water and start all over again." He made two passes before putting the sweep back in its resting place. "We use these to get the boat goin' and out into the current. The sweep on the stern is attached to the lazy board, that wooden platform Clyde is standin' on. We use that one to steer. Clyde's our best steersman. He knows these rivers like the back of his hand. Grew up on 'em," Pa smiled proudly. "Do you know what 'Mississippi' means?" Jennie shook her head. "The Algonquin Indians named it. It means Big Water or Great River," Pa told her.

Jennie looked back at Clyde, who seemed to be pretending not to listen.

"Pa, that eddy's comin' up here soon on the starboard side," Clyde said offhandedly.

"Just keep your eyes on it. Seems like last trip it was gettin' bigger."

"Yeah, but we'd just had a big rain then," Clyde answered.

"Right, right. Just call us up if you want some help." Pa turned around to head back down. "Introduce Jennie to the boat, but don't get distracted and forget that eddy!" he cautioned. "By the way, Jennie, can you swim?"

"Yes, sir. We had a big pond on the farm where we learned."

"Well remember, swimmin' in a river is a lot different than swimmin' in a pond. You have the current to worry about. We'll give you a chance to get into the river when it's not so cold. Just be careful." Pa disappeared down the ladder.

"So, my little brother, James, says you don't know anythin' about boats." Clyde ended the brief silence.

"No, not really. We have a Leavenworth yawl we use in the pond, but that's about it." Jennie wondered what she was going to talk about with this stranger.

"We have a yawl, too. You can see it tied up to the stern deck. Look." Clyde leaned over the back of the boat and pointed downward.

Jennie walked over to see for herself. "What do you use it for?" she asked.

"Sometimes we go huntin' or fishin' in it. If we have to tie up on the opposite side of the river from a town, we use it to ferry people and things across."

"Why would you have to tie up on the wrong side of the river?" she asked, genuinely interested.

"There might be too strong a current or, if there's not a dock, there might not be any good trees to tie to or the bank might look like it's gonna cave in. There's lots of reasons." Clyde stopped and looked at Jennie.

Jennie looked at him with a puzzled look on her face. "How do you know so much about rivers?" she asked.

"Been on the rivers since I was little. They're just a part of me. And I've studied Cramer's *Navigator* ever since I could read. It's a boatman's Bible!" Clyde quickly changed the subject, feeling like he'd gotten a bit too deep into it all. "Can you row?"

"I guess I can!" she answered defiantly. "I have older brothers to keep up with. They taught me a lot."

"Can you hunt?" he asked.

"Yes, but I don't really like to; only do it when my brothers dare me to." Jennie fell silent, her mind wandering back to the farm, her family, and especially her precious little sister, who, Jennie imagined, was receiving endless lectures about all the horrible things that await a young female runaway. "But I do like to eat wild game, especially venison!" Her mouth watered at the thought of eating a bite of venison cooked with wild berries.

"We don't do much deer huntin'; usually duck or geese." Clyde was running out of things to talk about. After a few minutes of silence, he started again. "My grandpa is a taxidermist."

"A what?"

"A taxidermist. You know, he stuffs dead birds and animals for people to hang on their walls."

"I know what you mean. My father has a deer head on the wall in our livin' room. What an awful way to make a livin'!" Jennie made a face just thinking about animal entrails all over the place.

"Well, he's also a teacher. Grandpa went to college in Ireland before coming over here. I can tell you, he makes more money from taxidermy than teaching!" Clyde added proudly. "A man's gotta make a livin' to support his family, you know. Whatever it takes. It's his responsibility."

"I didn't mean anythin' ugly. Just all that blood and mess makes me feel sick." Jennie sat down next to Clyde.

"Yeah, I guess. But once you've cleaned a few deer or some birds, it stops botherin' you."

"Do you like to hunt?" she asked.

"To tell you the truth, not really." Clyde looked around as if to be sure nobody heard him. "I'd rather sit down with a good book and learn somethin'. Grandpa gives me a box of books to read every time we take off down the rivers. He always tells me how happy it makes him that I love to learn things like he does. I don't know what I'd do without these books to read along the way. He picks them out special for me to help me get ready for college. He wants to be sure I learn about things like philosophy, history, mythology, and some of them are books he thinks I'd like, like *Tom Sawyer*. In fact, just this morning I dropped *Tom Sawyer* in the river when we were fishin'. I have to figure out how to dry it or Grandpa's gonna kill me!" Clyde got a worried look on his face.

And that's when it happened. Just that quick. Clyde had been paying too much attention to Jennie and not enough to the river ahead. It was too late by the time he saw it.

"Oh, my God!" he yelled, catching sight of the eddy just as the corner of the boat slipped into its circular motion. Clyde knew the eddy could rip the boat apart. "Oh, my God! To oars!" Clyde yelled at the top of his lungs as he stood and worked to steer the boat with every muscle in his body. His face turned bright red from the effort. "Jennie, stay down. Hold on!"

"Hold on to what?" she screamed as she felt the boat begin to turn.

"To me; hold on to my ankles!" Clyde had planted his sturdy legs on the lazy board and held them firm while trying to steer.

Jennie lay down and did exactly as she was told. They began to turn around and around, and she knew she was going to vomit. Luke and Pa had managed to crawl up and were attempting to use the side sweeps to help maneuver out of the overpowering whirlpool. Jennie saw the shoreline as it pitched and turned, with one side of the flatboat swinging up as the other sank down. She heard the whistling wind start in one ear and switch to the other as her position changed. Her hands were gripping Clyde's ankles so tightly her fingers began feeling numb.

"Luke. Hold her to the bow!" Pa screamed.

Hearing Clyde yell, "Pull her out!" Jennie couldn't hold it back another second and vomited all over Clyde's feet. The putrid smell made her gag and vomit again. She saw the chunky, beige liquid leave her mouth and disappear over the edge.

An unfamiliar voice, filled with fear, hollered, "She wants to break!"

"Ease up then, ease up!" Pa answered. "Steer her to the port side!"

"She won't go. I'm not strong enough!" Clyde's voice was strained and tired.

"You'll have to be, damn it! Do it!" demanded Pa, not a bit of sympathy in his voice.

All to no avail.

Round and round they continued to spin. Jennie could hear the clash of things being thrown around down below. She knew she was going to die.

It serves me right, she thought, *for leavin' my family. What was I thinkin'? Please God, don't let me die here in the middle of this crazy river with all these strangers. Please! I'll be good; I'll be better; I'll say my prayers. Just please don't let me die!*

"Hold on, Jennie!" Clyde yelled again.

Just as abruptly as it had sucked them in, the eddy spit them right back out with a force that sent them hurtling down the river in an eerie silence. Jennie let go of Clyde's ankles one moment too soon and was thrust to the edge where she clung for a brief second before being flung overboard. Her scream echoed down the river as she fell into the cold water that sucked the breath right out of her. She bobbed up to the surface in time to see Luke jump down to the back deck and almost join her in the water as one of his legs got stuck. Freeing his leg, Luke leapt into the yawl, panting hard as he headed out after her.

Jennie saw Luke coming as trees rushed by on the shoreline. She could hear his labored breathing as he rowed against the current with every bit of energy he had left after fighting against the eddy. She couldn't even yell as the current sent her slowly down the river toward him, but not as fast as the flatboat still moving with the extra help of the jolt out of the eddy.

Jennie was freezing. She was frantically treading water trying to stay afloat, but all of the clothes she was wearing made it impossible.

"I'm a comin', Miss Jennie! Hold on, I'm a comin'!" Luke yelled.

All she could do was whisper, "Please hurry!" *I've got to do somethin'*, she thought. *I'm so heavy! Take off my shoes; I can try that.* And she did. She let them go, then tried unsuccessfully to unfasten her dress.

"I'm 'most there!" Luke yelled. "Gimme your hand," he said, reaching out to her. But when he stopped rowing to grab her, the yawl slipped back a pace. He had to grasp the handles of the mounted oars and this time rowed just past her before trying again. "I gotcha!"

Jennie hung onto Luke's large black hand like life itself. He took hold of both her hands and pulled her next to the yawl.

"Hold onto the side and I'll get you in," he said. Jennie did just as she was told. Luke grabbed her around the waist and lifted her up, but her legs still hung over the side. Luke hurriedly flung them over, and there she was, at last, completely out of the frigid water.

With her teeth chattering as she tried to thank him, Jennie leaned against Luke, her head buried in his chest, and sobbed. Luke gently, yet strongly, wrapped his massive arms around her as the yawl floated down the river toward the flatboat.

Jennie could hear the faint sound of laughter coming from behind them. She turned around to see a group of young men on the shore pointing at them and laughing.

"What are they laughin' at?" she managed to ask quietly while sitting up.

"Us," answered Luke as he got hold of the oars and rowed downstream, catching up with the flatboat.

She could hear Pa yelling from the flatboat as they approached.

"Do you hear them laughin' back there? Do you know what they're laughin' at? A stupid pilot who got himself so excited talkin' to a pretty girl that he forgot to watch the river and nearly killed us all! What were you thinkin'? You risked all of us, not to mention the boat! If you can't keep your mind on the river when Jennie's up here, then she'll just have to stay down below!" Jennie, too weak to feel any anger herself, felt suddenly sorry for Clyde. "Ma, you and James okay?" Pa yelled down to his wife as he took over from Clyde.

"We're fine; a little shook up, but fine," she answered.

Clyde climbed down to the lower deck and helped Luke and Jennie onto the boat. She was shivering, tears still running down her face. Ma came out of the galley door to help.

"It's my fault," Jennie declared. "I shouldn't have talked to him so much. I'm awful sorry! I didn't know," she said, hoping to take some of the heat off Clyde.

Pa answered from up top where he had taken over the steering. "Of course you didn't know any better. And it's not your fault. But Clyde does know better. We'll just relieve him of his pilotin' duties long enough to clean up the big mess he made!" He pointed to Clyde. "I don't want to see you until this boat is in good workin' order again. Now get busy!"

Jennie tried again. "It really was my fault, too."

"Jennie, kindly stop takin' up for that boy. He knows better. He knows we depend on him to be responsible. I don't know what got into him. Now you'd best go inside the galley and get out of those wet clothes."

"Yes, sir," she responded through her chattering teeth.

CHAPTER 3

THE SLAVE

"Jennie!" Clyde yelled as he sat upright on the mat where he slept. He looked around and saw the familiar sight of shelves with pottery and knickknacks and remembered he was in the store. Sweat ran in a narrow stream down his temples, his hands tightly fisted. The boat was still tied to the shore.

"Jesus, Clyde," murmured a sleepy James who turned over on his mat next to Clyde's. "You scared the livin' daylights outta me!"

Clyde could barely see his brother's form in the darkness of the pre-dawn hour. "It was a nightmare. Jennie was drownin'—it was all my fault—I couldn't save her!" Clyde gasped.

"Doesn't sound like a nightmare to me; sounds just like what you did yesterday. I've never seen Pa so mad!" James put his hands beneath his head. Clyde could see the whites of his eyes shining.

"Don't remind me. He may never get over it. I feel so stupid!" His mouth felt dry and sticky as he spoke. "I've got to figure out how to get in good with him again."

"Could take years…" James replied with a certain gaiety in his voice.

"Shut up, James. You're just lucky I'm the oldest so you don't have to pilot this thing. God forbid we should all be in your hands!"

There was silence for a moment. Clyde lay back down and rolled onto his stomach.

"Did you see her...?" Clyde began, then hesitated. "Did you see her when she was standing there all wet, shivering and crying?"

"I guess everybody did."

"She looked so tiny and frail. I'll bet I could put my hands around her waist and my fingers would touch. I couldn't stop looking at her body...." Clyde's voice trailed off as he remembered her breasts heaving as she sobbed, and her ankles as she lifted the hem of her skirt to wring out the cold water that permeated every fiber of her clothing. She looked exhausted and afraid. He had wanted to rush over and put his arms around her and tell her how sorry he was—how he would take better care of her from now on, how she really could trust him.

"What are you thinkin' about over there?" James' voice spoiled Clyde's reverie. "Do you have a crush on Jennie? Huh? Do you?"

"Who wouldn't? She's beautiful!"

"So much for treating her like a sister...."

A few minutes later, Clyde could hear the heavy breathing of his sleeping brother. Deciding that he couldn't go back to sleep, he climbed the ladder to the upper deck, pulling his coat around him for warmth. This was where he could think. Up on top of the world, no one around to interrupt his thoughts, no brother around to argue with him. Quiet. Pure quiet.

He sat on the lazy board resting his elbows on his knees, his head cradled in his hands, and listened. He wasn't sure what he hoped to hear, but still he listened.

Sometimes there's a lot to hear in the stillness of the river at night, he thought.

The wind echoed with the voices of men who had lost their lives on this river. Hundreds, thousands of them buried in this pulsating ribbon of liquid mud. The river so strong and willful, moving in her own time, in her own way, with nothing to stop her.

The water lapped against the shore, running in bursts of energy and then retreating onto itself in a muffled sound of repetitive motion.

The wooden boat creaked and moaned in protest at its static position, yearning to be let loose to float down the river again.

Clyde closed his eyes to listen more intently. A dog howled off in the distance, or was he imagining it? Maybe it was a wolf. *Are there wolves along this stretch of the river?* he wondered. The loud reverberating noise of an owl hooting in the darkness startled him and made him shiver, his flesh now covered with goose bumps. It called out, "Whoo, whoo!"

"Good question," he said out loud to the night. "Who am I? A man who floats down the river only to be pulled back upstream again over and over. What a life; am I destined to repeat this for eternity like Sisyphus?" He had read about Sisyphus in a book on Greek mythology that his grandfather had given him and which he had read cover to cover a number of times. The character had been condemned by Hades to roll a boulder to the top of a hill, only to have it roll back down again, repeating this action for eternity. "Sisyphus was condemned to do it for eternity. He had no choice, but I do. I'm not doing that." He took in a deep breath and filled his nostrils with the familiar smell of musty dampness and raw wood. He rubbed his hand along the edge of the lazy board and remembered his father's words.

"All this will be yours one day," Pa had said proudly. "You know these rivers like the back of your hand. I'll leave the business to you and be proud to call you my son!" Pa had beamed at the thought; Clyde had felt suffocated.

"There's got to be more. I'm not gonna spend the rest of my life like this. I'm gonna sit up high in the pilot house of a fine steamer. And that's just the beginning. I'm gonna have a whole fleet of boats, and I'll be able to run my business like a college-educated man. I'll have a real house, a big house in a town where my children can run and play instead of working all day like I do. No, I won't end up like Pa, doing back-breaking work all day, drinking when no one's around to see, just to be able to keep goin'. I have ideas, dreams. I'm going to go beyond the river and make a better life for myself and my family. I swear!" He spoke out loud to the night. He told it to the hooting owl and the howling dog and the lapping water. He told it to the world. But most importantly, he told it to himself, and he meant it.

"Who ya talkin' to?" Clyde recognized Luke's voice, which seemed to come out of nowhere. Luke came walking toward him, rubbing his hands together in the early morning chill.

"Myself. Just talkin' to myself."

"Ya picked a good night for it. No one around to tell ya nothin' different." Luke stood looking at the trees.

"What woke you up?" Clyde asked.

"Thoughts I heard somebody talkin," Luke said. "Wanted to be sure everythin' was okay."

"Sorry I woke you up. I didn't know I was being so loud."

"No matter. It does a man good to get some fresh morning air from time to time." Luke sat down next to Clyde. His legs stretched out in front of him, he leaned back on his straightened arms and looked up at the sky and continued to speak.

"I tell you, I loves livin' on this here boat on the river. Every day there's somethin' new to see. Always movin', never stuck in one place too long."

"I guess," Clyde answered. "But don't you get tired of it, of a new town every day, of never stoppin' and stayin' anywhere?"

"Hell, no! I done been stopped and stayed before and it weren't too good," Luke answered.

"What do you mean?" Clyde asked. "Don't you miss your wife and your son when you're gone for months at a time?"

"I miss 'em all right, Sarah and my little Man, and when I sees 'em, we be real happy to be together. We be so happy the whole time I'm home. No fussin', no naggin', nothin' but good times. You know, when I be on the plantation with my firs' wife, she be hollerin' and cursin' and the like. She was one strong woman! And all the time I be havin' to listen to the hollerin' and cursin' of the boss man while I'm saying, 'Yezza, yezza' and actin' so happy and grateful when alls I feels was somebody holdin' a pillow over my face so I couldn't see where I was goin' and I couldn't breathe." He looked at Clyde. "It's all in how you look at it."

"That's kinda how I feel right now. Like I'm being smothered. How did you stand it?" Clyde was genuinely interested.

"I kep' my mind on where I wants to go and what I wants to do and didn't stop tryin' till I got there. And look where I am! A free man livin' an' eatin' with a nice white family and makin' enough money to send home to my family!"

"But Luke…"

"Don't you talk, just a-listen to me. There's nothin' freer than the river. I gets my freedom from this here river. She lets me go along for the ride. I can stay, I can go. I works real hard, but then I gets to sit back and rest as we floats along. Your ma and pa, they treats me like a man on this here boat. Not no lesser, but a man same's you. That's free. And if this ain't enough for you, you figures out what you wants and don't stop till you gets it. Don't let fear get hold of ya. And if ya gets lost along the way, just try somethin' else and keep goin'. If you don't, you'll be livin' somebody else's life, not your own."

"But Luke, you were a slave!"

"There's more than one way to be a slave, Mr. Clyde."

CHAPTER 4

THE COIN

There was always some business to be had in Randolph, Tennessee. A few hours after Clyde and Luke had shared the early morning air, the boat was tied up and alive once more, with the exception of Jennie, who had been left to sleep in after her unexpected swim in the Mississippi the day before. Later, Pa took her into town to replace her shoes, which ended up at the bottom of the river. Clyde followed later and entered the general store shortly after them.

"Hello," he greeted them.

Jennie smiled and said, "Your father is buyin' me a pair of new shoes! Isn't that wonderful?" She looked down at the brown shoes, twisting her foot to the right and left in admiration.

"Well," Pa began, "her old shoes are at the bottom of the Mississippi, thanks to you."

"I'm sorry, Pa," Clyde said. "Please don't talk about that here."

"Why not? Are you embarrassed about makin' a fool of yourself and almost killing your family? I sure would be."

"Pa, please! Not here. I'm sorry. I really am sorry." Clyde hung his head, embarrassed.

"Yeah, yeah. Sure you are," Pa replied, his tone still angry.

Clyde gathered everything on Ma's list and, with Jennie's help, carried it all back to the boat. As they approached the flatboat, they saw a wagon with four-foot sides filled to overflowing with…what? Were those white things jammed every which way onto the wagon really bones? They quickened their steps and in moments knew it was true. The wagon was full of bones.

How strange, she thought. *What would somebody do with all these bones?*

Jennie stood by the wagon, tempted to reach out to the bones, when a man came from around the other side and addressed them in a high-pitched voice. "Howdy! Name's Felix." He grinned, showing the worst set of teeth Jennie had ever seen. Her tongue glided along her own teeth as if to reassure herself that they were still there and intact. She shook her head.

"Hello. I'm Clyde. I guess you're looking for my pa."

"Is he the one owns this flatboat?" He snorted, rubbed his nose with the back of his hand, and left the residue on his sleeve.

"Yes, sir. He's not here, but he'll be here soon."

"No matter. I'll jes' sit here an' wait. Got all day. Been waitin' quite a spell for ya. Can wait a little longer, I 'spect." He walked up to the gray mare that had pulled the wagon here. The mare looked as much in need of food as Felix did of a dentist. He stroked the cowlick on the horse's neck and sat down next to her on the ground to wait.

Jennie went inside and found Ma in the store alone. "There's a man named Felix out there with a wagon piled high with bones! He says he'll wait to see Pa. I've never seen so many bones. Come see!"

They walked out onto the porch and surveyed the unusual scene.

"My word," said Ma, folding her hands across her chest. "That's a lot of bones!" Felix waved to them without moving. "You go and offer him a cup of coffee. Where is my husband?" She seemed to be speaking to herself.

"I'm not sure. He said he'd only be a minute behind me."

"I'll bet I know where he is," she mumbled quietly.

"How do people in these towns know when we arrive?" Jennie asked.

"Nothing much goes on in these small places. Somebody out and about sees us tying up and goes into town to tell everybody."

Felix accepted Jennie's offer, and by the time she reappeared with the tin mug full of hot black coffee, Pa had arrived and was talking to the man rather loudly and laughing, too. His joviality was exaggerated as he slapped Felix hard on the back.

"...and you say you have another wagon load?" Pa asked.

"Yes, sir. Been gettin' 'em from the new slaughterhouse and pilin' 'em up behind my cabin. I'm ready to cash 'em in and they say you buys most anything."

"That's the truth."

Clyde spoke up. "First I have to see if we have room in the hold for this much cargo, and then we'll have to see how much you want for your stack of bones. I'm not sure how much cash we have handy right this minute. I'll need some time to work this all out. Can you give us about an hour or so?" Pa had stepped back and seemed to be enjoying watching his eldest work.

"I reckon I can. I'll just tie my old mare to that tree over yonder. She could use a drink if you could manage it," he said, stroking her side.

"I love horses," Jennie chimed in. "I'll be happy to get her a drink and look after her if you want to go to town."

"I'd be much obliged," he answered. "Take her for a ride if you like. She ain't much to look at but she loves a good ride. Her name's Dolly." Jennie took the reins from Felix and tied her loosely to a tree.

As soon as Felix was out of sight, Jennie asked Pa, "What will somebody do with all these bones?" Standing next to him, Jennie saw how red his eyes were and began to wonder why.

"Lots of things," he laughed. "They'll be ground up and used in cleaners to scrub things with," Pa began, talking slowly and swaying slightly and then sitting down on the ground and rubbing his head.

Clyde was quick to pick up the conversation, eager to show off his knowledge. "They're full of calcium, so they can be used as medicine to make your bones stronger. And of course, there's bone china, among other things."

"I was wondering." Jennie looked down at her feet, afraid to ask permission to ride the mare. "Would it be all right if I went for a short ride on Dolly?"

"Sure, just don't be gone too long. Ma's gonna need your help." Clyde stood up, brushed off his backside, then walked onto the boat.

Jennie was thrilled. She was accustomed to riding most every day on the farm. Without hesitating, she untied the mare from the tree, jumped up on her bare back, straddled the mare and took off in a flurry of fabric and auburn hair. She saw Clyde staring at her in amazement as she sped past.

With the flatboat out of sight, she felt her first sense of complete freedom since leaving home. Dolly's back felt bony between her soft thighs and her gait was unsteady. Jennie urged her into a gallop and her gait smoothed out as her front hooves dug into the hard earth followed by the softer touch of her hind legs. Jennie sat her unkempt mount well, a testament to her years of racing across the pastures back home.

Emotion welled up inside of her and she closed her eyes. *I'm free*, she thought, *I'm really free!* The whisper of this inside her head didn't reach the part of her that felt so alive, that felt about to burst. "I'm free," she spoke loudly into the wind that bit at her ears. It still wasn't enough. "I'M FREE!" she yelled at the top of her lungs three times, her head back. Then, in an instant, the feeling of freedom that now enveloped her and held her so tightly morphed into fear of the unknown. "I'm free," she sobbed finally, still racing toward nothing in particular. She let go of the reins, hung her arms on either side of the mare, and rested her head on the horse's rocking neck as the thundering sound of galloping hooves slackened to a walk.

She kept her head down, her face feeling the coarse, dry mane that was wet with her tears. She smelled the moist heat of sweat and her ears filled with the sound of heavy breathing as the mare caught her breath. Jennie felt herself shivering.

She missed Leona and wondered how she was sleeping alone in their room. She missed her brothers, and even her father. *Are they looking for me? Are they worried about me?* she thought. *And Miss Dora, did they find out she deceived them? I have to write them, tonight! I want them to know I'm fine...and that I miss them.* Dolly walked on a bit, then stopped to nibble on some grass. Jennie slid off the horse and sat down on the ground where she landed, still holding the reins. She looked around at the rolling Tennessee hills and grasslands, not unlike her own Kentucky. It was a strange feeling, not really knowing where she was. She found a coin in the dirt beside her and picked it up. *Good luck? Is there really any good luck here somewhere for me?*

She rolled onto her back and looked up at the blue sky. There were a few wispy clouds that seemed close to the ground. In the center, it looked as if white flames were leaping from a fire of cotton buds, horizontal flames reaching out to touch the horizon.

It's going to be cold, she thought. *A clear day with the clouds moving in. I'd better get back.*

Before she left, she sat cross-legged, closed her eyes, and prayed that everything was going to work out all right for her. She put the coin in her pocket.

When Jennie arrived back at the flatboat, all the men were busy unloading the wagon. They filled burlap bags with the bones, tied the top with string, and carried them onto the boat, where Pa weighed them carefully. Clyde wrote down the amount, and Luke placed them in the hold.

Another Black man was helping Luke in the hold. Jennie didn't recognize him.

"Jennie," Pa yelled, "help those boys tie up the bags." She went to work and, for at least a short while, forgot her loneliness.

By dinnertime, it was cold. They all drank coffee to keep warm. It had been colder than usual that fall. The leaves had turned beautiful colors early on and there had already been some snow flurries. It was unusual for the Barbours to be on the rivers in the fall, but the shipyard wasn't busy and they needed the income.

The Black man that Jennie had seen earlier was named Esau. He ate dinner with his wife and little daughter in the deck room. They were traveling downriver trying to make it to Osceola, Arkansas, to see Esau's mother before she passed away. Pa said they could tie their yawl to the back of the flatboat and float downriver with them in exchange for helping out. They were to sleep in the hold. Jennie didn't think she'd get a wink of sleep down there, not with all those bones!

Jennie was starting to ache all over from the day's hard work. All she wanted to do was to finish cleaning the dishes and slide under the covers in her bed.

"Oh, I forgot something," Clyde added excitedly. He stood up and pulled a tiny bag out of his pocket. "Mr. Parks at the store gave me six pieces of peppermint...*free!* One for everyone! Oh, except Esau and his family." Clyde wasn't sure what to do about that situation.

"I expect they feel excited just to be on this comfortable flatboat of ours," Pa said.

"That was nice of Mr. Parks," said Ma as she washed another plate.

"Sure Ma, except he wasn't so generous until he saw our big order," Clyde answered.

The men talked while Jennie and Ma finished cleaning the kitchen. Jennie saw Luke step out to the deck room. She peeked through the doorway and saw him crouched down next to Esau's little girl, giving her his piece of peppermint. From the look on the little girl's face, Jennie wondered if she'd ever had any before and felt a warmth penetrate her deeply at the sight of this giving.

They stayed another day in Randolph. At the end of the day, Jennie sat in one of the two rocking chairs on the porch writing letters to her father, Leona, and Miss Dora before starting dinner. Pa, Clyde, James, and Luke were standing just inside talking and Pa was writing something in a small book.

"The big things are the two wagonloads of bones, seven barrels of scrap iron, nine railroad rails, and ten bushels of rags," he said. "We're loaded to the guards, so we'll head for Chickasaw Bluffs to unload, though I suspect we'll see the *Gray Eagle* or the *Rainbow* heading upstream before we reach there. If so, she'll take the load for us. Ma, hand me the till."

Ma rose from the other rocking chair and handed the metal box to Pa. He unlocked it and counted the money inside. When he was finished, she took the locked box and went to put it away. He looked concerned.

"Pa, isn't there something you need to tell the boys?" Ma asked as she reappeared in the storeroom.

He closed the book and cleared his throat, readying himself to say something important. "We're gonna do things a little different this year. Clyde's 19 now, a real man. I have decided that instead of both of you boys heading back home to Jeffersonville, James will go back alone, and Clyde will stay on the boat to help."

"But Pa, that's not fair!" James whined. "I don't want to go back by myself. Grandma will drive me crazy with just the two of us all those months! Plus, you need me on the boat!"

"What a thing to say about your grandma," Ma said. "She's taken care of you boys since you were born. She needs your help, and you need more schoolin'. I won't have a son of mine walkin' around without enough education!" This was the first time Jennie had seen her angry.

"I can't stay on the boat," Clyde protested. "I can't do this and study for my entrance exams for college. I need to go back to Jeffersonville, get back on at the shipyard part-time, and have time to study. You've known all along that was my plan. You can't do this to me now! I'm almost ready to start!"

"I won't go!" James shouted, stomping his feet.

"Listen, both of you," Pa said sharply. "The decision has been made, so stop your whining. James, you read like a baby, and you hate learnin'. It's time you grew up and acted more like your brother. And Clyde, Grandpa is meeting us to take James' place. He's bringing another box of books for you two to study together."

"It's not the same, Pa! When do I ever have time to really study on this old boat? I'm too busy doing everything else! I want to go to college!" Clyde's face was turning red.

"College? You know we can't afford that and what would you learn anyway that really matters? It's just another one of your fantasies. Grandpa went to college in Ireland, so you can just go to college on this flatboat. He'll teach you whatever you wanna know." Pa seemed quite proud of himself for putting all of this together.

"He went to college 40 years ago in a foreign country. What does he know about the world of business in 1894? Nothin', that's what. Nothin'! I have to study for this exam."

Jennie desperately wanted to disappear but couldn't without being obvious.

"Stop your yellin'! Don't you dare talk to me like that." Pa was poking his finger into Clyde's chest repeatedly. "The decision is final."

Pa stormed off the boat and headed to town. James ran off the boat and headed in the other direction. Luke slunk back farther into the boat.

"Oh, Clyde," Ma said, "I'm so sorry. He shouldn't have gone off like that. But we can't afford to hire a hand to take your place this year. You know how slow tradin' has been. The railroads are catchin' up with us. In a few more years, there won't be enough flatboat tradin' on these rivers and then I don't know how we'll earn a livin'." Tears were flowing down her cheeks.

"Aw, Ma, don't cry. But I won't spend the rest of my life tradin' up and down the rivers. I'm not gonna do it! I have ideas for where I want to go, and nothin' is gonna stop me."

"I know, son. And what I'm tellin' you is that in a few short years, we won't be doing this anymore. So, take heart." She put her arms around her eldest. His head hung low as she kissed his forehead.

"I need to get some fresh air. I feel like I can't breathe," Clyde said. When he stepped out onto the porch and saw Jennie there within earshot of all this, he quickly ascended the ladder to the roof, feeling totally humiliated.

Jennie took her writing papers, walked inside, and put them on her bed. She continued on to the galley to help with dinner. She was very uncomfortable at having been present during such an unpleasant family exchange. When Jennie walked into the galley, Ma was wiping tears from her face with her apron. Jennie was the first to speak.

"I hope me being here hasn't caused these problems. I would hate to think..."

"No, Jennie," Ma replied. "You bein' here is a blessin' to me, havin' your help and your company. And I think it's good for the boys to be around a female who isn't their ma. This is just life. Pa shouldn't-a talked to Clyde like that, but Clyde has to be more respectful to his pa. They'll have to get over it. This isn't the first or the last disappointment of my boys' young lives. Gettin' through this will help them grow and learn." She began to get things together for the evening meal. "You'll love Grandpa. He's kind and full of interestin' stories."

"Do you think..." Jennie began shyly, "would it be possible, maybe, for him to teach me some things, too?"

"Oh, yes. He would love to have such a pretty girl as his student! What do you want to learn?" asked Ma.

"Anything, everything." Jennie's mind was racing.

"That would be fun for both of you."

When it was time for dinner, Jennie went up top to get Clyde. She was embarrassed and wasn't sure what to say. He was sitting in his usual spot on the lazy board at the stern, elbows on his knees, his face cradled in his hands. She walked back to where he was and sat beside him.

"I'm sorry I heard all that. I didn't mean to. I'm sorry. I didn't know you wanted to go to college," she said quietly.

Clyde dropped his hands from his face, sighed, then spoke, not looking at her directly. "There never was much hope, but I always dreamed about it. Grandpa graduated from the University of Dublin.

Remember, I told you that he taught school in Jeffersonville, Indiana, where we have our home. He'd love for me to go to college, but Pa says it's a waste of time, and we don't have the money." He looked in her eyes, depleted and exhausted.

"You must feel awful! But you know, your ma said in a few years you'll be off this boat. At least you know you're not stuck here forever. That's why I left Kentucky; I couldn't stand to think of being stuck in a house with some old man I don't love." Jennie looked off in the distance as she shared her thoughts. "So, we're not stuck, either of us." She saw the river stretching on and on before them and felt the stillness of the cool evening descending upon them. She wondered what was going to happen to her. Would she ever be able to go home? Would she spend the rest of her life on this mighty river that dazzled in the moonlight as it moved tons of water so effortlessly? She knew so little of the world that she couldn't even have imagined what life had waiting for her. She looked at him and saw his disappointment.

"The way I see it," she continued, "this is a beginning for both of us—the beginning of the rest of our lives! We need to figure out what we want and use this time to prepare for that instead of wastin' it wantin' to be somewhere else. My mother used to tell me to enjoy every day because tomorrow, today is gone forever. I'm hopin' your grandpa will teach me some things, too. And you have lots of time to learn whatever you need to for college." She smiled at him.

"You sound like Luke," Clyde answered.

"Really?"

"Yeah, he said to decide what I want and keep going till I get it."

"Right! Why don't we do that? We could make a pact and even help each other get where we want to go." Jennie stood up and took something out of her pocket. "Here's a coin I found on the road yesterday when I went ridin'. I want you to keep it as our good luck coin. Every now and then we'll take it out and rub it!" She put out her hand that held the coin. "Let's shake on it."

Clyde stood up. "What exactly are we shakin' on?" he asked.

"That we'll help each other keep goin' until we get where we want to go!" Jennie beamed.

They shook hands, the coin pressed tightly between them. He held onto her hand. "I think I could do most anythin' with you helpin' me." He looked into her beautiful, glowing, hazel eyes, smiled at her, and released her hand, holding onto the coin.

Jennie could feel her cheeks turning red and was thankful for the waning daylight. But this time, she realized it was a pleasant burning she felt. When he let go of her hand, she laughed coyly and turned to walk away.

CHAPTER 5

THE GREENHORN

They let the lines go at 5:00 a.m., as usual. Jennie was on deck, catching lines in James' place; he was already on his way back to Jeffersonville. Pa yelled out, "To oars!" and let out his customary whistle. She had asked to help with the workings of the boat, but Ma didn't think it was right for a girl to be too involved with all of that. Catching lines seemed to be a good job for her, and after a few too many misses, she was starting to catch them with facility.

"Good work for a greenhorn!" yelled Grandpa, snickering at Jennie. Grandpa had arrived by train a few days after James left for Jeffersonville.

"What's a greenhorn?" she yelled back.

"A boatman making his first trip downriver. I'd say that applies to you!"

"So, Grandpa, is that supposed to be a compliment?" Clyde called down.

"You bet! There's no room for sniveling girls on this powerful river. Can't afford to give her the chance to pull you under," Grandpa continued.

"She's already showed us that won't happen," Pa added from up on top. "She learned that lesson early, with a little help from Clyde."

Clyde could hear his father laughing and could only hope Pa wouldn't go into detail about that incident.

"That's enough, Pa," came Ma's welcome voice from inside. "Now give me back my girl so we can get started on breakfast."

James hadn't been gone long, but Clyde had to admit, if only to himself, that he missed his little brother. He shared his sleeping space with Grandpa now, which wasn't quite the same as having a little brother to boss around—and who didn't snore.

Pa and Clyde had put James on the *Alice Brown* for the trip home to Indiana. Both Captain George Clark and his partner, Captain Robert Boles, were old friends of the Barbours and had often chaperoned the boys on trips home. They were fun people who didn't expect much in return for the favor. When James was ready to get on the towboat, Clyde pulled something out of his pocket and put it into James' hand.

"I want you to have this. It's only 23 cents, but it's all I have." Clyde had not included the coin Jennie had given him.

James looked at Clyde with disbelief. "Why?" he asked.

"You're my brother; isn't that enough?" James put the coins in his pocket and put out his hand, and Clyde shook it.

"Gee, thanks, Clyde."

"See you in a few months, little brother."

Everyone was pleased with how well Jennie and Grandpa got along. She had told Clyde that she'd never known either of her own grandfathers. Grandpa was happy to take their place. Clyde found himself feeling a little jealous at how much time they spent together talking.

Later that morning, during Pa's watch, Clyde spotted a coal boat left stranded on a sandbar. Coal was strewn all around it. It wasn't an unusual sight. Coal boats were made of very lightweight material with the weight of the coal balanced by the weight of the water to hold it together. They couldn't withstand any impact and would break apart easily, leaving their Pittsburgh coal, at $2.50 a ton, to be devoured by the river.

Clyde had spent much of the previous morning cutting wood for fires and cooking. The sight of all that coal gave him a great idea. He found Luke in the deck room and asked him to get in the yawl with him. Quickly, they rowed off to the sandbar and picked up a load of coal. They rowed back to the flatboat and emptied it. They were able to fill the yawl twice before the flatboat started to get too far away.

"The way I figure it," Clyde said to Luke, "we can use this instead of wood and save ourselves some wood-cuttin' blisters for a while!" Clyde was quite pleased with his idea. By the time they had finished getting the coal into the hold, Clyde looked about as black as Luke, who couldn't stop laughing.

"Guess you could be my chil'," he laughed, taking a piece of coal and smearing it on what was left of Clyde's white face.

"Only better lookin'," Clyde joked.

"Huh," was all Luke had to say to that.

Some of the big threats to the flatboat were the wind, bends in the river, and snags. It was the wind that day that was trying their patience. The morning had started out with a nice brisk breeze to their backs, helping to push them on their way. By the afternoon, however, the wind had picked up and was trying to decide on its own which direction the flatboat would go. Pa and Clyde took turns steering into the middle of the river. It was a weekday, and the river was full of steamboats and barges headed in both directions, which meant the middle didn't belong to them. Luke and Esau joined the other two on top to work the sweeps.

By the time Pa decided they would have to tie up and wait out the wind, they were in one of the long bends in the river. "How long is this bend, son?" he asked Clyde.

"It'll be about two miles, Pa." There were bends in the Mississippi up to ten miles long. They were nightmares for any boat, particularly in high winds.

"Jesus!" Pa shouted as another surge of wind from the starboard side caught his sweep. "We've got to find a bank!"

"But Pa, you know it's not safe to tie up on a bend," said Clyde, who had seen firsthand how the swift current could cut into the bank and collapse it, sending trees crashing into the river.

"There's no choice," Pa replied. "Let's pull real hard to starboard. Give it all you got!" Luke and Esau each worked one of the side sweeps, with Pa and Clyde now holding onto the tiller together.

"Push into it! Don't back off! Try to hold her!" Pa was yelling louder and louder as the wind stirred up the muddy waters, leaving little white caps across the width of the river. The river was like a tunnel, the wind hugging the banks, then pushing off to meet itself in the middle. Even the steamboats were moving more slowly, but they didn't face the potential consequences their flatboat did.

Out of the clamor of the moment, Clyde heard a loud crack and saw Luke fall to the platform. His sweep had broken in half. The flatboat quickly succumbed to the rushing current, moving out into the river. The determined wind was at their backs again, pushing them onward. There was no controlling the boat now.

It wasn't until Clyde almost fell overboard from the impact that he saw the sandbar barely visible just beneath the surface of the water. He heard someone scream downstairs as the boat came to an abrupt halt.

"Goddamn it!" yelled Pa, helplessly.

"Luke, are you hurt?" Clyde rushed over to Luke who was sitting down, looking himself over.

"Scared, mostly," Luke answered. "Never had a sweep break in two. That's some nasty wind!"

"And I can smell the rain coming. Next, we'll be soaked." Clyde helped Luke up and brushed him off. He looked around to get an idea of their location. "I hope nobody runs into us out here." He figured that they were about 150 yards from the outer bank. A towboat passed them on the port side, deckhands scrambling to keep the tow intact as they came out of the bend.

"I hopes we can get off this bar." Luke winced in pain as he took a step. "My knee don't wanna work too good." He limped over to the lazy board and sat down.

"Luke, you stay put. I'm goin' down to get started freein' us up."
Clyde descended the ladder and met the others, who had already
made it into the storeroom. Esau was holding his little girl, who was
crying, his wife holding onto him. Pa and Grandpa were arguing
about what to do next. Ma was helping Jennie up from the floor
where she had apparently landed when they hit. The flatboat was
slightly askew, the angles just off center enough to give Jennie an
unsettled feeling in her stomach. "Is anybody hurt?" Clyde asked. "I
heard somebody scream."

"That was me," admitted Jennie, looking a little embarrassed. "It
was just so sudden!" She straightened out her skirt and ran her hand
over her hair to smooth it.

"Pa, let's try to dig her out before she sinks any lower." Clyde was
ready to get going again.

Luke made it down the ladder and offered to check the hull
for damage. All the other men picked up a shovel or bucket and
gingerly stepped off onto the sandbar. Ankle- to knee-deep in the
icy water, they tried to move as much sand as possible away from
the stranded flatboat. Clyde's feet and hands were soon numb from
the blowing cold wind and even colder water. "I can't work fast
enough," he said out loud. "As soon as I move a good bit of sand, a
wave brings more!" They worked for over an hour, taking breaks
to warm their hands and feet, before giving up. Luke had found
no leaks.

"We'll wait out the wind then take the yawl ashore for some
saplings, supposing we can't get a tow off here before that. For now,
let's just warm up and have some dinner," Pa said. Clyde noticed how
old his father looked in his windblown state, his face dry and wrinkled
like an old sailor who has spent too many summers in the sun.

After dinner, the men sat at the table and discussed how they
would try again to free the flatboat in the morning. They dispersed
early, everyone exhausted from the day's adventures and eager for a
good night's sleep in their precarious position, before the morning's
work began.

Clyde noticed Jennie's door open as he made his way out of the galley, trying not to fall. He stopped and looked in slyly and saw her sitting on her bed writing. She looked up at him.

"Oh, sorry," he said sheepishly. "I saw the light comin' from in here and was just checkin'. Who are you writin'?"

"My family. I write often, especially to my little sister. I know she misses me a lot." She folded the paper and put it into an envelope.

Clyde thought he saw a reflection from her lantern that caught a tear rolling down her cheek. "What's your little sister's name?"

"Leona. Her name's Leona. Even before my mother died, she was my little shadow."

"You must be homesick."

"Yes. Oh, yes. It's much harder than I thought." She wiped her eyes with her right index finger while trying to hide a sniffle. "But my father was gonna make me marry some old rich man. And it wasn't the first time he tried to do that. He wasn't gonna let me say no this time. I couldn't live like that. I just couldn't!" Jennie grew more animated as she talked about her father. "I think I'll go to sleep now."

"Good night, Jennie. I'm sorry you're so sad." Clyde saw a stern, determined look come over her face and remembered their lucky coin, which he always kept in his pocket. He took it out to show her. "Here!" He walked over and held his hand out, holding the coin. "Let's think about where we're goin', not where we are. Where do you wanna go, Jennie?"

She took his hand and held it, the coin warm between them. "Someplace grand!" she announced, trying to smile.

"Then here's to someplace grand," said Clyde, shaking her hand several times. When they let go, the coin fell to the floor. "You keep it for a while now. I think you need it tonight." He picked up the coin, handed it to her, and then briefly touched her hair. He turned and left without another word.

As Clyde settled down to sleep on his lumpy mat, he held that brief moment in his mind. He smelled the hand that had touched her silky hair, but no scent lingered there. Instead, his nostrils filled with the smell of damp wood so familiar to him that he didn't really smell it at all. Outside, he heard raindrops and prayed the river would rise and float them out of their present predicament. He hugged his knees to his chest for warmth and dreamed of kissing that soft auburn hair.

In the morning, as usual, the men ate first in the lopsided galley so they could get to work. Even Esau ate at the table while they discussed how the day would unfold. Pa, Luke, and Esau took the yawl to shore, cut down some saplings, and brought them back to the sandbar to use as rollers. Once back at the boat, they worked for hours trying to shift the boat enough to get the saplings underneath. It took most of the day, but they were finally successful. The makeshift rollers in place, they tried unsuccessfully to push the flatboat back into the moving water. A passing towboat with no vessel in tow tied a line to their boat and tried to help move it, but even that didn't work. People on the river are always happy to pitch in and help; they know it could be their turn to need help at any moment. They were on the lookout for an empty barge onto which they could put the contents of the hold, making it easier to dislodge.

"There's nothing left to do but wait. Either another friendly barge owner will come along, or the river will eventually rise," said an exhausted Pa at dinnertime. "Let's pray it's not too long."

"It'll be fine, Pa," said Ma, mustering up her best reassuring tone. "We have what we need, and you men can always go huntin' and fishin' if we get hungry. We'll just make the best of this time and take it easy. It's not often we get that chance!"

"What about Esau and his family?" asked Jennie, concerned.

"Esau will have to decide for himself whether he wants to wait it out or go on alone," Pa answered.

"I hope he stays," Grandpa said. "He's a lot of help."

That evening, lanterns in hand, they all went up on top with blankets and jackets to keep them warm. The wind had calmed down and they sought out some crisp fresh air. Grandpa brought his fiddle and his tin cup with him.

"Be careful, don't slip," warned Pa. The boat's precarious position was not only a nuisance but dangerous.

"Oh, nonsense," Grandpa replied; it was his favorite saying.

Once up top, without any prompting, Grandpa started playing his fiddle and singing one of his favorite songs.

> "Oh, dem golden slippers.
> Oh, dem golden slippers,
> golden slippers I'm goin' to wear
> because they look so neat..."

There wasn't a still foot on the boat, all their tapping toes making a low rumbling that seemed to heat up the night. Ma started clapping in time, the motion catching on like fire around what was now a loose circle of people. Pa quickly snatched her up and whirled her around to the music, her dress gently billowing out as they danced a little jig in perfect time with the music they knew so well. They laughed as the tilted dance floor got in the way of their steps.

> "Golden slippers I'm goin' wear
> to walk the golden street!"

The lantern sitting on the deck partially lit all the smiling faces, but contorted by their own shadows, the faces looked gloomy and malevolent. Even Jennie's silhouette was bloated and absurd. Their extremities blended in with the grayness of the overcast night.

"That was fun!" Ma squealed as the song ended, catching her breath, which was visible in the air when she exhaled. "What's next, Grandpa?"

"'Camptown Races'!" Clyde said.

"'Oh! Susanna'!" said Jennie.

"'Old Folks at Home,'" Luke offered shyly.

"Hold on, hold on," Grandpa laughed. "We'll get to them all, but ladies first! Will you sing it for us, Jennie?"

"Yes, I will!"

And they were off, Jennie standing next to Grandpa, who was playing his heart out.

> "Well, I came from Alabama with
> my banjo on my knee..."

Everyone chimed in at the refrain.

> "Oh! Susanna, now don't you cry for me..."

Before the song ended, they were all on their feet dancing and swaying to the music as it echoed across the great emptiness of the Mississippi River. Their applause at the end could doubtless be heard all the way on shore.

"And now, out of respect for our revered steersman, Clyde Barbour, we will continue on with 'Camptown Races.' Jennie?" Grandpa grabbed her hand.

"Yes, sir?" she asked.

"Would you please teach that poor grandson of mine how to dance?" Grandpa smiled deep and long as he looked across at Clyde, then took a sip from his cup.

"I'll try." She walked over to Clyde and hung her head in embarrassment until the tune began. Clyde took her hand, and everyone watched as they began to dance. He held her hand and put his other hand on her tiny waist. He felt the soft touch of her hand on his shoulder. Her big hazel eyes caught the light when they turned into it, sparkling briefly, then were hidden in the darkness when they whirled away from it.

> "Camptown races sing their song,
> doo-da, doo-da..."

"Sorry," said Clyde when he stepped on her small foot. He felt clumsy and uncomfortable dancing, as he always had.

"No, I'm sorry. I think it was my fault." They looked at each other and started to laugh.

Clyde hoped the song would last forever. Usually, he loved to hear the music filling the air but would just as soon sit out the dancing. But the dancing afforded him an unparalleled opportunity not only to be close to Jennie but to actually touch her! *This dancing thing is not so bad,* he thought.

The song was soon over, and Jennie went to sit by Grandpa. She watched him take another sip from his cup and asked, "Is that coffee you're drinking?"

Grandpa giggled. "No, girl, this is my tonic."

"What kind of tonic?" Jennie asked innocently.

"His gin is more like it," Ma responded.

"A man needs his tonic, you know," he told Ma. "How about just a little more?" he asked, holding up his tin cup in her direction.

"If you promise to tell us one of your stories tonight, I'll get you some more."

"Get me a cup, too, Ma, while you're down there," said Pa. Ma didn't answer.

"I'm more than happy to oblige," Grandpa answered. Ma took his cup as well as Pa's, and disappeared downstairs.

"Luke, why don't you sing one for us?" Pa asked.

"Yeah, Luke. One of those old songs," added Clyde. Luke had a wonderful low voice but was a bit shy.

"I didn't know Luke could sing," said Jennie.

"Only if I has to," Luke said, smiling, seemingly pleased to be regarded as a chanteur. "How 'bout 'De Boatmen's Dance?'"

"Let's do it!" answered Grandpa as Ma returned with two full tin cups, trying not to spill any on the slanted deck. He took a long sip, put the cup down, and readied himself to play. Luke moved to sit next to the fiddler and began to sing:

"High row, de boatmen row…"

Luke couldn't contain his enthusiasm and stood up to dance a little jig as he sang.

When he finished, they all stood and applauded, including Esau and his family. Luke bowed formally, his face one big grin.

"Do another," Ma yelled over the noise. "Do that one we like so much; you know what one I mean."

"Yes, Ma'am, I knows what one you likes. Let me get a sip of somethin' firs'." He took a sip from his own mug, cleared his throat, and began to sing.

> "Swing low, sweet chariot,
> Comin' for to carry me home…"

The beauty and solemnity of the song that had just ended hung on the dense air surrounding them all. The briefest moment of silence followed, a silence that penetrated Clyde's soul as he was infused with the living, breathing energy of the river that wanted to consume him, this river of which legends were told. The Ohio River was beautiful and majestic, but the Mississippi was alive. It had a soul. It was part of him whether he liked it or not. He had grown up drinking her muddy water, swimming in her outstretched arms, and crying when she picked a fight and won, as she usually did.

"We couldn't end on a finer note than that. Thanks, Luke," Pa said as he stood up. "Grandpa's story will have to wait until tomorrow night. I'll see all of you when the sun comes up."

They took turns descending the ladder, except for Clyde, who needed his few minutes of solitude. He walked back to the lazy board and stood looking out at the darkness. "I don't care what he says. I don't care what anybody says. I am goin' to college. I'm gonna make something of myself. I'm gonna be a great provider for my family and do things Pa can't even imagine. I'm gonna own one of those mansions we see on the river."

CHAPTER 6

THE BARGAINING

A few days passed and the flatboat eventually eased itself off of the sandbar. Esau had decided that his family would wait it out but was eager to make it to his mother's side.

One morning, when Jennie woke up early, she heard the low mumbling of whispered speech. She wrapped her shawl around her shoulders and walked toward the sound, finding Esau, his wife, and daughter on their knees in prayer. She heard him pray that his mother would still be alive when they finally arrived at her side.

"I knows she's yours, Lord, and you gonna take her when you wants, but I pray you don't wants her today."

Jennie's mind traveled back to her own mother's passing. Her mother lay dying on her bed, the smell of death filling the air. She was pale and thin, looking as though she could be whisked away on the wings of a butterfly. Jennie could remember sitting next to that bed for hours, hoping to catch her mother awake and talk with her, never knowing when the last time would be.

"Jennie, please get out of this room and get some fresh air. The air in this room is full of sickness and not good for your young body," Mother had said.

Jennie had looked at her with a scowl on her face that made her mother smile. "You are so stubborn! A stubborn female will have a hard life. Men don't like that in a wife. Learn to give a little and smooth things out. That's a woman's place."

Miss Dora had come to see her mother almost every day. Having been friends since they were children, Miss Dora was not about to let her friend go off to the other side without being near her. Her nursing experience was a great help in caring for her close friend. But there had been nothing anyone could do other than keep her comfortable and wrapped in love.

"Good morning, Jennie!" chimed Ma, who came out of her sleeping quarters dressed and ready for the day. She seemed particularly cheery this morning. "I'm so happy to be off that old sandbar! Esau, we're finally on our way. Let's pray for fair weather."

Esau got up and helped his wife do the same. She pulled their little girl up into her arms and walked behind him out onto the porch.

They were headed straight for Osceola. There were so many little towns along the river that it wouldn't be possible to land at them all. Pa was eager to help get Esau back home.

They pulled into Osceola Towhead a few days later. Jennie heard the steamboat *Morning Glory* blow her landing. She imagined what it would be like to travel the river in such splendor. She loved the music these beautiful steamboats played as they steamed along with seeming effortlessness. They brought a festive feeling to the meandering river. The music brought smiles to the faces of many who found little to smile about in the doldrums of their own lives.

Life was hard for most of the people whose homes sat on either side of the river. Many were farmers taking advantage of the rich soil left behind by the Mississippi. It gave them the healthy fabric from which to sow nourishment for those who didn't live along its path.

Cotton was another mainstay. Jennie found the cotton fields beautiful and tranquil when the cotton was ready to be picked. Miles and miles of white, soft cotton balls in every direction. Mostly Black people picked the cotton and she had often heard them singing low, monotone spirituals to keep their minds above the arduous, monotonous task at hand. She had been told that if they picked from dawn to dusk, a good picker could leave the field having picked 400 pounds a day. That amount brought in 40 cents plus whatever monies other members of the family earned. Jennie couldn't imagine how anyone could feed a family on that little money.

They tied up just beyond town. Esau and his family said a hurried thank-you and were off. (A few months later, they were all happy to learn from Esau that they'd made it to his mother's bedside before she passed away.) The males went into town for provisions, leaving Jennie and Ma to unpack some boxes of items to sell and put them into the display shelves, hoping for some business.

Jennie loved looking at all the pretty things, especially the china. She thought how nice it would be to take some home to the farm when she returned to remind her of this tumultuous time in her young life. Leona had written that Papa had been so furious that no one was allowed to mention Jennie's name, that he claimed that she was gone to him forever. He punished Leona, certain that she must have known what was going on. Leona had kept her mouth closed, not admitting anything except that her sister had disappeared in the middle of the night. In her letter, Leona begged Jennie to come home soon. But that wasn't possible. The river had taken her hostage for the time being. Jennie wept each time she reread the letter.

Terribly homesick, she wanted to sleep in her own bed and roll in the luscious grass down the hill with her little sister. She found herself daydreaming about acres and acres of green grass and the fresh smell after it rained and endless amounts of water to drink and to bathe in. She wanted meat, and a lot of it, and fresh vegetables. She was tired of feeling unstable on her feet and knew now how it felt to be a hired hand. The Barbours were wonderful, but they weren't her family.

Before they stopped in Greenville, Mississippi, to trade, they had passed several plantation homes set a good way back from the river. Huge, white-painted wood or red-brick houses with wide porches stretching around the entirety of some of them, some with two-story columns. Jennie had never seen mansions before. She looked on them with wonder. "Clyde? What do the people do here to make enough money to build all these beautiful mansions?"

It was Grandpa who answered her as she sat up top watching the city approach. "Cotton, Jennie. They're all cotton farmers. This land's part of the Mississippi River Delta, which is perfect for growing cotton. See it being loaded onto those steamers?" He pointed to two steamboats that were being filled up. The one in front had cotton bales piled from the main deck to the boiler deck and beyond. It looked as though only the pilot would have a clear view of the river. "The *Natchez*, that stern-wheeler over there, is new. Isn't she a beauty? It was built at Howard Shipyards in Jeffersonville, where we live. It's a packet, so it can carry passengers and it can carry cotton. She can earn $2,500 a week in cotton season."

That night, Jennie watched as one of the side-wheelers was vying for crew members, by the light of odd hanging kerosene buckets. A man came onshore where 50 or so Black men were standing. She could hear the mate yelling, "$40 a month." Clyde was sitting with her on the porch. "What is that man doing?" she asked, pointing.

"That's the ship's mate. He's picking a crew to take upriver. He's offering them $40 a month to come onboard and work for him," Clyde answered casually, the sight being nothing new or unusual for him.

"$50 a month," the mate yelled.

"How will he know how much they want?" Jennie asked.

"Keep watching. When they're happy with the amount, they'll start walking onboard." Clyde seemed to enjoy this opportunity to play teacher.

"$60 a month." Nobody moved. "$70 a month." Still no movement.

When it got to $100 a month, a bewildered Jennie said, "That's a lot of money! What are they waiting for?"

"It's like a game of poker. Each side is trying to get what it thinks is the best deal."

At $140 a month, the Black men began to walk onto the stage. Jennie saw the mate pick this one and that one, leaving the others to go back onshore. She was amazed. "$140 for one month's work?"

"Yes, but that could be all that man will make until spring planting season begins." Jennie was impressed, as always, at his knowledge. They watched as the stage was pulled up and the steamboat took off.

Pa didn't show up for breakfast the next morning. When Jennie asked about him, all Ma would say was, "He's doing what he always does." Jennie had no idea what that meant.

CHAPTER 7

THE RICE

I t was time to turn around and head back upriver. It had been several weeks since they had left Greenville, Mississippi, and Jennie had sent word to her family and was waiting to hear their response.

On the last night they spent on the flatboat, Jennie decided to cook dinner for everyone by herself for the first time. There was some rice left, venison from a deer Grandpa had killed, and the makings of gravy which she would cook after frying the venison.

In the kitchen alone, she started the water boiling for the rice and began to prepare the venison for frying. She had watched Ma make rice; it was a mainstay of their diet. Unsure how much rice to add, she decided just to empty the entire container.

Ma came into the galley with a big smile on her face, delighted with Jennie's progress. "See there, you have learned something useful on this flatboat—cookin'!"

"Oh yes, ma'am! And I want to do it all by myself, so you just go sit on the porch and relax for a change," Jennie replied, quite pleased with herself. She set the table the way she had learned from her own mother.

On the stove, the covered rice pot was making sputtering noises. She lifted the lid and found the rice almost to the top of the pot with little water left. Looking around for ideas, she saw the soup ladle hanging on its hook, grabbed it, and took a scoop of the rice out of the pot. Flustered, she ran to the window at the rear of the flatboat and emptied the ladle into the river where the rice disappeared quickly. Turning back around to the stove, she poured some water from the pottery pitcher into the pot and put the lid back on. She went back to flouring the venison for frying. A minute later, the sputtering sound began once more. Removing the lid again, she saw that she had the same problem as earlier. Another ladle full of rice out the back window and more water added.

Ma stuck her head through the galley doorway. "Need any help?" she asked kindly.

"Oh no, thank you. Just a little bit longer." Her eyes darted back to the stove as she prayed for her teacher to leave.

"No rush, child, no rush," she added as she left the room.

Alone again, Jennie raced to the pot, removing two ladles of rice this time, running back and forth between each, and then adding more water. "It's bound to stop soon," she said out loud to herself. She started frying the venison, enjoying the rich smell of the meat. *No fish today*, she thought with relief.

Shortly thereafter the wonderful smell turned to a burned odor. The venison was barely browned. *It's the rice*, she thought. *Now it's burning!*

There was no logical place to move the very hot rice pot. Laying a kitchen towel onto the wooden countertop, she put the pot on top of it and began to scrape the bottom. Another ladle full into the river. As she ran back to the stove, Clyde came into the room sniffing. "Jennie, is everything all right in here? What's burning?"

She began to cry. "It's the rice. I've burned the rice. What am I gonna do?" Ma walked into the room, saw the two of them working together, and turned around and walked back out to give them some space.

"The rice keeps getting bigger! It keeps soaking up all the water and growing. I can't keep it in the pot!"

Clyde watched as she made her way to the window with a ladle full of partially burned rice and emptied it into the river. Trying hard not to laugh, he looked out and saw scores of fish jumping around in the water eating the rice. More and more fish came. He couldn't control himself any longer and began to laugh hard and loud, from way down in his stomach. Jennie cried harder. Clyde walked up to her and put his arms around her thin, shaky torso. Without thinking, she put her head on his shoulder and wept.

The commotion had caused everyone on the boat to run into the galley. Jennie quickly released her grip on Clyde, who called out, "Luke, go get the big nets; we have some quick fishing to do!" A tearful Jennie moved over to the stove to finish cooking the venison.

The men grabbed nets, Ma grabbed pails, and they went wild scooping up fish and rice, trying to get the rice out of the way, and putting the flapping creatures into the pails. "What a catch!" Pa said. "I've never seen anything like it!"

When they finally sat down to eat, there was venison and…more venison. Jennie's eyes were pink from crying, but she had calmed down and even began to laugh a little as the story was told and retold at the dinner table.

"The nets were so heavy you'd thought we were bringing in a baby whale!" laughed Grandpa.

"It's a good thing I was there to keep Clyde from fallin' in with his first net full of those jumpin' fish!" Pa added.

"The Lord took away part of our dinner and then gave us a boatload of fish," Ma observed with a smile.

Even Luke, who rarely spoke at meals, had to get in on the fun. "You knows you done somethin' right when the Lord fills your yawl with fish!"

Jennie went from feeling like the most disappointing cook on the river to feeling like the heroine in a novel who finds food just before they all die from starvation. The latter was a much better feeling, to be sure.

In the morning, the pots and pans and other kitchen supplies were packed away so they wouldn't shift in transit, as were other necessities for the next trip back down the rivers. The few clothes they each owned were packed to take with them. Jennie used her saddlebags. As she put all her things back in, that heavy feeling rose again in her heart. She felt her throat tighten as tears welled up in her eyes once more. *Why haven't I heard from Leona? It must be bad news.*

Bad news meant that her father wouldn't agree to see her or let her return home. She couldn't imagine that he would really do that. Had she lost her family forever? Where was she going to go? What was she going to do? An unmarried young female out in the world would have a difficult time surviving.

Jennie and Ma stayed on the flatboat as the men used the sweeps to get it across the river to the other side where the steamboat *Morning Glory* was moored. The pilot and his wife had been friends of the Barbours for a decade and often towed them back home. It was Clyde's favorite part of the journey, as it allowed him the opportunity to learn even more about piloting and even to pilot himself as he became more proficient at the task, and it afforded him more time to study.

On previous trips upriver, Ma and Pa were given a cabin to share while the males took bunks in the men's bunkroom. It had already been decided that Jennie would have a bunk in the women's bunkroom. Jennie had never slept in a room with a dozen other females before. The idea was both interesting and a little frightening.

The pilot's wife and Ma escorted her to the bunkroom. The bunks were stacked two high. The pilot's wife suggested that she take an upper bunk, as it would be quieter and more private. She chose an upper bunk at the end of the row. As Jennie was putting her saddlebags down, Ma said, "Why don't you leave your things in our cabin? I don't want you having to carry your things around with you all the time."

"There is a key for each bunkroom, and your things should be fine if you leave them here," said the pilot's wife.

Jennie didn't want to offend her, but the contents of her saddlebags were all she had. "I think I'll let Ma keep them for me. That sounds a lot easier." She smiled and shrugged her shoulders uneasily.

Once her belongings were stowed, Jennie took a walk around to absorb her new surroundings. She walked up the steps and onto the main level, where a large lobby was furnished with chairs and couches, and tables with curved legs. The grand chandelier dazzled her; the dangling crystals sparkled with such brilliance, reflecting the sunlight streaming in from the clerestory, that they took her breath away. The floor was stenciled in diamond patterns outlined with gold and yellow, and a Brussels fitted rug began where the dining tables sat covered in white linen tablecloths set for the next meal. At the opposite end of the vast space hung a large gilt mirror reflecting all the sumptuousness of the room. Deep-green draperies and valences added needed warmth to the beautiful but somewhat cold décor. Jennie sat on a floral couch to take it all in. The clerk's office was to one side, and on the opposite side was a small bar with a bartender sporting a mustache and muttonchops. He looked farcical to her. She covered her mouth with her hand to hide the laughter she was trying to hold in. She quickly diverted her eyes as she felt someone approach her.

"May I help you, young lady?" A man dressed in black tails was leaning over to speak with her.

"Oh, well, thank you. I was just finding my way on this beautiful steamboat," Jennie replied, wondering if she had ventured into a part of the ship that was reserved for people in real cabins.

"It's a beauty! I'm the head steward. Which cabin are you in?" the man inquired jovially.

"I'm with the Barbours," she responded quickly, not wanting to appear to be traveling alone.

"Jim and Annie Barbour? Have they joined us for the trip back up to Jeffersonville?"

Jennie was surprised that this man knew them. "Why yes, sir; we got on board today."

"I didn't know they had a daughter, just two sons—and Grandpa, of course."

"No, no, I'm not their daughter, just a relative," she answered anxiously, hoping he wouldn't have any more questions. She saw Clyde entering the Salon from the portiere and waved to him. He waved back and walked over.

"Mr. Clyde Barbour. Don't you look like a fine grown man!" The two shook hands eagerly.

"Thomas, this is Jennie Hobbs. She's been on the flatboat with us for the last few months. Jennie, this is Thomas. He runs things around here," said Clyde, smiling.

"It's a pleasure to meet you, ma'am." Thomas bowed to her.

"Thank you. How do you know each other?" she asked.

Thomas answered, "Most every year, we have the pleasure of their company on a trip back up north. And Mr. Clyde here always spends most of his time up in the pilothouse. Did you know he'll be a riverboat pilot himself before too long?"

"No, I didn't. Clyde, is that true?" Jennie was surprised she hadn't heard anything about this.

"I'm hoping so. I've been training most of my life to be a pilot on these rivers and piloting one of these big, beautiful steamboats has always been my dream." Clyde's gaze shifted so that he seemed to be staring far out into space. There was a brief silence while they let Clyde return from his quick sojourn into the future. "Sorry," he said sheepishly when he realized he was the cause of the silence.

"The captain says Clyde already knows more than most pilots twice his age. Mark Twain got his riverboat pilot's license when he was only 23. Clyde here may just beat him! How old are you now?" asked Thomas, who bragged as if speaking of his own son.

"I'm 19. I expect I will beat him. I hope I'll be a captain in about a year." His face shone bright with pride.

"Y'all excuse me; they need me over there. It was a pleasure to meet you, Miss Hobbs." He bowed and walked quickly across the room.

"He's very nice," said Jennie, watching him walk up to the clerk's office.

"Yes. I've known him for a long time…." His voice trailed off as he looked at the clock on the wall. "Quick, come with me!" He took Jennie's hand and led her, walking swiftly, out onto the veranda and to the bow of the boat. They ascended the stairs to the upper deck and stopped in front of the calliope. "We're about to shove off."

Moments later, Jennie jumped when the deafening music began to play on the calliope. The sound was very familiar to her now, but she'd never heard it at such close proximity. She released Clyde's hand and muffled her ears. She realized she was rocking her head from side to side in time with the music. Standing on her tippy-toes, she put her hand on his shoulder and strained to see the people on the shore waving as they took off up the Mississippi. She waved back furiously. Clyde put his arm around her waist to steady her, wondering if that was what it felt like to be in Heaven. She lowered herself back down and they began to dance around in a circle, laughing out loud. He marveled at her beautiful smile and funny laugh. They stopped, out of breath, still laughing and looking at each other.

"That was fun!" she exclaimed.

"I knew you would like this!"

They walked back down to the Salon where Jennie noticed Pa standing at the bar.

"There's your father," she stated as she pointed him out.

"Oh," said Clyde, his eyes darting back and forth, looking for an escape. "Let's go downstairs to the Tea Room and get something to drink. I'm parched."

"Don't you want to say hello to your father?"

"No. I'd rather not. Come on, let's go." Once again, he grabbed her hand and led her out through the portiere and down the stairs.

They sat in silence as they sipped their drinks. Clyde looked disturbed and distracted.

"What's wrong?" she asked, truly concerned.

"Haven't you noticed how my father disappears from time to time?"

"Well, yes, but I never gave it much thought."

"Pa is a drunk. There, I've said it. It's not an easy thing to admit." He hung his head and then put his hand on top of hers. She sat perfectly still, not knowing what to say, and that's how they sat for several minutes while Clyde composed his thoughts.

Jennie reached into her pocket and pulled out their lucky coin. Without saying anything, she put it into the hand that was resting on hers and smiled at him.

"Thanks," was all he said as he took it, rubbed it between his hands, and managed a smile.

CHAPTER 8

THE SHOW-OFF

I t was difficult for Jennie to sleep in that odd configuration of a bedroom. She was glad she'd accepted the upper bunk. It seemed a little bit more private, although privacy itself was in short supply in the bunkroom. She had never slept in a room with a stranger, much less a dozen of them. When she crawled into her bunk at night, she rolled over to face the wall to say her prayers and fall asleep. Her roommates would often come and go during the night. Every time the door opened, it woke her up. She hadn't complained, and tried to look at it as an adventure, one she surely wouldn't have had living at home on the farm.

The women were of varying ages and demeanors. Jennie had made friends with a 65-year-old woman from New Orleans whose tattered, bright-colored clothes seemed to speak of a colorful life in the French Quarter. She was headed to New Madrid, Missouri, where she'd been born, to live out her life with her brother and his family. She told Jennie stories she'd heard about the horrifying earthquake there at the beginning of the century. Mary, the girl who occupied the bunk under Jennie's, was heading to Memphis to join her fiancé, who had moved up there for a job in cotton. Mary had been an eager audience for Jennie's story about running away from home. It was cathartic for Jennie to have someone to share her recent history with.

Every day, the steamboat plied the waters of the Mississippi, drawing nearer to Hickman, where Jennie had boarded the Barbours' flatboat. All she knew at that moment was that Miss Dora would be there and would try to bring Leona with her. Her father had not yet acquiesced to allowing Jennie to come home without marrying Mr. Miller. The entire family had been humiliated, he told Miss Dora, and he wasn't about to add to that humiliation by letting her return with no consequences. Her brothers, as expected, followed in line with whatever their father was saying. Apparently, not enough time had gone by to heal that wound. *Will it ever heal?* she wondered. *What have I done?*

Clyde had been thinking about the same thing. He hadn't spoken with Jennie about what was going to happen when they arrived at her home landing. She had become a permanent fixture in his life, one that he liked very much. She had brought new life to the old flatboat and to Clyde's life in general. Everyone loved her; that was easy to do. He found himself missing her. The close quarters of the flatboat had been instrumental in the blossoming of their relationship. They had seen each other every day and often most every hour of the day until embarking on the *Morning Glory*. The idea that most of the day he had no idea where she was or what she was doing was unsettling. He felt the need to make sure she was all right. They had plans to go visit the pilothouse so he could show her around and hopefully impress her. They met in the Tea Room at 10:00 a.m. for her tour.

Clyde had purposefully arrived very early to be there before she was. When he saw her come through the doorway looking around for him, he was struck once again by how lovely she was. He stood up and waved. "Jennie! Over here."

She smiled and made her way through the tables to his. Clyde noticed that her head was slightly downcast, as if she was feeling shy. He pulled out the other chair at his table for her.

"Thank you, Clyde. It's nice to see you." Jennie sat down and he pushed in her chair.

"Did you sleep any better last night?" he asked as he settled across from her at the small table.

"At bedtime, Mary sat up in my bunk with me and told me stories her mother had told her. That helped me fall asleep faster." Jennie looked around the room. "I never see her anywhere but in the bunkroom. I wonder where she goes when she leaves the bunkroom?"

"There's no telling. This is a big boat!"

After a few moments of silence, Clyde asked, "Are you ready to go see the pilothouse with me? The captain said we could go up this morning anytime."

"I would love it!"

So the two found their way up to the pilothouse, where the captain was ringing a bell.

"What's he doing?" Jennie whispered, not wanting to disturb anyone.

"That's how he signals the engineer to adjust how fast we're going and which way to turn." Clyde spoke in a normal tone, which caused the captain to turn around to see who had entered his domain.

"Clyde. Get over here and introduce me to this beautiful young lady!" The captain held out his hand to shake Clyde's. He then gave a slight bow in Jennie's direction with a big smile on his face as he introduced himself.

"This is Jennie Hobbs. She's been staying with us," said Clyde.

Jennie blushed then raised her head to look out the windows that were on all sides of the small room. The view took her breath away. "We're so high up! It makes my stomach feel strange." She backed up a few steps with her hands on her stomach.

Clyde beamed. "Isn't it great? Look how far you can see. I love it up here." He got a dreamy look in his eyes.

"I had no idea the steering wheel was so big," Jennie said, looking amazed at the 9.5-foot-tall wheel the captain was standing next to.

"Yes, that's the wheel. A captain can stand on either the right side or the left side to steer. I like the left side," Clyde said.

"We have to do some sliding and guiding to get around this sharp bend," the captain said, ringing the bell a couple of times. Jennie could feel the boat idle then begin to reverse. It frightened her from this new perch of hers.

"What's happening?" she asked, wide-eyed.

Clyde was eager to fill in as the captain tended to the bells and steering. "Sometimes when you have a sharp bend, you have to go back and forward a few times and let the current help you make the curve." The pride in his voice made Jennie smile, which made Clyde smile, and then the captain.

"Take the wheel, son," the captain said. Clyde didn't miss a beat as he sidled up to the big wooden wheel and placed his hands just so.

Jennie was very impressed but also a slight bit hesitant for her friend to be in charge during what seemed a delicate operation. "How do you know what to do?" she asked.

"He's been turning these wheels since he was tall enough to reach 'em," the captain told her. "Isn't that so, Clyde?"

"Yes, sir, Captain," Clyde replied quickly while straining to see the river. The boat went forward again and back again, the bells signaling the engineer. Jennie could feel the soft change in direction under her feet. She was steadying herself with her hand that held onto a pipe jutting out of the wall.

In a few minutes, the boat had made the turn and was headed upriver once again. Clyde looked back at Jennie and smiled a satisfied smile. She smiled back and walked over to where he was manning the wheel.

"Come here," said Clyde, reaching out to her. She took his hand and he pulled her to him. He positioned her in front of him and put her hands on the wheel. He placed his hands on either side of hers. "Can you feel her, Jennie? Can you feel the rhythm of the paddlewheel? Listen…that's the sound of this powerful steamboat taking control of her path up the river." In the brief silence, he closed his eyes and took in a deep breath. "This is like Heaven to me."

Jennie was overcome with emotion as she felt his strong arms around her, saw his hands controlling their path, and realized her back was right up against his chest as they steered together. She could feel herself blush with her entire body, enjoying the thrill of being surrounded by his strength and confidence in his favorite place on earth.

The first mate entered the pilothouse. "Captain? Where would you like your lunch today?"

"Think I'll take it in my cabin. Clyde, would you like to come up here and help pilot while I eat? It should be smooth sailing the next few hours." The captain looked out in all directions, searching the water for untold hazards.

"Sure, of course, Captain. You know I will!" Clyde replied happily. "What time do you want me back up here?" As Clyde backed slightly away from the wheel, Jennie slowly edged her way to the side and Clyde replaced his hands on the wheel.

"Around noon, I'd say." The captain walked over to Clyde and took over the steering. "Feel free to bring Miss Jennie back up with you whenever you'd like. It's a pleasure to meet you, ma'am!"

"Thank you…Captain. It was a pleasure to meet you as well." Jennie curtsied and headed to the door.

The next day, they would finally stop at Hickman, where Jennie knew Miss Dora would be waiting to see her. She couldn't sleep that night, worried and wondering what to expect. Earlier, Ma had asked Jennie to come to the Barbours' cabin. It was quite small but adequate, and certainly much better than the bunkroom. The two of them sat on the bed to talk.

"Tomorrow's a big day for you. What have you decided to do when we get there?" Ma was holding Jennie's hand and speaking in a loving tone.

"It's very confusing," Jennie began. "I guess I expected Papa to miss me so terribly that he'd be happy to have me back home, but I'm afraid that's not gonna happen." Her hazel eyes were darting back and forth, and her forehead was wrinkled in thought. "I…I don't have any other place to go. I'll be homeless." The inevitable flood of tears began. She removed her hand from Ma's grasp and used it to try and wipe the tears away. Ma patted and rubbed her back.

"I know it's hard to imagine your future anywhere but on the farm where you grew up and that you love so much. But maybe you were never meant to live out your life there; maybe God has something else in mind for you. I don't believe things happen by accident. Life can't be that willy-nilly. Open your mind to other possibilities."

"But I'm scared! I'm so scared. A young woman all alone out in the world; I don't know how to do that." Jennie's words only made her cry harder.

"Everything you need you already have inside of you. Do you remember the powerful words written in Luke? 'Fear not, little flock; for it is your Father's good pleasure to give you the Kingdom.' God wants you to have it all." She smiled at Jennie, whose tears still flowed. They sat in silence for a few minutes, each of them absorbing what they needed from their conversation.

"Look at me, Jennie." Ma used her hand to move the young woman's face toward hers. "You have been a gift to me that I stopped hoping for a long time ago—a daughter! Havin' you with us has completed our family. I hope you know that you will always be part of us, and I would love nothin' better than for you to stay with us always. You never have to be all alone unless you want to be." Jennie looked up at this kind and generous woman and saw tears welling up in her eyes, compassion written all over her face.

As Jennie reached over to hug her adopted mother, the door suddenly burst open and Pa was standing in the doorway, swaying slightly. Ma stood up quickly and walked over to him. He was smiling like the Cheshire Cat with that sly look about him. She put her hand on his shoulder and looked him in the eye. "Jennie and I are talking about some important things. Go away and straighten yourself up!" Her hand dropped back down by her side and Pa grabbed it and held it tightly between his two large, rough hands.

"Let go, you're hurting me," Ma said in a low, gruff voice that Jennie had never heard.

"Aw, Honey. I just wanna hold you tight and never let you go!" He released his grip on her hand and put his arms around her just as tightly.

"Jim." Ma spoke calmly although her face showed fear and anger. "Stop it! You're scaring Jennie! Let go of me!" As he let go of her, he pushed her, and she landed halfway on the bed and halfway on the floor. "Ow!" she yelled this time.

Jennie sat frozen on the bed where only moments before, she and Ma had been exchanging thoughts and tears. She felt certain that he was drunk, although she'd never seen anyone drunk that she could recall. She wished with all her might that she could disappear and escape this horrific scene. She jumped up to help Ma off the floor but was stopped by Pa who inserted himself between the two women.

"You're such a sweet thing. Don't turn into a shrew like my wife here has done."

Jennie gasped to hear those words come out of his mouth. Never, ever...

"Hey there, Jim." The captain walked through the doorway and over to where Pa was standing. "Looks like Annie fell off the bed. Let's help her up, what do you say? And Miss Jennie, why don't you go on up to the pilothouse and see if Clyde can come down here to help."

"Yes, sir," Jennie whispered and she took off down the hallway, running all the way to where Clyde was helping navigate the boat. "Clyde! Come quick! Something's wrong with your father and the captain wants you down in their cabin." She was out of breath and suddenly embarrassed by the way she burst into the room.

"Here." Clyde handed the wheel off to the first mate, put his hands on Jennie's shoulders, and looked her square in the eyes. "Is he drunk?"

"I...I think so, yes, and your mother..." Jennie didn't have time to finish her sentence before Clyde ran off down the hallway. He yelled back, "Stay away. I don't want you there. Please!"

Jennie stood in the pilothouse with light shining in from all the windows and the grand old river and the wind trying to impede their every movement. The first mate turned back to look at her. "Miss Jennie, why don't you sit down for a bit?" And she did.

CHAPTER 9

THE ALCOHOLIC

Jennie stayed away as Clyde had requested. She really didn't want to get back into the middle of all that turmoil anyway. She had enough turmoil going on inside her own head wondering about the next day.

Certainly Papa will come; he wouldn't leave me on my own. He's just angry, she decided. *What if he still wants me to marry old Mr. Miller? I refuse!* She shook her head in vehement protest. *And I can't stay with the Barbours. I just can't! They would have to take me on like an orphan.* She shuddered, and her thoughts turned to Clyde. *I would miss him the most. He's so kind and smart. Oh, and handsome.* Her mind was turning things over and over.

At dinnertime, she went to the dining room to the table where she usually ate with the Barbours. Grandpa was the only one there. She hugged him from behind his chair and he stood up to seat her. She wasn't sure what he knew and wasn't going to bring it up.

"Grandpa, I haven't seen you in a couple of days. How are you?" She sat next to him and held his hand.

"Jennie, you're a delight to see as always!" He gave her a kiss on the cheek. "I've been busy helping around here so we don't look like freeloaders. Did you hear what we did with all that fish we caught on the flatboat when you were cooking rice?" He giggled at the memory.

"No. I don't know what happened to them."

"You know that a steamboat like this one needs a lot of food to feed all these people. So, Jim and Clyde and Luke and I put them in the yawl and rowed them to this steamboat and presented the captain with all those beautiful fresh fish!" Grandpa was talking excitedly. "He couldn't believe his good fortune. And he owes it all to you, sweet Jennie, who doesn't know how to cook rice!" This time even Jennie laughed. The idea that some good had come from all her embarrassment made it seem funny all of a sudden. "I've never in all my days seen anything like those fish jumping over each other to get to that rice!" He snorted and laughed even harder. Jennie was caught up in the moment and laughed along with him. Their laughter was contagious and soon many of the other diners joined in without even knowing why.

Ma and Clyde showed up just then and the jovial mood made even them smile.

"What's so darn funny?" asked Clyde as he pulled out his mother's chair then sat down.

"Oh lordy, it's the 'Fish Eating All That Rice' story that cracks me up every time!" Grandpa answered between laughs. The two latecomers to the table laughed as well. "Jennie didn't know she was the heroine in the end."

Pa's absence loomed large. Jennie wondered if Grandpa knew what had happened earlier.

"Where's Jim?" he asked.

"He's sleepin'," answered Ma with a snarl.

"He's sleeping? What is wrong with that man?" Grandpa had a disparaging look on his face. "I don't know what happened to make him love the bottle so much. I taught him better than that."

"Grandpa, not in front of the children," said Ma in a hushed tone.

"Children? I don't see any children at this table. Maybe this will teach them how horrible the whole thing is and not do it themselves." Grandpa banged his fist on the table.

"Ma," Clyde said. "You don't think I know what goes on when Pa disappears or when he gets all mean and ugly? Not just me. James knows, too! I'm sure Jennie has figured it out by now. He's a mess."

Clyde stood up to leave but Grandpa intervened. "Sit down. Let's reopen this chapter and see what we can do to change the outcome."

Ma was quietly crying, and Jennie was looking down at the table. All the people seated around them had gotten their food from the buffet and were engaged in their own conversations.

"Let's deal with the facts; Jim can't say no to alcohol. When he drinks too much, he does all kinds of things he wouldn't usually do. He's a nasty drunk. He's also my son and I love him. Take all that drinking away and he's a fine, responsible man. Maybe responsible is the wrong word...." Grandpa's voice trailed off.

"Yeah, I'd say you can't be a responsible man when no one knows when you'll disappear or how you'll act when you get back home." Clyde was angry. "When Grandpa isn't around, I have to be the responsible man around here, but still he won't let me make responsible decisions about my own life and how I want to live it."

"Clyde, I won't have you talkin' that way about your pa. He's been lookin' after all of us all these years. He's not perfect, but he's a God-fearing man and he's my husband!" Ma said resolutely. "He helps everybody who asks him. If he hadn't said yes to helpin' Dora Banks, you would never have met this wonderful girl who's stolen your heart."

There was an awkward moment of silence. Grandpa looked from Clyde to Jennie and back to Clyde again trying to think of something to say to ease the tension. "Listen to me," he began. "We're all fond of Jennie. I hope all this talk hasn't made her want to get off the boat in Hickman and never see any of us again."

"Y'all know that I have problems with my own father—different problems but still problems," Jennie said. "You are like my family now, even Pa. I don't know what my life would have been like if you hadn't taken me on board. I'd probably be married to some old man and cryin' myself to sleep every night." Jennie hoped she had said the right thing.

Clyde turned in his chair to face Jennie. "Ma's right; you have stolen my heart." He put his hand on top of hers and squeezed it, smiled at her, and then got up and left the table. Jennie didn't move and remained looking at the chair Clyde had occupied. Ma, still sniffling, excused herself and left the table as well.

Jennie and Grandpa sat as they had before. "Just as I thought, you and Clyde."

"So, what do you think?" Jennie asked.

"That you and my grandson have a spark between you!" He was smiling.

"I guess you're right. He's very sweet to me, and so smart! I don't think I'm smart enough for him."

"Nonsense. You're everything a man could hope for in a wife. I can see that you enjoy learning and that's what's important. Now Clyde, he's always been the smart one, ever since he was little. I taught him to read when he was about four years old; took no time at all. Always making things, coming up with new ideas. One day he was sitting on the flatboat playing with a rope. Said he wanted to try something. Before I knew it, he'd made a slipknot no one's ever seen before. I call it the Clyde Tie."

"He seems to know a lot about the river," Jennie added. "How does he know so much?"

Grandpa chuckled. "He's loved to read all his life; couldn't put Cramer's down. He read that thing over and over." He chuckled some more. "He's been traveling up and down the rivers for the past 10 years or more. He seems to take in everything he sees and remember it; damnedest thing I've ever seen, and I was around some very smart young men at university."

Jennie thought for a minute. "But he said he's tired of it."

"He's tired of the old flatboat, that's all. It's past time he piloted a steamboat like this; way past time." Grandpa shook his head.

"But," Jennie began again, "what about college? He wants to go to college!"

"And he should. He loves to learn. Give him a book, and he'll teach himself everything in it. He takes after me that way; that gives us a special closeness. It would have meant the world to me if Clyde's pa had been that way. He never cared much for books; same with

James. I guess it's just some people's nature to love learning and others not. But let's talk about you, young lady. I'm sure you've considered your options." Grandpa smiled at her.

"Yes, sir. If my father is there and wants me to go home…well…if he wants me to go home with him and not marry that old man…then I don't see as I have a choice. I won't go home just to become a slave to a man I don't love." Her defiant tone returned and her brow furrowed.

"It's not my place to tell you what to do. You've got a good head on your shoulders. What if he isn't there?" Grandpa asked, rubbing his beard.

"I don't know. I'm not gonna go home and beg him, but there's my little sister, Leona; she's depending on me to come back and take her with me." Jennie stared into the distance. "She's only 15; she's too young to be goin' off with a homeless girl like me." She bowed her head, determined not to cry. She kept shaking her head.

Grandpa held her hand again and she gripped his tightly. There was nothing else to say, no one else to make the decision. So much had happened. She wasn't the same person who had boarded the flatboat those months before wearing black mourning clothes, riding through the woods with her stomach all inside out. In fact, the only thing that felt familiar at that moment was her stomach, which always acted up when she was upset.

"Jennie, we all want you to stay with us until you're ready to leave. You can ride up to Jeffersonville with us and stay until we're ready to float down again. I don't think we'll be floating down the rivers too many more times. I want you to know that you do have some place to go and people that love you." Grandpa took his napkin and dried her face. She tried to smile.

"Thanks, Grandpa. I believe you. No matter what happens, my life changed forever when I got on that horse and rode away in the middle of the night. It was my choice. Now, I have to live with it, I guess." She stood up, kissed him on the cheek, and walked away.

CHAPTER 10

THE SHUNNING

It was a sleepless night for Jennie and for Clyde. She couldn't stop going over "what if" scenarios for the following day. Clyde couldn't stop thinking about the possibility that Jennie might be gone the next day—gone for good!

In the morning as she left the bunkroom, she could feel the steamboat slowing down at Hickman. *I guess we're almost at the landing.* She had decided not to take her satchel off the boat with her. It was packed and ready to go in the Barbours' cabin. She walked out onto the deck and headed for the bow to watch the landing and look for her family. Clyde came up behind her and tapped her on the shoulder. She turned to see a smiling Clyde, who reached out his hand to take hers. They stood holding hands for a moment and then headed toward the bow together. Just before they got to a place where they could see the landing, Clyde stopped, turned toward Jennie, took her other hand, and looked deep into her beautiful hazel eyes.

"Jennie," he began, "I just want you to know that you're like family to me. No, not family exactly, but like family. You make that old flatboat a nicer place." Clyde was frustrated looking for the right words. "I like spendin' time with you talkin' and readin' and learnin' from Grandpa. My whole family loves you, and Luke, too. I hope you're not gonna take off today and disappear forever."

Jennie had been thinking the same thing for days, but she had no answer for Clyde or for herself. After living on the river for months, new experiences around every corner, life back on the farm seemed so monotonous. And what about Clyde? What was it about him that made her heart beat a little faster? *So wise,* she thought, *and so smart and so sweet and…* Her thoughts were cut off abruptly when they heard people yelling from the shore.

"Clyde, let's go and look for my father." They walked swiftly to the bow holding hands and stopped near the front of the boat. Jennie strained her neck looking for her father. There were a lot of people milling about down there on the landing. There were carts and dogs and horse-drawn carriages. She saw boys playing on old barrels and another boy fishing from the wharf. These scenes had become familiar to Jennie after the last few months. She saw no tall man in the crowd. *Maybe he's on his way,* she thought, scouring the landing.

"Jennie!" Clyde was trying to get her attention. "Do you see him?"

"No, not yet. But that doesn't mean he's not coming. He could be late gettin' here." Knowing how timely her father was, she wasn't believing her own words. Having tired of looking, she turned to face Clyde, whose maudlin expression spoke volumes. "Clyde, I'm not sure what to say to you. It's all so confusing. It would be nice to know, if I have to go home, that you'd come back for me, in time. You're very dear to my heart!" She kissed him on the cheek and smiled a subtle but warm smile, a little embarrassed.

Clyde was overwhelmed. Of course he would come back for her, over and over if that's what it took. He knew at that moment that she was meant to be by his side forever. "Yes, Jennie, I'll come back for you. I'll send word when we float back down in the summer, and we'll stop. If you're not there, then we'll stop again when we come back up the river on our way home again. I won't stop trying until you tell me to." He was talking fast, knowing that this moment in time would be gone any second. And it was.

"Clyde, I see Miss Dora! I see her standing back from the crowd! It's her, I'm sure of it!" Jennie began to wave furiously hoping that somehow Miss Dora would see her waving amid the sea of outstretched arms.

Clyde felt his heart drop. All the mental preparation he'd done for this moment was of no help. He felt guilty but whispered a prayer up to God anyway, a prayer that she wouldn't go home.

"Let's go," she said and, still holding his hand, led them down to disembark. When they reached the gangplank, they saw Ma, Pa, and Grandpa standing there.

"We want you to know we're here if you need us," said Grandpa. Ma looked about to cry. "Do you see your pa?"

"No. No, I don't, but Miss Dora is here; I saw Miss Dora for sure!"

"Go to her and we'll wait right here." Pa was speaking now. His smile was sincere as he stopped Clyde from descending with her to shore. "We'll all be right here."

"All right, okay. Thank you. Clyde? I'll be back," Jennie said and quickly walked away. She spotted Miss Dora again and ran to her, arms wide open. Her friend finally caught sight of her and ran in her direction. The breathless women embraced and began to laugh the laughter of relief.

"Jennie, Jennie, Jennie," exclaimed Miss Dora, stepping back to get a good look at her. She furrowed her brow and mumbled under her breath before saying out loud, "You've lost weight. And you look tired. Have you been sick?"

Jennie was blushing from the scrutiny. "No, ma'am! I haven't been sick one day since I left! But never mind that, where's Papa?" She looked around again.

"He's not coming, dear," Miss Dora said softly.

"What do you mean he's not coming? Why not?" Jennie felt a pang run from her heart down to her stomach.

"He said you disgraced the whole family and unless you come back to the farm on your own and agree to marry Mr. Miller, he's finished with you." Her eyes filled with tears, and she put her hand on Jennie's shoulder. "I tried to get him to let me bring Leona to see you, but he said that he didn't want you to kidnap his baby girl and take her off to who knows where."

Jennie stood in shock and was almost run over by a horse-drawn cart with a driver who was clearly in a big hurry to get somewhere. It took her breath away; first she was just standing there talking with her mother's best friend, and suddenly the world had started spinning in an unknown direction. There were no tears, just a blank expression of disbelief. She was quiet for a moment, assessing the situation. She closed her eyes and sighed a deep sigh. When she opened them again, they glistened with tears. "What am I gonna do? What about Leona? I promised her I'd come back for her. Oh no, oh no, this can't be happening! Please God, tell me I'm dreamin'." Her sniffles turned to sobs that attracted the attention of passersby.

Miss Dora took Jennie into her arms, put Jennie's head on her shoulder, and stroked her soft auburn hair. The sobs kept coming. "Shhh, my sweet girl, shhh."

In a few minutes, Jennie's sobs had turned to sniffles. She stood up straight, as if that would help her summon the fortitude this dire situation would require. "All right. All right. I can't go home. I'll have to stay with the Barbours. But Leona, I have to see Leona no matter what!" Her eyes darted back and forth, searching the empty air for answers. "I'll go home just to see her. I have to see her. I promised. She must be worried sick what's gonna happen to me. That's what I'm gonna do," she said desperately.

"Well now, Jennie, let's think. Zeke and I rode here in the carriage, so we'd have room to take you back home in case you wanted to go. But how are you gonna get back on the steamboat?"

"I don't know. Let me go talk to the Barbours. Will you come with me to talk to them?" Jennie grabbed her hand and squeezed it.

"Of course. Let's go." The two women walked over to the steamboat and all four Barbours walked down the gangplank to meet them on land. After a lot of handshaking and hugging and thank yous, the answer was simple: Jennie could meet up with the boat at the next landing, which was Columbus.

"Maybe I should go with her," said Clyde, who was not willing to lose sight of her for any longer than necessary.

"No, no. I don't think that's a good idea," Miss Dora stated. "She's perfectly safe with me and Zeke. Let's not mix the pot any more than it already is."

Jennie agreed. "Clyde, that's very nice of you. Thank you, but I think it's better for me to go alone."

"We need to get going so we get there before dark. We can meet y'all in Columbus tomorrow evening. Does that sound right?" Miss Dora looked at Pa.

"Yes. Good. And if for some reason she's not coming back onboard with us, would you send Zeke to Columbus to let us know?" The practical-thinking Pa had shown up again.

"Of course, Jim. That's a good plan. Jennie, I know you have plenty of clothes at the farm, so I don't think you need to bring anything with you. Let's just get going now." Miss Dora did not want to show up at Jennie's home after dark.

"Well, I guess you're right," Jennie said. "I have my jacket on. So, we're just gonna leave now?"

"I think that's best." Miss Dora and Jennie said their goodbyes to the Barbours.

Clyde gave Jennie a hug like everyone else had and whispered in her ear, "Here, take the coin. It'll help me feel closer to you and give you good luck!" He slid the coin discreetly into her hand and they smiled at each other. She gave him a kiss on the cheek and was off.

It was a long ride back to the farm. The scenery was familiar, and the smell of the earth and trees began to fill her nose. It smelled clean and fresh and wonderful. She told Miss Dora stories about her adventures since they'd last seen each other. When Jennie told of her unexpected swim in the Mississippi and how Luke had saved her, she thought Zeke sat up taller. Jennie realized her feelings about Black people had shifted without her knowing it. In her past, had she intentionally kept them at arm's length, or was that just the way of the world all around her? She never thought of them as inferior or any less of a human being; they were just different. They looked different, they talked differently, and most didn't get much schooling. They seemed to live in the shadows, their heads bowed down ever so slightly.

The surroundings became more and more familiar to Jennie. They were skirting town to avoid being recognized and pulled into conversations there was no time for. It wasn't until they rode onto her land, her father's land, that tears began to flow. Her heart was singing but it was a song of yearning that came unsummoned. She longed for Leona, her brothers, her horse, her house that wasn't floating on water, her pretty clothes. When the house finally came into view, Jennie wanted to jump down and run all the way there. But she didn't. Instead, she worked to rid her cheeks of tears. There were no signs of anyone. She began to feel queasy. Then she saw her father and Leona step out through the front door. Leona stood in front of their father, whose hands were tightly clasping his daughter's shoulders as if to stop her from bolting. Her brothers were nowhere to be seen. Zeke stopped the horses and climbed down to help the two women dismount. Jennie ran to her family, smiling brightly at the sight of them both. As she approached, her father's right hand went up in a sign for her to stop. She slowed down to a walk, not sure what was going on. Leona tried to move forward to greet her sister but was held back by their father's firm grip on her shoulder.

"Stop right there, Jennie Hobbs. You are no longer welcome in this house." His voice was loud, stopping Jennie in her tracks. "You are a disgrace to this family and unless you're gonna behave and do exactly what I tell you to do, go back to wherever you came from." Leona began to sob, her little body shaking with emotion. Jennie moved forward to comfort her but was stopped by a now thunderous voice. "Did you hear me? I said stop! Look what you've done to Leona. What were you thinking?"

"I...I...oh Papa, I didn't mean to disgrace the family. I never wanted to hurt Leona. Please believe me!" Jennie was searching for the words. The speech she had rehearsed a dozen times had dissipated into the cool air.

"And why should I believe you, you selfish girl? You ran off in the middle of the night—a girl by herself out in the world. What did you have to do for these Barbour people to stay and live with them? I hope nothing immoral. God only knows." His booming voice had dropped to almost a whisper.

"Arthur, please," Miss Dora scolded. "She was living with a very nice family."

"And how do you know that?" asked her father rudely.

"Well," Miss Dora began, fumbling for words. "I met them at the landing. And they're friends of a family I know well from Indiana."

"Oh, and that makes you comfortable with my daughter in their care?"

"I'm just saying..." Miss Dora was cut off by a now angry Jennie.

"Papa! Don't talk that way to her. It's not her fault. She's just trying to help. If you wanna be angry with somebody, be angry with me!" She looked around in search of someone or something to grab hold of. Leona struggled to get out of their father's grasp and ran to Jennie. In seconds, they were hugging and kissing each other. In just a few more seconds, they were being ripped apart by their father, but they wouldn't let go of each other. Her father lifted Leona and, holding her on his hip with his left hand around her waist, raised his hand as if to hit Jennie, and Zeke, who had seemed a passive, uninterested bystander, rose from his seat on the wagon, glaring at her father.

"What do you think you're doing up there, boy? Ain't none of your business," he shouted.

Jennie summoned all the tomboy she had in her from growing up with a bunch of brothers and slapped her father across the face. "*Don't* talk to him like that!" She stepped back, well aware there would be consequences for her actions.

Her father walked to the front door, opened it, set Leona down inside and told her to stay put. He closed the door, stepped outside, and stood staring at the door for a minute. When he turned back to face them, his eyes were stained with tears, and he looked lost. He sat down on the stoop and put his head in his hands.

Jennie looked at Miss Dora for help then watched as Miss Dora approached her father timidly. "Arthur, please," she repeated.

Her father sat up straight, looked Miss Dora in the eyes and said, "How did we get to this? If only Jane was still alive, none of this would have happened." Leona sobbed behind the closed door.

"You're right, of course, Arthur. Everything would be very different. But she's gone."

He interrupted her, his voice shaky but steadfast. "She's not here and I have to take care of our family. I won't welcome a runaway back into my house until she does as she's told." He stood up and dusted himself off.

Jennie ran up to him and put her arms around his waist. "Papa, I'm part of this family. You can't put me out forever!"

He forcibly removed her arms from around him and held her at arm's length. "You haven't acted like it, so go back to your new family." He stepped back to the front door, looked at Miss Dora, and nodded. He slammed the door behind him and locked it.

Jennie reeled around to face her friend, her mouth agape. No words were spoken. She collapsed onto the ground and cried, rocking back and forth.

Her father appeared at an upstairs window and opened it. "And here are the rest of your things. I don't want anything left in this house to remind us of the Jennie Hobbs we used to know and love." He hurled down some clothes, shoes, and a few books. "I'll be selling your horse, too!" He slammed the window shut and disappeared.

Jennie had watched all this with astonishment. Her father had always been strict, but this was beyond her imaginings. Zeke jumped down and started gathering up the items that were strewn over the grass. Miss Dora walked up to Jennie and crouched down. "I don't know what to say to you, dear child. I'm sorry that I helped you leave. What have I done?" She wouldn't allow herself to cry. There had been enough crying. It was time to get moving. She stroked Jennie's hair softly and slowly. "Let's go on now." Jennie accepted her outreached hand and stood up, brushing herself off. "We'll spend the night at my house and get an early start in the morning."

Jennie was quiet. Her emotions had frozen, her eyes fixed on some far-off place. She stumbled as Miss Dora helped her make it back to the wagon and climb up. Zeke grabbed the last few items, stored them all in the back, and clicked the horses into action. Jennie watched her house as they rode away. She thought she saw Leona crying at an upstairs window and waved to her.

CHAPTER 11

THE UNION

Jennie woke with a start. She smelled biscuits and sausage and coffee. It took a moment for her to remember she was at Miss Dora's house. She put a shawl around her shoulders and went into the kitchen. "Miss Dora, it smells wonderful! I haven't had a breakfast like this in a long time! Is that gravy you're stirring?"

"Of course. Sausage gravy. I remember how much you love my sausage gravy!" Miss Dora had been hoping that a home-cooked breakfast might help distract Jennie.

With their stomachs full, a suitcase in the back of the wagon, and luncheon packed in a basket, the three took off again for Columbus. Hours later, when the landing and the steamboat finally came into view, Jennie was left with a crushing feeling of emptiness. The vessel's grandeur was pleasing to the eye, but the sense of adventure had slipped away. She really was an orphan now.

"Jennie? Come on, girl. I see the Barbours waiting for you." Miss Dora had already said every encouraging thing she could think of on the long journey. There was nothing left except to get Jennie back on the steamboat and on to her new life, whatever that would be. "Now remember, every time that you let me know you're passing by here, I'll come to see you!" She tried to sound enthusiastic.

"I'll remember. Thank you. Please be sure Leona knows that I'll be back for her in time." She stepped down from the wagon, brushed herself off, and gave her friend a long hug. The two walked together hand in hand to where the Barbours were standing. Clyde stepped forward, took her other hand, and Jennie let go of her friend. She studied him, trying to see something behind his kind eyes and soft smile. She wanted to trust him. She did trust him. But she'd trusted her father and look what had happened. She looked as deep as she could and saw nothing but kindness. *How do you ever know what a person is really like?* she asked herself, but her introspection came to an abrupt end as Pa started talking and taking over the rather awkward situation.

"Dora, thanks for bringing our Jennie back to us safely. You know we love her like our own kin." He kissed Miss Dora on the cheek. Miss Dora said her goodbyes and asked Clyde to walk her back to her wagon. Clyde looked from Jennie to his pa and back to Jennie again. He wasn't keen on leaving her side right then, but it would be rude to decline.

"Of course, of course. I'll be right back," he said directly to Jennie and patted her on the shoulder. "After you," he said and followed behind Miss Dora.

As they walked through the hubbub of the landing with the lively sights and sounds of loading and unloading, of buying and selling, and of reunions with friends, Miss Dora spoke to him. "I don't know you personally, Clyde, but I know your family. I think all of you want the best for Jennie." Clyde tried to interrupt, but Miss Dora put up her hand to stop him. "With all of the horrible things that happened in the last 24 hours, I could still see a spark in her eye when she talked about you. She told me how much she trusts you and how kind you are to her. Promise me that you won't let her down, that you'll be honest and truthful with her. That's all I ask. She deserves no less." Miss Dora's eyes were damp with tears as she turned to look Clyde in the face. "I am her mother and her father now. Please let me know if there's anything she needs. I will meet you every time you pass by here so that I can see Jennie. Keep her safe for me." She shook Clyde's hand and then leaned over to kiss his cheek.

"I love her; I'm pretty sure she knows that. I will take care of her, always. I will make all my decisions with her well-being in mind and never hurt her. And I'll be sure she sees you as often as possible."

They said goodbye and Clyde made his way back through the din of the crowd. His emotions were jumbled. He felt jubilant that Miss Dora would entrust so much to him, thrilled that Jennie had shown her feelings for him, ready to take Jennie as his own, and scared that he wouldn't be good enough for her. He knew he still had to win her all the way and vowed to himself that he would do just that.

Clyde rejoined his family. "Jennie, you must be hungry. Come with me and I'll get you something to eat." He took her hand and began to walk away.

"But my things," Jennie objected. "I have to put my things somewhere." She looked down at the suitcase Miss Dora had given her; it held everything she would ever have from her home.

"We'll take it to our cabin. You two go on now," Ma said.

So, Clyde and Jennie walked away hand in hand. He didn't ask her what had happened. It was weeks before she told him the whole story, weeks before she could speak of it and not fall apart. Her life was inexorably altered, never to be the same again.

Steamboating was an easy life. Jennie had no obligations to fulfill, no meals to cook, nothing to clean. She spent a lot of time studying with Grandpa. He might as well have been *her* grandfather, she loved him so much. She combed his long beard one day, and Grandpa so loved it that it became a sweetness that they shared often. Clyde joined them in their studies most of the time. He also spent a great deal of time helping to navigate the big, fancy boat. He planned to take his river pilot's license test when they got home to Jeffersonville. Jennie was planning to use the sewing skills she'd been taught by her mother to make some clothes.

It seemed to Jennie that every time they stopped or passed another river town, Clyde would tell her some history behind it. He said he'd learned it all from Grandpa, which made the old man feel good.

Cairo, Illinois, Grandpa had said, had served as a headquarters for Ulysses S. Grant. It was located at the confluence of the Ohio and Mississippi Rivers and had become a rich city as it was so ideally situated for steamboat traffic.

As they pulled into Henderson, Kentucky, Jennie saw long lines of horse- and mule-drawn wagons piled high with the tobacco that accounted for the many mansions that had been built there.

Next was Evansville, Indiana, where the local hardwood lumber was used to make more hardwood furniture than anywhere else in the world. It was also coal country. There were more mansions to see.

At Owensboro, Kentucky, Grandpa was quick to head onshore, as was Pa. "They're excited to go get some of the fine bourbon whiskey they make here," Clyde said. "Grandpa sips it and Pa gulps it down. We don't stop here on our way downriver when Pa needs to have his head clear to maneuver the flatboat." Clyde was neither smiling nor sulking, just stating facts.

The final landing of note was Leavenworth, Indiana, which was laid out in an oxbow of the Ohio River. The place was known for button-making and lime quarries. The city had been named for Zebulon Leavenworth, a famous riverboat pilot on the Mississippi who was friends with Mark Twain before Twain became famous. They had piloted the steamboat *Nebraska* together near Memphis at the start of the Civil War. "When they were told to stop, they kept right on goin' so the soldiers shot at 'em and the gunshots went right across their bow as a warning to stop," explained Clyde, who would always get energized when talking about the history of these places, and Jennie was eager to listen.

They arrived in Jeffersonville just as spring was beginning. The city was rife with trees that had only just begun to put out their greenery. The "City of Jeffersonville Ferry" went from Jeffersonville across the Ohio River to Louisville, Kentucky.

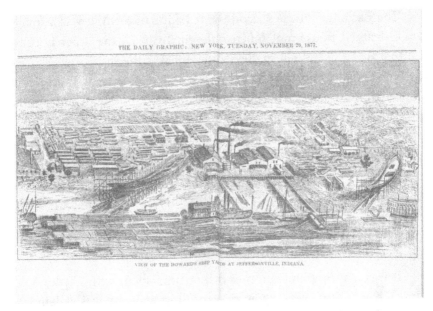

"From Paddlewheels to Propeller", Etching of Howard Shipyards,
Jeffersonville, Indiana

It was impossible to miss Howard Shipyards, front and center on
the north shore of the river. Jennie could see boats in the process of
being built, some on the wharves in the early phases and two floating
in the docks that were nearing seaworthiness. It was a massive place.
They had their own lumberyards and mill, a blacksmith shop the
size of the entire main level of a steamboat, and even their own steel
plant. Grandpa, Pa, and Clyde had all worked there at one time or
another. The majority of the townspeople worked in some aspect of
shipbuilding. They built more steamboats here than anywhere else.
"And they're damn good at it!" Clyde boasted, which made Jennie
giggle, as she'd never heard him swear before.

As was true of many of the river towns along the Ohio River,
Jeffersonville had its own connection to the war as an important
distribution center for the Union Army, as it not only had the river
but also three railroads.

The Barbours' house was on the outskirts of town. It was a small wood-framed house, not much different from all the other houses on that dirt road. What made it different was the inside, where Ma had made the plain and ordinary look pristine and pretty. There were cotton drapes at the windows and beautiful china and pottery on display, giving a touch of elegance to the space.

Through the spring and into the summer, Jennie busied herself with sewing, washing, and helping Ma cook. Her memory was refreshed on the canning of fruits and vegetables and the making of jelly. Knowing, as she did now, that they would actually rely on these canned things made the work seem that much more important. Cleaning, washing, sewing, and cooking left little time for leisure pursuits.

It was a spring and summer full of time spent with Clyde. Any time Clyde wasn't working at Howard Shipyards, he was at Jennie's side. He would help her if he could (he was terrible at sewing, and his cooking skills were not well honed), and often Ma would shoo them off to spend time together. They walked the town's asphalt streets, the smell of creosote strong when the temperature rose. Jennie particularly loved ice cream, so trips to the ice cream parlor happened most every week. The walk home was too long to take the ice cream with them, so whoever had the requisite number of pennies would go along with the two of them.

One Saturday, Clyde and Jennie took a walk to see the mansion that Captain Edmond Howard, the owner of Howard Shipyards, had built and which had just been completed. It was a heavy-looking three-story red-brick home in the Late Victorian style with seven chimneys and even a turret.

As they neared the entrance to the drive, Clyde pointed to the cannon and cannonballs, sitting as if protecting the beautiful mansion. Clyde began, "Pa and I brought this cannon and these cannonballs from Chalk Bluffs last year. If you climb all the way to the top of the bluff, there's a bunch of old broken cannons and cannonballs. We tried to break off a piece of one with a hammer, but it wasn't budging so we took the whole darn thing! I thought we were all gonna get killed trying to get that thing down the cliff and onto the boat. We gave them to Mr. Howard and he had them put here. He says he'll never move them." Jennie could hear the pride in Clyde's voice.

"How did you ever do that?" asked Jennie, amazed that the cannon could be moved at all without the help of at least a dozen horses.

They started to walk up the long, curved drive of Belgian Block, a step up from the commonly used cobblestones. "Even the drive is beautiful," Jennie remarked dreamily, stupefied by the grandeur of the place. "Why are we walking on their driveway? I'm sure they don't want a couple of strangers roaming around their yard."

"We're hardly strangers, Jennie. We gave Captain and Mrs. Howard the cannon because our families have been friends for a long time. I already asked permission anyway." They walked hand in hand, surveying the house and beautiful gardens. It was a bit of a walk up to the fountain that stood opposite the front entry. Leading up to the front door was a stately set of wide steps and an arched brick doorway with a deeply carved wooden door that bore the initial "H" in heavy script.

"I feel uncomfortable, like I'm snooping." Jennie put up her parasol to shield her face from the sun as well as recognition and looked around nervously.

"I just want to show you this fountain," Clyde insisted.

"Then we'll go?"

"Yes, I promise, then we'll go." He led her over to the fountain and ran his fingertips through the coolish water. Jennie followed his lead. "Look how tall it is," he said. Jennie was still feeling sheepish but she was enjoying the lovely surroundings. Clyde splashed the water with his hand then drew it out quickly. "Look, Jennie, I've found something!"

"Let me see, let me see!"

Clyde presented his clenched fist to her, knuckles up, then turned his hand over and opened it.

"What is that?" she asked, holding onto his fingers and moving his hand to better see the small, shiny object in his hand.

"I think…I think maybe it's a ring!" Clyde replied, a huge smile on his face.

"You're right. What in the world? I wonder whose it is?" Jennie was full of questions.

"Well, you see, really I brought it for you." He knelt down on one knee right there at the entryway to the Howards' new mansion. He took her hand and looked into her hazel eyes. "I've loved you since the first time I saw you. I never wanna be without you again. Please marry me, Jennie, and promise me you'll never leave me again!"

Jennie was overwhelmed. The world stood still again, as it had that horrible day when her father had hurt her in so many ways. But this felt completely different.

"Well…" she began, "What would we do? How would we do that? Did you ask your parents?" Jennie wasn't sure why the practical side of her came out first. "I…I…I wanna be with you…forever. Yes, I really do want that!" She seemed to be reassuring herself. "Oh, Clyde, marrying you would make me so happy! Yes, I'll marry you!"

So they kissed, a real kiss, a long kiss that made Jennie's insides feel squirmy. She looked deep into his eyes again and all the fear fell away. He slipped the ring on her finger. The ring was dainty and had been made with pieces of rose gold and yellow gold and silver laced together. "I designed it for you with scraps of gold and silver I saved."

The front door opened, and they turned toward it. Captain and Mrs. Howard were standing there with huge smiles on their faces.

"Congratulations!" the captain said. Jennie and Clyde walked up the steps to meet their unexpected company. There were introductions, handshakes, and even a hug for Jennie from Mrs. Howard.

"We wanted to be the first to wish you well on your new life together," said Mrs. Howard through a big grin. "And the first to give you something." She handed over a large, wrapped gift to Jennie. "Be careful; it's very fragile." Gingerly, Jenny took the package and unwrapped it. Inside was a large glass hurricane globe etched with grapevines with their leaves and clusters of grapes. Jennie was speechless. "The box will help you keep it safe until you have your own home to put it in!"

"It's beautiful! It's more than beautiful! I've never seen anything like it. We will treasure it forever! Thank you, both of you." Jennie was speechless again for the second time in a few short minutes. They were invited to come inside but declined so they could race home and tell their family.

They were married a few weeks later, on September 29, 1895. Jennie had time to sew a wedding gown of white linen damask with a few pieces of lace on the bodice. Captain Howard married them in the garden at the mansion. It was a small wedding, but large enough to make Jennie and Clyde feel special. At the end of the festivities, Captain and Mrs. Howard came up to the couple to say goodbye. "Just so you know, Mrs. Jennie Barbour," the captain began, "Clyde is not your average man. He is going places. I don't know where, but when he makes his mind up to do something, he won't stop until it's done."

CHAPTER 12

THE KNOT

It was the same flatboat with the same river lapping at its sides. It was the same people on the boat with the same ways they'd had before. It was the same smell of damp wood and river water that was so familiar—but nothing felt the same.

The only obvious change was that the bed in Jennie's cabin had been made bigger to accommodate the newlyweds and had a pretty, carved-wood headboard. She had slept in the same bed as her sister for as long as she could remember, so having a body lying next to her was not unusual. But this was a man's body, her man's body. His strong arms and hard chest comforted her. Lying in his arms, she felt safe, secure, and very much loved. She hated when he left their cocoon and looked forward all day to returning to his arms.

Their bodies were eager for each other, so finding their way through the labyrinth of sexual experimentation was life-giving. He was confident, sensitive, and patient. She was impassioned, inquisitive, and attentive. Their coupling was joyful.

Jennie now felt she was a real part of this flatboat and of this loving family that had taken her in. James, on the other hand, remained skeptical of the new family member and seemed a bit jealous of all the attention the newlyweds received from everyone.

"Seems like all anybody wants to talk about is Clyde and Jennie," James told Luke. Then, in a singsong voice: "They're so well matched! They look splendid together! They'll have beautiful children! Yuck." He was sitting on the railing and spat into the river in disgust.

"Now, Mr. James," said Luke, who was standing next to him, "why you don' like Miss Jennie? There ain't nobody don' like Miss Jennie. You don' like it your big brother done foun' hisself a woman and is happy?" Luke shook his head. "Your turn's a-comin' and I knows you gonna want everybody to be happy for ya. Do unto others, Mr. James, do unto others." Luke walked off toward town and didn't look back.

They had stopped at Caseyville, Kentucky, which had long been known for two things, gambling and coal mines. Gambling meant lots of whiskey and lots of fights. The coal mines provided the gamblers, and the pugnacious fellows who would liven up the night with their escapades. The mines also supplied the funding for these ever-present addictions.

The men headed into town at dusk. James was to return in two hours. Jennie and Ma sat on the deck in the rocking chairs. "Now that Clyde has his riverboat pilot's license, how many more trips do you think we'll make down the river with you?" asked Jennie with a heightened interest in the answer.

"He's been waitin' a long time to be called Captain. Pa's payin' him this time round—not much, but somethin'. Clyde needs to go on from here." Ma got quiet and Jennie wondered what it was that she wasn't saying. "He needs to use his license to make enough money to take care of his family now. It's gonna be hard for us to manage without him, but we will."

The sun was setting, and the sound of the night creatures began. The sounds echoed off the water to the trees and back off the water again, to be replicated endlessly in a hypnotic symphony of nature.

By the light of a gas lamp, Jennie held her left hand at arm's length and admired her ring. "How did Clyde get the idea for my ring?"

Ma looked at her and smiled to see her enjoying Clyde's design. "He's always been that way, always comin' up with new ways of doin' things or puttin' things together. He's the one who decided how he wanted your bed to look. One day he just made up a new kind of knot to help tie up the boat. I've seen him drawin' pictures of steamboats and houses; don't know where that comes from."

"Sometimes I wonder…" Jennie began, then hesitated.

"Wonder what, Jennie?"

"It's just that, well, you know, Clyde, he's so, he's so smart and all. He might get tired of me." The last sentence was spoken in a low tone full of trepidation. "He's been studyin' all that college stuff that I know nothin' about." She crossed her arms on her lap.

"God didn't make men and women to be the same. Do you know how to cook and sew and clean and take care of the family you're gonna have?" Ma got a quizzical smile on her face barely perceivable by the light of the gas lamp.

"Mostly I do. I'm still learnin'. But that's different. Women are taught to do all that growin' up."

"Yes, and men are taught to learn what they need to learn to take care of their families in their way. It all equals out. As long as you both keep tryin' and keep learnin', you'll be just fine. You're lucky to find a man with so much schooling; there ain't many of them around here." Ma was rocking again and looking out over the darkness once more.

James returned with stories of the goings-on in town. He was energized and his eyes sparkled. He reached over to pick up the can on the deck next to the railing, grabbed the string that was attached to it, and threw the can overboard. When he pulled the can back up it was full of river water.

"I don't think I'll ever be able to drink that river water," Jennie said with a look of disgust.

"I grew up drinkin' this stuff. Let it sit for a minute for the mud to settle and you're fine!" James said with the voice of experience. He picked up the can and took a big swig. "Ahhh!" he exclaimed and took a second sip then smiled up at them. "They say this water here can cure most anythin'!"

Luke returned and Clyde returned, but there was no sign of Pa, which wasn't unusual. They all went to bed knowing he'd show up eventually.

Several hours later, Ma quietly opened the door to Clyde and Jennie's room. Her heart sang when she saw the two sleeping in each other's arms looking so young and innocent. She hated to disturb them but had no choice. "Clyde!" she whispered. "Clyde!" She shook him lightly. He rolled over and looked at her, startled. He eased himself up to sitting and rubbed his eyes.

"What's wrong, Ma? Is everything okay?" he asked half asleep.

"It's Pa. He's still not here and he knows we need to leave at dawn. He should have been here by now." Ma still had her sleeping hat and nightgown on, and a shawl wrapped around her shoulders.

"Should I go to town and look for him?" Clyde asked.

"Yes. Let's try not to wake James or Jennie. I'll meet you on the deck." Ma left to let Clyde get dressed.

When he reached the deck, Luke was there and dressed. "Luke, you comin' with me?"

"Yes, sir. Don' want you goin' in there alone this time of night."

"Okay. Let's go. Ma, we'll be back as soon as we find him. Don't worry." Clyde kissed his mother on the cheek, and they headed off to town again.

Things had settled down a lot since the two men had left town earlier. The streets weren't teeming with pedestrians and horses and wagons. There were some men milling about and a handful of horses still stood tied to the hitching posts. Most of the buildings were dark inside and out. Two men stood outside of the saloon, each with his hat on, one with a mustache, the other with his hand on his hip smoking a pipe. They stared coldly as Clyde and Luke approached. A white man and a Black man walking down the street together wasn't a common sight. Clyde was rather short, but Luke was tall and wide and strong as an ox. It would have been unacceptable for Luke to go into the saloon, so he stood outside, at a distance from the onlookers.

Clyde walked through the swinging doors and into the poorly lit space. One man was standing, leaning on the bar talking to the bartender, who was cleaning up. Two men sat at a table, one with his head on the table asleep. A woman in a fancy green shiny dress was sweeping the floor. Clyde thought how odd it looked to see a woman in such an ornate outfit sweeping the floor. *I wouldn't wish that life on any woman. Never will my Jennie ever have to do somethin' like that,* he thought, with a familiar sense of determination welling up inside of him. Clyde knew the bartender, who was also the owner, and asked if he'd seen Pa recently.

"No, son. He was in here earlier, but that's all I know." The man went back to his cleaning and conversing.

Clyde was well aware that upstairs were a few rooms where prostitutes worked. *Oh Lord, please tell me he's not up there.* He walked up to the lady sweeping and asked if there were any men upstairs. Her answer was no. Clyde could breathe more easily.

The sheriff's office was just a few doors down from the saloon.

"Let's go ask the sheriff if he's seen him," Clyde said to Luke. The thought of his pa in the jailhouse was awful but didn't make his stomach turn as the last possibility had. Once again, Luke waited outside while Clyde went in.

The room was lit by a single kerosene lamp that sat on a desk. Behind it was a man asleep on a cot holding his rifle. *One false move and that man's gonna shoot me,* thought Clyde, as he tried to decide what to do next. To his right was the jail cell. It was divided into two parts, and there was a man sleeping on a cot on either side.

"Sheriff?" Clyde called without moving any closer. There was no movement. "Sheriff?" he said a little louder. One of the prisoners sat up, rubbed his eyes, and stared at Clyde.

"What you want, boy?" he asked, slurring from one too many at the saloon. The man's voice woke the sleeping lawman, who clenched his rifle and stood up quickly.

"Yes, that's me. Must a dozed off just for a second, son. What you need?" The sheriff straightened his clothes and patted his badge.

"Lookin' for my pa, Sheriff. His name's Jim Barbour. You may know him." Clyde walked closer and addressed the man.

The prisoner who had spoken to Clyde moments ago began to laugh, his cackle getting louder and louder.

"Shut up!" yelled the sheriff, which had only a momentary effect on the laughing man. "I told you to shut up!" he repeated, this time pointing his rifle at the man. Clyde stepped back, away from the quarrel as Luke stepped inside the office.

"Wee doggie, Sheriff, look at that huge thing done walked in here!" The prisoner stood up and held onto the bars. Clyde could see his nose was bloody.

The sheriff turned to look at Luke. "What you doin' here? I ain't got no use for you up in here." He walked past Clyde toward the door, and Clyde put his hand on his arm.

"He's with me, Sheriff. All we're doin' is lookin' for my pa."

The cackling began again. He pointed at the still sleeping cellmate. "There he is, boy; that there's your pa! He sure made a ass o' hisself."

"And what about you, you sorry fool. You were right in there with him." The sheriff walked over to the other cell, unlocked the door with his big ring of keys, and walked over to the sleeper, who was starting to stir. He pulled the small blanket off the man and motioned to Clyde to come. "This your pa?"

Clyde reluctantly stepped into the cell. A feeling of dread like a black cloud came over him. He saw his father's swollen and bloody face. He didn't know if he was more ashamed or concerned. "Yes, Sheriff, that's my pa. What happened to him?"

"Drinkin' and bein' a nuisance got him into a fight with that man yonder." The sheriff pointed to the still laughing man.

"And I say I came out the winner. Hardly a mark on me!" the man said proudly.

"'Cept that bloody nose you got," remarked the sheriff.

"Aw, that's nothin'. It'll be healed up by mornin'. Now Jim's face over there, that's gonna take a good long while I'd say." He laughed again then sat back on his cot.

"Let me fetch some water," the sheriff offered. He returned with a rag and a bowl of water. Clyde took them, kneeled next to the cot, and started trying to wash the blood off his father's face. Jim woke suddenly, yelling and flailing, which sent the bowl of water flying across the cell.

"What the hell's goin' on?" Pa asked. "Ow! Damn it. Stop that!" he yelled at Clyde. "Let me do that; you're killin' me."

"Well, the water's all over the floor now, Pa. Here, take the rag." Clyde handed it to him and walked out of the cell. "How long is he here for?"

"Until he sobers up," replied the sheriff. "You wanna take him, go right ahead. Be one less for me to watch."

Clyde looked at Luke, not sure what to do. Luke nodded and stepped farther into the room. "Luke and I will get him back on our boat. Luke, help me get him up."

"I don't need any damn help gettin' up," said Pa indignantly. He used the wall to buttress himself up to standing. Clyde reached out to steady him, but Pa resisted. "Nothin' a good night sleep won't cure."

They made their way back to the flatboat. Pa eventually let Luke and Clyde hold him up when necessary. Ma saw them coming and rushed to meet them.

"What in the world happened to you?" she asked, shocked at what she saw. Pa had no reply.

"Ma, he needs to lie down, that's all I know. He may have a broken nose. I'm not sure." Clyde was exhausted and humiliated. *At least we got him through town without a crowd of people seein' him. He's never gonna learn.*

They all went their own way, Clyde making sure Pa got onto his bed before quietly and softly slipping back under the covers next to Jennie.

"How's Pa?" she asked sleepily.

"It's nothing for you to worry with. Go back to sleep." He kissed her, wrapped his arms around her, and quickly fell asleep.

CHAPTER 13

THE QUARTER

The Ohio River was wonderfully calm. There wasn't much traffic on the river that day, so they were set up for an easy day of sailing. Clyde was up top reading a book and Jennie was inside mending and talking with Ma. Clyde called for Jennie, who was happy for the distraction. She nimbly climbed the ladder to the top and walked back to where Clyde was sitting on the lazy board. Pulling her heavy sweater closer to help shield her body from the brisk air, she sat next to her husband and kissed his cheek.

Grandpa came up behind Jennie and when he sat next to her, she pulled a comb out of her sweater pocket and began to comb his beard, making him smile. "What a good girl you are, Jennie Barbour!"

Jennie smiled and blushed ever so slightly. Their bond had become sweet and solid. He had become her teacher, her grandfather, and a sage old man she could talk to.

As they sailed along enjoying the day and the company, Jennie saw a monumental outcropping of large rocks downriver on the starboard side and pointed. "What's that?"

"Oh, that's why I called you up here. That's Cave-in-Rock. It used to be a hiding place for river pirates and other river rats," Clyde said. "I'll show you when we get closer."

"What's a river rat?" Jennie asked.

"A river rat is any kind of thief or robber or murderer livin' on or around a river."

"Are we safe?" asked Jennie, standing up anxiously.

"Yes, child, there's been no trouble around here since the sixties," Grandpa said. "It's mostly an attraction now for boaters passing by, but it has quite a bloody history." He was the only one who knew more about the history along the rivers than Clyde.

"Bloody? Really? It's not very ladylike to be interested in such things, but would you tell me some of the stories, please?" Jennie shifted to face Grandpa.

"Surely! You're a river girl now, so it's only fitting you should know some of the folklore. Let's start at the beginning. Around 1800, a river rat named Samuel Mason brought his gang here, and they set up a tavern and a gambling parlor right in the cave."

"It's the perfect place for pirates because the entrance is sort of hidden, but from the inside you have a great view up and down the river," Clyde added, not wanting to be left out.

James climbed up. "Grandpa, you tellin' stories? I wanna listen, too."

"Sit down, boy. I imagine you already heard these," Grandpa replied. "Mason could get the travelers to stop here for some whiskey, gambling, women." He looked over at Jennie who lowered her head, blushing. "Once he had them inside the cave, he and his gang would rob them, beat them up, and even kill them if they wanted. They say he had no conscience; he'd kill people for the money or just 'cause he felt like it."

"Why would he kill somebody for no good reason?" asked Jennie, confounded.

"This world's made up of all kinds of folks, Jennie, all kinds," Grandpa answered. "He did the same thing later on the Mississippi River and the Natchez Trace."

"What happened to him, Grandpa?" asked James, intrigued.

"They finally put a bounty on his head, $1,000 dead or alive. $1,000! So, what do you think happened, James?"

"I don't know, but if I'd seen him, I'd have killed him for sure to get all that money!" James was animated.

"Well, that's just what happened," Grandpa went on. "One of his own gang put a hatchet in his back, but he hadn't thought it through; the other gang members killed *him*, and no one got the money. So, Mason's gang eventually split up, and other pirates came to Cave-in-Rock."

Grandpa stood up and pointed to the site, which was now just in front of them. They all stood up and Jennie walked over to that side of the boat for a better look.

The entrance to the cave didn't face the river directly and was partially obscured by trees and bushes. The opening was the shape of a shark's open mouth and a narrow pathway in the center led into the limestone cave. The left front corner jutted out very close to the water. All along the shore, the gigantic rocks jutted out again and again, making this particular spot fairly indistinguishable from the rest of the outcropping. It was difficult to imagine that the cave hadn't been sculpted intentionally to serve as protection from the elements or the travails of frontier traveling.

Jennie and Grandpa stood silently watching as the cave's opening disappeared from sight. She felt an eerie sense of knowing that made her shudder as her ears picked up a noise, or many noises, coming from the shore. "What's that noise?"

"What noise?" asked James from across the boat.

"Listen. Shhh. It's like, well, somebody crying. They need help! I don't see anyone on the shore. Whoever it is, they need help!" Jennie searched the shore anxiously for any sign of life.

Clyde and Grandpa looked at each other and smiled, shaking their head in acknowledgment. Jennie looked over at them. "What is it?" she asked again.

"The story goes that some travelers on this river still hear the cries of the people who were murdered there. Some say it's just the wind blowing through the caves. It could be either one of those or maybe it's something entirely different. Who knows what it is, but there are so many things in this life that we don't understand," Clyde pronounced as he walked over to her and hugged her. "Nothin' to worry about." He kissed her. She held tightly onto her husband, who then led her toward the ladder.

"Let's go downstairs, get somethin' to drink. It's over now, or soon will be. It's probably just the wind blowing through." Clyde didn't like to see her upset. It was his job to take care of her. He wasn't going to allow her to be afraid. When they descended the ladder, Clyde took the can with the string and dropped it into the Ohio to get some water. "Here. Drink this."

She looked at him and started to laugh. "I don't think drinkin' that awful river water is gonna help me one little bit. No, thank you." They both laughed and her fear melted away.

As they made their way toward Cairo, Illinois, Jennie sat up top and watched the beautiful scenery. Many of the towns sat up higher than the river, the bare cliff faces topped by trees. The fall had brought out the vivid color in the leaves, gold and orange and red. Even after seeing mile after mile of these colors on either side, Jennie never grew tired of the sight. She collected leaves at their stops, which she kept in a box.

Their stockpile of miscellaneous items to sell had dwindled substantially, which meant a stop back in Columbus, Kentucky, where Jennie had returned to the steamboat after her dreadful stop to see her family. Miss Dora would be there the following day for a visit.

"Did you know, Clyde," asked Jennie, "that when the Frenchmen first came here and saw those rusty red-colored cliffs, they named it Iron Banks? It's pretty funny 'cause there's no iron anywhere around here." Jennie was pleased to have some history to share for a change. She figured the men already knew this, but it felt good to be able to bring it up.

Due to the white clay located close by and seen most vividly downriver at Chalk Bluffs, the area was home to a number of pottery plants. Jennie was familiar with this, as her home wasn't far away. Columbus was a big town with a large fish market full of catfish and spoonbills. One of the fish markets had burned a year and a half before, and remnants of some of the charred buildings still remained.

The newly enlarged Barbour family went en masse to buy pottery. It felt good to Jennie to be in familiar territory. Ma made her a real part of the decision-making process determining what to purchase. The men mainly looked around to see what was new but quickly got bored.

Jennie's meeting with Miss Dora was too short. The older woman had brought a long letter from Leona. The only real news was that her oldest brother had married his first love and the couple were already expecting a baby. At this point in Jennie's life, she was able to be happy for him; no jealousy or tears, just a wish to be part of the first grandchild's arrival. Their goodbye was sweet, knowing they would see each other again in the spring.

When they passed the landing where Jennie had first boarded the flatboat, she was sitting on her new bed wearing a new red floral dress she had made over the summer and a beautiful new ring designed for her by her husband. A bittersweet sense of great loss combined with a new hope for a future filled with love. She stared out the window and watched in silence until, even straining her neck, she could no longer see the landing.

They sailed on past New Madrid, Missouri, where the earthquakes of 1811–1812 had destroyed the town and much more. On the steamboat, Jennie had listened to her roommate's stories about the quakes and now she heard more—about how sections of the Mississippi River had actually flowed backwards and how the quake could be felt all the way up in Washington, D.C. She went to sleep that night amazed, once again, at how much a person could learn just floating down the river on a flatboat.

They passed Chalk Bluffs, where Fort Pillow was situated and from where the Barbour men had taken the cannon and cannonballs. The cliffs were beautiful and stood over 300 feet tall. They ran for 10 miles; it was a beautiful three-hour trip.

They stopped to trade at Harwood Point, Arkansas, the site of a large cotton plantation and a post office. Clyde and Jennie walked into the small town. They passed a Black man dressed in a coat and tie with a white starched shirt, the collar tips facing upward, walking into the post office. The two men exchanged smiles and greetings without stopping; it seemed the man was in a rush. Jennie could hardly wait to ask the obvious question. "Who's that Negro?"

"He's the owner of that cotton plantation and everything else you see around here. Very nice fella. It's the damnedest thing. Don't really know how he came to have so much money." Clyde shook his head in wonder.

Jennie was amazed. "Why, I've never heard of such a thing! This far south? That's, that's, well, that's a story I'd like to hear!"

"I plan to follow his lead and make lots of money," Clyde stated. "I'm gonna do that, you just watch!"

They sailed down through Greenville, Mississippi, passed Vicksburg and Natchez, and then stopped at St. Francisville, Louisiana, which sat atop a high ridge overlooking Bayou Sara. It had been the busiest cotton port between Memphis and New Orleans. They didn't stop at Baton Rouge, but as they sailed by, Clyde pointed out places of interest, including the beautiful Capitol Building. It was a busy port, with boats of all sizes moored and sailing up and down the Mississippi. Passing through Edgard, Louisiana, they saw cotton fields and plantations everywhere.

Finally, New Orleans was their next stop. Clyde was looking forward to showing his bride the Crescent City, which was bigger than any city she had ever seen. He told her, "It's called Crescent City because the Mississippi makes a big curve here, so it looks like a crescent moon." Jennie looked at him adoringly.

There wasn't much to see as they approached New Orleans. The land was flat with few trees, and the levees got higher. As houses began to appear on either side, beyond the high levees, it seemed to Jennie that their flatboat was higher than the houses. Pa explained that the city was basically at sea level and that the really old part called the French Quarter was actually below sea level, so the levees had to be built that way.

The river was so crowded at this point that the men manned the sweeps to keep their boat from running into others. They sailed beyond the docks where big steamboat after big steamboat was moored, all in a row. Smokestacks filled the sky as the boats were being loaded and unloaded. People and horses and wagons were everywhere and the shouts of the workers rang out in discordant echoes. There were hundreds of people and activity all up and down the docks. Beyond the docks lay the city, its crowd of multi-storied buildings in the distance. When they had passed all the steamboats and barges, they were able to maneuver their boat to shore and tie it off. Luke, Clyde, and Pa were to take turns guarding the boat and its contents, though nothing much was left. Luke had the first watch, so the Barbour family stepped off the boat and into the commotion.

Clyde was the consummate tour guide, having been to New Orleans many times growing up. He felt this was an opportunity to show Jennie how comfortable he was here in the big city. He also wanted to find out what other boatmen were doing now that flatboating was essentially a dying art. He was ready to pilot a steamboat from up on top in the pilothouse. He could make good money doing that.

They saw a half dozen flatboats being dismantled on shore. "Most of them are taken apart and the wood sold to make money to get back home," Clyde told Jennie. "Since we have so many friends on the river, we can always find a cheap tow back upriver, so we make ours to last."

Straight down from the levee was Jackson Square and St. Louis Cathedral, which was flanked by matching buildings with archways. On opposite sides of the square were long three-story buildings with balconies on every floor; the fourth side was the river. A statue of President Andrew Jackson on horseback stood in the middle of the square. With its steeple and two parapets, the cathedral was taller than all the buildings in the French Quarter. Clyde took Jennie to sit on a bench in the square, where he told her what he knew of the place. The clock on the cathedral struck three o'clock, and Jennie looked around with awe. The sound was very loud but clear and seemed to hang in the air for a long time.

They walked around the Quarter past endless buildings, each two or three stories high, all attached to one another. There were beautiful wrought-iron balconies, many with plants on them trailing downward. The entire Quarter looked a light gray, from the dirt streets to the facades. The people were every shade of beige and brown and black. At the edges of the Quarter were narrow little houses with flat, very plain facades and a few steps leading up to the door. On one set of steps sat a little Black girl holding a rag doll. The girl wore an old yellow dress, and her hair was in pigtails. As she sang quietly to her baby, she rocked it back and forth. Jennie smiled at the child, held Clyde's arm more tightly, and whispered in his ear, "I hope we'll have a little girl someday!"

Clyde felt a rush of pride that this beautiful woman had chosen him and wanted them to have a family. His next feeling was of responsibility, but not in a negative way. He stood up straighter and taller and relished the idea of taking care of his family, *his* family. He was a man now who had a wife, and they would have children and anything else Jennie wanted.

They headed back to the boat, where Ma and Jennie cooked dinner. It was noisy that night as they tried to sleep. Steamboats seemed to be coming and going all night long and Jennie got the impression that the city never slept. The next morning, Pa gave Clyde a few hours to show Jennie more of the city while everyone else stayed at the flatboat to work.

The couple headed toward the opposite end of the French Quarter. They stepped from the narrow dirt street onto the paved, bustling Canal Street. Turning the corner from Royal Street onto Canal, Jennie felt she had been transported to a completely different time and place. In the middle of the street was a broad boulevard where streetcars running on electricity had recently been added. Electric lines ran in several directions overhead. Tall buildings lined either side of the boulevard, each having a distinct, elaborate facade and large windows.

At the end of the street was a statue of a man. Pedestrians walked every which way, horse-drawn wagons followed a somewhat more organized path, and trollies came and went constantly; it was a lot for Jennie to take in. She had never seen anything like this. She felt at the same time frightened and curious. *What are all these people doin' and where are they goin'?*

Clyde smiled at the look of wonder on his wife's face. It was quite a scene for someone from the Kentucky countryside. He'd been here more times than he could remember. He thought it was a beautiful city and loved all the fancy buildings, trollies, statues, and, of course, the French Quarter.

"Who's that statue?" asked Jennie.

"You'll find that interesting. Let's go look." He took her hand, and they walked through the crowd to the statue. "It's Henry Clay!"

"Henry Clay? But he's a Kentuckian. He was a famous politician where I come from." She was delighted to see something in this thriving city she could relate to.

"Yep. He was in both the US Senate and the House of Representatives, and he was Secretary of State for President John Quincy Adams. He ran for president three times. He liked to spend winters down here to get out of the cold weather. He visited New Orleans and other parts of Louisiana many times, and his brother once lived here."

"Still seems kind of funny that the only statue I can see on this whole street is of a man who's not even from Louisiana!" She walked around the statue to see it from all angles. They could hear a steamboat sounding its landing. "Don't you think we should get back to the boat?"

"I guess so. I wanted to take you down to Maison Blanche."

"What's that?"

"It's a store that sells just about every kind of clothes you can think of," Clyde told her. "Very fancy. Very expensive. It's real pretty. You'd like it." Clyde wanted to be the one to introduce Jennie to the finer things in life.

"Next time, next trip. I'll save up some money!" Jennie laughed at the thought of having any money of her own to save.

"How about if I save up some money since Pa paid me this time round? You just wait; we'll have plenty of money." Clyde was pleased to have more than a few pennies in his pocket. They walked off toward the flatboat hand in hand. "I'm still thinking this is gonna be our last trip on that old boat. I'm a riverboat pilot now, and I'm ready for us to move on."

CHAPTER 14

THE LOSS

The flatboat was being taken back upriver by the towboat *Alice Brown*. The sternwheeler had two black hinged stacks between which hung a large symbol of an anchor. A sign above the sternwheel read "Alice Brown of Pittsburg PA" and on both sides was painted "Brown's Line." On the upper deck, or Texas Deck, a railing ran all the way down both sides; here were the cabins where the captains and the crew slept. Towboats didn't ordinarily take on passengers, so there were no frills.

This was not the first time Captain Clark and Captain Boles had towed the Barbours back up to Jeffersonville. At the beginning of this trip, there was only one empty barge and their boat in tow. While they were welcome on the *Alice Brown*, the Barbours would stay, for the most part, on their flatboat. On occasion, when food was plentiful, Ma would cook a big dinner and invite the captains.

Clyde had resigned himself to the fact that they would be tarring the roof of the flatboat. He had been able to talk Pa into waiting until the trip upriver. Tarring was perhaps the most awful job that had to be done on the flatboat. It was a smelly, sticky, hot mess. Clyde and Luke got the wash boiler and put it on the stove. They filled it half full of tar and started the flame. In order to be spread on the roof, the tar had to thin out, which would take a while, so they went down to start salt-curing the wood in the hold. They were hauling a 25-pound keg of gunpowder, 4,000 gun caps, a barrel of lime, and a barrel of coal tar, and they had places to sell all of it.

Jennie sat on the swing on the porch and Ma had joined her, sitting in the rocking chair. Jennie was remembering how at first, being on the swing when the boat was underway had been almost nauseating. The swing would be swinging, the clouds moving in one direction, the shoreline in a different direction, and the water in several directions, all at once. Sitting in the rocker had always been somewhat better. Now, she hardly even noticed as she sat on the swing and watched the banks pass, wondering what was going to happen this time when they stopped at her Kentucky home. Her heart ached every time she let herself think about her family. She wrote Leona frequently and from time to time would hear back.

"What is that horrible odor?" Jennie asked, her mind returning to the present as she pinched her nose shut.

"It's the tar heatin' up for the men to use on the roof. It's a nasty job. Smells horrible, too!" Ma did not feel the same need to pinch her nose. "I wonder where Pa is?" she asked more to the air than to Jennie.

"Haven't seen him in a good while. I guess he's with Grandpa and James on the towboat. That smell is nasty! How do you stand it?"

Before Ma could reply, a crewman from the towboat jumped onto their porch, yelling, "Fire! Fire!" The man ran all the way back through the cabins and into the galley. Jennie saw heavy smoke coming from the galley window.

"Ma! It's a fire in the galley!" Jennie yelled, jumping off the swing and heading inside.

"No, girl, it's just smoke from the tar. No fire." She followed Jennie inside, and they moved quickly toward the stern, Ma moving more slowly, feeling no need to rush. In the galley, they saw the man desperately trying to get the boiler off the stove.

"There's no need…" Ma began, but it was too late. They watched helplessly as the unstable pot fell over and onto the floor, covering the man's hand with hot tar. He screamed, looking around wildly for something to wipe off his hand. Ma grabbed a towel from a drawer and started to help the man when the first flames ignited on the floorboards. The fire looked manageable for about two seconds but then started to spread quickly.

At that moment, Clyde and Luke appeared in the galley. "Ma, Jennie, get out of here!" Clyde shouted. "Run! Run fast!" He pushed them both to the storeroom and pointed to the porch. "Hurry! Hurry!" He disappeared back into the galley where the flames were spreading.

Ma and Jennie made it to the porch and carefully climbed aboard the *Alice Brown* using the tow knees and the railing. Ma was yelling for Pa and Grandpa, who quickly found the women, heard what was happening, and rushed off to the flatboat. Ma held James back from getting any closer. By this time, more smoke and now flames were visible on the far side of their boat.

Back in the galley, the men worked frantically to put out the fire. The crewman had jumped screaming into the river to cool his hand and to escape the flames. As the tar spread out, it carried the flames along its edges, setting everything in its path on fire.

"Thunderation!" Grandpa yelled.

"The damn tar; it's the goddamn tar setting everything on fire!" Pa roared.

"Mr. Jim! We gots to get that gunpowder off this boat or it'll blow!" Luke shouted. Without hesitating, he ran to tackle the problem.

"You've only got two or three minutes," Pa called after him. "Forget it!" But Luke wasn't listening. He was already manhandling the barrel of gunpowder.

Captain Boles was now on the boat trying to douse the flames. Captain Clark was in the pilothouse and yelled down to Ma, "Don't you worry, Miss Annie. We'll git it, we'll git it!"

That was when James reminded Ma that there was a barrel of gunpowder on board.

"Oh heavens. God save us!" she whispered. "Pa! Grandpa! Everybody off the boat. The gunpowder…!"

There was no stopping the fire's advance. There weren't enough buckets or enough people, and there wasn't enough time. The flames had spread to the sleeping cabins, inching their way toward the front.

"Abandon ship! Abandon ship!" Captain Boles yelled. "We got to cut the boat loose. Come on!" He brusquely got Grandpa and Clyde to the porch.

"Go on, Grandpa, get onto the towboat!" Clyde demanded. As Grandpa quickly climbed off the boat, Clyde scurried back inside.

"Luke! Luke! Come on!" he yelled. . "Pa, Luke won't listen! Tell him to come on!" Clyde pleaded.

"Get the hell off this flatboat! You have a wife waitin' out there! Go! Go! I'll get Luke!" Pa pushed his son toward the porch. This time Clyde acquiesced.

Pa looked at Captain Boles, who was still working to contain the flames. "This is *my* ship! You get off here and let me handle this." The captain nodded and raced to his own vessel to untie the burning boat.

Luke was struggling to get the barrel of gunpowder through the doorway and roll it to the porch and into the river. Pa jumped over the barrel and got on the porch side to help upend it. Suddenly, they heard loud pops coming from the hold. The pops so startled Luke that he let go of the barrel and turned to see what was happening behind him.

"The gun caps," yelled Pa. "Luke, come on. We have to go *now!*"

Half the flatboat was in flames. The boat listed toward the bow as pieces of the boat dropped off into the water. Water was overtaking the burned parts of the boat. Just as Luke let go of the barrel, a sudden lurch knocked the two men over and sent the gunpowder rolling toward the flames.

"*Jump!*" Pa screamed, leaping from the boat to the empty barge alongside and covering his head with his hands. He landed with a thud as the flatboat exploded, sending burning debris in every direction. It had been untied to keep the fire from spreading to the towboat, but still, flaming pieces landed on the deck, igniting the wood in several places. The crew ran about putting out each new fire.

"Pa!" Clyde yelled. "Are you okay?" They had seen him jump but now couldn't spot him. Pa stuck his bloody head up but said nothing. Clyde cautiously climbed onto the barge and got to his father. "Pa, you're bleeding!" Clyde wiped the blood off with his hands and wiped it on his pants. "Say something to me. Pa!" Clyde watched as his father slowly and painfully turned his head toward what remained of their floating home and cried out loud, " Luke. Oh, Luke! No, no, no!" He sat down next to his father and put his arm around him; they cried together.

The *Alice Brown* tied up at Kenner, north of New Orleans. Everyone on board felt their pain. However, a boat exploding on the river was not uncommon. Steamboats often suffered boiler explosions, which would maim and kill passengers and crew alike. At this point in time, 1895, steamboats were becoming dinosaurs. Railroad tracks began to replace them as more reliable and faster transportation for goods and people.

That was the world Clyde found himself in after the loss of their flatboat. Armed with his new riverboat pilot's license, he had thought he would have the world by the tail. But with steamboats in disfavor on the big rivers, he had to reinvent his future. He would not be sitting high up in the pilothouse of a sternwheeler sailing up and down the Mississippi and Ohio Rivers as he'd imagined all his life. How many nights had he spent dreaming of being the captain of such a craft? He had watched his dream evaporating as he watched new rail lines being constructed but hadn't dealt mentally with this new reality.

"Y'all need to move on out to the bayou country in south Louisiana. That's where you'll still find a need for your kind of business," offered Captain Boles, and Captain Clark agreed.

But they had lost everything on the boat, except for the clothes on their backs, literally. Even the little bit of cash that Ma had sewn into the hem of one of her dresses was at the bottom of the Mississippi, as was the money sewn into one of Jennie's dresses. The box full of money, the cargo, all the items that hadn't sold on their way down to New Orleans, and Grandpa's books were now all part of the river lore, as was Luke. He had lived many years on the rivers, and when he died, he became an intimate part of them.

Ma, James, and Grandpa stayed on the *Alice Brown*, whose captains offered to take them home, no charge. Pa, Clyde, and Jennie stayed behind. Pa and Clyde had to get some kind of business going, and Jennie refused to leave her new husband.

"Jennie," Clyde had said, "we have no idea what's gonna happen or how long it's gonna take to get our lives back on track. Please go back to Jeffersonville with Ma."

"I will not!" This was a side of Jennie she had kept well hidden. "We are a family now, you and me, and I won't go back to Indiana and wait to be called!" She crossed her arms and looked away.

Clyde didn't know whether to laugh or cry at this new stubborn side his wife was showing. "All right," he said slowly, not sure what to say next. "It won't be easy, but having you with me would be wonderful." And so it was decided.

Nothing brings people together quite like a catastrophe. Their friends came forward to help them from up and down the rivers. They had always been well liked and accepted everywhere. Even though Pa was known to over-imbibe, he was such a fair and honest man that he was still admired. It was well known that he never missed an opportunity to help someone in need, Black or White. This paid dividends when they needed it most.

Both captains on the *Alice Brown* lent them money. Captain Boles lent Clyde some money and added a bit extra as a wedding gift. Captain Clark lent money to Pa. With each loan came an IOU, which gave Clyde a tightness in his throat that he'd never felt before. He'd never been in debt. For Pa, it was just another transaction, a debt he would repay as soon as he got back to work, whenever that was.

The family decided that Clyde and Jennie would visit Luke's widow to tell her in person what had happened and to give her whatever money they could. Word spread quickly up the rivers of Luke's death because he was not just another man blown up on a boat—he was the kind of man, regardless of his skin color, whom people remembered and liked. He was always right there with Pa, helping whenever needed. The Black man who owned everything in Harwood Point, Arkansas, had sent money for Pa to give Luke's widow. That made the idea of the trip by train to see her all the more possible. Pa would go back to New Orleans to try and figure things out while Clyde and Jennie headed to Oakton, Kentucky, by train.

CHAPTER 15

THE VISITANT

They found a train out of New Orleans that stopped in Kenner, Louisiana, and would take them to Luke's home. It was about a 10-hour train ride. Luckily, since the train started in New Orleans, its first stop was Kenner, so they left around 9:00 a.m. and would arrive at a reasonable hour. The loud noise of the locomotive and the thick smoke from the engine fire made it a less than optimal means of transportation. On the flatboat, loud noise consisted of the music from a sternwheeler or the calliope calling its landing at a new place. The incessant noise of the train was almost more than Jennie could stand, before the clickety-clack and the rocking side to side finally lulled her to sleep, her head on Clyde's shoulder.

Oakton was not situated on one of the rivers. There was no hotel in this small town, but there was a boarding house that, according to the station master, had a few empty rooms. They walked the quarter mile to the house and found shelter. Their visit to Luke's widow, Sarah, could surely wait until the morning.

Only a few hundred people lived in Oakton, so houses were thinly spread out. Luke's house was not quite a mile outside of town. Luckily, Clyde had found a wagon to rent for the trip out there. The bumpy road made the ride uncomfortable, but riding was far superior to walking all that way and then having to turn around and walk back to town.

Luke's house was a cute little light-blue house with a front porch on which hung a swing. The grass was sparse, but several full trees provided ample shade for hot summer days. They sat silent in the wagon, neither of them wanting to be the bearer of horrific news. Clyde jumped out and helped Jennie climb down.

Clyde had never met any of Luke's family. He knew this was Luke's second family after he'd been separated from his first family when he lived on the plantation. He knew that they had a little boy Luke always referred to as "my little Man" and that Luke adored his son and his wife, Sarah. Luke had enjoyed telling stories about them both.

As they left the wagon, the only sound was a little boy singing a song unfamiliar to them. Slow and repetitious, he filled in with made-up words. Jennie followed Clyde to the front door, which was ajar. "Hello? Hello?" A little boy opened the door. Indeed, his face looked quite grown up for a five-year-old, which explained his nickname, Man.

"Hey Mister, Missus, what you doin' here?" he asked, his head cocked toward his shoulder, looking at them suspiciously. "Ma! There's folks here! Ma! No kiddin'!" the boy yelled.

"Who dat at my do'?" said a strained female voice from back in the house.

"I'm lookin' for Sarah Brown," Clyde said, loud enough for the woman inside the house to hear him. "My name's Clyde Barbour, and I'm here with my wife, Jennie."

"Clyde Barbour? You's Clyde Barbour?" the soft voice from inside the house asked.

"Yes, ma'am, I am."

"Man, you come here," the voice said, and the little boy ran inside. Jennie and Clyde could only hear whispering.

Clyde looked at Jennie, who took his arm in support. She shrugged her shoulders, unsure of their next move. Man came back to the door and asked them to come inside. "Ma ain't been feelin' so good. I's takin' care of Ma!" he said proudly, holding his head high. "She says come on back to her room."

They followed him into the front room then into an adjoining room, which was a bedroom just big enough for a bed and a small chest of drawers. A chair had been pulled up beside the bed, taking the place of a bedside table. The room smelled of sickness; sweat, musty bed linens, damp wood, and alcohol.

"I's Sarah Brown," she said weakly without sitting up. "And you's Clyde Barbour? Come here."

Clyde went to stand next to her bed. Her dark brown skin was ashen, and her eyes were glassy and lifeless. Her lips looked chapped and hard. She only moved her head to look at him. Her mouth turned up slightly in an effort to smile.

"Don't you look mighty fine, Clyde Barbour? All I hears is what a good boy, I mean man, you be. My Luke, he thinks you made the werld!" Sarah spoke softly, stopping at the end of each sentence to breathe.

"I don't know 'bout that," Clyde stammered.

"I'm Jennie, and I'll tell you, Luke thinks the world of you, too," offered Jennie, still standing at the foot of the bed. "I feel I know both of you from all Luke's stories."

During an uncomfortable silence, Sarah looked back and forth from Clyde to Jennie. Her slight smile slowly melted into a frown as she turned to look at Man on the other side of her bed. "I needs you to go sit on de swing for a bit." Man stomped his feet in defiance. "No time for dat. Go on." The little boy hung his head and obeyed, leaving the front door ajar. "So why is you here and not my Luke? Where he be?" Sarah spoke each word laboriously.

Clyde put his hand on her shoulder. As a tear slowly ran down his cheek, he replied, "Sarah, your Luke has gone to be with the Lord."

As the realization of what happened hit her, she called out Luke's name and sobbed in a frail and ghostly manner. Jennie rushed to the opposite side of the bed, sat down on the bed, did her best to embrace Sarah, and cried with her.

Man ran into the room and pushed Clyde aside. Jennie sat up to give him space. "Where's my Papa Luke?" he asked his mother. "Why you cryin' and callin' for my papa?" Sarah tried to reach her arms up to hold him but didn't have the strength. Man dried her tears with her sheet. He climbed onto the bed, grabbed her tight, and looked at her, nose to nose. "Ma! Ma! Ma!" he cried.

Jennie reached across Sarah's chest and held one of Man's little hands. "He's gone to be with the Lord, Man, and he's lookin' down on you right now, so proud of how you're takin' care of your ma."

"That true, Ma? That true?" he asked his mother, whose wailing and crying had become inaudible, her breathing more labored. He began to shake her, a river of tears running down his face. Clyde grabbed him around his chest with one arm and pulled him back off the bed. Jennie scurried over to where they were standing and took the trembling and sobbing boy into her arms.

Clyde returned his attention to Sarah. "He died tryin' to save us all from being blown up. He did save us, but he lost his life in doin' so. He went down with the boat on the Mississippi near New Orleans." He wasn't sure how much detail to give her, or if she could even hear him. "Some people on the river gave me money to help you out. My family loved him. Without Luke and without the flatboat, I'm thinkin' it's time to move on to somethin' new. Don't know how we'd manage without Luke." Immediately after he said that he regretted it. Their lives would go on and Luke's place would eventually be filled up with others; Sarah's life was unalterably changed forever.

Her silent lamenting turned into coughing, a guttural and lingering cough. Clyde handed her the glass of water on the chair by her bed, but she waved him off.

Jennie, who was consoling the crying boy, asked him who took care of his mother. "Miss Becky...she come by...no doctor," Man replied between sniffles.

"Where does Miss Becky live?" she asked, but it was a long time before he could answer.

"Down da road," he answered. "She live down da road to town."

"Do you think you could help your ma and show us where she lives? I think your ma needs some help." Jennie realized that Sarah needed help, and now.

"I don' know. Maybe," was all he offered.

"Okay, I think maybe you and Clyde Barbour should go fetch Miss Becky and I'll stay here and take care of your ma till you get back," Jennie said.

"I's not goin' nowhere. I's the one takes care of Ma!" Man insisted.

Clyde had overheard their conversation and stepped in to help. "Man, I need your help. I can't find Miss Becky without you. Your ma's lookin' real sick, so we gotta hurry!"

Sarah's whisper could hardly be heard as she tried to sound strong. "You go on now, you hear? Clyde Barbour's wife gonna take care a me."

"No, Ma. Don' make me. I wants to be with you, Ma!"

"What did your Papa Luke always say, little Man?"

"First thing is I gots to take care a my ma, that what he said." Man had stopped crying but wanted nothing to do with leaving.

"Then you better go along with Clyde Barbour and help your ma," Sarah whispered again.

"We have somethin' important to do, Man. Let's go and get it done." Clyde took his little hand. "We'll be back faster than lightnin'!"

"Ma, I gots to go. I gots to take care uh you. You take a rest and when you wakes up, Miss Becky'll be here." He walked over to his mother and kissed her goodbye. "Now you stop that coughin', hear?"

Jennie set about cleaning up Sarah and the sick room as best she could. She talked to Sarah as she worked, fearing that if Sarah fell asleep, she might not ever wake up. "Luke was learnin' to read and gettin' real good at it, too! He wanted to surprise you with it; always talked about teaching Man to read when he was still little, so he'd feel smart and important."

Sarah watched Jennie and tried to find a smile underneath her grief and exhaustion. Jennie's nervous activity helped greatly to fill a void for both of them. When Sarah closed her eyes for a few minutes,

Jennie tiptoed to her side to check her breathing. She remembered seeing a Bible on the chair next to the bed, picked it up, and went into the front room to read it. It looked as though it hadn't been read much, if at all; it smelled of new paper, crisp and clean. Jennie sat and read the Bible, waiting for Clyde and Man to return.

Jennie awoke from her unintended nap to the sound of the horse and wagon arriving and the talking of the riders. Man came running through the door and into his mother's bedroom. "Ma! Miss Becky's here. Ma!"

Miss Becky, a short, stout white woman, had served as a nurse during the War and used those skills to help the sick whenever she could. After a brief introduction, Miss Becky walked over to see Sarah. Man, lying on top of the covers next to his mother, put his little hand on her face. He told her about the trip and how fun it was to bump all around riding in the back of the wagon. His young mind had been easily distracted from the horror that surrounded him.

Miss Becky stood over Man. "Come on now, honey, let me check out your ma." She coaxed him off the bed and sat down in his space. Clyde and Jennie left the room to give them some privacy. "Man, you go outside and play. Go on. I need to tend to your ma. Go on now." Slowly, he left the room, walked out the front door, and sat on the steps.

Clyde and Jennie sat in the front room reading the Bible. Man sat on the front steps drawing in the dirt with a stick. Time seemed to pass ever so slowly. Jennie got up to look for something to eat. Clyde pointed to a basket Miss Becky had brought with her.

"She brought some food; said since Sarah is sick, she knew there wasn't much food in the house." They waited for Miss Becky to reappear and hand out the food and drink. A Coca-Cola had been added for Man, who ate his food outside on the porch.

"How is she ever gonna get better?" Jennie asked.

"She's not," answered Miss Becky in a serious, nurse-like tone. "She's got consumption. I'm surprised she's still alive. She's always been a frail thing. She's 'most gone." Clyde had managed to tell her that Luke had died without letting Man realize it. "We been waitin' for Luke to come home so he could take Man back with him."

"Well, that's not gonna happen," replied Clyde flatly. "Where will Man go?"

"I don't know. Nobody 'round here can take on another mouth to feed. I can talk to the preacher. I just don't know." Miss Becky was shaking her head looking desolate. "It's horrible to think that he'll lose both his parents at such a young age. He's smart and sweet and dedicated to his ma. She's been his whole life."

They heard a noise from the bedroom. Jennie stopped Miss Becky from getting up, saying she'd take a turn. She saw Sarah trying to reach over toward the chair. "My Bible," Sarah was saying. "My Bible."

"I'll get it, Sarah. Clyde and I were reading it." She fetched the Bible and handed it to Sarah, who couldn't hold it, so Jennie rested it on Sarah's chest.

"I can'ts read but I holds it and turns the pages. Luke give it to me." She started to wail again in a near silent desperation. Jennie sat on the bed. Clyde walked in and sat on the other side. Sarah's coughing started again.

"Sarah," said Clyde in a soft but stern voice. "Sarah. Your crying is making you cough and that's bad. Try to calm down." He held her hand. "Where's your family?"

"I don't know. They all gone somewheres," she whispered. "All gone...."

"Friends?" asked Clyde, searching.

"We's pretty much alone out here. Miss Becky, she's kinda a friend. She so sweet and good to my little Man." She started to cry, but more quietly now. "I's gonna die and my baby got nobody." The crying got harder; the coughing started again.

"Sarah. Stop. Listen." Jennie looked at Clyde and shook her head no, to stop being hard on her. Clyde ignored her. "What do you want us to do with Man? I mean...who should we take him to? I promise we'll get him wherever you want him to go."

"There's nobody nowheres wants a little Negro baby boy. Nobody! Less'n they wants to treat him like a slave! Oh Jesus, no, that can't happen!" She grasped Clyde's hand the little bit she could.

"No...no...no. That's not gonna happen. Not to Luke's boy," Clyde insisted.

All this talking had worn Sarah out. She let go of Clyde's hand and closed her eyes. They both sat there for a minute waiting for her to fall asleep. Clyde looked at Jennie and nodded his head toward the front room. As they got up to leave, they heard Sarah's whisper of a voice again.

"Clyde Barbour," was all she said.

"Yes, Sarah, I'm still here." He walked back to her bedside. "Do you want some water? Are you ready to try and eat some of Miss Becky's soup?"

"No, Clyde Barbour. I wants you," Sarah said.

"I'm here, really I am."

"I wants you to take our little Man. I wants him to go with you and your pretty wife."

"You want us to take him? Well...I hadn't thought about that." He looked at Jennie. Her face looked as stunned as his.

"For me and my Luke. Please!" Her begging, though only a whisper, cut right through to Clyde's heart. He could see tears in Jennie's eyes. "He's a good worker and a sweet boy. He'll make a fine worker for you." She closed her eyes and breathed deeply. "When he grows up, he'll see how you saved his life. Please, Clyde Barbour, take him with you now. He don't need to see his ma die. The Lord be ready for me now."

"I think you're right; the Lord is ready to take you," said Jennie. "Of course, we'll take Man with us and watch over him. I know he'll make you and Luke both proud."

"But please keep his name; I wants to be able to find him when my spirit returns next time," Sarah whispered.

Clyde and Jennie were sitting on opposite sides of the bed. Jennie took Sarah's hand and held it to her chest. Clyde held Sarah's other hand. No more words were necessary. They were as one now, coming together to save a little boy from what would have been inevitable cruel servitude.

Suddenly, Sarah loosed her hands and reached toward the foot of her bed, crying out for Luke. Her eyes and arms seemed to follow something invisible until she was looking in Clyde's direction. Her chin lifted up and her eyes closed, as if being stroked like a kitten. Sarah opened her eyes, smiled, and murmured several times, "Yes." She tried desperately to sit up but could only stretch her arms out as she started to cry and call out in an agonized voice, "Luke, don't go; please don't leave me, Luke!"

Clyde and Jennie looked at each other not knowing what to think or say. Clyde had noticed that the room had quickly turned cooler during this exchange and he'd felt an undeniable presence there with them. *Was that Luke? Could that have been Luke?*

"Luke, are you here?" Clyde asked out loud.

"He's gone," cried Sarah. "He's gone!" Her eyes closed as she continued to weep.

Clyde reached across her to hold Jennie's hands, which were cold; her eyes were wide open. "Did you see anything?" he asked Jennie quietly.

"No, did you?"

"No, but I could feel a presence right in front of me!"

Sarah stopped crying. "It was Luke all right. He wants you should take Man with you."

"Of course, we will. Yes, don't worry Sarah, we'll take really good care of him." Clyde took her hand, squeezed it softly, and looked into her eyes, smiling.

Jennie wanted to stay with Sarah until she died. She could remember holding her mother as she passed away. Clyde said they didn't have the luxury of time for that; they had to get back to Pa in New Orleans and start working. Tearing Man away from his mother was bound to be awful.

Clyde and Jennie spent that night at Miss Becky's while Miss Becky stayed overnight at the house with Sarah and Man. Finally alone, they were able to revisit what had happened earlier in Sarah's bedroom. As they lay in bed, they talked quietly.

"Do you think Sarah really saw Luke?" asked Jennie.

"Yes, I do. Back on the flatboat it wasn't unusual to hear of people seeing ghosts. Remember Cave-in-Rock? Not only do people hear the cries of those who were killed, many have seen ghosts of them and the pirates."

"You saw ghosts at Cave-in-Rock?" Jennie asked, anxious to hear more.

"No, not there. Actually, it's happened more than once." Clyde looked shy, not knowing how his wife would react. "I mean, on the river you're always hearin' about ghosts and stuff."

"Really? I always wanted to see Mother after she passed, wanted her to come tell me she was okay, but it never happened." Jennie rolled over to face her husband. "Who did you see?"

"I didn't recognize her. She was on the other side of the porch, sitting in the rockin' chair smiling at me. All the time the rockin' chair was moving back and forth. I walked over to try and touch her, but she just disappeared, vanished into the night. There've been other things, but none quite as real as that." Clyde looked off into space, recalling the apparition.

"You weren't scared?"

"Nope. Just interested." Clyde cuddled up next to his wife, ready for sleep. "Let's stop talkin' about all that stuff and get some rest. It's bound to be a long day tomorrow with Man."

The next morning, Clyde suggested that Jennie stay at Miss Becky's while they dealt with Man. Although Jennie desperately wanted to distance herself from the trauma, she wouldn't allow herself to do so.

When they arrived, Miss Becky was asleep in the front room. Clyde gently shook her to wake her. Man was asleep next to his mother. The three grownups went into the bedroom, which woke the little boy. He looked around and saw that the room was full of people. Man kissed his mother's cheek to wake her up. "Ma. Ma. We all here at the same time! Look, Ma!" Sarah opened her eyes. The silence was deafening.

"I sees them, my little Man. They's all folks that loved your pa and wants to take care of us," Sarah whispered.

"I bets Clyde Barbour done got lots a money he can share!" stated Man unequivocally.

"I wish that was true," answered Clyde.

Jennie interrupted, "We don't have lots of money, but we do have lots of love in our hearts for you. We want you to come live with us." Her sincere smile and heartfelt words fell on tiny deaf ears. It was all she could do to hold back all the emotion swelling up in her as she remembered her mother's passing, a feeling similar to what she now felt every time she thought of her own family.

"That'd be silly since I needs to be here taking care of Ma, you know?"

"But your ma is real sick," said Miss Becky, "and needs me here all the time now. I can't take care of you *and* your ma."

Man got quiet, and they could see his mind working hard. "I can fend for myself; I ain't goin' nowheres! Besides, I promised Papa Luke I'd take care of her. He's gone and 'specting me to do my promise." He had already sat up in bed next to his mother. He crossed his arms and looked from one adult to the next. "You can't make me." No one said anything. "I don't wanna go and you can't make me."

Sarah, who looked to be asleep, spoke up in her soft tone. "Baby boy, you don't know, but your papa was here last night, standin' next to my bed. He wants you should go, only till I gets better, that's all." She gave her best smile.

"What you mean Papa was here? Papa passed, you told me so."

"It were his spirit come to say bye and say you needs to go with Clyde Barbour and his pretty wife. We has to do what Papa Luke tells us, right?"

"But Ma, I's the one cares for you, not Miss Becky." He looked indignantly at his mother's nurse.

"Now, Man, I'm a nurse so I know how to take care of sick people better than most anybody. I will take care of her as long as she needs me. I promise. And since your papa passed, Mr. Barbour, he needs your help. When she gets to feelin' better, we'll send for you."

Clyde chimed in. "Have you ever been on a train?" Man shook his head. "Have you ever been on a steamboat?" Man shook his head once more. "Well, you'll have to take a train with us to get to our steamboat!" Clyde's enthusiasm seemed to be rubbing off on the little boy.

"Sounds like you's gonna have a big time, my little Man!" Sarah added.

"And I gets to do it again when I comes home!" Man added as the adults looked on with sadness.

And so, it was decided. Right before they left the next day for New Orleans, Man decided it was a big mistake. But the bravest mother in the world, Sarah, assured him all was well and made him go.

CHAPTER 16

THE REBEGINNING

The trip up to Oakton had been somber and pensive. The trip back down to New Orleans was anything but. Man had cried all the way to the train station. When the train engine came into sight and blew its whistle, he jumped into Jennie's arms, screaming with fear, clawing at her chest as if to crawl inside of her to hide from the approaching monster. Getting him onto the train took coaxing from four adults. When the porter picked Man up, let him hold the whistle and blow it himself, he finally got onboard in the porter's arms and thought nothing more about it.

Back in New Orleans, Pa had been sleeping wherever he was offered a space. Rivermen helped each other, waiting for their turn to need assistance. It was easy for him to get by with a few dollars, eating once a day and drinking with his buddies on their boats, where he knew he wouldn't be called upon to pay.

If it had only been Pa, Luke, and Clyde, it would have been a lot easier to strike out on their own, but with a female in tow, things would have to be more settled. Pa wondered how he was going to make that happen. The introduction of a child into the picture was still unknown to him. When he saw the young couple walking down the docks with a Black child in tow, he was more than a little puzzled.

Jennie hugged Pa and kissed him on the cheek, Clyde shook his hand, and Man began asking questions.

"Miss Jennie, who dat mister?" he asked. "What is does mens doin' over dair?" then added, "Clyde Barbour, you gonna teach me to swim? What if I falls into dat big water?"

It took only a few minutes for Pa to realize who this child belonged to; it was Luke's baby, Man. "Clyde Barbour?" Pa asked.

"Pa, I keep tryin' to get him to call me Mr. Clyde, but…well, I'll tell you later."

Pa squatted down. "Hello, you must be Man, pleased to meet you!" He held out his hand to shake, but Man wasn't so sure. "I'm Clyde Barbour's pa," he said.

Slowly, Man put out his little hand and shook it. "Is you the one knows my Papa Luke?" he asked.

"Yes, I am. Your papa was with me for 10 years!"

"Then I'm guessin' you's a good man," replied Man with conviction. The adults chuckled.

"Why don't you call me Mr. Jim? That's what your Papa Luke called me; he would like that, I'm sure of it." Pa smiled at the little boy and stood back up. "Looks like we'll be needin' a proper place to stay."

All this talk about his father made Man cry. Jennie picked him up and walked down the dock with him so the men could talk. As she walked away with this Black child on her hip, it struck her how easy it had been to take him not only into her arms but into her heart. Now that she was thinking about it, she could feel her heart contract and a feeling of uneasiness creep up her body. She closed her eyes, took a deep breath, and said to herself, *His pa saved my life. His pa was part of Clyde's family. His pa was a wonderful man who just happened to be a Negro.* She held Man tighter, put his head on her shoulder, and kept walking.

While they'd been gone, Pa had managed to do some good reconnaissance in between his bouts of drinking. He had scoured the town for ideas and settled on transporting merchandise up the bayous, mainly from The French Market, which held a sprawling produce market and many treasures that men beyond the reach of any real commerce would appreciate. A roof covered most of the stalls, while other peddlers sat on the ground with no cover, displaying their wares. People milled around in a disorderly fashion looking at the produce, the little trinkets and treasures, and even candy that was being sold.

He had been to the Post Office and found a letter for Jennie from her sister Leona and another one for Grandpa from Grandma. When he handed the letter to Jennie, she smelled it, hoping for some lingering scent of her home, and then held it to her heart. She put it in her pocket to read later.

Now they needed a boat. A longtime friend of Pa's had a second, smaller sternwheeler he was willing to rent to Pa, with the understanding that Clyde, with his riverboat pilot's license, would be the captain. That put both Pa and Clyde in awkward positions, but that was the new reality.

Sarah had insisted that Clyde take most of the money given to her; she knew she wasn't going to need much more. Clyde had promised to use it only for something that would benefit Man. Sarah responded, "Clyde Barbour, I trusts you to do what you needs with dat money, just likes I trusts you with my baby boy." That money helped them rent the boat and buy some merchandise. They also paid a pittance to an older man named Broussard, who had grown up on the bayous and could help them navigate. Clyde turned out to be a great negotiator and made it all come together for their first trip, with a few IOUs sprinkled here and there. In a few short days, they were off on the journey of a lifetime.

They were heading to Bayou Teche and in particular a town named Franklin. Opportunities for them in that area were said to be vast. It took days to get there. They turned west off of the Mississippi near Baton Rouge onto Bayou Plaquemine, and then headed into Grand Lake and finally onto Bayou Teche near Morgan City, Louisiana. The land was flat, and trees full of moss and vines lined the waterways. There were exotic-looking birds they had never seen before. In the evening, they could hear the sound of these singing birds and croaking toads, often unpleasantly loud.

There was nothing familiar about this new landscape. As they made their way through what Broussard told them was a swamp, Clyde noticed a smell of wet vegetation and cypress, and Jennie felt the world closing in as the canopy got lower and the moss thicker. It was like being in a cave, Clyde decided. Eerie but interesting. Jennie was happy there was adequate space inside the boat to help ease her feeling of the swamp swallowing her whole.

They passed men in pirogues and canoes with guns and traps, whose enthusiastic hellos sounded like nothing any of them had heard, except, of course, for Broussard. He told them, in his own unfamiliar, heavy accent, that most of the people on the bayous and in the swamps speak a form of French called Cajun.

"I hears they comes from as far north as Canadia or some such place, but I don' believes it. I thinks they's just here all by theyselves and they made up some kind of talk so no one from not 'round here can understand what they saying," Broussard explained.

Clyde had heard this kind of talk many times in New Orleans and had been given basically the same explanation. He had learned about Canada at school in Jeffersonville, but nothing about any of those people going down to Louisiana Bayou Country.

That day in the swamp, Broussard spotted an alligator on the bank and made sure everyone saw it. Clyde and Pa looked on with fascination; Man seemed partly afraid and partly fascinated, but Jennie began to shake. *What if one of us falls in that water the way I did that one time on the Mississippi?* She shuddered and went back inside, thinking of how her brothers would love such an adventure.

Franklin, Louisiana, looked much like all the other river towns they'd passed. Several sternwheelers were docked there, and the dock was alive with activity. It was a major sugar cane and lumber port. The cypress swamps were being stripped of valuable lumber that was both insect resistant and moisture resistant. The lumber salesmen spoke of there being no end to the forests in the swamps around there; the locals knew all too well that wasn't true.

They tied up at the municipal docks, everyone happy to get back on land. Jennie looked around carefully before she got off the boat to be sure no alligators were lying in wait. There were two places to dock, the Main Street dock and the Adams Street dock. Jennie scurried around figuring out where and how to display their merchandise, most of which they still had onboard, even after several stops along the way. The pralines and taffy Jennie had been so excited about were old hat to these people. The millinery goods were more appreciated, as were the bananas they had purchased green in New Orleans and that Jennie had babied all the way here. Now they were the perfect combination of slightly green and lemony yellow, making them ready for purchase.

A friendly riverboat pilot had some advice for the young Captain Clyde: "Why not try farming? Most all the plantations you see on the bayous belong to farmers."

Clyde replied, "Oh, no, sir, I'm no farmer. I'm tied to the water, not the land."

The next day, Clyde and Jennie strolled down Main Street. Gas streetlamps were evenly spaced all down the narrow boulevard. And the houses! Each seemed more beautiful than the last. There was a Methodist church, a Catholic church, and a beautiful courthouse that stood stately and strong in the middle of the square. The Black people would step aside to let the young couple by while smiling politely. It seemed that everyone was equally friendly. Jennie couldn't see how they would find a place to live in such a town as this, but Clyde was not put off.

"We just have to get our bearings, and everything will come together; you'll see. With a whole lot of hard work, we'll have a cute little house here in no time. I can see it in my mind!" he told his wife with a far off look in his eyes, imaging the life he knew was coming. Her only response was a loving smile. His confidence gave her the courage to share something amazing with him.

"Clyde? I'm pretty sure I'm gonna have a baby." She looked around anxiously.

"Really? You and me…a baby? Us?"

"Yes. I think so!" As Jennie answered, Clyde lifted her by her waist, spun her around, and put her feet back on the ground.

"We need a place to live, that's what we need first." Clyde furrowed his brow, and with a serious look on his face, continued. "I can't have a baby without having a job. I need to find a job quickly!"

Jennie was smiling. "If I'm right, the baby won't be here until the first part of the summer so there's plenty of time to find a house and a job."

"A house? Oh, Jennie, it's gonna be a while before we can get a house. My ma made our flatboat into a home every time we set off downriver. We'll do that. Our first home will be a steamboat." Clyde's mind was racing ahead. "I can tow some of this sugar cane and cypress lumber we see everywhere. You heard what Broussard said; there's more trees in the swamps around here than could ever be cut down by men."

Captain Clyde Arthur Barbour was off and running.

CHAPTER 17

THE PATRIARCHY

1896

The rental boat served as both their home and their workplace. Man slept on a pallet in the galley. Every morning when Jennie came in to get breakfast and coffee started, Man would sit up, rub his eyes, and say, "Miss Jennie, I hongry!"

Jesse Collins Barbour was born that summer, 1896, on the steamboat they temporarily called home. He was a happy and healthy baby. Clyde would beam every time he saw the new bundle. He had carried on the Barbour name with his first child. Jennie's favorite time of the day was sunset when she'd sit out on the deck in a rocking chair and nurse Jesse to sleep. One evening in particular she watched as the sun became an immense ball of crimson, doubled as it reflected off the surface of the water, turning it into liquid gold. Then the moon would rise. *I love the blue moonlight,* she thought. *It looks like God took a little dot of light blue watercolor and brushed it very softly over the moon!*

There was so much to see along the route. Everything about the Bayou Country was different from anything they'd ever known. One of the things that most intrigued them was the sight of an abandoned manor house just north of Franklin on Bayou Teche. They both found it hauntingly beautiful in its derelict state. They would stop every time they passed it and came to know that it was called Oaklawn Manor and had long ago been a sugar cane plantation.

They plied the waters of Southern Louisiana on the rental boat, back and forth on Bayou Teche from New Iberia all the way to New Orleans. Although their first trip hadn't proved very fruitful, Clyde and Jennie got a feel for what was needed along this route and within a few short months, they were making enough money to pay the rent on the boat and their living expenses, with a few dollars left over.

Clyde made a deal with the Sears and Roebuck Company to deliver their catalogue orders out of New Orleans to landings all the way down to New Iberia. The rest of the space he filled with groceries and household items. Clyde didn't believe in having an empty boat, no matter which direction he was sailing. On his way to New Orleans, he would take some handmade items, especially the beautifully intricate baskets woven by the Chitimacha Indians near Franklin. He had found a market for them in the French Quarter, which was always full of visitors wanting something unique. There were often paying passengers going in either direction. The accommodations were basic: pallets on the floor with biscuits and sausage gravy and coffee for breakfast. That was the only meal provided.

They also took people from one landing to another for a fee. Nothing was too small or too inconsequential for Clyde to transport for a fee. When one of the planters bought furniture on Royal Street, Clyde brought it out to them. In fact, when Captain William Kyle, owner of the Kyle Lumber Company, bought a piano in New Orleans for his daughter's birthday, it arrived late at the store. In order to ensure the piano was in its place in the Kyle mansion on the day of the festivities, Clyde agreed to make a special trip just to retrieve the piano. The owner of the piano store came along as well to be sure it was tuned properly once it was placed. Jennie took such good care of the gentleman that he promised to use their services whenever he needed to send a piano somewhere on the water.

Captain Kyle recognized the entrepreneurial spirit in Clyde and decided to take a gamble on him. The lumber mills were always in need of boats to bring the lumber in from the swamps.

"I like the way you do business, young Captain," the captain told Clyde one day. "I've just built my own mill, and I don't wanna let a smart man with a savvy mind like yours get away from me. How about I let you buy one of my boats, pay me a little every month, and you go pick up some of my lumber for me. It's steady work and it pays well. And there'll be lots of room for your family on board."

Clyde bit his lip for a moment while he thought. "Thanks for the offer. I need to talk about it with my wife and my pa first."

"Now son, I respect how you feel, but you need to rearrange some of that thinking if you're gonna make it in this tough business world here on the bayous. You need to use that brain of yours to take care of that young family and remember it's you who's in charge; you've got the responsibility to make it all happen." Captain Kyle patted him on the back. "Let's talk again tomorrow."

Walking back to his boat, Clyde kept hearing those words going through his head, over and over again. *He* was in charge now, not Pa. *He* was the breadwinner and had to be sure decisions were made in a way that protected his little family and their future. *He* was the one with the knowledge and know-how to move up the ladder of success he was already climbing. He was a man now, a husband and a father, and it didn't scare him at all.

Back at his boat, at supper, he told Jennie and Pa what he had decided. "Captain Kyle has offered me a good deal. He wants to sell me one of his boats to haul lumber for him and to live on. I only have to pay him a little bit every month until I pay for the boat."

"That sounds wonderful," said Jennie.

"Will you make more money than you are right now? Things are goin' well on that New Orleans to New Iberia route we've been workin'," Pa observed.

"That's why I've come up with a plan to do both. Pa, you get some help and keep doing the route we've been doing, and Jennie, Jesse, and

I will move onto the Kyles' boat and start doing some logging. It pays well, and that way we'll have a lot more money coming in."

"Now, Clyde, I'm not a pilot," Pa protested. "We're gonna have to find one. And all those people along the route, they like talkin' to you, not me; they like dealin' with you, not me."

"Come on, Pa, you made friends with hundreds of people all up and down the rivers."

"But that was when I was younger and better lookin'." A smile crept onto Pa's face. "It's real different down here, not the same at all."

He was right. Different people with a different language in a different environment with different weather and different customs and even different food. Clyde found it fascinating. Apparently, Pa wasn't as captivated.

"Pa. Everything has changed. My dream of being the captain of a big steamboat on the Ohio River with hundreds of passengers and a load of cotton is never going to come true. My dream of having special living quarters for me and Jennie and our children on this big steamboat sailing down the Mississippi and being greeted by everyone as the man in charge isn't going to come true either. But something else is gonna happen. I'm not sure exactly what, but I feel it unfolding more every day." Clyde leaned across the table to get as close to his father as he could. "Ma and Grandpa and James will be down here in just a few weeks. There'll be plenty of family to go around and plenty of work to do. We need to put down some roots here and call this our new home."

Captain Kyle gave Clyde his signature boat, the *William Kyle*. They moved their few belongings onto their new steamboat. It was newer and nicer, and their living quarters were larger.

"Plenty of room for another baby, don't you think?" Clyde teased Jennie.

"You better hush!" she replied, blushing as she placed the old green and white Ice Water pitcher Clyde had bought her and which she loved on the countertop.

Man had come with them and was awestruck, once again, by another even larger steamboat. "I bets Papa Luke would know just how to make this big ole boat go!" he claimed. "He coulda drove this thing all the way to N'Orlens I bets."

Jennie and Clyde chuckled, and their hearts were warmed by this little boy's bragging about his father. "You know he could!" Clyde agreed. "I never saw nothin' your pa couldn't figure out." Whether it was true or not didn't matter. They had all loved Luke and all wanted his child to know what a special person he had been. At the same time, Clyde was keenly aware that in the world beyond their steamboat, Man was a Black male and would need to know his place or his life would be lonely and disappointing. It had been different with Luke; a grown man, he had already learned how to navigate each part of his life in a manner that best served him. Man would have to learn to do the same.

They began sailing deep into the swamps to where the swampers were cutting down mostly cypress trees, but also poplar, gum, oak, and willow. The swampers were paid a 10-cent stump fee for every tree they cut down. Wooden calipers were then used to measure the width of the trunk, which determined, along with the tree's length, the total amount the swampers were paid for each tree. The lumber companies owned most of the land, and there were mills up and down the bayous. On Bayou Teche, mills were scattered all the way down to Morgan City where Bayou Teche met Six Mile Lake.

The swampers were a different breed of people. Their olive skin, unkempt dark hair, and soiled, tattered clothing made their dirty existence look even grimier. They were happiest out of doors—fishing, hunting, and working. They were rugged, quick, and strong. The processes of cooking and eating were like a religion to them, the omnipresent sharing of victuals a sacrament. Clyde seemed to know just how to relate to them. He had grown up around people from all stations in life and was fairly comfortable in all those different settings. He found these new people very much like the river people who lived near the small landings they had often visited. A work ethic built by necessity and a love of the Earth built on an intimate relationship with her.

Broussard proved invaluable, as he now became navigator through the Atchafalaya Basin. The closest logging sites were on Six Mile Lake and Grand Lake, but some of the best forests were around Big Pigeon Bayou and Little Pigeon Bayou, which were farther up the basin. Plying the waters of these swamps and bayous was very different from traveling the big rivers Clyde was accustomed to. From time to time, the cypress trees would engulf the sternwheeler. Alligators were not uncommon, and there were birds that neither Jennie nor Clyde could identify.

The sight of a sternwheeler pushing logs was ordinary to people who traveled the big rivers. Making the turns and working with the currents made losing some of your logs inevitable. But the swampers had their own way of making huge rafts, or booms, with the lumber to transport it to the mills. Clyde even saw a pirogue resting on top of one, perhaps for hunting the shores or catching an errant piece of lumber. One time on Bayou Teche, he had seen some youngsters trying to cross the bayou, but the very slow and lengthy boom made them decide to put their canoe on top of the logs, walk across carrying it, and put it back in the water on the other side. It seemed very dangerous to Clyde, but with the boom's rate of speed at one mile an hour, it was certainly understandable.

They pulled up on Little Pigeon Bayou to where a sternwheeler was being fitted with its timber cargo to push back up to Kyle Lumber Yard. Standing on the Texas Deck, they could hear the sound of squeaking metal wheels and whistling coming from far into the forest. Broussard pointed to an enormous log hanging on a thick cable making its way toward the boat. Two swampers on the ground maneuvered it down, releasing it so it fell into the water to be pulled into place beside the other logs waiting to be carried away. Here came another. The whistling continued and seemed repetitious. Broussard explained.

"That whistling? It's how they signal when to stop and start the lines. The tall tree the lines are hooked up to is way back there, so they signal each other whistling in code."

Jennie was standing on the deck next to Clyde holding Jesse. They watched the logs being placed next to each other, held together with a long wooden strut that looked like a comb with the tines protruding on either side of each log. These struts were angled in different directions to accommodate the different lengths of the logs. Swampers were on the side getting the logs situated in a group, then adding them to the boom.

Every so often, they could see what looked like manmade canals running back into the forest. Swampers were floating logs down these canals to be added to the lot as well.

Jennie was intrigued by all of this. Clyde's discerning eyes were taking it all in. It seemed like organized chaos. There were no idle bodies as the logs came from different directions but were shuffled together to become one massive body of logs. She was asking Broussard questions while swaying in an effort to keep the baby content as he sucked on a rag filled with a bit of sugar. Man shuffled out of the galley carrying Clyde's wading boots.

"Okay, Man. You stay here and take care of Miss Jennie and Jesse for me. Oh, and, if one of the crew needs anything, you help 'em."

"You knows I will, Clyde Barbour," he said, handing Clyde the boots. Clyde and Jennie laughed.

Jennie knew her husband well enough by now to know he wouldn't return until dusk. She knew he was in his element down there with the locals learning yet another set of skills. No doubt he would absorb the information and shortly know more about it than anyone other than those actually doing the labor. He thrived on the acquisition of knowledge of all kinds. He read every night; something, anything. Jennie enjoyed talking with him about his latest interest. He was always ardent and ebullient. Though often he lost her in the first few minutes of one of these conversations, she nonetheless listened happily and tried her best to ask a question or two.

These were the nights he would be especially passionate in bed. His enthusiasm always spilled over into his love for her. She relished his attention as he gently and carefully removed all of her clothing and made love with her. Finally, they would sleep wrapped in the warmth of knowing they were on this difficult yet amazing journey together.

The next morning, Clyde was up before dawn. Jennie cooked breakfast for her husband and all their crew, as usual. Man was trying to talk his way into going along with the men for the day. He did not appreciate the "No!" in response to his many requests and went off alone. The men were sharing stories from yesterday. Several had been doing this work for years and enjoyed the status of the well-entrenched. Those who, like Clyde, were new to this business listened intently, asking questions along the way. Jennie heard whispering and tried hard to hear their secrets.

"They do what?" she asked with an incredulous look on her face. The men stopped talking abruptly and turned to look at her.

"Now, Jennie, that's not a story ladies need to hear. Men, let's keep our talk around my table to things everyone can hear," Clyde told his workers.

Jennie couldn't let go of what she thought she'd heard one of the men say. She asked Clyde to step outside with her for a moment, then whispered, "The swampers pee on their hands? Really? That's awful," she said, but her intrigued expression belied her pretense at shock.

"Yes, they do. It helps toughen their hands for the hard labor of felling trees. I'm sorry you had to hear that."

"Oh, Clyde. Stop it. I'm your wife. We can talk about anythin'. And it's kinda interestin'—in an ugly way." She chuckled, then hid her face in his chest and laughed harder. "We can't let Man hear any of that or we'll likely be hearin' it at the most inconvenient times!"

They were there for four days. When all the logs had finally been placed, they took off for Kyle Lumber Mill at the appallingly low speed of one mile an hour. It was a long journey back.

Within a few months, Clyde had the lumber transportation business all figured out. He had put together his own group of swampers who worked solely for him. He took on another sternwheeler to help fill in the time lapse from picking up the lumber and getting it back to the mill. Clyde was in his element.

CHAPTER 18

THE FEVER

The next year, 1897, the Kyle Lumber Mill burned down. It didn't take much to burn down a business based solely on lumber. While he had no insurance, with the financial assistance of Edward Hanson and Frank B. Williams, Captain Kyle was able to rebuild that same year.

In the interim, Clyde kept rolling along. The lumber he would have been taking to Captain Kyle he took to Albert Hanson Lumber Co. and F.B. Williams Cypress Co., which stepped up their production to accommodate what was to them a fortuitous, if temporary, opportunity. Clyde was now transporting lumber for two mills that were new to him. He took advantage of the situation and was able to add more boats to the Barbour Line of boats, which eventually became the Teche Transportation and Fuel Company.

Fortunately, Grandpa, Ma, and James had returned. Grandma had passed, so their return had been delayed. It was truly a family business, with everyone doing what they could. It seemed to help Grandpa's grief to be able to throw himself into a new adventure, although he never seemed to quite get his gumption back. James, however, continued with his whining ways that irritated everyone. Not one to be left out, Man had his say on the subject. "Mr. James, he needs ta keep his mouf shut! He sound like a baby to me." Jennie let Man know that his thoughts on the matter were better kept in his little head.

It was also the year that a yellow fever epidemic came to Louisiana. They had already been plagued by the flooding of the Mississippi River in April that spread all the way to Bayou La Fourche and by a hurricane in September that devastated Abbeville. Late that summer, the epidemic began in New Orleans and Baton Rouge but only barely touched Franklin. In Baton Rouge, all public institutions as well as businesses were closed, and no public assembly was allowed. They heard it was like a ghost town. Franklin saw only a handful of cases, including Mayor Tarlton, who was the fourth person to catch the fever, the first three having died. The mayor somehow survived. The cool weather of October and November stopped the spread of the disease.

In the middle of the heat that summer, Jennie had become pregnant again. There was a combination of delight and then fear when yellow fever came to town. Clyde insisted that she not step foot on land, hoping that would keep her and the child she was carrying safe. He was secretly hoping for a girl, and so was Jennie.

It wasn't the easy pregnancy the first had been. Fits of nausea kept Jennie off her feet for many days. She was glad that the heat and humidity of the long summer were gone before her problems began and before she was heavy with child. She felt the baby way up in her chest and had difficulty breathing at times. Luckily, Ma was there to take up the slack with Jesse and with Jennie's other household chores.

"That's what mothers-in-law are for!" Ma would often say as she tucked Jennie into bed, an empty bucket Jennie's constant companion.

The baby came on a beautiful March day in 1898 full of cool air and sunshine. Dr. Beverly Smith came onto the boat when the baby was ready to be delivered. Given that Jennie looked scarcely six months pregnant when the baby came, he wanted to be present just in case. Ma was holding Jennie's hand. Clyde came in and out of the bedroom to give encouragement, even though the doctor felt his presence was unnecessary and distracting.

"Doctor, this woman is my life! You can't keep me from her," Clyde proclaimed, and the doctor fell silent on the issue. So, Clyde was there, wiping her brow with a damp cloth and yelling above her cries his words of love and support. After many hours of pushing, he was there when the final push released her body's hold on the baby and the doctor eased out a small baby that gasped for its first breath of air then cried to announce its arrival.

"It's a tiny but healthy and loud baby girl," the doctor assured them. "Congratulations!" Both parents had gotten their wish, unbeknownst to the other.

"Can we call her Lena, for my sister Leona?" Jennie asked in an exhausted yet exhilarated voice.

"Whatever you want, Sweetness. Whatever you want," answered her relieved husband, who watched as the mother of his first daughter held her for the first time and suckled her.

Jesse wasn't sure how to react to this new addition, this tiny, soft, loud critter that now slept next to his mother. He decided that ignoring it was the best course of action.

Two days later Jennie was still bleeding heavily and was very weak, so Dr. Smith came by.

"I don't like your color; you shouldn't be so weak, and you shouldn't be bleeding this much. You need to stay in bed and take this iron medicine, and I have a tonic to help stop the bleeding. Be sure she drinks a lot of water," Dr. Smith told Ma.

"Yes, Doctor. I won't let her get out of bed." Ma looked at Jennie sternly.

"Good. I'll be back in three days. If she seems to get worse, come and get me." The doctor closed his black leather bag and left. Jennie's symptoms subsided in two days, and she was allowed to get out of bed and ease her way back into her routine, which now included two children.

In October, when Lena was sleeping through the night, yellow fever returned to Franklin. This time, it was of epidemic proportions. Dr. Henry R. Carter, the United States Marine Hospital Service's quarantine officer, established a headquarters in a hotel, as well as a detention camp and a hospital on the other side of Bayou Teche, away from the city.

Franklin was officially quarantined against all the towns above it. Anyone who wanted to leave the city had to first stay in quarantine for 10 days to reduce the spread of the disease. No one had any idea that a mosquito was to blame.

The Southern Pacific Railroad refused to stop in Franklin, fearing that the towns farther along their path would refuse to let the train stop at their stations. Most of the provisions the citizens, as well as patients, needed came from New Orleans. If the trains from New Orleans wouldn't stop in Franklin, the city would be in even worse straits. What were they going to do without the medical supplies and drugs for the ill, not to mention the everyday supplies they depended on to live?

The residents gathered at the courthouse and decided they would have to give the railroad an ultimatum: either trains would stop in Franklin as usual, or the railroad would find its tracks torn up above the town so they couldn't go any farther. The threat worked.

Most of the young doctors in town fell ill, and the mayor felt it was his duty to help out. The undertakers would make caskets for the dead but would not transport them in their hearses, afraid of contagion. The mayor got a wagon and a horse and found an old Black man who had survived the fever in years past and wanted to do his part; it was believed that you could only get yellow fever once. He would drive the wagon with the caskets to the cemetery for burial.

It was Jennie who was stricken with the fever. Clyde refused to let her go to the detention camp, arguing that he could take better care of her.

"Clyde," said Ma, "you have a newborn baby on this boat and two other children. You can't risk everyone else getting sick. Try to understand."

"Then I'll go with her."

"And who's gonna do your work and keep this family going? Make the best decision for your family, not just you."

Jennie was sent to the camp that day. No goodbye kisses or hugs, just tears. Clyde moved the family onto another boat while the *William Kyle* was fumigated. He was miserable.

Jennie, along with others who were ill but well enough to write, sent notes to their families via the pirogue that crossed the bayou several times a day with food and supplies. It left everything on the bank just up from the camp, from where it would later be retrieved by one of the guards whose job it was to keep in those who were ill and keep out those who were not.

Jennie and Clyde made a vow to see each other every day at noon. They would stand on opposite shores to wave and blow kisses. Clyde could always spot her from a distance as her beautiful golden highlights caught the sun. After a few days, it took all of her energy to walk to her spot so she would sit on the bank. As long as he saw her, he could return home with the knowledge that she was still alive. Clyde sent her something every day on the supply boat—a flower, a piece of candy, a lock of Lena's hair. The men on the pirogue were more than happy to take things across for a few extra pennies and to find out for him in which tent she slept.

Then came the day she didn't show up. Clyde waited an hour. He tried to bribe the supply boat to take him over, but the answer was "No!" Clyde didn't like that answer. They brought back a note from Dr. Carter. Jennie's condition had worsened. She was bedridden and her fever was high. That's all it took to get Clyde in the frame of mind he was becoming known for, in which "No!" was not an option.

At 2:00 a.m. the next morning, Clyde sneaked off of his sternwheeler and into a pirogue, alone. He took a large piece of ice and an ice pick as well as some coins to use for bribes. He was single-minded.

There were enough clouds to help hide him from any curious eyes but few enough to let the moon come shining through at times to light his path. He came across a sleeping guard and continued on. The ice was bulky and melting with the heat of the night. He saw no one around, so getting to Jennie's tent was not difficult.

He stepped into the dark tent where he knew she was and put the ice down. There was a candle burning, which he picked up and, going from bed to bed, found his wife. When he woke her, she smiled a faint smile and reached out to him. He took her hand, kissed it, and held it tight.

"Go away," she whispered with great effort. "You can't get sick. Please go." Although her face was streaked with sweat from her fever, he could still make out the tears coming from her barely opened eyes.

"Ice. I've got ice. Hold on," Clyde whispered. He retrieved the ice and put it on the ground next to her cot. He picked off small pieces of ice and fed them to her. He also rubbed some ice on her face and head. He kissed her beautiful auburn hair as he doused it with drips from the ice. She began to shake as he rubbed ice over her limbs and torso, trying to lower her temperature. He went about his business knowing that the shaking would only do her good. Soon she drifted off to sleep.

Clyde looked around to see the three other female patients in the tent with Jennie. One opened her eyes and tried to cry out "Help me!" but no sound came out. He took the ice over to her bedside and did for her what he'd done for Jennie and continued until he had, at the very least, given each of the other three some ice and some cooling down. He went back to his wife and started all over again until the combination of the heat of the night and fever had melted the ice away. He woke her to say goodbye.

"I must be dreaming," she whispered.

"Yes, you are. And tomorrow night, you'll have the same dream!"

As he quietly exited the tent minus the burden of the chunk of ice, he saw a nurse headed straight toward him. He knew by the startled look on her face that she had spotted him. He ducked back into the tent and she followed.

"Who are you and what are you doing here? This area is strictly forbidden for anyone except the sick and those of us taking care of them," she whispered harshly. The women didn't stir.

"Please. Listen. I came here to help, too," he replied, trying to gauge his response. "That's my wife over there, Jennie. Doc said she's doing awful. I came with ice," he said as he pointed to the ice pick, "and gave all these ladies ice chips and tried to cool them down. Look; see the little puddle of water there next to her bed where I put the ice?" He pointed to the ground.

Before she spoke again, she took a look at each of her charges in the tent. Clyde wasn't sure whether to run or try to get her on his side. He waited.

"Of course the ice helps, but everyone over here needs ice." She spoke a little above a whisper now.

"I can't get enough ice for everyone over here, but I'll help whoever I can. I had enough for all four of these poor ladies in this tent," he said, matching her volume. "I could bring ice every night. How would that be?" He looked for signs in her face that was so darkened by the night, signs that would give him hope of returning to Jennie. He could feel the sweat rolling down his face.

"You know that's not possible. It isn't allowed, not allowed at all," she replied staunchly. "You'll have to be quarantined now like the rest of them. That's what we'll have to do."

"But ma'am, this woman right here is my life!" he began, searching for the words that would make everything all right. "She had to be stripped away from our newborn little girl who still needs to be suckled. And a little boy who's two. Then there's the little Negro boy we've taken in 'cause his mama died and so did his pa." At least she was listening. "I have some money. I could bring some money."

"Your money can't save these people and it can't keep you from getting the fever."

"Yes, but the ice could help save them; all four of these ladies might be saved with my ice. You'd be helping to save their lives! Isn't that what you're trying to do? My children will have a mother, and I'll have my wife back." Clyde watched her face soften as his words connected.

"That's all well and good but you could catch the fever and spread it around town. What about that?" she asked, showing a glimmer of compassion.

"Well, let me think…I could, no, maybe…." He was wracking his brain to think of a solution. "What if I quarantine myself on my boat? I could do that!"

She thought for a moment. "And how will you get the ice from the iceman?"

"I know him, he's a good man. He could leave it on the dock, next to my boat. I'll pay him extra to bring it at nighttime. I'll bet he would do that." Clyde was feeling more confident with each new thought. "My family already moved off the boat Jennie was on when she got sick. We fumigated it. I'll stay there by myself until Jennie gets well!"

"What if she doesn't get well?" the nurse asked, not afraid to look him in the eye.

"Oh, but she will. That's not an option. I won't let that happen… never, ever," he said with such conviction as to convince God Himself.

They stood in silence, each wrapped in his and her own thoughts, pondering the options. He waited and prayed while he gave her some time to think.

"Let me tell you how it's going to be," the nurse said. "I will meet you in this tent at 2:30 every morning. I don't have time to wait around. I've heard about you, Captain Barbour, how you're always helping folks. You gave my nephew a job. He had nothing, knew nothing, but you taught him what he needed to know and now he's so proud! I'll go along with your hijinks because I believe you. If I hear you're out anywhere in town, I'll turn you in, and you'll be over here living in one of these tents."

"That's fair. That's more than fair. I promise I won't disappoint you. Thank you, thank you, thank you!" He kissed her hand and her feminine side emerged and she became shy. "You seem to know a lot about me, but I don't even know your name."

"Lucile; my name's Lucile. Now get out of here and don't get caught. I'll see you tomorrow morning." He left her there to do her work, and he stealthily retreated from the camp and back to his pirogue.

He told his family that he wasn't well; that he didn't have any fever but just to be sure he was moving back onto the *William Kyle* until he either got the fever or recovered from whatever was making him ill. The adults thought it rather strange but didn't question him. Ma was happy to take care of the children and would bring him his meals and leave them on the dock.

His trip that next night went as planned. Lucile was in the tent when he arrived.

"Jennie, she's not doing well. Her fever is very high, and she can't eat or drink anything."

Clyde rushed to her side. He was carrying a metal box containing the ice surrounded by sawdust; that would help it last longer. Jennie was very hot to the touch and was moaning softly as she turned in her bed. He was unable to awaken her fully, but she would take the ice chips into her mouth. Lucile took ice to the other three women as Clyde concentrated on his wife. He whispered to her as he bathed her in ice water and fed her ice chips. She always loved to have him rub her head and hair, so he took time to do just that, hoping that somewhere deep inside she would know.

Lucile came over and patted his back. "There's only so much you can do, Captain Barbour. She knows you're here and that's more than anyone else in this godforsaken camp can say. Now leave before somebody finds you here."

"I can't leave. I won't leave. I have to save her. I can't live without her!" He knelt down next to her cot and prayed. He couldn't remember the last time he had gotten down on his knees to pray, but he didn't know what else to do. He knelt for quite some time, then stood up and rubbed her head again. "I love you, Jennie Hobbs Barbour. So do little Lena and Jesse, even Man. You light up all our lives with your smile, your pretty face, and that beautiful auburn hair of yours. Fight, Jennie, fight! Do it for all of us who love you. *Please!*" He held her face in his hands, still beautiful beneath the sickness ravaging her body. He kissed her forehead, tears from his own eyes dripping onto her cheeks and down her face.

He left her there; he had no choice. He was distraught and not paying enough attention to his surroundings. He lifted his head and saw the guard standing a few feet in front of him.

"What the sam hell is you doin' out here in the dark? Is you sick?" The guard was standing right in front of Clyde, using his lantern to look him over and stopping him from proceeding. "You don't look sick."

"No…I'm not sick…just here delivering ice." He showed the guard the tin ice box he was carrying.

"Well, that ain't right. Nobody's supposed to be comin' through here."

"I've been delivering ice here for a while now. Every time I see you, you're sleeping. Didn't want to bother you." Clyde waited for his reaction.

"Sleepin'? Me? Here? Huh."

"I have permission to bring this ice; it's for my wife and some other fine ladies who seem like they're dying." Clyde hung his head, not wanting any emotion to show.

"Who gave you permission?"

"The nurse who takes care of my wife. Look. I don't want to get in any trouble, and I know you don't want to get into any trouble since you have this important job and all. Here, take this." Clyde took some coins out of his pocket and handed it to the guard, who looked the coins over and smiled to himself.

"That seems fair and all, but I can't let you get any of the townsfolk sick on account a me." Clyde could see the man struggling with himself.

"You don't have to worry about that. I'm in quarantine over on my boat. I won't be getting anybody sick, and I'll bring you some more of those, too." Clyde pointed to the coins.

"Well maybe…maybe…I guess if you're quarantined it'd be okay. When you comin' back?" The guard pocketed the coins.

"About 2:00 tomorrow morning. I won't bother you." Clyde was slowly making his way past the guard just in case.

"Okay."

For another three harrowing days, Clyde hardly slept. Every night he sneaked over with the ice. Two of the women seemed to be getting better after those initial two nights. Jennie's fever didn't break for another two days, and even then it came down very slowly. After almost a week of nightly trips across the bayou with ice, a greatly improved Jennie convinced Clyde not to return. Every time he came to the camp, he risked getting the fever himself. He obeyed, rowed back to the boat, and slept for an entire day.

Jennie was able to return home after another five days. Clyde had kept himself away from everyone for a few days as well, just to be sure. When they were finally reunited on their sternwheeler, it was a day of celebration.

The yellow fever epidemic in Franklin that year made 600 people sick and killed 11.

CHAPTER 19

THE WHIPPING

1899–1900

In the dead of the Louisiana heat of 1899, another baby was born to Clyde and Jennie. The pregnancy was once again fraught with morning sickness, and once again when it was time for the baby to be born, Jennie looked scarcely six months along. Dr. Smith was prepared after her last delivery and had already been treating her. She was still weak and had trouble pushing and pushing for hours. This time Clyde stayed by her side and did everything he could think of to help, which wasn't much. The small bundle that the doctor helped pull out of Jennie was another boy. She fell asleep instantly. The doctor cleaned her up and put a poultice between her legs to help stop the bleeding. Clyde woke her before the doctor left and helped her ease up enough to nurse their newborn son.

"I'd like to name him Clyde Arthur Barbour, Jr.," said Clyde. "I wasn't sure I wanted to name one of our sons after me, but this could be our last boy." A very fatigued Jennie smiled and nodded as she nursed.

Having already spent so much of her pregnancy in bed, Jennie couldn't bear the thought of an extended convalescence now that Clyde, Jr., was born. Dr. Smith wanted her in bed for another five days, to which Jennie agreed in his presence. However, two days later she got out of bed, wanting some fresh air for herself and the baby. She sat on a chair out on the deck and breathed deeply as she put the baby to her breast. She fell asleep.

Clyde found her out there asleep and was angry. "Jennie, what are you doing out here? You're supposed to be in bed! How do you think you're gonna get better if you don't do what the doctor says? Let me help you back to bed." He took the baby into his arms, then helped Jennie up. As she stood up, Clyde saw that the back of her nightgown was soaked with blood and there was more of it on her chair.

"Ma!" he yelled at the top of his lungs. "Ma, quick, come here!"

She came running onto the deck, saw the blood, and quickly took the baby from Clyde's arms. The baby began to cry that soft, tender cry of a newborn having been torn away from his mother's breast. "Man," he called. "Go get Dr. Smith. Hurry!" He picked his wife up into his arms and carried her to their bed.

Man took off to get the doctor. Clyde helped Jennie remove her nightgown. Ma took Jesse and Lena into town.

Dr. Smith was even angrier than Clyde had been. "What were you thinking?" he demanded.

"I had to get out of this room and the baby needed some fresh air," she answered stubbornly.

"Well, you've just written yourself a prescription for another week in this room," the doctor told her. When he had Jennie settled and was ready to leave, he called for Clyde. "Close the door behind you. We need to have a talk."

He moved closer to Clyde. "I want the two of you to give some serious thought to not having any more babies. You have three healthy children; let that be enough. Jennie's body has been through enough."

Jennie held her tongue until the doctor was gone. "I will *not* stop having babies. Next time I promise to be smarter and more patient after the baby is born."

"I don't think this is the right time to talk about it, Jennie. You get some sleep, and we'll talk about it later. I'll be here if you need anything, okay?"

"Okay. Now go back to work and don't worry about me. I've learned my lesson." Jennie rolled onto her side and fell asleep.

It was at the end of that year that Clyde received a large, official-looking envelope in the mail. As soon as he saw that the return address was Bryant & Stratton College, he knew what it was. He asked Jennie to have the whole family for dinner that night, not an unusual request. He bought a bottle of whiskey in town for dinner as a treat. As they all sat around talking before dinner, Clyde opened the whiskey, poured each adult a taste and said he had something to tell everyone.

"This came in the mail today. It's something I've been working on for years." He took the envelope, opened it, and held up a document for everyone to see. "It's my diploma! I've finally finished my studies. I now have a college degree in finance from the largest national business college in the country." He was beaming, ecstatic that he had done it. He had his degree. Already he felt smarter and more imbued with the knowledge he needed to set himself above the crowd of men trying to outdo one another in this intense battlefield of business on the bayous.

Everyone cheered, including the children, who weren't sure and didn't care what they were cheering about. They toasted and talked loudly and excitedly about the future. Ma had made dessert just like on the flatboat. That took the conversation back to the old times and what seemed two lifetimes ago. The meal lasted until the only ones still awake and left at the table were Clyde, Grandpa, Pa, James, and his new wife, Mary LeNain.

"Grandpa, this never would have happened without you," Clyde said to his grandfather, who seemed genuinely happy for the first time since he'd buried Grandma.

Pa stood up, a little off balance from the additional alcohol he had consumed before arriving for dinner. He slammed his glass down on the table. "No thanks to your pa, huh? I was the one taught you to work hard. I was the one put you on the rivers when you were a baby and helped you learn your way on the water. And 'cause I needed you to help me on the boat instead of going to college, I'm the one done you wrong, I guess."

"Pa, you're gonna wake the babies," Clyde began. "I'm not blamin' you for anything. I know you were doing what you had to." Clyde stood up and walked over to his father. As he went to put his hands on his father's shoulders, Pa raised his arms to push Clyde's arms away.

"You're an ingrate, plain and simple. 'Oh, Captain Barbour!' I'm so sick a hearin' that, like you're somethin' special, better than me."

"Pa, why are you sayin' that?" asked Clyde.

Mary began crying softly.

"Son," said Grandpa, "that whiskey's making you into an ass like always." Pa began to stagger toward Grandpa, but Clyde moved to stand in his way.

"Stop it, Pa. Do you hear me? Stop it! This is about me, not about you. Go home and get some sleep." Clyde was pointing to the door.

"You ain't gonna tell your pa what to do, hear me?" Pa started.

Something snapped in Clyde at that moment. He saw Jennie's face come peeking around the corner and lit into his father.

"That's enough!" he shouted. "This is *my* home. You will not come into *my* home and act like this. If you want to drink yourself to death, go away and do it where you won't interfere with our lives!"

Everyone was silent. Even Pa stopped talking.

"Go on, leave! I don't deserve to be talked to like that, and my family doesn't need to always be making apologies for you when you're drunk. You need to get sober or get out!" The look in Clyde's eyes was frightening. Jennie saw it and retreated to their bedroom.

Grandpa began, "Let's go, Jim. Everybody's tired and mad. Let's go." He tried to put his hand on Pa's shoulder to lead him out, but Pa shook it off and headed out the door, stumbling as he walked away in silence, Grandpa following at a distance. As he exited the galley, he turned to Clyde. "I'm sorry, son, that your pa could never see clear to leave the whiskey alone, and that's no excuse for acting the way he did here tonight. I'm very proud of you, son!" James followed him out without saying a word, followed by a frightened Mary.

The new century began and with it, the usual dispute as to when it should be celebrated; the first of January 1900 or the first of January 1901. Clyde and Jennie felt certain that the first of January 1900 was correct and acted accordingly, as did most of the country.

They moored in Franklin to enjoy the city's festivities, including a parade down Main Street and fireworks. Even the boats were decorated, making Bayou Teche come alive in color and pageantry. Red, white, and blue were everywhere. Jennie had even made herself a new dress, a shirt for Clyde, hats for baby Jesse and Lena, and a blanket for Clyde, Jr., all with the stars and stripes of America. Pa was nowhere to be found, but Ma, James, Mary, and Grandpa celebrated with them. Grandpa had protested at first, preferring to stay back at the boat alone.

Whiskey flowed more freely than usual that night. No one was surprised to see an upstanding neighbor not standing up so well. The townspeople gathered at the Willow Street dock to watch a rare display of fireworks over the bayou at midnight. Hoots and hollers and gunshots rang out across the countryside as people found their own style of celebration. Children, never seen on the street at midnight, screamed in delight at all the excitement.

When the fireworks ended, people began making their way home. Ma had been living on the *William Kyle* with Clyde and his family, while Grandpa, James, and Mary were living on another sternwheeler owned by Clyde. But Clyde and James weren't finished celebrating. They joined a group of men heading for the bars in town. With all the trade on Bayou Teche, four bars had opened in Franklin. At times, such as that night, it was a rowdy place.

In a short period of time, Clyde had made a name for himself as smart, driven, and innovative. He was also a kind and helpful man, well liked in the community. However, rivalry between captains was alive and well, and Clyde had been on the receiving end of some of this jealousy-inspired anger. Fortunately, he was skilled at the art of self-deprecation, which he used to extricate himself from such awkward situations as well as to ingratiate himself with townspeople.

Captain Taylor owned several sternwheelers that worked the same routes as Clyde. To Taylor, Clyde had become a thorn in his side as he watched this newcomer win so much business—some of which Taylor felt was his by right.

The bar was livelier than usual that night, with everyone in a jovial mood. The piano even seemed livelier. Clyde and James got drinks at the bar. When they turned around to let the next men get their drinks, Captain Taylor was standing there with his feet shoulder-width apart, his hand on a pistol he carried in his belt. Instinctively Clyde's hand went to his own. At 200 pounds and six feet tall, Taylor outweighed Clyde by 35 pounds and stood three inches taller. Clyde was a solid man and no shrinking violet, but he usually knew when to step away. However, he wasn't the most insightful version of himself at that moment. Taylor began slinging insults directed at Clyde, who stood his ground, glaring at the man. The noise in the bar gradually diminished as men began to realize an argument was taking place.

"I can't hear your nonsense, Taylor. Everybody but you is having a good time in here." Clyde raised his full glass to the crowd who raised theirs back, everyone then emptying their glasses and shouting. Taylor slapped the glass out of Clyde's hand, and it broke when it hit the wooden floor between the two captains, splashing its contents on both of them.

The bartender, seeing a ruckus about to break out, yelled to the men. "Captain Taylor, Captain Barbour, take your fight outta my bar!" He pointed to the door.

James, excited by the thought of watching his big brother in a real fight, called out, "Yeah, let's take this outside!" and pushed Clyde toward the door. The other patrons agreed and began shouting for them to go outside, not to get the argument out of the bar but to get the argument going so they could watch. Clyde could see no way that this was going to turn out well.

The two captains, followed by James and most of the patrons from the bar, stepped out into what had been the cool calm of the night. The cooler temperature helped Clyde sober up a bit. It was dark outside, the only light coming from inside the bar and the moon overhead. He saw someone taking Captain Taylor's pistol and felt James remove his own pistol from his belt. This wasn't a duel; it was a fight. James was talking nonstop to Clyde, whose brain hadn't quite caught up to events. He was very strong, but Taylor had the reach on him with those long arms.

Clyde got the first punch in fast, an uppercut to Taylor's chin. Taylor looked dazed, then furious. He reached to his belt and produced a horsewhip. Clyde backed up more and more as Taylor drew the whip back to make a pass at Clyde, whose hands went up in defense. The whip snapped through the dark night, burning his hands and drawing blood as he grappled with it, the smell of leather filling his nostrils. Taylor pulled the whip back over his head to strike again.

"You lousy, Yankee son of a bitch! You ain't comin' in here takin' *my* business!" He slashed the whip again, this time hitting Clyde on the waist. He doubled over in pain, unable to defend himself.

The crowd went crazy. All Clyde could hear was noise, not one recognizable word. Then he thought he heard James telling him to run. *Run? I can't run.* He managed to grab the whip long enough to pull Taylor to the ground. Taylor got up even angrier and moved the whip faster so Clyde couldn't catch it. He got another few whips in before Clyde fell to the ground, bleeding and in terrible pain.

The sheriff appeared, yelling at the top of his lungs to be heard over the crowd. "What the hell you doin', Taylor?" He grabbed the whip. "That's enough! I'm tempted to land a blow on your head, maybe knock some sense into you! Get outta here before I put you in jail."

Taylor walked over to where Clyde was writhing in pain and said, "Hope you learned your lesson; stay out o' my business!" He stared down at his victim for a moment and walked away.

"As for you, Clyde, what got into you?"

"Too much whiskey, for one thing," Clyde allowed. "Thank you, Sheriff."

As the crowd dispersed, James helped Clyde, wincing and bleeding, to his feet. Partly to divert attention from his role in the debacle, James began to talk about what an ass Taylor was; how no one could have predicted that he would have a whip, and how clever Clyde had been to get in the first blow.

Clyde said nothing, only moaned as he looked himself over with his bleeding hands. He thought about the slaves who endured whippings much worse than his. He wasn't surprised when Dr. Smith appeared.

"Clyde Barbour, what were you thinkin'?"

"This is what happens when you let your little brother do your thinkin' for you," replied Clyde between gasps of pain.

At the doctor's office, Clyde was cleaned up and bandaged. As James helped him slowly back to the *William Kyle,* he babbled nervously. "Don't you worry, Clyde, we're gonna get Taylor back in a big way!" Clyde looked at James and shook his head in disbelief.

It was after 2:00 a.m. when James got Clyde back to the boat. As they tried to sneak on, they could hear Jennie singing on the deck:

> "Go to sleep my little one,
> Until the rising of the sun.
> When the sun comes out to play,
> Thank the Lord for a brand new day."

It was one of Jennie's favorite nursery rhymes. Clyde had come to love it, too. He didn't have to see her to know she was gazing down with total love at their baby, who would stop from time to time and smile up at his mother, his tiny lips outlined with his mother's milk. It was the most beautiful sight Clyde had ever seen. He felt ashamed of himself. "Please, God, help me not ever drink liquor again!"

Clyde had lost the fight that night, but he'd gained even more respect from the town.

In August, James and Mary had their first child, a son. When the infant passed away shortly after his birth, the entire family was devastated. The St. Mary *Banner* printed the following: "We sincerely console with Mr. and Mrs. James Barbour who lost their infant son on Monday morning."

Ma had been with Mary for the birth and stayed with her after the child was gone.

"I know this won't really help, but I want you to know that Pa and me lost a son."

"I didn't know," Mary answered softly.

"Well, we did. His name was William Cilas. He was born two years after Clyde. We lost him when he was five years old." Ma had a pleasant look on her face. After all these years, she could, at times, remember her son without hurting deep down inside. "Then I had James. So, you see, you'll have plenty more babies before you're finished." She kissed Mary's head and smiled down at her.

The next month, on September 8, Galveston, Texas, was hit by a monstrous hurricane. It flattened every structure on the island. The population of the entire island at the time was about 40,000. Of those, between 10,000 and 12,000 people lost their lives, and property damage reportedly amounted to $20 million to $30 million (approximately $710 million to $1 billion in 2023). The two railroad bridges and the wagon bridge to the mainland were destroyed. This most horrific of natural disasters would lead to one of Clyde's biggest successes.

Jesse and Lena Barbour Early 1900s

CHAPTER 20

THE INITIATE

By 1900, the Port of New Orleans had dropped from the fourth to the twelfth largest, in terms of cargo, in the country. It was the only major port Clyde was familiar with, having sailed in and out of there most of his life. He knew the slow pace of the city and loved the grace and pizazz with which the ordinary citizens lived their lives. There was always music playing, food being eaten, and people frolicking in the streets, particularly in the French Quarter.

Clyde loved to have his palm read by one of the many readers in New Orleans. He had a favorite on Royal Street whom he had visited many times. He could understand why many people thought it foolish, but he felt there had to be something to it. After all, on several occasions, he'd been unnerved by what the palm reader had been able to divine about his life and his future from his hands. Growing up, on the way down the Mississippi, he would try to save up the requisite coins for a visit to the palm reader and to Café du Monde where, from an early age, his parents allowed him to enjoy a cup of café au lait and to share an order of beignets. There was the occasional fight with the powdered sugar canister that would end in Pa threatening that to be their last visit to the Café. It never was.

When time and money allowed, he would ride the streetcar up St. Charles Avenue to gaze at the fabulous mansions, imagining the life led behind the front doors. From time to time, Ma would accompany him, but James and Pa thought it foolish and a waste of time and money. Clyde also enjoyed getting out in the middle of a ride and walking past to get a better look. He had always had an eye for detail. When he took in one of these mansions, he studied it in detail. He noticed the colors, the curves, the Neo-Classical fluted porch columns with ornate cornices and pediments, the paneled wooden front doors with side lights and the fanlight above, and the Queen Anne style with its corner turret. He noticed which way the roof sloped, the shape of the columns, and whether the entablature had dentil work or perhaps corbels in the corners. Studying this type of architecture was a passion of his that he kept under wraps. It was at these times that he would visualize what his own mansion would look like someday. Over the years, on two occasions, Clyde had been invited inside by someone living in one of the houses he was studying so intently. He had always had a calm, intelligent look about him that made people accept him readily. Each time he was invited inside one of these mansions, he was awestruck at the beauty of the furnishings and the politeness with which the inhabitants spoke to each other and to him. That's how he would behave.

On this trip, less than two weeks after his fight with Captain Taylor, he had been invited to dinner at Captain LaSalle's home on St. Charles Avenue—not the biggest house or the fanciest part of the street, but still, it was on St. Charles Avenue. Jennie hadn't wanted to accompany him, which Clyde could not understand. He never thought of her as particularly shy, but when these sorts of occasions arose, she always found a reason not to go along.

He was especially well dressed this evening. He loved to wear a suit; it made him feel intelligent and successful. Intelligent he had always been, and success was already knocking on his door.

He arrived a few minutes early, as was his custom, and was the first guest there. He was shown inside by a servant and waited in the parlor for his host. Clyde wished that Grandpa could see him here, starting to be accepted into this world of wealthy, intelligent businessmen. He stared at a portrait of a middle-aged man with a rugged, angular face whose eyes were dancing but whose mouth was set firm. He heard footsteps approaching and turned to see his friend, Captain Steven LaSalle, entering the parlor. He walked up to Clyde smiling and they looked each other in the eye as they shook hands firmly.

"I see you looking at my grandfather's portrait. He was quite the sailor!"

"I find it interesting that his eyes seem to show a fun side to him that his mouth knows nothing about!" answered Clyde, smiling.

"Very observant of you. He was quite a complex man." LaSalle chuckled. "What happened to you?" he asked, noticing the fresh scars on Clyde's face and hands. "Looks like you got into a fight with a drunk sailor." Clyde was relieved when the doorbell ended their conversation abruptly.

There were 10 men at dinner that evening, all of whom Clyde either knew personally or had heard about. He refused the temptation to feel smaller, less important, less worthy than his dinner companions. After all, he'd been invited because they thought he had something to bring to the table. He was not going to let any insecurity keep him down.

Had ladies been present at the meal, there would have been no business talk. That not being the case, soon after the appetizer was cleared away, LaSalle proposed a toast to the men at the table, saying he hoped they would all prosper together. That's when he made his announcement.

"I don't know if any of you have heard the news yet, but two days ago, the oil finally came in on Spindletop Hill in Beaumont; the biggest gusher ever seen, they say!"

"They've been drilling over there since at least '93," said Captain Morris.

"Yeah. I heard the oil sands kept messing them up," added Captain Clark.

LaSalle continued, "It only made sense they'd find some oil in those salt domes. Old Lucas was right all along! The story is the mud came bubbling up. Then a couple tons of drill pipe came flying out of the hole, but then it got all quiet. Next thing they knew more mud, then gas, then oil came gushing out 100 feet high! No telling how long it'll take them to cap it off."

"Wish I'd seen that. Imagine the look on those roughnecks' faces! How deep did they have to drill to find it?" Captain Morris asked.

"Somewhere around 1,100 feet," LaSalle replied. "A good lesson on sticking with what you believe."

"Was it on Gladys City Company land?" asked Clyde, wanting to be part of the conversation.

"Right next door. You know Lanier and Higgins left the Gladys City Oil Company in '95. They must be crying their eyes out and kicking the dog!" LaSalle laughed.

"You think that's bad, imagine what their wives are doing to them!" said Captain Brennan. They all chimed in and had a good laugh.

"It's a strange mix of characters over there," LaSalle continued. "None of this would be happening without Lucas being so convinced the salt domes were full of oil. But you can't get the oil out without the money from the Mellon family and the know-how of the Hamill brothers to get the drilling done. It's a lot of moving parts."

The conversation got louder and louder as the men grew more excited about the prospect of this prodigious discovery, practically in their backyard. There was talk of starting an oil company of their own, but none of them had any experience. Then the conversation went on to investing money in it, but in which part and how much? Would it make sense for them to do this as a group? At that point, Clyde was ready to go back to his boat to be alone where he could think.

"There's a lot to think about. We have to do this quickly, so who's in and for how much?" Clyde asked.

He, LaSalle, and Brennan decided to invest some money in the Lucas Gusher as quickly as possible to beat the inevitable influx of thousands of wildcatters. Clyde left his boat with his crew at the dock in New Orleans and went by train to Beaumont with LaSalle and

Brennan. Though Clyde's investment was a small percentage of what the other two men put in, they nevertheless treated him as an equal.

When they arrived in Beaumont, although it had been about a week since the gusher blew, it had still not been completely capped off and there was activity in most every direction. They spent three days there and every day the place grew more and more crowded. When the three men had finished their transactions, Clyde told his partners that he felt he should go down to Galveston Island, where the hurricane had leveled most of the island only months earlier. Grandpa had expressed a desire to go and help those poor displaced people, but his bad health held him back. Throughout Clyde's life, he had watched Grandpa, time and time again, go toward danger unconcerned for his own well-being in order to help those affected by a catastrophe.

Captain Brennan was in a rush to return to New Orleans, but Captain LaSalle went along with Clyde to aide in the recovery efforts. They boarded a train for Houston and changed trains there. Knowing they would find no provisions of any kind on the island, when they stopped in Houston, they purchased some inexpensive work clothes and other provisions they deemed would be helpful at their destination, but nothing could have prepared them for the devastation that had once been Galveston Island.

There was a wide variety of people on the train headed south to the island. Both sexes, all ages, colors, and stations in life. People chatted with a mix of emotions: excitement, anticipation, anger, fear, grief, and sadness, all rolled up together. The bridge connecting the island to the mainland had been washed away by the hurricane, so the only way in was by train and then ferry.

The moment they exited the ferry, the entire world changed. Clyde had seen nothing like it in his life. The total destruction and the smells of stagnation, rotting wood, and mold overwhelming any scent of the fresh salt air breeze took his breath away. He stopped short, not knowing how to proceed. Captain LaSalle appeared to do the same. They looked at each other.

"Steven, what the hell?" said Clyde. LaSalle just shook his head, his mouth agape.

They made their way, along with many others from the train, to where The Red Cross was set up. It had been four months since the hurricane had swept through and some organization had sprung up. It was difficult for the men to imagine that after four months of cleanup, there was still so much work to be done. What rescuers hoped was that the body found about a week before their arrival would be the last discovered. Clyde was grateful for the fact that it was January, when the air was cool, and not August, when the sweltering heat and smell of decaying bodies would have overcome a large percentage of the workers.

Wooden planks were in piles all around. Here and there were houses that were half gone or leaning like a tree in the wind or cut into pieces which had been strewn in all directions. Clyde imagined that if he could see all of this from high above the earth that it would resemble a gigantic ant farm. People were scattered all over like soldier ants, some pulling large timbers off of piles with ropes, some piling the scraps high on wagons, and others driving the heavily laden wagons away. It sounded like an enormous construction site with hammering and sawing and yelling of orders across the island.

The Relief Corps had set up hospitals. Some saloons had reopened, along with several places to eat, and the telephone and water had been restored to some extent. The city had determined that it had to build a 17-foot concrete retaining wall along the beach and elevate the entire town, but work on those very expensive and time-consuming efforts had not yet begun. Looking down the beach, they could see only one house still standing. A few ships were coming into the harbor with freight. It seemed a strikingly odd mélange of devastation and resurrection.

They stayed in Galveston for almost two weeks, spending their days tearing down and building back up. They found they were most useful helping to build rafts and boats to ferry people and things around. It was Clyde's idea that they start to build a fleet of fishing boats to help feed the people on the island and get that commerce going again. It was here, in the company of other boatmen, that they heard talk of the Galveston Harbor and the need for a harbor farther inland, protected from the inevitable storms served up by the Gulf of Mexico. Talk had been going on in Washington, D.C., for years about dredging the channel to deepen and widen it. Perhaps this natural disaster would make that come to pass.

The trip home was long and laborious. They took the railroad back through Houston and on to Louisiana, where Clyde disembarked at New Iberia. When he and LaSalle said their goodbyes, it was with tears in their eyes at everything they had been through together. This trip forged a lifelong friendship between the two captains.

Clyde hoped that Jennie would be at the depot. Only yellow fever had kept them apart this long. So much had happened, much of which he felt would be better left untold. He wanted to kiss her and hold her and tell her how much he loved her and missed her. Of course, he also wanted to see their children, but that could wait.

And there she was, standing on the platform, her auburn hair full and pulled back into a soft chignon. Her radiant smile turned to laughter as he approached. She had her girlish figure back and smelled as though she had just taken a long bath. Clyde felt dirty and unkempt after his adventures but didn't hesitate to take his lovely wife into his arms and kiss her deeply.

The *William Kyle* was moored down the street on Bayou Teche. As they approached the boat, all three children came running toward them, Clyde, Jr., doing his best to keep up. It was a sweet reunion complete with a large family dinner cooked by Ma, after which Clyde took a very long bath and Jennie put the children to bed. Jesse was determined to stay up and talk more with his father, but she told him it was time for the grownups to have some time alone.

When Jennie emerged from putting the children to bed, Ma had disappeared into her cabin. She found her husband clean and in his nightshirt, making notes about something. He stopped immediately when she returned to focus all his attention on her.

"I saw thousands of people with nowhere to go, nothing to eat, alone. The misery was everywhere. But they kept going; the people who were left kept going. And there were all these people who went there to help, strangers mostly. It was an amazing thing to be part of. I'll never look at my life the same, or the people I love. I never want to be away from my family again!" He leaned over and kissed her passionately.

"But you will. Our life will go on and you'll go where you need to go, and we'll be just fine!" She smiled at him and brushed his hair back away from his face with her hand. The moon, framed now by the window, caught her attention. "Look! A blue moon! You know how I love the blue moonlight!"

Clyde grabbed her shoulders and pushed her down onto their bed. She giggled, pretending to be shy. But this was not a night for shy lovemaking as he hurriedly removed her clothes and rubbed her soft skin with his rough hands as the moon lit up their room. He touched and kissed every part of her then stared at her naked body in the blue moonlight. She rolled on top of him and when they could last no longer, they ended with a sexual healing perfectly in sync, one with the other.

CHAPTER 21

THE QUEST

1901–1902

They were underway first thing the next morning. The *William Kyle* had never before seemed so spacious and comfortable to Clyde. He was the last to wake up, which was unheard of. He woke to the sound of Jennie singing in the kitchen. He smiled and said a prayer that God please spare them the kind of pain he'd witnessed in Galveston. Maybe it was time to start going to church again. He even mentioned it to Jennie, who thought it a splendid idea.

As they approached Jeanerette, Clyde gathered his family for a fun ritual. As a treat for children who lived on the bayou, Clyde would blow the whistle as they approached a residential area, and when the children came running, those on the boat would throw pieces of peppermint sticks to them. It wasn't clear who enjoyed it more, the children receiving the candy or those throwing it. Jesse, who was almost five, under the tutelage of Man, could throw it far enough to reach the children if Clyde could maneuver the boat close to the shoreline. Lena, barely three, did her best but mainly the candy ended up in the water where, surprisingly, the fish would sometimes eat it. Clyde, Jr., who would be two that summer, mainly jumped up and down laughing and clapping.

They passed the Indian Reservation at Charenton Beach, and then Baldwin before making the turn onto Irish Bend. They tied up in front of the old, abandoned plantation home that had always caught their eye. Often, they would sail by slowly and make up stories about who lived there and all the ghosts that must inhabit a place like that. They'd been told it was called Oaklawn Manor.

Clyde had planned a treat. They would picnic under the oak trees in front of the columned mansion, which certainly in the past must have hosted the wealthiest landowners from all around. Ma, now officially known as Grannie, had prepared the food.

"Jennie!" Clyde called from up in the pilothouse. "Jennie, come up here!"

Man, now 10, began to help Grannie get the food and the children off the boat while Jennie went up to find her husband. He was standing to the left of the steering wheel, as always, with a big smile on his face. "Come here, woman of mine," he said with a playful tone.

She went to him laughing and put her arms around his neck. "Yes? What can I do for you?" He grabbed her around the waist and pulled her to him for a passionate kiss.

"I have a surprise for you." Clyde's eyes were smiling. He brushed the hair off her forehead and left his hand on the back of her head. "Look outside."

"What are they doing out there?" she asked when she saw Grannie, all three children, and Man walking away from the boat.

"A picnic! Right there on the grass under the oaks where we can see Oaklawn. I've been away so long I wanted to spend some time with my family before going back to work."

They went downstairs and were exiting the boat when Man came sulking up to them. "Clyde Barbour, I don' wants to eat on the ground. That's what po' folk do."

"Man, it's called a picnic, and many Negro families and white folk enjoy it," Clyde answered.

"I don' care. I ain't doin' it," he said, stomping his foot on the ground for emphasis, his arms crossed.

"You don't have to, but we'd like you to," Jennie told him, smiling warmly.

"I thanks you, Mrs. Barbour, but I's goin' fishin.'"

"Go get yourself something to eat first and maybe we'll have fish for dinner!" said Jennie.

It was a nice, cool day. The grass was patchy underneath the oaks, with only a dappling of sunshine reaching the ground. Grannie and the children were laying out the meal as the couple walked up to them.

"Mama, not yet! We're not ready," cried Jesse to his mother, who stood back obediently and waited. Shortly, they were invited to come and sit down on the blanket, which had been moved into the sunshine as the temperature was so pleasant. They sat together, ate, and laughed, and the grownups told stories. It was at that moment that Clyde felt overwhelmingly like a father and a husband, like the head of his own family unit. It made him proud.

They all took a walk through the trees, close enough to the house to see but not intrude should someone actually reside in that dilapidated mansion. They stood looking at the front of the house. Six large Doric columns spanned the front porch, which rose two stories high. A second-story balcony with wrought-iron railings ran almost the entire width of the front. A wide set of brick steps led up to the elevated porch. A wrought-iron fence enclosed the bottom of the steps, along with a few trees and what may have been a garden at one time.

"Daddy?" Jesse asked Clyde. "Why is that fence around the steps?"

"Good question. The only thing I can think of is to keep animals from getting up on the porch."

On the first and second floors, there was a large center door with side lights and a fanlight above. On either side were two sets of French doors. There was a large, plain pediment, in the center of which was a set of French doors that had been boarded over many long years before, leading onto a small wrought-iron Juliette balcony that was partially detached from the house.

The facade was worn and peeling, making it look a dull shade of brown. The shutters that remained were missing many slats and hung at odd angles. And although it had the appearance of a ramshackle mess, it gave off energy of strength, stability, and permanence. It was still grand and noble.

"I scared!" cried Lena, clinging to her mother's skirt.

"It is scary looking," said Jennie, who was carrying Clyde, Jr., in her arms and couldn't pick up her daughter. "Just think how beautiful it was!"

"Come here." Clyde disentangled Lena's little hand from Jennie's dress and picked her up. Just then, a cow came strolling out through the open and partially broken front door.

"Look!" shouted Lena joyfully. "A cow house!"

Grannie laughed. "And a mighty fine cow house it is!" They all laughed loudly.

They gathered up their things and headed back to the boat, Clyde and Jennie lagging behind, holding hands and surveying the once-grand mansion again. Clyde stopped and kissed Jennie on the lips. "Jennie, someday this is going to be ours!" He felt it deep in his soul; he knew it without pause, and he was ecstatic.

Oaklawn Manor, Franklin, Louisiana about 1901 or "The Cow House".

In April, James and Mary had another baby, a boy whom they named James R. Barbour, Jr., after his father. Mary, having lived through the horror of losing an infant child, reveled that much more in her newfound motherhood.

The oily seepage that oozed up in the bayous and swamps dated back centuries and had been used for many purposes. It had been used in oil lamps, for medicinal purposes, and even as a lubricant. In the late 1800s, it was thought to portend the presence of oil and gas. After the explosive gusher at Spindletop, the country, and most especially the southern states, were alive with speculation. That spring in Jennings, Louisiana, five prominent businessmen of that town got together and formed the Jennings Oil Company; seepage there in the Mamou prairie was enough to convince these men to invest a lot of money up front on infrastructure to be prepared for the oil to start flowing. They laid miles of four-inch pipeline from there to the Mermentau River, to be transported by boat all the way to Plaquemine, Louisiana, where it could be put on barges on the Mississippi River.

W. Scott Heywood was responsible for the drilling. He had achieved notoriety in the discovery of gas and gold. Having heard this, Clyde used some of his profits from Spindletop to invest in the Jennings Oil Field. When they had drilled to 1,000 feet, where the oil was found at Spindletop, and found no oil, many investors backed out. Clyde had put his money on Heywood and wasn't going to back out now. The remaining investors agreed to drill to 1,500 feet but still no oil. More stock was sold, of which Clyde bought what he could, priced now at only 25 cents per share. On September 21, 1901, when they had reached 1,700 feet, sand and gas came spouting out of the well, followed by oil. It was the first producing oil well in Louisiana. Being one of the few and the faithful who had stood behind Heywood as they drilled deeper and deeper, Clyde was in the perfect position to talk to the men who started the Jennings Oil Company about using him to be in charge of their oil transportation on the water. It was the beginning of yet another successful business for Clyde.

The charter for the Teche Transportation and Fuel Oil Company was signed on February 25, 1902. The Board of Directors consisted of Clyde (president), Joseph Birg (secretary/treasurer), and William W. Sutcliffe (vice president). The purpose of the company was to purchase steamboats and barges for a general transportation business but especially for towing and distributing fuel oil to customers. Clyde raised $10,000 to get this new company going.

It was in April of that year that Jennie felt certain she was pregnant again. She was ready for another girl to balance out the family. Clyde was thrilled! He was in love with the idea of raising a big family to carry on not only the family name but also the many businesses Clyde had become involved in. This baby would come at the end of the year.

Jennie didn't know that Clyde had been thinking about buying a proper house in Franklin for his growing family. He had waited until he felt he had the money to not only buy a house but to give Jennie the life he wanted her to have, with a cook who could also help with the chores and the children. He would surprise her with the house but knew that she would need to choose the cook herself.

They had begun to attend the Methodist Church after Clyde's mission to Galveston. They would get all the children in their carriage and drive to church dressed in their Sunday best. After lunch, the children would be off to nap, which gave the couple a bit of free time alone. Grannie made sure of it.

This particular Sunday, the children down for their naps, the two went off for a buggy ride. Light gray cumulus clouds spoke of rain, and the air felt heavy. Some of the confederate jasmine had begun to bloom, sending a sweet scent of spring into the air. They passed the beautiful courthouse and rode on down Main Street to the other side of the square and down a short way to Iberia Street, where they turned right.

"Are we going anyplace in particular?" asked Jennie, her arm laced through her husband's and sitting right next to him.

"Yes. It's a surprise. You'll see!" Clyde's heart was pounding in his chest. They drove a few blocks and stopped in front of a precious wooden, one-story, yellow cottage. Three brick steps led up to a porch and the front door.

"What a pretty little house! Do you know the folks that live here?" Jennie asked.

"I do," replied Clyde as he got down from the carriage and put his arms up to help his wife get down. "You're gonna like them a lot!" he added, grinning.

When they reached the front door, Clyde knocked politely. No answer. He knocked again. "Hello? Anybody home?"

"Are they expecting us?" asked a puzzled Jennie.

"Well, yes, they are," answered Clyde, opening the front door.

Jennie grabbed his arm and pulled it back. "Clyde Barbour, what are you doin'?"

Clyde pushed the door open and bid her enter with his left hand. "Welcome home, Mrs. Barbour!" He chuckled and touched her back to get her over the threshold.

"What do you mean?"

"This is your, I mean our, house! I bought it yesterday. We now have a proper home for our family. What do you think?"

Clyde watched his wife as she began to wander aimlessly around the place. He followed her into the kitchen. When she turned around, he could see that she was crying. Her cheeks were damp, but her eyes shone with wonder and her smile was wide. "Ours, really? This is ours? I thought...." He silenced her with a kiss, grabbed her hands, and they waltzed through the kitchen with Clyde humming some imaginary song as they danced clumsily and laughed. She noticed some items on the counter and walked up to them—some peanuts, a bunch of beautiful bananas, a bag of popcorn, and two bottles of Coca-Cola. "All my favorites! You put all of my favorite snacks in our new kitchen. Let's celebrate!" Clyde opened the bottles; they clinked them together and toasted with every sip until they ran out. Clyde had her turn around and pointed to an open shelf where the old green and white Ice Water pitcher sat proudly. "Now I *know* it's ours!" she laughed.

Clyde took his wife on a tour of their new home. There were three bedrooms and a little wing off the back with steps down to the small backyard. He showed her the attic and walked her back to the front room. Jennie was dizzy with excitement, talking about this piece of furniture and that set of curtains she would make. He had never seen her more joyful over anything except their children. He rested his back against the wall, crossed his arms, and watched her. "If you weren't pregnant…." He smiled at her, his eyes looking back toward their new bedroom. Jennie laughed playfully and kissed him deeply. "Come with me." Clyde walked into their new bedroom with Jennie following behind. "Close your eyes." She did as instructed. "Now open them!"

When she did, she saw he had turned on the light. Blue light filled the room from the lightbulbs in the chandelier. "It's beautiful! How did you find those?" She walked around staring up at the chandelier.

"I want you to always have what you love. Now you can have blue moonlight anytime you want!" Clyde was very pleased with himself, as was Jennie. "I love you," he said softly, smiling contentedly.

"Clyde Barbour, you are the most amazing man! How did I find you?" she asked.

"I knew you were coming!"

Green, White and Gold Ice Water Pitcher

That night it was foggy. The air was very still on Bayou Teche. Jennie was so excited about the new house that she couldn't sleep. She sat on the deck in the quiet until she heard a foghorn. It was a long, low, lonely sound that filled her chest and resonated in her ears. The sound bounced across the bayou from side to side, stretching far up and down the water. It was a soulful melody being played. She closed her eyes and smiled. She knew she would miss that sound.

Within two weeks, they had moved into their new little yellow house. Only under duress did Jennie agree to hire someone to cook and clean; she thought it much too extravagant. She chose Elizabeth, a Black woman who had been recommended by someone at their church. She was about Jennie's height but much heavier, which was assumed to mean she was a good cook.

"I don't think anyone would hire a skinny cook!" Jennie told Clyde, who smiled heartily, happy to see his wife helping to make decisions about their life.

Elizabeth had been born and raised in Mississippi and had the deep accent to prove it. She had been married for 30 years but had no children, allowing her to take on the children that she watched without prejudice to her own. Clyde had purchased a white, ruffled edge maid's apron that Elizabeth loved. "Cap'm Barbour, he sure 'nough know how to make folks happy!" she declared when presented with the apron. She wore it every day and kept it looking like new.

Grandpa's health had continued to decline. Clyde had asked him to move into their new house with them, but he had refused. "I'm happiest on the water, you know that," he answered. Dr. Smith said it was grief combined with old age that was wearing him down.

Jennie visited him almost every day. He didn't get out of his bed anymore, so she would pull up a chair and talk with him, combing his beard as she'd always done. One particular day a tear rolled down her cheek. She loved this old man who'd taught her so much and loved her so much. Grandpa saw it, reached over, and wiped her cheek clean. "We'll have none of that, girl. It's my time. I'm an old man who's lived a grand life, but the woman I shared it all with is gone, and I want to join her."

"But Grandpa, who will I talk to when things get confusing? I need you here."

"Jennie. Do you ever feel like your ma is here, right next to you? Are you ever suddenly reminded of a fun moment you shared with her and wonder where the thought came from? Your ma is here, right next to you, everywhere you go. Her soul will never leave your side, and neither will mine when God takes me away. Just sit still and quiet and think of me and I will be there, I promise!" She lay down next to him on his tiny bed, her head on his chest, his hand rubbing her thick hair. He kissed the top of her head. "Now go on, my beautiful Jennie Barbour. Your children are surely wondering where you are."

Pa hadn't been seen in over a year. Clyde, although content at the time with his father's absence, felt obligated to find him before Grandpa's imminent death. He had the word out all along the bayous and rivers. He hadn't been seen in Jeffersonville or New Orleans. He seemed to have disappeared off the face of the Earth. It pained Clyde to think how it would feel for Pa not to have the chance to say goodbye to his father. It had also occurred to him that Pa's return might rally some zest for life in Grandpa.

For Jennie, of course, it inevitably brought back memories of when her mother died, leaving them that day to go be with God. Her father had shown little emotion. *Maybe he cried when no one was around,* she hoped. She had wanted so badly for him to break down in tears there in front of everyone. She had needed to see that he was vulnerable, struggling to keep his emotions at bay. She didn't get her wish. He had rarely shown any tenderness before her death, and the absence of her mother hadn't changed that. Now that she had children of her own, Jennie had a better understanding of how a mother could get enough joy from her children to offset an unthoughtful husband. *I will never have to worry about that with my dear, sweet Clyde,* she thought. *Not for one minute!* She rubbed her hand over her pregnant belly. *And my children will never feel unloved or abandoned, I swear!* She tilted her head back, looking toward the heavens, her hands came together in prayer, and she kissed the tips of her elongated fingers.

Early one morning, about a week after Jennie and Grandpa had had that special moment together, Mary came running into Jennie's house crying. "He's gone. Oh, Jennie, he's gone."

"What are you talking about?"

"Grandpa. He didn't wake up this morning. He's gone." Jennie held Mary in her arms and they both sobbed. Elizabeth was there and took the three children out into the backyard. "Clyde's already there. He told me to come get you." So, the two women, related only by marriage to this old man, William Barbour, wept together. Grandpa was to be buried next to his wife and the baby, William Cilas, in Jeffersonville, Indiana.

Clyde was having a new boat built there on the bayou. However, he had to buy the machinery for it in Memphis. He decided to take Grandpa's body to Indiana and then stop at Memphis to pick up the parts for his new boat. He left James in charge, hoping the responsibility might help him grow up and become more serious about his life. Captain Kyle and many others were happy to be on call should any member of Clyde's family need help.

It was a month before Clyde returned. He and Jennie talked for hours about the low points (burying Grandpa) and the high points, which were many. Having a new boat was like having a new baby.

Before Clyde went to bed to get some much-needed rest, he produced a large rectangular package for her. "I have a surprise for you!" He smiled a big smile with a twinkle in his eye. "Go on, open it, but be careful, it's very fragile."

Jennie opened it slowly and carefully and gasped when she finally pulled out the etched glass hurricane globe that the Howards had given them as a wedding present. "Where did you find it?" she asked as she rubbed her hand over the globe.

"It was still at Grandpa and Grandma's house where we left it when we sold the house in Jeffersonville. We should have it with us." Clyde walked over and admired the beautiful piece.

"I'm so excited to see it again! What a day that was when you proposed to me back at the Howards' amazing mansion. You are one romantic man, Clyde Barbour." She kissed him and he began removing Jennie's nightdress to look at her lovely body. He smiled at the baby bump and rubbed it. He got down on his knees and put his ear on it. "He must be sleeping; I don't hear a thing!" mused Clyde as he kissed her belly.

"Don't you mean 'she'? It's a girl, I'm sure of it," Jennie responded, her hand on her husband's head.

It was Dr. Smith's orders: no sexual intercourse while she was pregnant. There had been too many complications in the past. The chemistry between them was as fervent as ever. He used his hands like paint brushes, being careful not to miss a single spot as he moved around her body. She grabbed him and pulled him even closer. She breathed in his essence as she kissed his neck and ears. They moved to the bed to continue, and even though they followed the doctor's prescription, they were more than satisfied when they closed their eyes and fell asleep entangled.

Clyde continued to put his hand into many different businesses. He had begun buying small parcels of land around southern Louisiana. There was an increasing demand at that point for cattle, hogs, and other livestock. He and Mr. Peterman from the Kyle Lumber Company bought a parcel of land of about 6,000 acres on Lost Bayou over Grand Lake to raise livestock on a large scale for the commercial market. They sent 250 head of cattle there to start and planned to send more. They hired Mr. Alfred Mequet, Sr., as overseer of the ranch and to set up headquarters there for the company, called Peterman Barbour Cattle Company. Clyde had already figured out that he didn't need to know a business from top to bottom to get involved in it; what you needed were trustworthy, intelligent, and seasoned men to work for you.

By November of 1902, when Alfred visited Franklin, he told the *St. Mary Banner* that the cattle were fine and healthy, and the company was constantly increasing its already large amount of livestock. The newspaper went on to brag, "In a few years, Franklin may boast of having several cattle kings!"

At 8:00 a.m. on December 31, Jennie gave birth to another beautiful baby girl. She was small and delicate. She didn't cry when she entered her new world and was not easy to rouse. Jennie began to be fearful. "Why isn't she crying? Is there something wrong? What's happening?" she begged as Clyde went over to where his newborn daughter was being checked over by Dr. Smith.

"Doctor, what's going on?" asked Clyde, relying on his inner calm.

"She's not breathing well. Please give me some room to work," the doctor answered brusquely.

Clyde stepped back to his wife, whose color had changed to white, her neck craning to see her baby. "You need to breathe, Jennie." He looked down and saw blood still trickling out of her. Their newborn began to cry and even seemed a bit angry.

"That's the most wonderful sound I've ever heard!" said a relieved Jennie. "Please bring her to me!"

Dr. Smith handed the tiny package to her. "Mrs. Barbour, here's your little princess!"

She cuddled the newborn, kissing her and putting her to her breast. "She's so blue," stated Jennie, trying to help her latch on for some needed nourishment.

The doctor put his hand on the tiny cheek and neck. "She's doing fine now. Her blue tone will go away soon as her body gets some more oxygen."

"She looks like a little blue moon," said Jennie, smiling.

"Your favorite," replied Clyde, taking this new life into his body and soul. "Maybe we should call her Blue."

"That's not funny," Jennie pouted. "Remember that nurse that helped me when I had yellow fever? Her name was Lucile. I'd like to name her that."

"I was thinking we should name her after Mrs. Lilly Lucile Berwick. She's such an elegant, fine, wealthy woman. After all, she named her black horse, Clyde, after me!" Clyde started to laugh, realizing how ridiculous it sounded.

"I do love to watch Mrs. Berwick in town and at church. She's a very kind woman, too. So how about it? Lilly Lucile Barbour. I think it's beautiful!" Jennie smiled, a far-off look in her eyes as she thought of this little bundle growing up to be a fine lady.

Dr. Smith busied himself cleaning Jennie up and hoping to stem her flow. "I'll be back tomorrow. Do *not* get out of bed!" he ordered loudly, at which Jennie smiled demurely.

In the middle of the night, Clyde woke to Jennie moaning quietly. "What is it? What's wrong?" When there was no reply, Clyde jumped out of the bed and turned on the light. He could see his poor wife moving her head from side to side and the blood on the covers from her waist down.

"Ma, help! *Ma!*" he called for his mother. Grannie came running as if she'd been in wait. "The blood, it's the blood." Grannie removed the covers and gasped at the amount she saw. "We have to get her to the Sanitarium now! Go wake up Man and have him bring the carriage around."

Clyde was glad to have his mother there, her wits about her as always. It took Man and Clyde no time to get the horses hooked up to the wagon. Clyde picked up his bleeding wife. Man helped them into the carriage, the wheels of which had been painted yellow to match the house.

"Drive quickly but no bouncing. You hear? Smooth, that's all." Man, who loved Jennie like a mother, had tears in his eyes but never took them off the road, trying to keep the wagon ride as smooth as possible. Iberia Street, where they now lived, was downtown and close to the new Sanitarium. When they got to the entrance, Man jumped down, startling the horses.

"I's sorry, Clyde Barbour, I didn't mean to spook 'em," declared Man as he helped Clyde down, his arms filled with the woman who was his life. He didn't reply but hurried right inside to where help was waiting.

It was their first trip to this facility. The nurses wouldn't let him go back with her.

"You can't keep me here!" he yelled at the two nurses barring the door marked "Patients Only." They stood, arms crossed, in their white uniforms with pointy hats like starched origami pointing skyward, their nostrils taut in an effort to stay the smell of alcohol that permeated the still air.

Clyde stomped his foot like a child having a tantrum and his face turned a reddish purple in anger. "Let me back there!" he yelled.

"Captain Barbour, if you can't calm down, we're sendin' you home. There're sick people back there don't need your yellin'," one of the unyielding nurses said firmly.

Clyde stormed out through the front doors. Man stood next to the horses and ran to him for news. "She gonna be okay, Clyde Barbour? Please tell me she gonna be okay." Man sobbed, tears running down his face.

"Of course she is; don't be silly. Now take the wagon back on home and put the horses up. I'll be stayin' here the night." He patted Man on the back and motioned for him to get moving.

Clyde walked around the building and easily gained entrance through a back door that put him at the end of a hallway. Being sure to act as though he was meant to be there, he eventually found his wife being cared for by a doctor he didn't recognize. He crept into the room and stood, his back to the wall.

A nurse entered the room carrying supplies. She saw him and asked who he was and what he was doing there.

"I'm Captain Barbour, this woman's husband!" The words came out strong as he attempted to take control of the situation.

"Who let you in here?" she asked.

"I don't understand your question." He approached the bed and stood between the doctor and another nurse. "Jennie, it's me," he said softly.

Her eyes opened briefly. "Clyde...."

"You need to get back so we can tend to your wife. You want to help? Go stand over there," directed the doctor as he pointed to where Clyde had been. This time he obeyed the order, happy to at least be able to see Jennie and know what was being done.

An hour later, the doctor tapped Clyde on the shoulder and motioned for them to go into the hall. The doctor looked tired. "She should pull through this. It will take a while. But you need to understand, Captain—if she has another baby, she won't survive." There was silence in the hallway. "I see how much you love her. You must have gone to a lot of trouble getting past my nurses to find your way back here. You want to have a long life with her? No more babies." He patted Clyde on the back and left.

Jennie was all right after a few weeks of rest. Lilly Lucile remained the princess the doctor had proclaimed her to be, and Clyde was afraid to touch his beautiful Jennie.

Clyde Arthur Barbour about 1903

CHAPTER 22

THE MORES

In January of 1903, Clyde was accepted into the Shriner's Lodge in New Orleans. He traveled there with his friends from Franklin who were already members: Fred Marsh, J.R. Todd, and Henry and Tom McCardell. He had worked his way up quickly at his Freemason's Lodge and was easily accepted into the Shriner's Lodge. He had been raised to have a sense of personal philanthropy, having witnessed his parents and grandparents doing the same. Even his pa, who loved his alcohol more than himself, always stopped to render aid when the opportunity presented itself. Clyde loved what the Freemasons stood for, their motto being "Liberty, equality, fraternity, solidarity," and was ready to take the next step to become a Shriner. He was also well aware that all serious businessmen were Shriners.

Later that evening, Elizabeth cooked dinner and the family sat around the table without Clyde. This was a normal state of affairs, as he was often gone for days at a time. Elizabeth always set a place for The Cap'm, as Jennie required, even though they knew he might not be home for dinner. Every day in the late afternoon, Jennie made sure the children were dressed, clean, and ready to greet their father. Everything should be just right because the Captain was coming home. Jennie loved when he was referred to as such and enjoyed calling him that herself when she wanted to make a fuss over him. Whether they were expecting him or not, the same routine applied.

"Now children, is everything ready for your daddy?" she would ask them.

"Yes, ma'am," they would respond, often in unison.

"But Mama, why do we set a place for daddy when we don't know if he's coming home for dinner or not?" asked Jesse.

"Do you think your daddy's the best daddy ever?" Jennie asked him.

"Yes, but...."

"Who works hard every day for us?"

"Daddy does," replied Lena.

"And what does Daddy like to see when he gets home after working so hard for all of us?"

"A tidy house with clean children who are quiet and peacefully," Jesse recited.

"I think you mean peaceful," Jennie said, smiling at hearing Jesse repeat her own words.

"No, Jesse, don't you know anythin'? This is how it goes, 'Everything needs to be just right because The Captain is coming home.'" Lena did her own recitation with her arms crossed, staring at her big brother.

"Lena, don't talk like that to your big brother. You listen to him; he's older than you and knows a few things you don't." Jennie knew that as the oldest male, Jesse would be in charge of the family someday. He was levelheaded and listened to everything Clyde told him. He adored his father and wanted to know all about his world, even at this young age.

Lena was another story. She seemed to have been born fussing and arguing and wanting the spotlight shining on her. Her hair was thick and wavy like her mother's but was a dark brown like Clyde's. Clyde tended to find her amusing and often didn't scold her when Jennie felt he should have. But that was for Clyde to decide; she followed his lead on everything.

This particular evening, Clyde walked through the front door while they were eating and went to join them. He had an air of excitement, his eyes sparkling, smiling from ear to ear and light on his feet. He kissed the back of his wife's head, patted his mother's shoulder, and sat at the far end of the table. The children jumped up and greeted him with hugs and kisses.

"Jesse, how was school?" he asked.

"Daddy, the carnival's comin' to town!" He relayed this most important piece of information with a look of sheer joy on his face.

"I am not going to that carnival. I heard they're bringing snakes with them," said Lena.

"Oh, Lena, hush up. Daddy can't stop them from bringin' their prize snakes," Jesse responded.

"Jesse!" said Clyde in a loud and stern voice. Jesse jumped in his chair. "We don't speak like that to each other in this family! We are polite and kind to each other. I won't have that kind of talking in my home." Clyde's happy demeanor had quickly changed. "We are people with pride and substance; we want to be looked up to as a fine example of a family. Apologize to your sister!"

"Sorry, Lena," Jesse said quietly, Lena enjoying every moment of this interaction.

"I couldn't hear you," Clyde said.

"I'm sorry, Lena," Jesse said, more clearly and sincerely.

"That's okay," Lena responded, smiling like the Cheshire Cat.

After a few minutes of silence, Lilly Lucile could be heard crying the still sweet, and lilting cry of a newborn. Elizabeth came into the dining room. "I gots her," she said.

"Let me," said Clyde, pushing his chair away from the table and standing up.

"Ain't no need, Cap'm," Elizabeth continued.

"No, no, I want to." He walked out of the silent room. They could hear baby sounds coming from the bedroom. Jennie exchanged glances with Grannie and Elizabeth, who shrugged their shoulders.

Dinner finished quickly. Jennie took the children and got them ready for bed. Afterward, she herded them into the sitting room as Clyde walked in carrying a fussy infant. "I think she's hungry," he stated as he carefully handed the bundle over to his wife.

"I'm sure you're right," she answered, then settled down in the rocker to nurse their baby to sleep.

"Children, let's all sit together and I'm gonna read to you. Let me see," Clyde said as he looked through books on the bookshelf. "Here. 'The Boatman's Horn.' That'll do." He sat in his big chair, and the three children sat on the floor at his feet, ready to listen. This had been a family routine since Jesse was a baby and had become a sacred time that took place on no particular schedule. "It was written by General William O. Butler in 1821. He was a Kentuckian," he continued.

"Just like me!" added a proud Jennie.

"That's right! When he was 21, he volunteered to fight in the War of 1812. He got captured by the Indians, let loose, and then guess what he did?" Clyde asked.

Lena, as usual, was the first to answer, regardless of her knowledge of the topic under discussion.

"He went home and got married!" she said.

"No, Lena, he went back to fighting," answered Clyde. "He was very brave. He helped Andrew Jackson in the Battle of New Orleans, and then went back to Kentucky to study law and work to help the people of his home state. He almost got to be their governor. Then guess what he did?"

This time Jesse wasted no time in spurting out his answer. "He went back to fightin'!" he answered excitedly.

"That's right! Good thinking. After all that time, he joined the army to fight in the Mexican-American War. He was 55!"

"What was he thinkin'?" asked Grannie out loud.

"Grannie, he was thinkin' he didn't want those Mexicans to win!" Jesse continued.

Grannie, Jennie, and Clyde could be heard chuckling quietly.

"Okay. Enough history lesson. He also wrote a bunch of poems and here is one of them." Clyde cleared his throat and began to read out loud, slowly and with much vivacity.

As was usual when Clyde told stories of his youth or read things about the rivers, he ended with tears in his eyes. There was silence. Even Clyde, Jr., knew they weren't to interrupt their father when he talked or told stories. Halfway through the poem, Clyde, Jr., had lain down on the floor, his head in Lena's lap, and closed his eyes. Jesse did a good job of paying rapt attention for most of the reading. Lena had listened briefly before succumbing to the desire to fidget and scratch, then soothing her little brother in an unusual show of motherliness.

Jennie reveled in this living picture of family life, her family life. She had never been happier and didn't believe she could be. Her family was the ultimate expression of love and acceptance she had always dreamed of. *I will never let anything or anybody come in here and hurt my family,* she thought, her brow furrowed and her head shaking back and forth ever so slightly. *Never ever!*

When all the children were tucked in and Jennie retired to the bedroom, Clyde was in the bed reading. He slammed his book closed, smiling widely at his wife. "I've been waiting all night to tell you. Come here. Sit down." He patted the bed next to him. Jennie hurried over and jumped onto the bed next to him and put her arms around his neck.

"Tell me, tell me!" she begged.

"I'm going to be on the Board of Directors of the new bank opening up in Morgan City. Me!" He was almost giddy. "It's happening. Just like I knew it would, just like I saw it in my mind. These men look at me and see a man they want on the board of their bank; they don't see a barefoot boy who grew up on a flatboat." He stood up and walked around the room.

Jennie sat on their bed watching him and listening to his every word as she always did. She knew better than anyone, except maybe Grandpa, who was no longer around to dance in the glory of the news, how big Clyde's dreams were. He had come so far and accomplished so much, yet he still had so much more he wanted to achieve. She loved to hear him outline what all he was going to do and where they were going. None of that mattered to her, as long as they were going there together.

It had been a few weeks since the carnival had come and gone. Franklin had gone back to its normal bustling ways. The First National Bank of Morgan City opened its doors in March, with Clyde one of the directors.

His cousin, Milt Campbell, had moved south from Indiana to work for Clyde's Teche Transportation Company as a steamboat pilot. Milt and his twin brother, Ira, had both spent time on the Barbour's flatboat many years before. They were two years older than Clyde and had both worked for Howard Shipyards since they were boys. Ira was happy building ships, but Milt wanted to be on the water.

One evening in the late spring, Milt was piloting the steamer *Joseph Birg* on Bayou Teche, towing oil. He'd quickly become known for the pipe that rarely left his mouth, giving his speech a muffled quality. He blew for the floating bridge at Willow Street to swing open.

James was also onboard, working up in the pilothouse. "Have you ever seen this many lily pads?" he asked Milt. "I think I could probably walk bank to bank without even gettin' my feet wet!"

"Maybe you could get the ladies thinkin' that you walk on water. That for sure would make 'em want you, boy!" Milt laughed.

"I ain't no boy and they already want me," replied James, licking his fingers and running them through his hair, then striking a smiling pose.

"What they like is a real man, like me!" Milt copied James' moves and started laughing heartily. James chimed in, slapping his knee.

That's all it took—those few moments of nonchalant piloting sent them ramming into the bridge, which had failed to open properly, sending both of them lurching forward.

"Goddamn it!" Milt shouted.

"What the hell?" asked James, righting himself.

"The bridge didn't swing open. It's those goddamn lily pads!" Milt was sending the signal down to the engineer to reverse.

"You blitherin' idiot!" said James, a look of disgust on his face that quickly turned to a one-sided smile as he continued. "Wait till Clyde hears about this," teased James.

"So, it's my fault you were actin' like a idiot?" Milt returned the insult.

"A idiot? You callin' me…." James started when the engineer entered the pilothouse.

"The hull is banged up. She's gonna need a repair. Let's get her docked, and soon as the bridge gets pulled open, we'll take her and get her fixed up," the engineer said.

Since it was nighttime, the men went to Clyde's house looking for him. Both felt the other was at fault for the accident and came to clear his name. At this late hour, they went around to the back and knocked on the kitchen door. It took a few tries before Clyde appeared.

"James. Milt. Why are you here so late? What happened?" Clyde looked the men up and down for signs. "Come in. Here…sit down." All three men sat at the kitchen table, the two uninvited guests sweating, but not from a spring heat wave.

"Well, Clyde, it's those damn lily pads," Milt began.

"Yeah, and you know them floatin' bridges ain't worth a damn," added James.

"Ain't that the truth," agreed Milt, the pipe between his teeth bobbing up and down.

"I think that crazy…" James was cut off by Clyde.

"Just tell me what happened." Clyde was tired and in no mood for this.

"We ran the *Joseph Birg* into the Willow Street Bridge," Milt blurted.

"No 'we,' Clyde. He was steering."

"And you weren't pestering me or nothin," Milt said. "You wasn't acting like a idiot I guess, neither."

"Now, Clyde, do you think…" James tried to take his turn.

"*Stop!*" Clyde snapped. The following silence weighed heavily on both guilty parties. "So, you're telling me you wrecked my boat on the bridge? 'Cause of the lily pads gumming up the works on the swinging side? How bad is it?"

"Well, yeah, Clyde, it kinda happened two times," Milt said slowly and quietly, looking down at the table and holding his pipe.

"Yeah, can you believe it? Two times?" James began but was cut off by Clyde.

"*Twice?*" he yelled. "You hit *two* bridges?" Clyde banged his hand on the wooden table, stood up, and began to pace back and forth. Milt puffed rapidly on his pipe while James sat silently, his shoulders hunched, staring at his hands on the table.

"But *he* was steerin', not me. I…" James said, speaking quickly.

"*Stop!*" Clyde yelled again. "Yeah, Milt, *you* were the pilot. But you, James, you grew up on the water with me. Didn't you learn anything? The river…the bayou…can change in a second! The only thing you have that the boat doesn't have is your eyes and sometimes a brain; your eyes have to be watching all the time."

Milt tried to get a few words in. "But Clyde, it was a long day, I was tired, and those lily—"

"Milt, why were you so tired? Did you get any sleep last night or were you and my little brother out carousing?" Clyde was standing face to face with Milt, staring him in the eye. He pulled the pipe out of Milt's mouth and set it loudly on the table. "You used to build boats for a living. You know how much they cost to repair." He turned to face James. "Do you know how much money you lose in revenue when your boat's laid up? Do you?" James shook his head. This time the silence lasted a few minutes while Clyde paced some more, thinking. "We've already got the *William Kyle* in the shipyard for repairs; that makes two of my fleet unable to work, and pilots like you two sitting around with nothing to do!"

Milt opened his mouth to say something, then changed his mind and shut it tight. He saw Jennie out of the corner of his eye as she stuck her head into the kitchen and quickly turned back around.

"No pay for either of you until the boat's fixed, and that hardly begins to pay for the damage. If you weren't my damn cousin," he stated as he looked over at Milt, "and you weren't my damn little brother," he added, turning back to look at James, "I'd fire you both. As it is, I want you both helping to do the repairs, for free!"

"Now Clyde," James started.

"What? Now what?" Clyde sighed and shook his head. "I know those godforsaken lily pads are making the bayous almost impassable. Their roots are long and strong. They've got to get rid of those swinging bridges and move up to the turntable bridges. That would help the problem some." He was quiet for a moment. "You two get the *Joseph Birg* to the shipyard tomorrow, you hear? First thing in the morning." Clyde walked out of the kitchen and away down the hall.

"Phew, that coulda been a lot worse!" said Milt, picking up his pipe from the table.

"Yeah, but you don' know how mad he is. I hate when he gets mad; it makes me feel bad," said James. They left the way they had come in.

In two weeks, the boat was repaired.

CHAPTER 23

THE ARMISTICE

February 1904

A year later, on a fine February afternoon, Clyde was piloting the *Joseph Birg* in from the swamps carrying a full load of lumber. Captain Kyle was standing on the wharf, his arms crossed as he watched Clyde smoothly pilot his boat to his mooring spot. Clyde disembarked and walked up to Captain Kyle. The two men shook hands hardily.

"That's a mighty big tow of fine lumber you got there, Captain Barbour; mighty fine." Kyle slapped Clyde on the back hard.

"Just for you, William. Gotta keep you wanting more!" Clyde responded with a smile, looking back at what was often called one of the finest crafts on the bayous. He felt a surge of pride that he, Clyde Barbour, could own such a fine towboat, much less also have the *William Kyle* and another in the pipeline. He wished Grandpa were there to take pride in all that he had accomplished.

A man about Clyde's age, in work clothes, approached him as he was leaving the lumber yard. "Captain Barbour?" the man asked.

"Yes? What can I do for you?" Clyde shook the man's hand and noticed he was fidgeting and a little shaky.

"I been told you was a helpin' kinda man." He stopped, rubbed his temple with his dirt-stained fingers, then continued, "So I come here to ask fer yer help."

"What's your name?"

"I's Billy Broussard, ole Broussard's my cousin. He's the one what helped ya get here the first time ya came here."

"Nice to meet you, Mr. Broussard. How can I help you?"

"Well, Captain, I owns some acres of sugar cane out by Baldwin; got my first good crop goin'. I needs a crane to get those stalks up onto my wagons to haul 'em to the sugar mill. Gotta get mine crushed quick, ship off the syrup quick, get paid quick, and get that next crop planted." As Billy began to talk about his business, he livened up and looked Clyde right in the eye. Clyde loved to talk to men about their business and see their whole persona change as their excitement and dedication shone through. "Gotta do it; yes, sir!"

So Billy Broussard and Captain Barbour mapped out a plan and shook on a deal that served them both. Clyde lent him the money and would tow his cane syrup down the bayou for the normal fee he charged all the farmers. Clyde also knew that this gesture would add another person to his arsenal of those he could count on in the future.

Jennie and her sister, Leona, had been writing to each other consistently over the years. In 1898, Leona had married Douglas Carver, who had proved to be a violent husband of few words. They had a daughter, Cora, born in 1900, whom Leona devoted her life to, hoping against hope that she would be able to shield her daughter from the wrath of her father.

It had been almost 10 years since Jennie had seen her family. She heard from her brothers from time to time, but the ache to go back had long disappeared. Lilly Lucile was now 18 months old. Her family now complete, Jennie felt ready to return. Clyde had encouraged her to go throughout the years, but he'd always been met with a non-negotiable, "No!" He seemed as excited as the children were to be heading off to Kentucky in the late summer. He insisted they take a steamer. Even though most of his children had been born on and lived on the *William Kyle*, they had never experienced the luxury of a Mississippi River sternwheeler appointed for passengers.

"Your mother and I fell in love on the Mississippi," Clyde told Jesse and Lena. "She was the most beautiful girl I had ever seen!"

"I knew he was smitten the minute he laid eyes on her," Grannie added.

"And he was the smartest boy I ever met," added Jennie, "and he still is!"

"Mama, he can't be smarter than Captain Kyle; he owns that whole lumber yard," stated Jesse.

"Or the principal at school," added Lena. "He must gotta know everything to be principal." Lena was adamant. Clyde and Jennie laughed.

They had sailed to Baton Rouge and would soon be boarding the *Morning Glory* for their trip upriver. As they approached the boat, Clyde turned to Lena. "Can you read the name of this boat?" It was written in big letters on the side.

"It says 'Mor...,'" Jesse began, and Clyde hushed him immediately.

"Let Lena try," said Clyde, wanting his six-year-old to show her skills.

"Well, Daddy, it starts with a 'm-o-r,' which sounds like m...m... mo...mor...." She hesitated.

Jennie protested to Clyde, "Don't make her nervous with all that right now."

"Mama," Clyde answered, "she needs to learn how to sound it out. I won't have any of our children not able to read." Jennie stopped talking.

Clyde, Jr., began humming "Mmmm," mimicking Lena. "Stop it, Clyde! You don't know how to read," said Lena, wanting all the attention.

"Lena," Clyde said, "sound it out. Come on, you can do this."

He smiled at his little girl, which melted away her trepidation as she proudly said out loud, "Morning!" Clyde picked her up and put her on his shoulders.

"What else? What's that other word?" he asked.

Lena was silent for only a few seconds before admitting, "I really don't know, Daddy."

"The second word is *glory*. The name of the boat is the *Morning Glory!* Good job," Clyde said, patting Lena on the head.

They made quite an entourage. Clyde, Jennie, Grannie, and four children. They had two staterooms next to each other. It was no surprise that Clyde knew the pilot.

After they had moved into the Little Yellow House as it came to be known, Man and Elizabeth had grown close and the two of them decided that he would move in with her. Having no children of her own, she was pleased to finally play the role of mother, at least in a way. Man was still young enough to be excited to have a mother figure in his life. Before embarking on their boat, the whole family had gone to the train station, where Clyde bought tickets for Elizabeth and Man to visit where he had been born and where his mother was buried. Man knew his mother had died shortly after they left her. This was his chance to visit her grave. He also knew that his father's grave was the bottom of the Mississippi River.

Clyde felt at home amid the usual hustle and bustle of the boat being made ready for the trip upriver. He smiled as he herded his family along. Jennie felt overwhelmed at the prospect of keeping track of four children and was delighted that Grannie was with them. Jesse hurried to keep up with his father. Lena questioned Grannie about everything. Clyde, Jr., was content to hold Jennie's hand, and Lilly Lucile was on her hip, crying from discomfort in what, to her young mind, was a loud, unfamiliar environment. She didn't settle down until they were in their staterooms—Grannie with the three older children, and Jennie, Clyde, and Lilly Lucile in the other.

The Grand Salon was beautiful. The children were awed by the size and grandeur of the place, the chandeliers, gilded everything, and the beautiful carpet. For a time, that helped them behave appropriately. Once the novelty wore off, however, they were more difficult to handle—except for Lilly Lucile, who was not at all accustomed to being on the water. She tolerated the stateroom and eventually warmed up to being on the deck, as long as she was being held. The favorite time of day was at dinner when the band played and people sang along, clapping and having fun.

Clyde spent a lot of time in the pilothouse and walking around talking with workers whom he knew. He hadn't had this kind of time away from his business with his family since he could remember. A part of him wished his pa were there to reminisce, but no one was sure where he was. Clyde would gladly have spent all his time up there, so high above the Mississippi. Jennie joined him up there on a few occasions.

At night, as he lay in his bunk, his ears filled with the rumble of the engine and the splash of the buckets in the water over and over and over, he would recall bits and pieces of his very own "Life on the Mississippi." Unbidden memories of the smell of Ma's cooking as he sat up on top taking note of every little thing in and around the river. Hunting in the yawl, shooting his gun off too early and taking heat for it for days, sitting at the kitchen table with Grandpa learning to read before he started school, sleeping on the floor under the counters with James when Grandpa or other visitors were staying on the flatboat. He remembered once tying up to the wrong tree and Pa coming out with a litany of curse words that would shame a sailor. Pa was always better at the business side of the flatboat; Clyde was better at feeling the water and the wind and remembering the subtleties of each bend in the rivers. They had been a good team, for the most part, but he didn't need his father anymore. He had taken over his place in the family, leading it to a more stable and peaceful existence. He would never embarrass his family the way his father was apt to do. Well, maybe only that one time when he and Captain Taylor got into that fight.

He found that he missed his father from time to time. He missed the spoken and unspoken praise that Clyde had become such a wise pilot. What he didn't miss was all the drunken nights and anger outbursts that could end in someone getting hurt. Clyde had had one main goal as a boy: to impress his father and make him proud. At that he had been successful.

In Jennie's mind, a trip upriver had always carried with it the possibility of going home and seeing her family. For years she wouldn't, couldn't, let her mind travel back to the last time she'd been at home and her father had sent her away. Now, standing on the deck, Lilly Lucile on her hip, the memory came rushing over her. It enveloped her and took her breath away. It felt dark and heavy and smelled of their farm, the sweat of the horse, and the wood of the wagon. She closed her eyes and shook her head in an effort to make it go away, but in that darkness, she saw the fury in her father's eyes and the tears streaming down Leona's face.

She started when Clyde put his arm around her shoulder. "I didn't mean to startle you." He smiled and kissed her on the cheek. "How's my Lilly?" He reached over to take Lilly in his arms, but she protested. He took her anyway and she quickly settled down. "You look like you've seen a ghost," Clyde continued.

"All of a sudden, I don't know why, but all of a sudden I was remembering my last trip home." Jennie went quiet.

"That was a long time ago. Everything is different now. Even if he wants to be ugly, he wouldn't dare do that in front of me. Leona says it's fine. I will never let anyone hurt you, ever," Clyde said, squeezing her shoulder and looking deep into her eyes. "I promise."

"Me, too, Mama! Me, too!" said Jesse, who was standing on the other side of Clyde. Jennie bent down to kiss the top of his head.

"That's right, Jesse. You'll be the head of this household one day. Promise me you'll always take care of your mother first," Clyde said in a deep, serious-sounding voice.

"I promise, Daddy. You know I will!" Jesse answered proudly.

Grannie walked up carrying Clyde, Jr., and holding Lena, who was talking nonstop, by the hand. Lena let go of Grannie's hand and ran up to Clyde and pulled on his trouser leg. "Daddy? I wanna hold Lilly. It's my turn."

"Okay, Lena, okay." Clyde handed the toddler to Lena.

William, Jennie's oldest brother, and Leona were waiting for them when the boat docked. Clyde insisted that Jennie go down first and have her private hellos. She didn't know if she was feeling more anxious or excited as she made her way down to her two siblings. When her eyes met Leona's, all the anxiety melted away and she ran into her little sister's arms, wanting never to let go. William wrapped his long arms around his sisters and kissed Jennie's head. Jennie was laughing, Leona was crying, and William was talking away. A few minutes later, they were all three smiling and talking.

"Oh, Jennie, are those your children?" Leona asked as she saw Clyde, Grannie, and the children approaching.

"Yes, those are all mine!" Jennie replied happily. "And this is Clyde's ma. We call her Grannie."

The ride to her childhood home seemed longer than Jennie remembered. The wagon was filled with children and grownups and laughter and excitement, but it was uncomfortable to Jennie, who had become accustomed to the smooth ride the water generally provided. Clyde and Jesse sat up with William, who was driving the horses. Eventually things settled down and the younger children slept, along with Grannie. William told Jesse about the trees and plants and animals that inhabited the forested trail.

As the children slept and things quieted down in the wagon, fear and anxiety filled Jennie to her core. She became very quiet and even closed her eyes in an effort to remove herself from the outside world, which bore the reality of what was about to happen. *Why did I do this? What was I thinking? My children: how will my father treat them? I should never have brought them here. Oh Lord, please help us! Did I bring them to shield me from him? Oh, please no. I'm supposed to shield them! How selfish I am.* She tried to hide her tears, but it was impossible in that small space.

"Jennie, honey, what's the matter?" asked a concerned Leona, wrapping her arm around her big sister's shoulders.

"I...I...I'm just overwhelmed...with happiness...it's..." Jennie offered, trying to find something suitable to say.

"Well, of course you're overwhelmed," added Grannie, patting Jennie on the knee. "This is a big step for you—and it's the right thing to do." She smiled at Jennie, that warm, soft smile that enveloped and cushioned the receiver in goodness and love.

Even if she'd still had her eyes shut, Jennie thought she'd know from the feel of her skin and the smell in the air that they were on her father, Arthur Hobbs', land. Memories fell upon her like an avalanche, one after the next. She caught bits and pieces of each one as they swirled from her subconscious to her conscious mind. She was galloping across the hills; she was swimming in the pond; she was hunting; she was hiding from her brothers in the woods; she was picking blackberries with Leona, their faces and teeth stained with the dark blue juice of the fresh berries. She smiled. *I can't let the few awful things make me forget all the good things that happened here.* She took a deep breath and closed her eyes to thank God and her mother for all of it.

Jennie's father had remarried. She knew her old home was once again filled with young people. Remarrying after the death of a spouse was a common occurrence then, but the idea of strangers at home in the bedroom she'd shared with Leona was very uncomfortable to her. Leona had been around from the beginning of that marriage and so was accustomed to it all. When Leona married, she moved close to town, to a small wooden house with a front porch. She missed the countryside and so spent a lot of time at their father's house escaping both the city and her unfriendly husband until finally divorcing him the year before. Now Leona and Cora, their daughter, shared a room in a boarding house. She began to sew for a living. Their mother had been one of the first to have a sewing machine in their town, so both girls had learned to sew well at an early age. Being a seamstress was a respectable way for an unmarried woman to earn a living.

As they passed by the edge of the pond, Jennie realized they were almost there. What kind of reception would they have? Would their father even be there to greet them, or would he be angered to the point of violence? Who is this stepmother named Margaret? Leona and all the grandchildren called her Ma Margaret. Jennie closed her eyes to pray but didn't know what to say. *Lord, please bless our trip here*, was all that came to her.

She saw them from a distance as they walked out the front door and stood on the porch; Father and Ma Margaret along with two children, both of whom looked close to Jesse's age. As the wagon got closer, the children ran out to meet them, then ran alongside the wagon the last few hundred feet. Jesse jumped out as soon as they came to a stop and started shaking hands with the young girl and boy as they introduced themselves. Jennie's stepmother came up, smiling, and introduced herself. "Hello! I'm Ma Margaret." She tried to take Lilly Lucile from Jennie's arms so she could get down from the wagon, but Lilly Lucile was having nothing to do with this strange woman and began to wail. Clyde came up to retrieve the crying baby, and William helped Jennie and Leona down. The two sisters dusted themselves off and Jennie followed Leona's lead as she hugged their stepmother, introducing herself and her children, who were scattered about. She turned to see her father watching her as if discovering her for the first time. His gaze was contemplative—no joy, no sadness, just thoughtful.

"Father," Jennie began nervously, "it's really good to see you." She used her hand to smooth back her hair. She put her hands lightly on his shoulders and hurriedly kissed him on the cheek. He stood motionless. Jennie stepped back and busied herself with her children to fill the awkwardness she felt down to her soul. Her father's lack of emotion sent shivers down her spine. *Why did I come back here? My children...oh Lord, please help me!*

Clyde was painfully aware of the tenuous situation his wife was confronting. He was standing behind her and reached around to shake hands and introduce himself to Jennie's father, who reached out and shook his hand firmly.

"Clyde Barbour. Nice to meet you, Mr. Hobbs." Clyde was his charming self, smiling and engaging Jennie's father in a light conversation to allow Jennie to settle in her awkward situation.

"Call me Arthur. I hear you pilot steamboats." Jennie's father seemed interested.

"Yes, sir. I grew up on the rivers. They made me who I am. And my middle name is Arthur!" Clyde felt he'd gotten a little deep and changed the conversation quickly by bending down to pick up Clyde, Jr., and introduced him to his grandfather.

Arthur returned the favor by introducing Clyde and Jennie, who were standing close by, to his two children, Bessie Lee, who was nine years old, and George, who was seven, the same age as Jesse.

It had been decided that Jennie and her family would stay in the room she had occupied with Leona as a child. There were two beds in that room now, so the adults would all have a bed to sleep in and the children could sleep on pallets on the floor. Since Jesse and George had already taken to each other, the two boys would stay in George's bedroom.

The rolling hills and woods of the Kentucky countryside were very different from their home in Louisiana. The children spent most of the days outside running and playing. Jennie's nieces and nephews had always called her father "Grandpa Hobbs," so her children did as well. He was a tall, straight, black-haired man who rarely smiled. That didn't seem to bother Jesse, who spent time with his grandfather learning to shoot a pistol. Lena was extremely upset that she was not allowed the same privilege, but Clyde felt she was too young. Instead, Ma Margaret took her to the barn and taught her how to milk a cow and feed the chickens. Clyde took Jesse, Lena, and Clyde, Jr., to the stables most days to teach them how to ride, even though Clyde, Jr., was much too small; he would sit on the saddle with his father sitting behind him.

Jennie and Grannie spent their days helping with the cooking and cleaning alongside Jennie's stepmother, who had seamlessly taken Jennie into what was now Margaret's home and made her feel welcome. It was her father who made Jennie squirm. She avoided him as much as possible, afraid that she might stir up some unwanted ugliness in him. She visited her mother's grave several times and wandered around in the woods when time allowed. In those woods, she relived her childhood, thought of her mother, and tried to figure out her future. She would never have dreamed that her life would be so full and happy and satisfying. Now, she prayed it would stay that way. She had a loving husband and four beautiful children, but how were they going to keep that closeness without that feeling of total oneness that came from their coupling? They enjoyed other ways of pleasuring each other, but it wasn't the same. *It's not the same at all.*

One morning, she and Leona joined the family shooting contest. Grandpa Hobbs, Clyde, Jesse, and George had set it all up and the two women wanted their turns.

"Your mother used to be a good shot," Leona told the boys proudly. "I wasn't that good, but I've had a lot more practice now!"

"Mama, I've never seen you shoot a gun," said Jesse, curiosity on his face.

"I don't need to," Jennie responded. "I have your Daddy to take care of me!"

She went first, aiming her pistol at the tin can on the left. She held her right arm out straight, supporting it with her left hand, aimed, and fired. She missed.

"Looks like that bullet went the way of my daughter, disappeared into the woods," Jennie's father said, staring into the distance.

"What's that mean, Mama?" asked Jesse.

Jennie was holding her breath, unable to speak. *Did he really say that?*

"Arthur," said Clyde flatly, "she's here now. Isn't that what matters?"

Leona began to cry. "Father, please don't spoil everything," she begged.

Arthur grumbled some things under his breath, aimed his rifle, and shot the can right off the fence.

"Wow, Grandpa Hobbs, that was a great shot!" Jesse sang out.

"Watch this," said George, who took a great deal of time aiming his rifle before his shot rang out, his bullet grazing the side of one of the remaining cans.

Clyde felt sure he heard George say, "Damn!" under his breath but thought it prudent not to say anything about it. "That was a great shot there, George!" he said, patting the boy on the back.

"Yeah. Not bad," said Arthur to his son. "Next time don't take so long aiming, boy; it knocks off your timing."

Jennie was trying to regain her composure. Luckily, Jesse was busy with his rifle. "I want a turn," he said loudly. "It's my turn!"

"Go on, son," Clyde replied, squatting to be level with his son, talking to him about lining up his shot.

Although he'd been practicing, the recoil sent Jesse's shot way over the fence. Jesse stomped his foot in frustration and looked ready to throw his rifle to the ground. Jennie stepped over to stand next to him and put her hand on his shoulder. "It's just one shot, Jesse, that's all. Just one shot. Guess we're just townsfolk." She smiled down at him.

"You'll need to do some more practicing," Clyde told his son. "Let's let Aunt Leona have her turn." He turned to his sister-in-law, whose tears had abated, and motioned to her.

Leona took little time getting off her shot, which sent another can flying. She jumped up and down, laughing, and was soon surrounded by the two boys jumping around in circles shouting with joy.

"Now that's my girl," said Arthur, grinning. Leona looked angrily at her father and handed her rifle to Clyde.

"I've never been a good shot," said Clyde as he shyly took the gun. "I was always getting into trouble when I was a boy hunting with my brother, James, and my pa. I would shoot too soon and frighten the animals away before they got a chance to shoot. I can still hear them yelling at me, Pa cursing up a storm!" He was laughing and doing a good job of distracting the onlookers from the rude comment Jennie's father had made. "Guess I'll try." He took a shot and barely missed the tin can. "Just another townsfolk," he said.

That night after supper, Grandpa Hobbs had a real war story to tell. Jennie knew the story well and told her husband she thought it inappropriate for children.

Clyde responded, "It's a true story of what happens when men are foolish enough to go to war. It won't hurt 'em to be saddled with a bit of reality."

It was a warm August night, so the family settled down on the back porch, listening to the cicadas and praying for a breeze. The smell of dinner lingered in the air, mingling with the musty smell of wet bluegrass. Jennie sat in the far rocking chair, Lilly Lucile in her lap, not wanting to be there at all.

"I had a brother name o' John. We joined the Union Army, the 8th Virginia Volunteer Infantry," Grandpa Hobbs began, leaning forward in his chair. "He and I married sisters; two brothers marrying two sisters." He laughed, then looked at Ma Margaret, who seemed unperturbed by the comment, which she'd heard many times before. "Minerva came to see me many times in the field. It was the only comfort we had.

Our first was The Battle of Bull Run. Not a special looking piece of land; mainly flat, a few trees, with the crick running through it and a house standin' off to the side where an old woman too sick to move was. We was sittin' pretty 'cause we had more men and brought in the big guns." Grandpa Hobbs took a deep breath, giving George the opportunity to step in with the details.

"We had four rifled 10-pounders and two of them Howitzers, right Pa?" he added, smiling at his father, who seemed tickled by the intrusion into his story.

"Good thinkin' there, son. That's right. Them Confederates had none o' that but they did have the railroad station surrounded. We was beatin' the daylights outta them when John and me, we got separated. You see, before the fightin' broke out, John says to me, 'Arthur, if I get shot during this battle, I'm gonna put my hand on the wound so's you know it's me out there in the field.' I said okay. Them damned Confederates got another 11,000 soldiers and they just ran us out o' there; we was retreatin' over the top o' those folks what came to watch the battle in their fine clothes and wagons. It's a wonder none of them got shot. When the shootin' stopped, I walked all around lookin' for

John. There were dead bodies all over the ground, almost 5,000. Then I find him dead, lying there on the ground on his side, his little finger sticking in the wound in his head. I tell you I cried, right then and there, kneeling on the ground." He ended looking down, as if seeing his brother lying at his feet there on the porch.

No one said anything, not knowing what to say after such a tale. Clyde, Jr., solved that problem when he began to cry. It was unclear why he was crying. Clyde went over to his namesake and picked him up. But the story was not yet over.

"During the War, I was in 26 engagements. I served our country for 3 years, 6 months, and 20 days," he said with a flourish, seemingly satisfied that he had done his duty.

"What happened to that sick old lady?" asked Jesse.

"She got wounded by bullets and died. That's all I know," answered Grandpa Hobbs.

Jesse sat there, engrossed in a seven-year-old's thoughts on the subject. Clyde, Jr. had settled down, and Lena, who as usual couldn't sit still, sprang up, grabbed Cora by the hand, and led her off to the barn. Lilly Lucile had slept through the entire recitation and was now awake and ready to play.

Jennie found herself feeling proud of her father and his service and wondered how someone could be so noble and yet behave so cruelly to his own daughter.

During their many hours of talk, Jennie and Leona had discussed Leona and Cora returning home with Jennie and her family to live. She would get away from her ex-husband, who would never really leave her alone, and start fresh, Jennie there to hold her hand. Clyde agreed, and when it came time for Leona to tell her father that she was leaving, she was afraid. Clyde went with her. Her father didn't make the fuss that Leona had feared, but he looked angry.

"So, Mr. Barbour," he said sarcastically, "you're taking another one of my daughters away from their home. Fine, that's fine. I'm gettin' too old to be takin' care o' so many people. You go on, Leona, and you just pray that this man don't turn on you, too." Leona didn't seem surprised at her father's response.

"I assure you, Arthur, that I am a man of character, and I'll be sure nothing bad happens to Leona. She's part of my family now, too."

When it came time to return to their home in Louisiana, Jennie was content that she'd seen her brothers, Miss Dora, and friends from when she was a girl. She also shed tears at her mother's grave. She couldn't wait, however, to be back in their little yellow house, this time with her little sister and niece in tow.

CHAPTER 24

THE FAIR

September 1904

Shortly after they arrived back in Franklin, Leona and Cora neatly tucked away with an older couple from their church, Clyde left again. He was headed back up north with James Peterman (of Kyle/Peterman Lumber Company) and Joseph Birg (who was now the president of the bank) to see the St. Louis World's Fair. It was to have opened in 1903 to commemorate the hundredth anniversary of the Louisiana Purchase—its official name was the Louisiana Purchase Exposition—but due to the extensive amount of building that took place to allow for exhibits from around the world, it was not until 1904 that the gates were opened. It was well worth the wait.

When the three men arrived at the fair in September, it had been open for over six months. Still, the crowd was large at the entrance, where they waited their turn to pay 50 cents each to enter. Immediately upon crossing into the grounds, their view, between two buildings, was of the Louisiana Monument and beyond that to the Grand Basin waterway. Festival Hall stood on the other side of the water, with its beautiful water cascades in front of the round neoclassical building outlined in columns. One reason it had taken so long to get inside the fair was delay caused by the awestruck tourists who, once inside, stopped immediately to take it all in. Everywhere you looked were beautiful, ornate white palaces and buildings, most with columns and obelisks. The three men had never seen anything like it. They walked past a small building on their right and onto the grass between the Palace of Manufactures to their left and the Palace of Varied Industries to their right. They put their suitcases down and took a look around.

"We've entered another world here," said Clyde, feeling alive with expectation and curiosity.

"This is unbelievable," said Joseph Birg. "How did they do all this?"

"Where did they get the money to do all this, is my question," added James Peterman.

"It's incredible," Clyde almost whispered, smiling deeply.

They decided to check in to their hotel and get rid of their suitcases. There was only one place to stay at the fair, the Inside Inn at the east end of the property. They took the Intramural Railway, a double track line that ran for 15 miles around the fairgrounds. They passed Model City, which was a study in city planning, and then there was the beautiful, heavily decorated Palace of Liberal Arts with its Roman arches and Doric columns. The stately US Government Building was outlined with colonnades of gigantic Ionic columns situated on high ground with the slope of the hill covered almost entirely by staircases with statues, clipped hedges, and flowers. A collection of smaller buildings represented many of the states: Missouri, Ohio, Massachusetts, Minnesota, Iowa, Mississippi, and Arizona. They exited the train at the Indian Territory. As they walked past, carrying their bags, they looked over and saw someone they later learned was Geronimo, shooting arrows at a target they couldn't see.

The Inside Inn was a massive, fortress-like building with 2,257 rooms, which rented for $1.50 to $5.50 a day, depending on the room and the meals included. It was three stories high, with two large towers about seven stories tall at the entrance, atop which American flags flew. It sat on a hill with an imposing view of the Plateau of States. With two restaurants, a lounge, a drugstore, a haberdashery, a shoeshine parlor, a newsstand, and a barbershop, it put even the French's Floating Palaces, from back on the Mississippi River, to shame.

The men had decided to share a room. As the youngest, Clyde was obliged to sleep on the upper bunk. James won the coin toss with Joseph and chose the double bed, leaving Joseph to sleep on the lower bunk.

Refreshed and ready to go, they still had a few hours before the palaces would close for the day. One of the places they all wanted to visit was the Palace of Transportation. It was at the opposite end of the fair and just across the way from The Pike, which was where most of the entertainment took place. They would enjoy the palace until it closed at 6:00 p.m., then walk over to The Pike for dinner and fun.

The Palace of Transportation resembled a train station, with elaborate arches and high turrets that gave the building a feeling of substance and strength. The red roof stood out in stark contrast to the white structure, the green grass surrounding it softening the look.

"What kind of plaster are all these buildings made out of?" James asked no one in particular.

"I read it's called 'Staff,' and it's made by mixing plaster of Paris and hemp fibers," answered Clyde, opening the fair brochure to check that he was correct.

"You know most of these buildings are gonna be torn down come January," Joseph added. "It's hard to believe."

"I read an article saying some of these palaces are getting worn down by the weather," Clyde said. "Look up there." He pointed to the top of one of the archways. A piece of the ornamentation overhead was missing, but rather than looking as if it had been broken, it looked more like it had melted.

They entered into the fifteen-and-a-half-acre exhibit hall. There were few walls, and the ceiling was held up by hundreds of exposed metal trusses. There were 14 railroad tracks running the length of the building. In the center was a massive revolving turnstile supporting a 160-ton train engine and coal car. The men walked up to it and read on the side "The Spirit of St. Louis."

"Just think of the size of engine it takes to move that thing around in circles. Maybe they'd let us have it when they tear this all down and we could use it on that damn Willow Street Bridge. Think how fast that bridge could open with this much power behind it," said Joseph. They all laughed.

"Yeah, and it could cut right through all those damn lily pads," added Clyde. "Save my boats."

"Well, it would help if Milt could keep his mind on the water and off any young lady who catches his fancy," James laughed.

"That and drinking will be the death of him," Clyde commented. He didn't know how right he was.

They walked over to where French automobiles were on display. As the world's leading car manufacturer, de Dion-Bouton's exhibit was large. The stark metal trusses provided an interesting backdrop for their beautiful cars, many with luxurious finishes and interiors shining brightly.

On the other side of the building was the American automobile exhibit. In stark contrast to the French exhibit, here the ceilings had been draped with striped fabric in an undulating pattern like an open Roman Shade, billowing in the breeze. Ramblers, Fords, Studebakers, and Oldsmobiles were the names they recognized, but there were a dozen manufacturers they weren't familiar with, such as Baker Motor Car, Knox Automobiles, Pope Motor Car Company, Consolidated Motor Company, and many more.

"Look at that old thing!" said Clyde, walking over to a car standing off by itself. He read the plaque: "First successful gasoline powered automobile created in 1893 by Elwood Haynes of Haynes, Apperson Company of Kokomo, Indiana." The wheels were large and there was only space for the driver to ride. "It looks like somebody just took away the horses from my old wagon and fancied it up."

"You had to sit up mighty high with not much to grab onto, and back then the roads were made for wagons. Looks dangerous," said Joseph, stepping back and shaking his head.

There were 160 cars on display, many of which were for purchase. Ford was showing off its latest, the Model C. It had a front and a back seat, along with two side oil lamps and a large horn attached to the post. Another version had a leather top that was lined with cloth and had side curtains.

"That's mine right there. Might be able to keep some of the mosquitos out with those curtains. I could fit my whole family in there!" Clyde said as he walked over to the other side and opened the door, this time stepping inside and sitting down.

James stuck his head in. "Never knew you were such a fancy man there, Clyde. You better hope business stays good if you wanna be buying such nice things."

"It's only gonna get better!" exclaimed Clyde, smiling grandly and looking off to the side.

They could easily have spent a few more hours in the Palace of Transportation but were forced to cut their visit short and walk over to The Pike, where the evening entertainment was already underway.

The Pike was the hub of entertainment at the fair. It was a mile long and could accommodate more than 20 people walking abreast. Unlike the rest of the fair, The Pike was meant not so much to teach as to amaze, frighten, and engage. When they arrived at the east entrance, they were greeted by the amazing statue by Frederic Remington, "Cowboys Shooting Up a Western Town." The statue consisted of four cowboys wearing their hats, on horseback, all with their arms extended up into the air, holding pistols and firing.

"Have you ever seen anything look so real?" asked Joseph as they stood in awe.

"Each one has a personality," Clyde observed.

"The cowboys or the horses?" asked James.

"Both," Clyde replied seriously. "And look at their legs—one… two…three…four…five…six, look, only six hooves are touching the ground. How is that possible?"

James shook his head. "Looks to me like they was having a fine time!"

They all laughed and agreed. They entered the Cummins' Wild West Show, where they saw a reenactment of the Custer massacre at Little Bighorn. They were told that some of the Indians in the reenactment had been present at the actual battle.

Clyde, having helped during the cleanup after the Galveston Hurricane, was curious to see how it would be depicted in the "Galveston Flood" exhibit. The exterior resembled a large fire station. Inside, a combination of miniatures and murals made for a realistic look of the town. There were trains running, boats sailing, the sun shining, and then it all changed. Heavy clouds gathered, and the wind and rain bombarded the city. The exhibitors had decided not to show the gory details of the tens of thousands of deaths, but instead ended with the new and better Galveston that had come out of the ruin.

"That narrator was really good," said Joseph.

"Well, Clyde, did it look like that?" asked James.

It was difficult for Clyde to disengage his mind from that horrible ordeal he had witnessed. "Yeah, it sorta looked like that." Clyde shook his head, hoping that would clear his mind.

"Hey! Look! Let's go do some shootin'!" James cried, pointing to a sign that read, "Hunting in the Ozarks."

"Sure. I'll wager you I can outshoot you with my eyes closed," Joseph bragged.

"You're dreamin'? When have you ever outshot me?"

"Well," Joseph answered, "there was that time...."

"You just keep dreamin'. Let's go! What's your wager?" James put his hand in his pocket and took out some coins.

Joseph thought for a moment. "Fifty cents."

James laughed heartily. "Not much for a sharpshooter like you!"

"Okay, okay, a dollar," Joseph said.

"You're a real high-stakes player, aren't you? Okay. A dollar it is." The two men shook on it.

Clyde had been silent throughout this exchange. "You both know what a lousy shot I am. I'll leave y'all to do the shootin'; I'm going over to have my palm read."

"You know those fortune tellers on Royal Street are better than some pretender in St. Louis," said James.

"I know, I know, I just like doin' it. It'll be interesting to see what she says."

The men separated, and Clyde found himself in the familiar surroundings of a palm reader's milieu. After her initial perfunctory sentences about his being married and having a big family, she stopped and looked him in the eye for what seemed like a long time.

"I see water all around you. You are not drowning. I see you floating; yes, you are floating. Look at your face; you are smiling, even laughing. You love this water." She sat back in her chair but did not release her grasp on Clyde's hand. He remained silent, intent on her every word. She released his hand, reached back, and produced a crystal ball, which she placed in the center of the table between them. "All this water could be telling me you're an Aquarian, but I don't see that in you; you're too determined." She placed her hands on either side of the ball and sat gazing, engrossed in examining some vision she saw inside of the ball.

"Why is the water so green? I see it flowing down a waterfall and collecting into a pond; now it looks like a lake, now an ocean." She made a motion over the crystal ball with her hands and looked again, deeply, into Clyde's eyes. She raised one eyebrow and smiled a devilish smile. "Ahhh, now I see more clearly. It is money, lots of money. It shall be yours, this money. Your determination will make you a very wealthy man; yes, very wealthy indeed!" She waited for a response, but Clyde didn't want to interrupt her stream of consciousness.

She returned the crystal ball to the table behind her and reached, once again, for his hand. "Your Leo personality will help make this possible," she began again, looking at his palm. "But here, what can I say? It will be fleeting." She took his hand and put it between her hands and squeezed it. "Enjoy your life, every day of it."

Clyde, recognizing that she was finished, asked her, "What is fleeting?"

"Everything in our lives is fleeting; enjoy this day." She stood for him to leave.

"What's your name?" he asked.

"My name is not important. You will not see me again. Your confidence, your eagerness, and your determination will win you the world, but there are things we cannot change."

Clyde paid her and gave her a large tip. He walked outside into the cool night air, feeling almost dazed. He wanted to remember every word she had said.

"Fleeting. What will be fleeting? What did she see?" he said out loud to himself.

He looked for a place to sit and find his center, but The Pike was packed full of pedestrians. Instead, he found his way to the shooting gallery and went inside to find his friends.

Inside the "Hunting in the Ozarks" exhibit, he walked around until he first heard, then saw, his two friends firing at iron animals that popped out all around.

"Can I join the party?" Clyde asked as he walked up to them.

"This is somethin' else," said James, smiling. "It's even harder than huntin.'"

"Aw, that's just an excuse 'cause I beat him," Joseph laughed.

"How do you figure?" asked James.

"The numbers don't lie," replied Joseph. "I'll take that dollar now!" Joseph opened his hand and James, fumbling in his pocket, produced the requisite dollar, and with great solemnity, handed it over to Joseph. They exited to The Pike.

"What the hell?" Joseph said as the three men came upon a camel parade. Each camel had a rider trying to stay atop a large, very elaborate saddle.

"Which one of you gentlemen would like to go home with a story of a camel ride?" called the barker.

"That'd be Clyde," said Joseph.

"Not me," Clyde replied. "I'll stick with horses!"

They stopped into the Alexandria Café but, not enjoying the food at all, left almost as hungry as when they went inside.

"I just cannot get past the smell; those spices turned my stomach!" James said.

"Oh, come on; the lamb was tasty," Clyde objected.

"I'll stick with their bread. What did they call it? Here, I wrote it down: *eish merahrah*. What about them using it like a damn fork?" Joseph added.

"I say we go back to the Inn and get something American to eat!" James said.

The Intramural Railway got them to their destination. Along the route, they saw the Palace of Electricity, which was a stunning sight all lit up in the darkness.

"I wonder how much it costs to keep that building lit up like that all night?" Clyde mused.

"I'm just glad I'm not payin' the bill," Joseph replied sleepily.

It had been a long day. Their stomachs full, they decided to retire to their room and get some sleep.

They spent their days wandering from exhibit to exhibit, palace to palace, and country to country. They saw the Liberty Bell, brought in from Philadelphia. The log cabin President Lincoln lived in as a child was on display. Next to the Palace of Agriculture, the beautiful Floral Clock was 112 feet in diameter. The Temple of Fraternity attracted all three men, who were Masons. The huge Philippine exhibit was very popular. The United States, having recently acquired the islands as spoils of the Spanish-American War, used this opportunity to show off this latest prize. They ate lunch in the Great Anthracite Coal Mine, which was underground, simulating a real coal mine. In Festival Hall, they saw the world's largest pipe organ.

"Imagine the sound of that thing coming across the bayou!" said Clyde.

"Every gator within 10 miles would find cover!" James laughed. "I bet you could play that thing in the middle of the Atchafalaya Basin and folks would hear it clear to New Orleans!"

Clyde went off on his own from time to time. His friends weren't interested in seeing pieces of Queen Victoria's Jubilee gifts, which included jewelry made with magnificent precious stones; carved boxes of ivory and ebony, gold, and silver filigree; and even the world's finest elephant saddles. He marveled at the craftsmanship and wondered how many years it had taken to make just one of these pieces. He longed to show it all to Jennie and to be able to adorn her with a piece of exquisite jewelry. *I will*, he thought. *Just watch me!*

Clyde shamed his traveling companions into visiting the Palace of Fine Art.

James complained, "You know, Clyde, paintings and sculptures are a little too highbrow for me."

"I have to agree with him for a change, Clyde. There's nothin' that makes me want to spend time in here," Joseph said.

"A little culture will do you good. I'll give each of you a quarter if you don't find something in here that you like, or at least appreciate. Humor me."

"Okay," said James, "I'll use your quarter to buy one of those hot dogs I see all over."

"Right! And I've been wantin' to try one of those ice cream cones," said Joseph. "I can walk around eatin' my ice cream and seein' the sights!"

They spent hours there. It took some coaxing from Clyde to get them to start really looking at the beautiful paintings, etchings, sculptures, and the like, but after some time, they were all three going through the rooms unhurriedly.

When they exited the building, James took a quarter out of his pocket. "Here you go! You were right. A little culture didn't hurt us."

"But…" Clyde began.

"Yeah, here's mine," said Joseph. "Just don't tell any of our friends back home!"

"I didn't say you had to pay me if you liked it," Clyde reminded them.

"Seems fair, that's all," said James. "Now let's go undo some of this culture!"

They strolled to The Pike and gawked at their first belly dancer, tapped their feet to the new ragtime music of Scott Joplin, and became familiar with the words to "Meet Me in St. Louis, Louis!" Clyde bought them all hot dogs followed by ice cream cones, which they ate while watching the Devil Dancers from Ceylon perform their ritual dance.

Their last stop was the Ferris wheel, which was called The Observation Wheel. It had been made for the Columbian Exposition in Chicago in 1893 and made its way to St. Louis for this fair. It stood 264 feet tall and made four revolutions per hour. There were 36 wooden cars, each with an attendant. If all the riders stood up, 2,160 people could ride at one time. Many weddings had been performed here.

"Now this is something to see," stated Joseph as they finally made it to the top.

"Good thing I'm not bothered by heights or surely I'd pass out," James said.

Clyde wondered how he could describe this to his children back in Franklin.

As they exited the ride, they happened upon an automobile parade. Clyde was excited at the prospect of what this new mode of transportation was going to mean for all of them. Each car was remarkable in its own way.

The next day, Clyde talked them into going to the Irish Village. His family had come from Ireland only two generations before. "My grandfather came here from Sligo, Ireland. He graduated from the University of Dublin." So, Clyde played tour guide, explaining things as they went. They entered through a large archway, a replica of the St. Laurence Gate of Drogheda. It had two high towers with crenulations from atop which they had a clear view of any potential threat from the sea.

Outside was a replica of the Blarney Stone. There was even sod and soil brought over from Ireland to help with the effect.

"What's that big rock?" asked Joseph.

"That's the Blarney Stone! They say if you kiss the Blarney Stone, you'll get the gift of 'eloquence,' which means smooth talking," explained Clyde, laughing.

"So that's where you get it," replied James.

Just then, a large Irish band began to play "A Nation Once Again." Clyde was elated, and, to his friends' amazement, started to sing along. When he finally finished, his friends teased him.

"Captain Clyde Barbour, famous Irish singer and storyteller," James marveled, and then began to laugh heartily.

"Who taught *you* to sing?" asked Joseph.

"You're both jealous that I have a heritage to be proud of," Clyde said.

"So that's what it is, heritage," James replied. "I thought it was the mating call of the red-tipped, striped-belly vulture."

Even Clyde had to laugh at that.

For lunch, they ate Irish stew and soda bread in a reproduction of the Old Irish House of Parliament. Afterward, they went to the shops for Clyde to buy some small things for his family, who, he realized, knew almost nothing about their Irish roots. There were fine linens, silks, flags, and small Blarney Stones, of course.

As they were leaving, the band began to play "The Wind That Shakes the Barley" and both men pushed Clyde to the exit without comment.

Clyde's last solo outing was to the French Pavilion. They had passed it many times, an impressive reproduction of the Grand Trianon, which had been one of Napoleon XIV's favorite residences. The grounds were beautifully planted, many of the plants and trees sent over from France. On the ground floor, he strolled through the picture gallery, each painting more beautiful than the last. He saw the billiard room and the many salons full of delicately carved furniture with lavish upholstery. There were elaborate paintings on the ceilings with ornate molding outlining each one. He studied closely the ornate pieces of Sevres porcelain that filled two rooms, as well as other rare vases, statues, jewelry, and glasswork. There was even what was said to be a lock of Napoleon's hair. Clyde was skeptical.

He lingered longest in the Grand Central Salon, an imposing room lined with Gobelin tapestries. He walked down the center of the salon, awestruck. The wide room was devoid of furniture except for three large upholstered oval benches with a back cushion in the middle and heavy fringe that hung to the floor. The ceilings were, once again, covered with frescoes and intricate molding. Elaborate sconces hung on the walls in between the tapestries, and on the walls opposite them, large curtained windows let in the light.

He sat on one of the fancy stools and gazed intently at the tapestries; the colors, the faces, the detail. He shifted around to take it all in. He sat on each stool, then walked up as close as the rope would allow him and examined the work more closely. He did this with each tapestry in turn, fascinated and intrigued.

"G-o-b-e-l-i-n!" He spelled the name out loud. "Jennie has to have one of these, too!" He grinned and exited the salon on his way to rejoin the real world.

The trip home was uneventful but fun as they relived their time traveling around the world in St. Louis. It would be difficult to describe to the people back in Franklin—impossible probably. The world now looked different to these men whose eyes had been opened to possibilities they'd never even dreamed of. Clyde realized how little he really knew and how much he wanted to travel and witness for himself all the spectacle the world had to offer.

CHAPTER 25

THE CONSEQUENCES

"Lena, fix your little sister's dress. Clyde, Jr., put your shoes on. Where's Jesse?" Jennie was doing her best to stay focused.

"Jesse's lookin' for his hat, Mama," said Lena.

"His hat? He doesn't need his hat! Jesse!" Jennie called out. "Come here!"

"Mama," said Jesse as he came into the front parlor, "look, I got my hat!" he said proudly.

"Jesse, we're not goin' anywhere; you don't need your hat."

"But Mama, you said to get all dressed up, and men, when they're all dressed up, wear hats!" Jesse answered emphatically, patting the hat on his head.

"And you look very handsome. Does your daddy wear a hat when he's inside the house?" Jennie asked her firstborn.

"Well," he thought, "no…I guess not. But I like it!"

Jennie finished tying his brother's shoes and then walked over to Jesse. She put her hand on his shoulder and spoke, a serious tone in her voice. "Well, you know it's not polite to wear a hat inside a building. See that small book on the table over there?" She pointed to the table. "What's the title?"

Jesse stepped over to the table, picked up the book, and read the title out loud: *Etiquette for the Lady and the Gentleman.*

"Yes. And if you look inside, you'll see where it says that gentlemen take their hats off before goin' into a building. Do you want to be a gentleman like Daddy?"

"Of course, Mama. I wanna be just like Daddy."

"Then take that hat off your head and put it back in your room quickly. Daddy will be here anytime now." She patted him on the back, and he slowly returned to his room. Grannie purposefully stayed in her room to give the family special time with their returning father.

Clyde had been gone for two weeks. It was a longer than average time away, and Jennie missed him terribly. Elizabeth was in the kitchen cooking shrimp stew, which gave their little yellow house an extra measure of welcoming. Everything had to be just right because the captain was coming home!

Lena was the one who heard the carriage pulling up to the house. With much giggling, they all got in place where Jennie had told them to stand so Clyde could see them all clean and dressed and smiling.

The door opened and Clyde stepped inside, took off his hat, and stood smiling at his progeny. "These can't all be my family! How could one man have such a good-lookin' bunch of children and such a pretty wife?" He got down on one knee, opened his arms wide, and the children all ran to him. In short order, he was covered with love from the adoring bunch. He stood up and, walking over to Jennie, took her into his arms, bent her back, and gave her a long kiss on her lips. The children all laughed and ran up to them. Jennie stood up, rearranging her hair with her hand and blushing deeply.

Man, now the official "chauffeur," stood at the door smiling, his cap in his hand. "This gots to be the craziest white folk I ever did see!" he claimed, laughing.

"Come on in, Man," said Clyde.

"No, sir, Clyde Barbour. I's hongry so I gots to put up that ole horse and get back to de kitchen," Man replied.

"Okay, me too!" Clyde said. "It smells delicious in here. What's Elizabeth got on the stove?"

"Shrimp stew," said Elizabeth, who had just stepped into the parlor. "And it's ready to eat. Welcome home, Cap'm Barbour."

"Thanks, Elizabeth. I've had some strange things to eat lately; can't wait to have your good home cookin'! Let's go eat!" Clyde said to his children, and they all headed to the dining room, each one trying to get his or her father's attention.

Clyde entertained his family with stories of the World's Fair. "It was like a huge city that somebody had painted all white! Big, beautiful white buildings everywhere you looked. And one gigantic lake they made called the Grand Basin. There were boats brought all the way from Italy that were in that lake. Things from all around the world."

Clyde's stories didn't end until it was well past their bedtimes. With them all tucked into their beds and Elizabeth and Man gone, the two adults finally had time alone. He took his shoes off and sat on their bed watching her. She was telling him what had happened while he was away, but he didn't hear a word she said. He watched as she unpinned her hair and brushed it. He stood up, took the brush from her hand, and brushed it for her, knowing how much she loved that; her mother had brushed her hair and sung softly to her when she was a child. Her eyes closed and she leaned back against him. Clyde whispered in her ear how much he loved her and had missed her. He kissed her ear. She turned to face him and fell into his embrace. They kissed, hungry for each other, every inch of their bodies pressed together. He put his hands on her buttocks and pushed her deeper into him. She rubbed her hands up and down his back and kneaded the back of his neck.

"Come to me," he said, picking her up and carrying her to the bed where he playfully threw her down. She laughed softly. He leaned over her and began to unbutton her white ruffled blouse. She sat up and returned the favor, unbuttoning his shirt. As they undressed, they threw their clothes around their bedroom. When finally they lay together naked in each other's arms, Jennie was eager to please her husband. It was their new way of making love, all the intimacy life could afford them without the ultimate connection of his being inside of her. Doctor's orders. In their bliss, in their longing, perhaps they went too far.

As they fell asleep still entangled in each other's arms, Jennie hoped they hadn't been too careless; Clyde prayed his lapse in judgment wouldn't cost the woman he loved her life. He barely slept.

The next morning when the children were eating breakfast, Clyde walked in carrying some bags. He stood at his end of the table and with a big smile on his face, said, "Good morning! I bought each of you a little present at the World's Fair." Jesse pushed his chair back to run to his father's side, but Clyde stopped him. "Hold on there, son. Wait your turn. Ladies first!"

Grannie, being the matriarch of the family, was first, followed by Jennie. Everyone had a turn, including Elizabeth.

"I need to get going. Where's Elizabeth?"

"I'll get her," said Lena, who returned holding Elizabeth's hand.

"Look at all dem gifs," she said, seeing paper and trinkets all over the table. The children all vied for her attention.

"Hold on, hold on," cried Clyde. "I didn't forget about you and Man." He handed her a circular fan with a painting on it.

"Why, Cap'm Barbour, it's the Gold Dust Twins painted on this here fan!" Elizabeth was smiling from ear to ear. "This gots to be the prettiest fan I ever did see! Look at all that gold on there!"

"It says, 'The Gold Dust Twins at the World's Fair St. Louis USA 1904.' I thought you'd like it!" said Clyde.

"Like it? I loves it!" she exclaimed. "I thanks you kindly."

"You're welcome. Now, please tell Man to bring up the wagon and I'll get to working!" Clyde said.

The children accompanied him to the front door and all hugged him goodbye. The yellow wagon pulled up with Man driving the horses, and Clyde was gone.

"Hello, Man. Thanks for taking such good care of my family while I was gone," Clyde said as the two sat up on the wagon. Clyde wanted Man to feel important in this world, where a young Black man was lucky to be a servant rather than a day laborer out in the field.

Both were a big step up from being a slave, owned and beholden to some white man for his very existence, something Clyde had always wrestled with internally. He owed it to Luke to take care of Man, and he felt it deep down in his soul.

"Thank ya, Clyde Barbour! I tries my best!" He was smiling at the compliment.

"I brought you somethin' back from the fair." Clyde handed Man a small metal container. Man turned it over and over. "That's one of the palaces there. That palace had all kinds of things about mines and metal. Look what it does." Clyde took it back, took off the top and expanded the bottom into a cup. "It's a travel cup, Man! You fold it all up and keep it in your pocket. You'll always have a cup on you!" Clyde was obviously excited about this gift.

"I never seen nothin' like it!" Man exclaimed. He collapsed it then opened it up again several times. "This musta cost ya a bundle! I'm gonna hide it somewheres so nobody steals it." He got a serious look on his face.

"No, no!" exclaimed Clyde. "I want you to use it all the time! You'll be the only man around with a metal cup he keeps in his pocket!"

"That's a crazy idea, Clyde Barbour, but I likes it!" He folded it up and put it in his pocket. "I thank ya. Now we needs to get goin'," Man said as he signaled the horses to move on.

It was now 1905, and Clyde was building his businesses and starting new ones. He bought one of the first automobiles in Franklin, a Model C Ford like the one he'd seen at the fair, and had learned to dress the part. He had begun to enjoy dressing up, wearing suits, ties, and hats. He made quite a statement driving down the dirt road in his new car; everyone stopped to gawk, and Clyde enjoyed the attention. He had paid $1,000 for the car. He didn't tell Jennie how much it cost; he knew she wouldn't understand. He also knew that in order to be wealthy, he needed to look and act wealthy. He looked at the automobile as an investment in their future. Sometimes, when he visited another city on business and took his Ford, it was written about in the newspaper. He liked having his name in the paper; he'd worked hard to be someone of note and planned to keep going, no end in sight.

On a cold, wet day in February, Clyde got home early to find Jennie on their bed crying quietly into her pillow. "What happened? Come here," he said, as he lay down next to her and pulled her close.

"Well, I wanted to be sure before I told you," she said meekly.

That was all it took for Clyde to know exactly what she was talking about. "Oh, no, Jennie. Please tell me…not that, please!" he begged.

"It's true. I'm pregnant." That was all she got out before beginning to cry again.

"Let's think. Let's think," was all that Clyde could say.

"Think about what? We're havin' a baby and there's nothin' else to say." Jennie sat up, wiped the tears from her eyes, and smoothed out her hair. "Clyde, we're supposed to have this baby, or it wouldn't be comin.'"

"Or I was just too stupid to act like a man. I'm so sorry I didn't take better care of you. I'm so sorry!" Clyde's eyes filled with tears. He sat up next to her and held her hand.

"My sweet Clyde, we both made this baby. We know what's gonna happen, so we'll do what needs to be done." She got that determined look on her face that showed up so rarely those days.

They waited until the next month, March, to tell the children. As had always been the case, it was exciting news to be adding another sibling to the pack. No one knew how frightened the parents were.

They went together to see Dr. Smith. "We talked about this after your last two deliveries. Do you remember what I told you? Jennie almost died when Lilly was born. I may not be able to save her this time. I'm so angry with both of you—but especially with you, Clyde. It's the man that leads the sex; you and I both know that." The doctor shook his finger at Clyde. "I'm inclined not to deliver this baby. I don't want to be part of all this. You've put me in an impossible situation!" He got up from behind his desk and paced back and forth a few times.

"Dr. Smith, I'm embarrassed that this happened. I can promise you it will never happen again," Clyde said, which made Jennie begin to whimper. "I can pay you whatever you need!"

"Pay me? Is that what you think? That you can buy your wife's safe delivery? It doesn't work that way. Only God can make that happen!"

"I…I just meant…if there's something special she'll need that might help, I will buy it. You know Jennie. You're the only doctor we would trust. Please tell me you'll help us. Jesus was merciful to those who wronged him and repented. Please, Doctor!"

The silence that followed seemed to go on for hours. Dr. Smith sat down in his chair, rested his head in his hands and thought… then thought some more. "I feel it's my duty to deliver this baby. But I tell you now, I won't deliver another one, Jennie. You'll have to have this baby in the hospital and stay there after it's born until I say different. And no sneaking in, Clyde…no sneaking in. You hear me? Both of you?"

They accepted the terms in tandem.

"I want to see both of you here in my office once a month. Hear me?" Dr. Smith spoke with authority.

"Yes, sir, we will. I promise," Clyde replied. Dr. Smith looked at him with his head to one side, as if to mock the promise.

"Maybe we can figure out what makes your bleeding get so bad. No promises. Do *not* disappoint me again," said Dr. Smith, who stood to dismiss the nervous parents. "Go to church and pray to God. That's all you can do now." And they did.

CHAPTER 26

THE GRIS-GRIS

March 1905

The next month, Clyde was to travel to New Orleans to attend a meeting of the Mystic Shrine. Dr. Smith was one of the men in the entourage, along with an additional eight upstanding businessmen from the area. Clyde planned to keep his distance from Dr. Smith.

While he worked hard to be a part of their club, he still had to make a conscious effort not to feel inferior. Mostly, he didn't want to leave Jennie, but it was his job to be out providing for his family; no one was going to do it if he didn't. He knew that a large part of success is who you know. His raw wisdom and charm, along with his devotion to his various ventures, were what had propelled him so quickly up that ladder.

Was it vision or good luck? Maybe it was the shamrocks! When John D. Rockefeller of the Standard Oil Company bought up all the independent fields around Beaumont, the money Clyde had scraped together and borrowed to buy into Spindletop early on came back to him many times over. Some of that money he used to buy more boats, some to buy property where he planted the new crop of St. Mary Parish—rice. It actually grew better here than in what were called the "ideal rice parishes." Farmers began planting rice around 1903, when the sugar cane crop became less profitable as the price of sugar went down. His rice fields were very profitable, as were the hundreds of acres of sugar cane fields he also owned. The livestock business was a solid business but had yet to show the profit he had expected. The island where they grazed was inexpensive real estate, and although it was a little remote, he had all the boats he needed to take the livestock to market.

There was no stopping Clyde. In April, he was appointed vice president of the new Riggs Cypress Company, Inc., which was formed in Franklin. His friend, Wilson Peterman (president of the Kyle Lumber Company), now a senator, was elected president of the company. They bought out most of the existing cypress timber from companies and individuals and purchased the Trellue Cypress Lumber Company, all for $245,750. The new company would be using the Trellue sawmill plant and updating all of its facilities.

The next month he bought stock in Planter's Hardware Company in Franklin. The capital stock of $25,000 was cut up into 250 shares at $100 each. Clyde was put on the Board of Directors. He knew that the more sources of income he had, the better. It helped stabilize his financial portfolio and balance the risks.

Still, his mind wandered to Jennie. What would he do without her? How would he live with himself if she died in childbirth? He had to do something. While he was in New Orleans, he took time to visit his favorite palm reader for help. He'd been in and out of New Orleans most of his life and knew all about the voodoo practiced there. He'd seen people of all ages and backgrounds get help from the local practitioners, of whom there were many. The palm reader said she could help him and knew what he needed before he asked.

"It's for your wife, I know. She makes too much blood when the baby comes. I will make a special gris-gris for her to wear and one for you, too. Be sure to rub it every day to bring out the blessing. Come back in an hour and they will be ready."

Clyde found himself shaking as he walked out into the daylight to have some lunch. His stomach wasn't in the mood for a lot of food.

He went down Royal Street, took a right on St. Peter's, and headed to Jackson Square. Café du Monde would be perfect. There was never a bad time for hot café au lait and beignets. After reading *The Times-Picayune*, he returned to Royal Street to retrieve his gris-gris.

She handed him two small muslin bags tied at the top. "What's in here?" Clyde asked.

"It is my special blend for both of you. Rattlesnake root for protection from sudden death; very important motherwort, which is a very strong protector; lavender to protect the baby; clove for a catalyst and many other powders, a talisman, and things that you do not need to know about. Both of you should wear it near your heart and be sure to rub it every day to freshen it. I put something different in yours—alfalfa for success in money, and bergamot, which will bring you luck through your intuition."

Clyde thanked her several times. He paid her the $2 she charged, then pulled out his wallet a second time and gave her an extra dollar, feeling that somehow that might make the gris-gris work even better.

When he returned to Franklin, he sat on the bed with Jennie and explained to her what he had done. "There has to be something to all of this. People have been doing this for hundreds of years," he explained.

"It won't hurt," Jennie agreed. "What do I say if the children see it?"

"They'll be excited to hear you have a good luck charm around your neck," Clyde laughed.

"Yes, and that won't scare them. I don't want to have to start talkin' about hexes and stuff." Jennie put it around her neck and wore it as she was told. *If Clyde thinks it's important, then so do I.*

As of July, Clyde refused to leave Franklin. The baby was due in the middle of August. Everything was planned. Jennie had told the children that she would be having the baby in the hospital for the first time. They even went to see the hospital. Grannie would be at home with the children, along with Elizabeth and Man. Jennie wasn't sure which would be more comfortable for the short ride from the Little Yellow House to the hospital, the buggy, or their new automobile.

Clyde decided on the yellow buggy. He busied himself trying to prepare for all possibilities.

On August 14, Jennie's water broke. Man went to find Clyde, and the excitement grew as they waited. Jennie found herself caught up in it until she remembered what lay ahead. She spoke to each child individually. Lilly was not letting her mother go without her. She gave some directions to Elizabeth that they both knew were unnecessary, but it kept Jennie busy.

When Clyde arrived at the house, flustered, he raced to Jennie. She smiled warmly, took his arm, and kissed his cheek.

"Are you wearing your necklace?" She nodded. "Let's go," he said. "Now, you children behave. You can all come see the baby after it's born." He held Jennie's elbow and led her out the front door. Lilly was crying and holding onto Jennie's skirt. Jennie couldn't bend over, so Clyde picked the child up, soothed her, and let her kiss her mother before turning her over to her very capable grandmother.

It took both Man and Clyde to get Jennie into the buggy. "I be drivin' mighty slow, Clyde Barbour, so I donts bump y'all too much," said Man.

"Good," Clyde said. He put his arm around his wife, and she rested her head on his shoulder. No one spoke a word.

"Captain Barbour," said the nurse at the reception desk. "We've been expecting you!" She smiled at Jennie and then turned to Clyde. "The doctor arranged a special room for you to sit with your wife until the baby's ready to come. Follow me." The special room was partly for Jennie's comfort and partly to keep Clyde from interfering with the orderly flow of the place. *Maybe being a Shriner like the old doc is paying off!*

He walked to the front door and told Man he could go home. Jennie and Clyde followed the nurse through the once-forbidden doors and back into a hospital room that had a bed and a chair. The nurse helped Jennie change into a hospital gown and got her comfortable in the bed. Her contractions had begun and were coming five minutes apart. She was very uncomfortable. Clyde held her hand and told story after story to try and keep her mind off of her pain. Twice, the nurse told Clyde it was time for him to go, and twice Clyde refused. She appeared once again to check Jennie. As she straightened the sheets, she gasped and then tried to pretend that nothing had happened.

"Let me go get Dr. Smith so he can check on you," said the nurse with what she hoped was a smile.

"What is it? What's wrong?" demanded Clyde, who never missed anything.

"I'm sure it's fine; I'll just get Dr. Smith."

Clyde pulled back the sheet and saw blood—a lot of blood—on the sheet. "Oh my God, what's happening?"

"You know, Captain Barbour, that women bleed, a lot, when they're giving birth, so calm down," she said authoritatively as she quickly left the room.

Clyde and Jennie stared at each other blankly. "You're going to bleed; we both know that," he said in a matter-of-fact tone.

"Clyde, Clyde, I'm scared," she said softly as another contraction hit.

Dr. Smith came swiftly through the door and took over. "Clyde, sit down," he insisted. Clyde obeyed as the doctor examined Jennie. He gave the nurse some orders and she left the room. "It's time to get this baby out. She's bleeding before the birth this time; that's not good."

"Jennie, I'm here. I love you. We'll do this together like we always do!" Clyde tried to comfort his wife.

"We're taking her into the operating room. And you, Clyde, cannot come in there, do you hear?"

"I will not—"

The doctor cut Clyde off. "You will do exactly what I say. I can't deal with you and your wife. For Christ's sake, stay here or go out front."

Clyde went over to Jennie. "I'm gonna wait right here. I will pray, and I will know that both of you will be all right. It's the good luck of the Irish! Let's both rub our gris-gris." He tried hard to smile and so did she.

"Clyde, I love you. You're my hero. You saved my life more than once. I'll bet on the good luck of the Irish." They kissed and she went into another contraction. And then they whisked her away.

Clyde sat down again and put his head in his hands. As he raised his head, he saw drops of blood on the floor. He got down on his knees, closed his eyes, and prayed to God. He began to cry. Once again, he rubbed his gris-gris intently and held it to his heart.

After some unknown amount of time, the nurse walked into the room. Clyde stood up quickly in a daze. In her arms was a baby swaddled up in a blanket. "Here's your son, Captain Barbour. He's healthy and beautiful." She handed the bundle to him, and he smiled through tears of relief and joy.

"Hello, son. I'm your daddy!" Clyde said softly as he stroked the baby's face. He looked at the nurse and asked, "How's my wife? Can I see her?" The nurse took the newborn from him. "She's doing as well as she can be," was the deflecting answer. "You'll have to wait until Dr. Smith says it's okay to see her."

"Please, would you please go ask him now?"

"He's still working on her. You'll have to wait a little longer." The nurse left the room with the newborn.

Clyde couldn't wait any longer. He looked out the door and, seeing no one, proceeded down the hall toward the operating room. He knew that if he made it to that door, he could get in there to see her. As he opened the door, the nurse came rushing out of the OR. "Don't you dare go in there!" she hissed. "I'm going to get the other doctor for help."

She raced on and Clyde entered the room. "What the hell are you doing in here?" asked the doctor brusquely.

"I had to see her. I had to see how she's doing," Clyde answered meekly.

"It's just like last time—I can't stop the bleeding. If you're gonna be in here, try to calm her down," said Dr. Smith. "Take that chair over there and sit next to her. If she's calm, she won't bleed as much."

Clyde gladly did as he was told. Jennie seemed only half-conscious. She could feel his presence and whispered his name. "Clyde!"

"Jennie, I'm here. You had a beautiful baby boy! He's so tiny and so wonderful." Clyde was stroking her hair. He sat with his back to the doctor so that he wouldn't have to see what he was doing. "Where's your gris-gris? Here, let me rub it. It's working, Jennie, I know it is!" he said, trying to sound confident. He rubbed his again, too.

Jennie began to moan, her head moving from side to side on the bed. She screamed in pain and the doctor started talking to her. "I'm almost finished, Jennie. Hold on a little longer. Give her some more laudanum," he told the other doctor who had arrived to assist. It quickly put her to sleep, but Clyde was not moving. He kissed her cheek and held onto her hand.

He remembered the first time he'd laid eyes on her back on the flatboat; her beautiful auburn hair and sad eyes. Memories flooded his mind; Jennie falling into the Mississippi River and Luke saving her; the first time she gave him their lucky coin; the flatboat burning; bringing Man home with them; the majestic plantation, Oaklawn, that he'd promised her; the beautiful family that they'd made together.... *Please, God, don't let her die. I'll do anything!*

He became aware that the doctors were talking, which brought his mind back to the present. "What's happening?"

"We have it stopped for the moment. That's all we can do." He turned to the nurse. "Take her back to her room. Clean her up without getting near the dressing. Keep the baby here at the hospital. In the morning, we'll try to get him to nurse; that helps tighten up the uterus. Don't let her move. If she wants to see the baby, let her; it will calm her. Any bleeding and you need to send for me."

So Clyde spent the night in a chair next to her bed. He slept off and on, waking whenever Jennie moaned or moved. She was in and out of consciousness and in pain. He was startled awake by the nurse who came in with a tray of food.

"Captain Barbour, you need to eat," she said as she approached him. She put the tray down on a table next to the bed.

"Thank you, but I'm not hungry," he said softly.

"Captain Barbour, you have to eat somethin'." She walked over to him and put her hand on his back. "You can't take care of her if you don't take care of yourself. You have a big family expecting to see you fit as a fiddle. They don't need to be worryin' about their mama *and* their daddy. Here," she handed him a fork; he stared at it. "Come on, Captain." The nurse began to push his chair over to the table.

"You're right, you're right. I just don't know if I can even swallow." He took a small bite, chewed it well, and swallowed.

"Just take it slow. No hurry." She left him to eat.

As he was taking a few bites, Jennie woke up, turned her head, and saw Clyde eating.

"I'm glad you're eatin' somethin'," she said softly.

Clyde stopped abruptly and stood up to see his wife. "Jennie! You're awake!" he said, kissing her on the lips.

"I'm not sure if I am awake. I feel strange. My head hurts," she said, rubbing it. "My whole body hurts."

"Dr. Smith has you all fixed up to stop the bleeding, so be still," insisted Clyde as he stroked her hair. "Does that help?" he asked. "Are you thirsty, hungry, uncomfortable?" Clyde wasn't sure how to help.

"Well," Jennie began, "I'm real thirsty."

"Here, I'll give you some of my water." He held her head up enough to sip the water until she was satiated. "There."

"I'm havin' trouble rememberin' what happened. That's right, we have a new baby boy! Isn't that wonderful?" She smiled through her obvious pain. "Remember we decided if it was a boy, we'd name him William, after Grandpa; William Ellsworth Barbour. Perfect!"

"And he's a fine baby! Now our family is complete." Clyde smiled at his wife. "Three boys and two girls."

Jennie began to cry, overwhelmed by it all. She cried harder and harder. The nurse came in and worked to calm her down.

"Now, Mrs. Barbour, gettin' yourself all twisted up in knots is not gonna help any. You need to calm down so I can bring your precious little boy in here to nurse. You'll be hurtin' there, too, before long if we don't get some of that milk out." She straightened the pillows and the bedding, and she and Clyde got Jennie on her side to nurse. Having something important to do calmed her down and she was eager to see her newborn.

The nurse returned with William swaddled in a soft cotton blanket. She placed the warm bundle next to Jennie, who teased his mouth with her nipple to interest him in nursing. It took a few tries, but in her experienced arms he began to suckle, those first few minutes always so painful. Jennie was happy for the familiar pain in her breasts as her milk rushed in. She knew why they were hurting, what to do about it, and that it would go away in a few days. She knew none of that about the other pain surging through her body.

They fell asleep together, mother and child, each needing the other as Clyde witnessed this living masterpiece, the two of them lying there cuddled together, having enjoyed one of humankind's most primal of instincts.

"Captain Barbour? Why do you stay in here with your wife? This isn't a man's world back in here; it's where women and doctors belong," the nurse asked, puzzled, looking down at him as he sat in the chair next to the bed.

"If it's my wife's world, it's my world. I wouldn't be anywhere else," he answered.

"You're a different kinda man than I've seen here before. A different kinda man." The nurse shook her head as she picked up the newborn, and looking down at William, she continued. "In the nicest kinda way."

Clyde smiled and thanked her as she left the room. It was time for him to go home, change his clothes, and see his other children. He didn't want them to worry about their mother. He stood up and adjusted Jennie's covers again. Something caught his eye. He pulled back the covers and saw bright red blood. He raced to the door and yelled after the nurse, "She's bleeding! Hurry!" She handed the baby to another nurse, told her to get Dr. Smith, and ran back down the hall to Jennie's room.

Jennie was moaning quietly. Clyde wanted to scream, to ask God why this was happening. He wanted answers and he wanted them now. Why was He punishing Jennie? *Please, God, punish me, not her. I knew better. She doesn't deserve this! I beg you! Take me, not her. I'll do anything you want!*

Dr. Smith rushed through the door and pushed Clyde aside. The doctor was talking to the nurse in a soft monotone. Clyde stood back and watched as another nurse rushed in with a rolling cart full of metal objects. He had to remind himself to breathe.

Although she was moaning, Jennie luckily was not awake. Clyde's legs felt limp and he sat down on the floor, resting his back on the wall. It was a strange perspective from down there. The ceiling light cast strange shadows around these very large-looking people. He wanted to see Jennie's face, but knew he needed to stay put, so he hung his head down and thought about the family they had made. He could see the children playing in the front yard of the Little Yellow House with the yellow buggy parked in front. He remembered the ecstasy on Jennie's face when he showed her that house for the first time. That was it! He'd buy her a new house when she was better! A bigger, newer house! He would surprise her with it again!

Then his mind went blank, as if it had been unplugged from a wall socket. He searched for Jennie in the nothingness. He heard her cry out! He heard her again. *I have to go to her; I have to hold her hand and talk soothingly to her; I have to at least touch her.* He stood up and then he could see her, could see her face, so white and tortured. He left the security of the wall and walked toward her bed. One of the nurses saw him and guided him into the chair he had occupied earlier. It was no longer next to her bed, but being able to at least see her face was comforting. He could also see the bloody sheets and bandages. There was so much blood! *All because I wasn't careful enough, man enough to leave intercourse alone. Oh, Jennie, please don't leave me!* Tears ran down his face. He leaned forward and reached out to try and touch her or at least her bed, but his arm was knocked out of the way when a nurse walked between him and the bed. He stood up only to feel the nurse's hand on the top of his head pushing him back down. He closed his eyes and prayed. *I'll never do that again!*

Was it hours that went by? Clyde wasn't sure. All the commotion had died down. He stood up again and was able to reach Jennie's bedside without being interrupted. He found himself afraid to touch her. He didn't want to hurt her. He put his hand on her shoulder and when she didn't flinch, he rubbed it lightly.

Dr. Smith stood next to him. "Clyde. We stopped the bleeding again. She's not to move around. The nurses have cleaned her up. I can't promise the bleeding won't start again and if it does, I don't know if we'll be able to do anything else for her. Just pray and try to stay calm. I'll come back in about an hour to check her."

"I don't know what to say, Doc. I'll do anything you say. I'll stay with her every minute, so she has whatever she needs." Clyde was adamant.

"No, Clyde, that's not a good idea. The nurses will be with her constantly. Please go spend some time with your family. You're only minutes away."

"I won't let her out of my sight," the nurse told him.

So, a conflicted Clyde kissed his sleeping wife, told her how much he needed her, and headed home. He thought about his children at home, wondering what was happening. How would he manage with five children if something happened to Jennie? How would he ever live with himself knowing it had been his weakness that led to an unthinkable outcome? He began the walk home. He forced himself to see a world with Jennie in it months from now. He imagined their smiling baby William in her arms. He saw his children smiling and playing. That's how it was going to be. He could feel it. He would be sure it turned out that way.

"Captain Barbour! Where are you headed on this lovely day?" Clyde looked up to see Mrs. Lilly Lucile Berwick, one of his daughter's namesakes, driving her fancy carriage with the horse she had named Clyde, after him.

"Yes, it is beautiful! Jennie's just had another baby boy, and she's staying at the hospital for a bit. I haven't been home since yesterday, I think." Clyde had stopped walking and approached the carriage to talk.

"Climb up and let me give the new father a ride!" She smiled and patted the seat next to her. Clyde thanked her and climbed aboard. As Jennie had said, Mrs. Lilly Lucile Berwick was a beautiful woman, somewhat older than Clyde, and was always immaculately dressed. Today was no exception, her ruffled hat tied under her chin. "You have a full house now! Five lovely children! I've always been sad that the Lord didn't bless me with any children," she said, the smile disappearing from her face.

"I'll lend you one or two from time to time if that would help!" joked Clyde, trying to lighten her mood, even though his was even heavier. "I tell you what; I'll lend you your namesake if you'll lend me mine. An extra horse from time to time couldn't hurt!" They both laughed heartily.

She stopped next to the yellow buggy in front of the Little Yellow House. As he thanked her and said goodbye, she kissed him on the cheek. It startled him and he could feel he was blushing.

"Just a good luck kiss for a fine man," she said, her eyes sparkling. "Oh, don't be such a bluenose," she told him as he looked at her questioningly. "Let me know if I can help while Jennie recuperates."

Clyde was speechless. He managed to compose himself and responded, "How could a man be anything but pleased with a kiss from such a good-looking friend? Thank you for the ride!" Returning to the real world, he dismounted, waved, and walked to the front door, drawing in a deep breath before he entered.

He had barely opened the door before the children came running to him, all talking at the same time. He crouched down and took them into his arms. Elizabeth came out of the kitchen, drying her hands on her apron.

"Cap'm, it's good to see you! How's Mrs. Barbour doin'?" The children stopped talking to hear the answer to that question.

Before he could answer, Grannie appeared and went to Clyde's side. She hugged him. "You make your mama very proud!" Clyde was overwhelmed. He wanted to talk to her and be comforted by her, but there just wasn't time and he was a man now; he should be doing the comforting.

"Little William Ellsworth is doing just fine! He's a cute little thing who just wants to nurse, like the rest of you did!" Clyde began, a smile on his face. "Now, your mama is still feeling poorly. Dr. Smith wants to keep her in the hospital a few more days so he can take extra good care of her!" He hoped his tone was sufficiently upbeat.

"When can we see Mama and the baby?" asked Lena.

"We can all go see William. We'll have to wait another day or so to see Mama," he answered.

"I want my mommie," said Lilly Lucile, who began to cry. Grannie picked her up.

"Your grannie is here, and I'm your daddy's mommie. I promise not to leave you until your mommie comes home. She'll be home soon." That was at least a little bit of solace to Lilly Lucile, whose crying began to abate.

"Cap'm. I know you ain't been eatin' up there, so I'll get somethin' together for y'all to eat. Then y'all can go on to see your new little brother." Elizabeth went back into the kitchen, followed by Clyde, Jr., who was ready to eat.

They made quite an entrance at the hospital, the six of them. Lena and Jesse went straight up to the desk, demanding to see their new little brother. Rather than have them wake up the entire hospital, the nurse found a room for them to congregate in while seeing the baby. Clyde took him first and realized he'd had almost no time with this newest addition to his family. The nurse and Grannie helped all the children hold the baby. Grannie held him and talked to him for a long time.

As they were leaving, the children began to ask to see their mother. The nurse told them she was sleeping, and that Dr. Smith wanted them to wait another day or two before visiting her so she could get her strength back. Lilly Lucile began to cry again and buried her wet face in Grannie's shoulder. Clyde, Jr., began to protest, but Clyde put a stop to it quickly. "We have to do what the doctor says. He's in charge here." And that was that. "I want y'all to go on home. I have some work to do downtown."

"But Daddy, who's gonna drive?" asked Jesse.

"Grannie can drive."

"Grannie is an old woman; she can't drive," Jesse answered emphatically.

"What? Grannie taught *me* to drive! If you don't think your grannie can drive a buggy, you don't know your grannie very well!"

As soon as the buggy—with Grannie driving—was out of sight, Clyde walked back into the hospital. No one tried to stop him any longer from walking through the once-forbidden doors. He walked down the hall to Jennie's room and peeked inside. She was propped up slightly, nursing William. He walked in silently so as not to disturb the suckling duo. Jennie lifted her head and smiled at him. Her warm smile was in stark contrast to her very pale lips. He could see her in there behind her smile, the Jennie he loved and cherished. Tears ran down her cheeks and when she spoke, he could barely hear her.

"I'm gonna be just fine, I know it!" she whispered.

"I know; we still have a lot of life to live together. And don't forget we have to buy Oaklawn and fix it up! You just stay here and do what Dr. Smith tells you to do. Will you do that for me, for all of us? No cheating, okay? I know you're not very good at following orders!"

Jennie smiled and laughed the slightest of laughs. Clyde smiled and felt, for the first time in days, that it was going to work out. *It has to work out!*

After two long, scary weeks, Jennie and William came home. The children had been able to visit her briefly from time to time in the hospital, and now she would be theirs again.

CHAPTER 27

THE NAMESAKE

Yellow fever came to Franklin again in August of 1905. Just weeks after baby William and Jennie moved back home, an outbreak was declared, strikingly reminiscent of 1898 when Jennie almost lost her life. Clyde, as the manager of his Teche Transportation Company, was mentioned in the local newspaper: "Our energetic townsman… donated to the town of Franklin in present emergency 100 barrels of crude oil." Many of the businessmen in town donated what they could, but none were as generous as Clyde. His generosity did not go unnoticed. The townspeople stayed in their homes except when absolutely necessary. This time, no one in Clyde and Jennie's family was affected by the deadly disease.

When the yellow fever scare was over, people began coming to meet the newest addition to the Barbour family. Jennie was still weak and tried to limit her visitors to one or two short visits a day. At times, Leona played hostess and let Jennie sleep. It was one of those days when Milt, still known for wrecking the boat as well as his wandering eye, came to pay his respects to his cousin/boss's newborn. The children, having grown tired of the endless need for polite conversation with the visitors, had been sent off to play at Mrs. Berwick's, who spoiled them all.

Leona opened the front door and was surprised to see a big, burly man with rugged good looks and a friendly smile. She felt herself blushing and invited him in.

"I'm Milt Campbell, Clyde's cousin from Indiana." He took off his hat and walked into the house.

Leona closed the door. "I'm Leona, Jennie's sister from Kentucky." She was holding William and so couldn't shake his hand. "Come in. Do you want some coffee?"

"That'd be real nice," he answered, sitting down on the couch.

Leona went into the kitchen to ask Elizabeth for help with the coffee.

"Let me see the little guy," said Milt enthusiastically. Leona sat next to him on the couch to show him off. "Can I hold him?" he asked, to Leona's surprise.

"Well, okay." She handed the bundle to Milt who looked at once ridiculous and cute cooing to the baby in his arms.

Milt overstayed his welcome, which was fine with Leona, who thoroughly enjoyed his attentions. The children returned while he was still there, including Leona's daughter, Cora, whom she wasn't ready to introduce as such just yet. But when Cora came over to Leona, gave her a hug, and said, "Mama, what's for dinner? I'm hungry," her cover was blown.

"So, this is your daughter? I didn't know you were married," Milt said, a bit perplexed.

"Actually...well...I'm not married now. This is my daughter, Cora." Leona always felt ashamed when she had to relay this piece of information to people.

"Oh." He smiled at Cora. "Hi! I'm Milt Campbell." Cora smiled politely but wasn't the least bit interested in this male stranger.

"He's Uncle Clyde's cousin!" Leona explained as Jennie walked into the room.

"Milt! Good to see you. How's your wife?" Jennie asked, as she had quickly picked up on the energy between Milt and her sister.

"Marguerite is doing just fine. She'll be by to see the baby soon." Milt got up from the couch and walked toward the door. "Thanks for all the hospitality, Leona!" He smiled his big, friendly smile at her. "Bye, all you Barbour children. See y'all soon!" He closed the door behind him. Jennie sat down next to her shocked sister and took William into her arms.

"He's married? Really? I never would have known."

"Yes, he's married, but he takes up with other women," Jennie whispered in her sister's ear. "Stay away!"

Clyde made the trip back to Jeffersonville to take ownership of his latest sternwheeler, the *Jennie Barbour*, and bring her down to Franklin. Since he expected to be away for about a month, he left his brother, James, and his cousin, Milt, in charge of the family. He knew well that his mother, now forever to be known as Grannie, could handle anything that came their way and, along with his Jennie, the two of them would be fine. Even so, he wouldn't have left without some men around to help.

"How much will she set you back?" James asked Clyde before he left.

"$17,000 (Approximately $575,000 in 2023.) and worth every penny," Clyde responded. "After all, it'll be the *Jennie Barbour!*"

The first week of November, the entire family, including Jennie for a change, raced over to the Willow Street docks when they received word that Clyde and his new sternwheeler had moored. She was a beautiful boat with *JENNIE BARBOUR* in capital letters on the sides and smaller lettering on the pilothouse.

"It's a beautiful boat," said Grannie, her pride clearly evident.

"Mama, it has your name on it!" said Lena, always proud to show off her talents.

The sight of the beautiful new boat with her name on it took Jennie's breath away. *How can he love me so much?* she wondered. Her schooling was largely incomplete, she hadn't traveled much, and now they couldn't even get lost in each other's bodies as they always had. Yet, there he was, moving quickly to her side with all the love and caring a man could possess. His long kiss made the children laugh, as always. She knew she needed to say something.

"Oh, Clyde, she's beautiful!" she exclaimed.

"This is all for you and because of you. I love you, Jennie Barbour!" He lifted her up and spun her around.

"Are you talking to me or that new boat of yours?" Jennie asked, and everyone laughed.

The "Jennie Barbour" Sternwheeler

Before the end of that year, Clyde decided there was a possibility of making some money in the tin and sheet iron smithing business; he saw a need for it. He met with Rudolph P. Riddeck, who was known for his expertise in this business and wouldn't require a lot of supervision, and offered him the job of running it. Rudolph accepted, so Clyde went to New Orleans and invested $300 in tools.

More boats meant more manpower. Clyde had begun using convicts to fill the unskilled labor posts on his boats a few years earlier and found it both an inexpensive source of needed workers and a benevolent way of helping others. Milt was working for him, as were James and other more removed relatives and acquaintances. Clyde was known for his firm hand, as well as his equanimity and fairness. Man wanted to work on the boats, but with as much time as Clyde spent away from his family, he needed Man right where he was. Man was not above sulking about his predicament to anyone he thought might he sympathetic. Elizabeth often scolded him, saying, "You got it real good here at the Cap'm's house. You best be quiet and get along!"

Jennie had been seeing less of Leona than usual. One morning, she had Man drive her in the carriage to where Leona and Cora lived. Cora was in school, and Leona was nowhere to be found. Jennie left a note. They drove around Franklin looking for her, but there was no sign. Jennie began to worry. Leona should be at home doing her sewing or maybe at the mercantile buying supplies, but no. Then she spotted her sister, walking hastily up Willow Street from the docks, alone.

"Leona, where have you been? We looked everywhere!" Jennie said when Leona was settled in the yellow carriage.

"Oh, I was just…out, you know, gettin' some air." Leona wasn't looking at Jennie but instead looked down the street.

Jennie knew something was going on. "You better tell me what you're up to, little sister." She turned Leona's head so that they were facing each other.

Leona dropped her head and looked down. "I'm a grown woman. I can do whatever I like!" Her quietly defiant tone surprised Jennie.

"What are you talking about? Of course, you can do what you want. So tell me, what were you doing that's so secret?" Jennie asked. "Is it a man? That would be wonderful! Who is he?" Jennie was suddenly ecstatic at the thought that her sister had found a man.

"Well, yes, sort of," Leona responded. "He's not quite available… you see…he's getting a divorce."

Jennie's hands went up to her mouth and her eyes opened wide in horror. "Please tell me you're not secretly seeing Milt Campbell! Leona, please, no."

"If you tell anybody I'll…I'll…I'll be very upset!" stated Leona emphatically. "We love each other, and we're going to be married! There, I said it. Say what you like, you will never change my mind!"

"But he's married! What about Marguerite?" Jennie was stunned.

"You don't know anything about their marriage. I do! He's been unhappy for a long time. She's very selfish and unkind, and Milt is a wonderful man!" Leona got a dreamy look in her eyes.

"Oh, Leona, I am very sorry for both of you. They have a family together. How will you explain all this to Cora? She'll want to know," Jennie insisted.

"I'll figure it out. We'll figure it out. I've never been happier. Can't you be at least a little happy for me? Don't I deserve to be happy, too?" Leona asked.

"We all deserve to be happy, but not if it means hurting other people. So, when is Milt getting his divorce from Marguerite?" Jennie was shaking her head and feeling guilty. After all, she had brought Leona down here to live.

"In April, and we'll be married in May." The carriage had stopped outside Leona's house, and she quickly descended. "Nobody knows. Please don't tell anybody."

"Don't worry, I don't want to be the one who has to explain this to everyone," replied Jennie. Then she told Man to take her home.

Milt divorced a shocked and horrified Marguerite on April 19, 1906, and married Leona on May 3.

On the last Sunday in July, Clyde and Jennie went for a ride in the car. The sight of an automobile on the streets of St. Mary Parish was still a novelty, so they received a lot of waves and smiles, which they happily returned.

Back in Franklin after their drive, Clyde pulled up to a two-story house just outside of downtown with a long driveway. Built in 1850, the large house at 307 Main Street was set far back from the street and had a covered front porch with latticework for the railing. Three thin, one-story, white columns on either side of the porch were connected by arches at the top. The upstairs jutted out, matching the porch with two large windows in the center.

"I've always liked this house," said Jennie, smiling. "It's so grand! Are we here to call on Mrs. Bloch?" Mrs. Bloch, a widow in her late sixties, had owned this home for a long time. As they drove up the long driveway, Mrs. Bloch came out, waved to them, and waited.

"Mrs. Bloch," said Clyde, removing his hat, "how nice of you to meet us!" Clyde kissed her hand, making her blush.

"Oh, Captain, I'm so excited. Mrs. Barbour, your drive has made your cheeks the prettiest shade of pink," she exclaimed, shaking her hand.

Jennie's hands automatically went up to her cheeks. "Please call me Jennie. Whenever I go by your house, I think how lovely it is!"

"Well, that's just perfect. Come on in, both of you." Jennie walked in and Clyde held the door open for Mrs. Bloch.

The inside of the house was wrapped in the warmth of wood and jewel tones. A beautiful solid mahogany staircase rose up toward the second floor, its newel posts handsomely carved. The oak floors showed little wear. They followed their hostess into the front parlor, beyond which a sunporch jutted out. The large room was sparsely furnished with modern pieces that Jennie found appealing. A housemaid brought in coffee on a silver platter and Mrs. Bloch served them. Their small talk consisted of the house's history, the Barbour children, and the captain's latest steamboat.

"The *Jennie Barbour*...that's so romantic!" Mrs. Bloch sighed. "You're a lucky woman, Jennie!"

Jennie noticed Clyde giving their hostess a nod. Mrs. Bloch stood up and went over to the chest in the corner and pulled out a wrapped package. She took it to Clyde, who handed it to a perplexed Jennie. "It's for you!" Clyde was smiling mischievously.

Jennie quickly opened the box and withdrew their green, white, and gold Ice Water pitcher. She held it by the handle and looked questioningly at her husband. "I don't understand," she said.

Clyde, seated next to her on the settee, put his hand on her shoulder. "Where was the last place you saw this pitcher?"

"Our Little Yellow House," she answered.

"And before that?" Clyde coaxed.

"Well, before that we used it on the steamboat. I plan to use it in every house we have for the rest of our lives," stated Jennie emphatically and then stopped abruptly. "Are you telling me that this is our house?"

"That's why it's here," said Clyde as he stood up, took the pitcher from his wife, and set it down on the table next to the silver service. He helped her up from the couch, held her hand, and made a grand gesture. "This is our new home!"

Jennie gasped. "What are you talking about, Clyde Barbour?"

"I bought this house for you, for us! Mrs. Bloch will be moving to a smaller house at the end of the week." Clyde seemed more excited than Jennie, and Mrs. Bloch was teary-eyed with happiness tangled up in her sadness at moving on.

"But, but it's so big! And lovely, of course. And very grand." Jennie began to walk through the rooms joined by Clyde. Mrs. Bloch left them alone to explore their new dwelling.

Afterward, they drove home and told the children the news. To their surprise, there was little enthusiasm from the youngsters, who mainly wanted to know why they should move from the perfectly good house they already had.

Once they were established in their new house, Clyde had a sidewalk poured all the way from the street to the garage with lights at either end. A telephone was also installed. Only the best and newest for Captain Barbour's family! At night, the children often lit candles, put them on posts, and roller skated up and down the long driveway until they were made to go inside to sleep.

In the backyard was an old cistern, the top of which had been cut off and to which a door was added. Lilly Lucile used it as a playhouse where she spent hours. She especially enjoyed serving Cambric Tea there, which consisted of hot water, milk, and sugar, and reading the Little Colonel series of books to her little brother, whom they now called Will. For his birthday, Jesse was given a St. Bernard, which he named Rex. Lena began to learn how to play the piano, and Clyde, Jr. began to perfect his powers of persuasion.

Clyde diversified even more by putting his friend Ulger Romero, who had been the mill foreman for Kyle Lumber, into the shingle business that continued for many years. Captain Taylor, the man who had horsewhipped Clyde, now had the B.C. Taylor line of boats under contract to Sterling Plantation, which freighted coal, fertilizer, and cooperage materials. Clyde had no problem being happy for Taylor; there was plenty of business to go around.

In April of 1907, it was Clyde's turn to be ill. He was home for several days fighting influenza. When his illness was reported in the local newspaper, it gave Jennie the opportunity to tease him relentlessly about his newly achieved high standing in the community. The biggest problem his illness presented was trying to keep Lilly from contracting it. She had been sick more often than not. Dr. Smith had been closely monitoring her; she seemed to become ill easily and was becoming more and more frail. Luckily, the new house was large enough that Jennie could easily keep the two of them apart.

On June 3, Leona gave birth to a healthy son whom she and Milt also named William and called Billy. Clyde was displeased and embarrassed that his cousin, whom he'd brought down here for a better life, had divorced his wife to marry Jennie's sister. With the birth of their baby, Clyde supposed he would have to change how he felt about the subject, at least outwardly.

Soon after Clyde recovered, he got word from James and Mary, who were living in Houston, Texas, that Pa had shown up in a terribly disturbed state and needed help immediately. Clyde and his mother, Grannie, took the train to Houston together. It had been years since anyone knew Pa's whereabouts. The news that he was still alive brought with it a mixture of relief and dread. "What'll I say to him?" Clyde's mother asked, not looking at her son.

"Ma, he's the one that needs to say something, not you." Clyde put his arm around her shoulders and hugged her.

They arrived at James' house to find that Pa had gone out that morning, so they'd have to wait. The familial banter was forced, and everyone was ill at ease. Ma kept looking out the window for Pa. "Here he is," she stated just above a whisper. He walked through the front door, saw the visitors, and entered the front parlor, smiling as he made his way to his eldest son.

"Clyde!" Pa said enthusiastically. Clyde stood up and embraced the haggard, emaciated, and confused man he barely recognized. "What are you doin' here?" His eyes darted from Clyde to Ma and then to the rest of the people in the room. The smell of alcohol emanated from his pores.

Clyde stumbled over his words. "Came to see you...and Houston. Been hearing this is the place to be to make money!" He faked a smile and in polite deference to Pa, spoke to him as his son. "What about you, Pa? How long have you been here? What are you doing these days?"

"Too many questions, son. Let me take a breath or two." Pa was smiling.

"We're gonna go let y'all three have some privacy," said James. "The wife'll get you some coffee."

Pa sat down in an easy chair, seemingly exhausted. "I've been workin' and workin' and workin' with no time to rest." He put his head back and rested it on the top of the chair. "When you're the man in charge, Clyde, somebody's always wantin' somethin'." He sighed, sat up, and put his hands on his knees. "I own a little place down the street. If it gets any busier, I'm gonna have to hire some more help." He stared out the window.

"What kind of place, Pa?" asked Clyde with trepidation.

"You know the kind of place. A little of everythin'," answered Pa, his words flat. "Have to send money home to your ma."

"I never got any money from you, Pa," answered Ma with a mixture of hostility and bewilderment. "I never even knew where you were!"

Pa stood up, glaring at Ma. "Ma'am, I don't know who you are, but you don't know nothin' about my business with my wife!" The sentence ended in a shout. "Now, I've got to get back to work." Pa started toward the front door.

"Pa, wait!" Clyde jumped up to join his father. "I'm coming with you."

"Oh, no, you're not, son. Nobody there wants to see you. They're like my family now. They can't understand why my own family left me to die in that yellow fever camp. I can't stand to think about it." Pa's expression was that of a wounded soldier trying with every breath to keep himself alive. He began to cough and cry. James came out from the kitchen, looked at Clyde, and shrugged his shoulders. His face distraught, he leaned over to Clyde and said faintly, "There is no place, no store." He went over to Pa and helped him into a nearby chair.

The coughing worsened so much that Clyde thought Pa would stop breathing. With much effort, the brothers got Pa into their carriage and headed to St. Joseph Infirmary on Crawford Street. Before they arrived, his coughing had ceased for the most part, but he was left wailing and crying out for help.

The two men took him in through a gate adorned with a large cross overhead. Pa's coughing resumed as they got him up the steps and into the building, where a nun rushed up and led them into a tiny curtained-off space with a bed on which they placed him. After the brothers had explained the situation, the nun took over and asked them to wait on the other side of the curtain. A doctor nodded at them as he went inside the enclosure. Clyde tried not to listen to what was happening in there.

James told Clyde that Pa had been suffering from delusions. At times, he knew exactly what was going on around him, but at other times he made up crazy stories of people and jobs and all manner of things. And of course, he did a lot of drinking. Grandpa had enjoyed his liquor, too, but Clyde wouldn't have described him as a drunk.

James, however, couldn't hold his liquor at all. Once again, Clyde was reminded why he was especially careful when he did drink alcohol.

When the doctor reappeared, he motioned the men away from Pa's enclosure. "He's asleep now. We'll need to keep him here. His lungs sound good, so I'm not sure where the cough is coming from. Tell me about his drinking."

"I haven't seen him in years," Clyde replied, "but he's always been a drunk. My brother sent word that he'd showed up at his house half crazy, so Ma and I got here as fast as we could. One minute he knows who we are and the next he's telling lies about some business he's running and about us leaving him in some yellow fever camp, and that didn't happen. Oh, and suddenly he doesn't know who Ma is and starts yelling at her. I've never seen anything like it." Clyde felt mentally exhausted.

"That's how he's been since he showed up a week ago," James added. "Okay, then not okay. Then he gets loud and scary. I'm sorry, Clyde, but I can't have him in my house anymore. Mary is pregnant, and it's too much."

"I don't blame you. He's my responsibility, too. Ma and I will stay with you until we figure out what's gonna happen."

Clyde and Ma stayed in Houston for 10 days. The doctor wouldn't allow anyone to see Pa. It had been decided that his cough was a result of a general lack of self-care and probably living in unsanitary conditions.

"His alcohol problem is obvious," the doctor told Clyde and Ma on the last day, "but there's something else going on, some kind of disturbance in his brain. Could have been brought on by his drinking so much for so long." The doctor shook his head, thinking quietly for a minute. "We'll keep him here. He needs to be tended to. I'd say give us four weeks; then come back and we'll see how he's doing."

"Can we see him before we leave?" asked Clyde. He wasn't at all sure he wanted to see his father, but he knew that Ma wouldn't want to leave without doing so.

"No. That will only upset him. Go back home and let us care for him. We'll see you in a month." The doctor patted Clyde on the back, smiled at Ma, and was gone. They left for Franklin the next day.

While they were in Houston, Clyde had made the rounds of the city. He had been there on a few occasions before but only briefly. He was enthralled with all the people and different kinds of commerce. The flat geography reminded him of New Orleans, but nothing else was similar.

He was especially perplexed by what people in Houston meant by "bayou." When Clyde thought of a bayou, he pictured cypress trees and gators. The area in downtown Houston where Whiteoak Bayou and Buffalo Bayou met was called Allen's Landing, but to Clyde, the waterway looked more like a small river. There were plenty of boats making their way up and down the bayous. He decided to return in a few weeks and spend all his time at Allen's Landing before returning to the sanatorium to see Pa and figure out what to do about his nightmarish situation. All he wanted to do right now, though, was to kiss his children good night and sleep with his arms around Jennie.

Back Row: Lena Barbour and Friend,
Front Row: Lilly Lucile, Will and Clyde, Jr.,
Main Street Residence, Franklin, Louisiana about 1908

CHAPTER 28

THE RELOCATION

1908

A few weeks after their return to Franklin, Clyde was notified that his father had somehow sneaked out of the infirmary and couldn't be found. Clyde's emotions were everywhere. He was angry for his mother. *Ma has never done anything but stand by his side, and now he does this.* She cried for days and even the children couldn't make her smile. He was ready to wash his hands of his pa forever.

"I wanna go back to Jeffersonville. That's where I belong," Grannie said when asked what would make her feel better.

"But, Ma, there's no one left up there to take care of you," Clyde objected.

"The children would be very upset if their grannie left," Jennie added. "What would we do without you?"

Grannie teared up, and shaking her head, sank onto a kitchen chair. Her elbows on the table, head in her hands, she took a deep breath. Jennie sat down next to the woman who had been her mother for many years, and Clyde stood with his hands on her shoulders. "I know how you love New Orleans. I need to go down there to see an eye doctor. How about you and Jennie come with me? You can go shopping and have lunch and do whatever you want with no one to take care of but yourself."

"And who's gonna take care of my grandchildren?"

"Elizabeth will take care of them," Jennie assured her, "and Man can take them to school and home. Mrs. Berwick is always wanting to help. And there's Leona and Milt." Clyde raised his eyebrows at that, but only Jennie could see. "Will stopped nursing months ago. We'll be gone for less than a week. It's settled!" Jennie stated with conviction.

The three of them set off for New Orleans, Jennie hiding her tears at leaving the children behind.

The Monteleone Hotel in the French Quarter on Royal Street had become so popular that by 1908 it had to be rebuilt to accommodate more guests, which was unfortunate timing. Clyde had always wanted to stay there but had never had the funds. So he'd made reservations at the Grunewald Hotel, which had just added a new tower at the cost of $2.5 million and was said to be fabulous. Taking their finest clothes, the three hitched a ride on the *Jennie Barbour*.

The Grunewald's lobby was so elaborate that Jennie and Grannie stopped dead in their tracks upon entering, making it impossible for Clyde not to literally run into the back of them.

"Keep moving, ladies," Clyde said, smiling big at his ladies' awe.

"But I've never..." Jennie began.

"I can't..." said Grannie.

Clyde chuckled as he ushered the women up to the reception desk. Clyde felt excited in this lavish environment, never ill at ease. He knew he was meant to be in this elegant place. He could talk with anyone, regardless of their level in society, and seemed to attract those in high society with his good looks, confidence, smile, and intelligence. As Jennie and Grannie did their best to disappear into the background, Clyde shook hands all around.

He heard a "Good afternoon!" behind him and turned around to see a small man in a beautifully tailored suit. "I'm Louis Grunewald, the proprietor of this hotel. Whom do I have the pleasure of meeting?"

"Captain Clyde Barbour from Franklin, Louisiana." The men shook hands and talked for a few minutes. Clyde turned to the women and introduced them. Mr. Grunewald bowed and said, "Please treat my hotel as your home. If there is anything you need, be sure to ask and somebody will get it for you!"

The family followed a bellman to the elevator. Grannie held her breath and closed her eyes when the door closed behind them. Jennie was fascinated but quiet. They were on the 14th floor—the top floor of the new tower. Grannie couldn't hold her breath that long.

Mr. Grunewald had upgraded them to a suite with two bedrooms, a living room, and a bathroom. When the bellman left, Clyde sucked in a deep breath and whistled. "I don't know what to say." He wondered if his daily rate had gone up, as well, but he didn't really care if it had. *I have a feeling that meeting Louis Grunewald will make it worth whatever I have to pay.*

"I'm afraid to touch anythin," admitted Grannie. They all laughed.

"I'd be happy just to stay in these rooms the whole time we're here," said Jennie, eagerly checking out the suite. "Did you see the bathtub?" It made Clyde swell with pride to see his wife so excited and to know that he had been able to provide this for her. She enticed Grannie into her own room. A metal half tester bed adorned with white linen and lace stuck out at an angle from one corner. The windows had sheer curtains on them, which concerned Grannie until she realized there wasn't another building that tall in all of New Orleans, so there'd be no peeking in from outside. The view down to the street left her breathless again, and she sat down in the rocking chair.

There was a knock on the door, and Clyde went to answer it. A bellman was carrying a small box and, handing it to Clyde, said, "Compliments of Mr. Grunewald!" Inside the pretty wrapping and ribbon was a box marked "Grunewald's Creole Pralines." A printed sheet explained that they were made with only Louisiana cane sugar and pecans and, being pure, were good for your children! They were no strangers to pralines after all their years in Louisiana, but never had they seen any this fancy. Grannie wanted to save them for the children, but Clyde protested and grabbed one before he could be stopped. The ladies followed his lead, promising to get more for their children later.

Jennie and Clyde slept well, but Grannie was fitful in the middle of the night over her absentee husband, whom she had finally found and so quickly lost again. She had forgotten what it was like to share her bed with a man. *I don't guess I'll ever do that again.*

D.H. Holmes, with its famous clock on the facade, was the largest department store in the South and was located across the street, just blocks from their hotel on Canal Street. Although it was new to Jennie, Grannie had walked past its glass doors dozens of times, peering in for a glance at the wealthy patrons. Clyde sent the ladies there to buy something.

For a special night out, Clyde let Jennie choose between the long-standing Antoine's Restaurant on St. Louis Street or the new Galatoire's on Bourbon Street. Taking no reservations, the latter required patrons to wait their turn in line outside. Jennie chose Galatoire's. Their wait was quite short, and the trout almandine melted in their mouths. They returned to Franklin feeling that the weight of the world had been lifted from their shoulders, at least temporarily.

That summer, Clyde returned to Houston, alone this time; the trip was to be all business. He had made some contacts when he was there tending to Pa and wanted to find his niche in the booming city. Clyde knew that the Gulf of Mexico, Galveston Bay, the Houston Ship Channel, and all of those Texas bayous offered a lot of opportunities for a water transportation man like him. Commerce on the bayous in Louisiana seemed to be slowing down, so this was perfect timing for Clyde.

His first meeting was with four men who, along with Clyde, would form the Galveston, Harrisburg & Houston Transportation Company. It was chartered in Houston with $100,000 of capital. Thomas C. McCain, William T. Palfrey, Henry S. Palfrey, James H.E. House, and S. Tallaferro joined Clyde in funding the new company, which would be carrying cargo on the Houston bayous, as well as to Galveston.

Several of Clyde's friends were long-time politicians who had become well known. That fact, combined with his Masonic friends (many of whom were both Masons and politicians), gave Clyde solid connections in many areas of business. John N. Pharr, whose family were Scotch-Irish, was a sugar planter and refiner, who owned Orange Grove Plantation in Iberia Parish. He had been big in the Whig party until after the Civil War, when he and most of the Louisiana sugar planters organized the "Lily-White" Republican Party in Louisiana, which only existed from 1892–1896. He'd had unsuccessful runs for both governor and the US Senate, but was nevertheless an important ally. When the old man died in 1903, he was the largest landowner in Louisiana. Though Clyde didn't have a long relationship with him, his son, Henry Newton Pharr, took over many of his father's enterprises, including Pharr & Williams Lumber Mill, which the senior Pharr had started with F.B. Williams. Henry was a director of the State National Bank of New Iberia, so he and Clyde shared many of the same interests.

In April of that year, Lt. Governor of Louisiana, Jared Young Sanders, Sr., who was a Franklin man and another friend, had been elected governor, a post he held from 1908–1912. Clyde was exceptionally well positioned to strike out into the world of business outside of southern Louisiana, leveraging all his connections.

Governor Sanders had no trouble getting Clyde an appointment with the Mayor of Houston, Horace Baldwin Rice, nephew of William Marsh Rice, the man who endowed Rice University. Mayor Lewis of Franklin also called on Clyde's behalf. When Clyde had initially sat down and laid out these connections on paper in an organized fashion, he was amazed at all the well-connected people he knew. Seeing it all written down made it come alive. He was more than ready to tackle the ideas that were constantly filling his brain.

He stayed with James and Mary, who had a new baby girl they named Lucile. James, Jr., was now seven. Clyde had always loved having a new baby in his house, but he found that someone else's baby, even your brother's, wasn't nearly as cute.

His planned weeklong stay became almost two weeks. With the building of the Galveston Causeway to begin the next year, Mayor Rice was eager to finish up those plans. Clyde, with his many boats and men, as well as the others he could enlist to work with him, was an attractive opportunity for the mayor. He had also found Clyde's character to be above reproach—not always an easy thing to find in the construction business. He scheduled a meeting for Clyde with Galveston County Judge Lewis Fisher to get his opinion on Clyde's business acumen. At the time, Judge Fisher was planning to run for Mayor of Galveston the next year and was particularly interested in having the beginning phase of the bridge construction go off seamlessly. Rice and Fisher agreed they would give Clyde's new company, the Galveston, Harrisburg & Houston Transportation Company, the contract to deliver all the sand and gravel to make the concrete that the 10,675-foot-long and 119-foot-wide bridge would require. It took a herculean effort for Clyde to sit calmly when he was given this news by Mayor Rice, with the caveat that if they could pull this off, there was a lot more work that would come his way.

Although not the main topic of conversation with these men, it was mentioned many times how their real obsession was the Houston Ship Channel. Clyde had that same obsession ever since he had traveled to Galveston after the hurricane of 1900.

Back home, Clyde felt a sense of pride well up as he entered the new Franklin Courthouse. As the head of the Teche Improvement Association, he was approaching the elected officials who ran St. Mary Parish, hoping to get an appropriation to survey Bayou Teche to see how much money it would take to dredge the bayou to a depth of 15 feet. Once the cost was determined, they would ask the US Congress for the funds.

"The cost of the survey is $2,500, and y'all know we'll get that money back many times over from more boats using it and bringing in more commerce, as well as from fewer of our own boats getting damaged and having to be repaired or replaced," Clyde argued. The committee agreed.

Two weeks later, the Mayor of Franklin, John C. Lewis, appointed Clyde one of the delegates to the Convention of the Interstate Inland

Waterway League in New Orleans. A few years before, Clyde had begun volunteering for these sorts of committees, and by this time, he was one of the first men to be asked to participate.

Clyde was off and running, putting together what he needed for his new project in Houston. He was surprised when Jennie wasn't as elated as he was. "What's wrong, Jennie? What is it?" he asked.

Jennie was silent for a moment before she said, "You see, you're already gone so much. This new job sounds like more work than ever. And it's in Houston! Will we ever see you?"

Clyde smiled and took her in his arms. "I'm glad I'm so missed! Yes, you will see me. We'll figure it out; we always do!" They kissed and Jennie sighed, wondering nevertheless.

Clyde met with a steamboat builder from Morgan City, Louisiana, whom he hadn't used before, to build a seagoing tug. Drackett & Terrebonne Steamboat Builders signed a contract with Captain Clyde Barbour for $20,000.

A few months into 1909, the entire Barbour family went to visit Houston and stayed at the Rice Hotel. Lilly Lucile was in second grade and was still often ill, and Jennie wouldn't dream of leaving her behind with Elizabeth while the rest of them went on this adventure. Houston held unpleasant associations for Grannie, and she didn't want to go, in the end joining them only so she could stay at the hotel to care for Lilly Lucile if she wasn't feeling well.

Clyde combined the trip with a meeting at the Masonic Lodge in Houston. When Clyde was working, James and Mary took over as tour guides. Given that business was going so well in Houston, Jennie felt certain that Clyde was secretly looking for a place for them to live there—and she wasn't sure how she felt about that idea.

The building of the frame for the Galveston Causeway began in the fall of 1909. With a signed contract, Clyde took the train to New York City in search of major funding for that and other large projects he was in line to receive. His partners had agreed unanimously that Clyde should be the one to represent them in New York City.

To get to New York City by rail, it was necessary to ride into the Pennsylvania Railroad's Jersey City station, Exchange Place station, and then board a ferry to Manhattan without leaving the building. It was an immense, well-run place. Once across the water, Clyde found himself in the heart of New York City. It was overwhelming, even to a man accustomed to traveling; he was awed by the size of it, the number and height of the buildings, and the mass of humanity bustling around. There was a mix of trolleys, automobiles, and even horse-drawn wagons. The men's attire seemed to be mostly white shirts, ties, and lots of knickers, many with suit coats. The ladies wore mostly darker-colored dresses. The facades of the buildings were covered in signs. It seemed a tangled mess.

Clyde had chosen to stay at the Cosmopolitan. It had been around a long time and was recommended to him as a business hotel. Located on the corner of Chambers and West Broadway streets, it was a nice-looking six-story brick building that had been painted beige. The entrance was a two-story portico, and trolley lines ran on both sides of the building. The roof boasted a massive American flag. Although certainly not sumptuous like the Grunewald Hotel, it was nonetheless more than adequate. Exhausted from his travels, Clyde stayed at the hotel for dinner and retired early.

His appointment at Gotham National Bank was the next afternoon. He'd wanted plenty of time to prepare and extra time in case his train was delayed. He arrived at the bank 30 minutes early. It was an ornate skyscraper that had just recently been opened. Large Corinthian columns ran the length of the building and were connected several stories up by arches. Toward the top of the building, the protruding windows, framed by columns, were stacked and staggered like a pyramid topped by an elaborate entablature. It was stunning! The interior did not disappoint either. There was an enormous amount of marble and granite, the rooms large, airy, and grand. He took it all in, enjoying the flurry of financial transactions going on all around him; the din was like the inner workings of a clock, everything running effortlessly and perfectly synchronized.

He tried to imagine what all these people were doing there. The energy being generated was contagious.

The dapper Captain Barbour had chosen his suit and tie with great care. He carried his dark-brown leather briefcase in one hand and his hat in the other.

Clyde's appointment was with the vice president, Mr. Steve Hilton. He was a tall man, and seemed even taller standing next to Clyde, whose small stature rarely mattered to him. At that moment, however, it was a bit unsettling. Dealing with bankers was nothing new to Clyde—after all, he was on the board of a bank himself—but this felt different; it was unfamiliar in its familiarness. The banter included no talk of food, no family references, and definitely no Cajun jokes. He wondered if Mr. Hilton found him at all backward. He couldn't— wouldn't—let himself think that way.

"So, the name of your company is…." Mr. Hilton fumbled to find the letterhead.

"Teche Transportation Company is mine, and I've partnered with three of my business associates to form the Galveston, Harrisburg & Houston Transportation Company."

"So, you own the Teche Company?"

"Yes, sir. I bought out the interests of all the stockholders for $68,000, which included all steamboats and barges." Clyde waited patiently while his interviewer looked through the papers Clyde had brought for him to review.

"So, this contract is for all the sand and gravel needed to build a two-mile causeway connecting the island of Galveston to the mainland just south of Houston?" Mr. Hilton continued to peruse the papers.

"That's right. It should take about two years to complete. The other contract is for Houston's answer to La Gare d'Orsay in Paris." Clyde was pleased with the homework he had done. "Did you read that Paris flooded earlier this year?" He watched as Mr. Hilton raised his eyebrows and looked over at Clyde, a sly smile on the man's face.

"Yes, I heard. Maybe you should make yours waterproof!" Both men laughed and Clyde felt the mood relax. "So, this will be called

Union Depot and will be in the middle of Houston?" Mr. Hilton asked, surprised.

"Yes, sir. They're razing some expensive homes in the process. The city is serious about making Houston the southwestern center for railroads," Clyde added excitedly.

"Makes sense, makes sense," said Mr. Hilton, rubbing his chin with his thumb and forefinger. "So, what's next for you, Captain?"

"Mexico. They discovered oil inland, which means it'll have to be transported to the Gulf...."

Two hours later the deal was structured and the terms agreed to. All that remained was for the president of the bank to sign off on the agreement, which he did. Clyde left the bank walking on air. He wanted to scream hallelujah and throw his hat in the air, but he controlled himself. He found the nearest telegraph office and sent one off to Jennie. "I got them both!" Now, all he had to do was figure out how to make it happen, and that was his favorite part.

When Clyde returned home, he sold most of his businesses in Louisiana to raise capital for his new ventures in Texas and moved his family to Houston, where they lived at 205 Avondale Avenue, a new residential area in the city. They joined the United Methodist Church on McGowen and sent the children to the Fannin School.

205 Avondale, Houston, Texas about 1910

CHAPTER 29

THE FOUNDATION

1910

Jennie was exhausted. Clyde had been gone more than he was home. Lilly continued to be frail, and the unpacking in Houston seemed to go on and on. There was so much to do. Elizabeth could not be swayed to leave Franklin, so Clyde had hired a cook/housekeeper named Josephine. Man had become so attached to Elizabeth, and to Franklin in general, that he had announced that he was staying behind as well.

"But Man, you've been part of this family for so long!" Jennie had said. "I can't leave you back here!"

"Mrs. Barbour, you's been like a ma to me. I loves ya and Clyde Barbour and all the chil'en, but Miss 'Lizbeth, she be my real ma now. I just has ta stay and takes care a her."

Tears trickled down Jennie's face. The little boy whose dark eyes had rained tears when they'd taken him from his dying mother wasn't a little boy anymore.

"Now if you tells me I *gots* ta go, then I be goin'." He straightened up, stood tall, and looked Jennie in the eye.

She took one of his hands in hers and cleared her throat. When she looked at the teenager, she saw Luke and Sarah, Man's mother, and the determined little Black boy protecting her. She thought about the picnic at Oaklawn Manor when he didn't want to participate, and the times he'd driven her to the hospital. The way he looked out for the children. She knew they owed it to Luke and Sarah to let Man stay where he was happy and felt at home.

"No, I won't make you go to Houston. I'm happy you've found your home. I'm ready to find my own." Jennie hugged him long and tightly and kissed his cheek. "We'll send for you and Elizabeth to come to Houston to visit."

"I hears that's one big city. Not sure I'd like it," he responded, "but a visit, now that would be just fine."

The first night in their new home, when all the boxes had been unpacked, Clyde was there. Jennie felt lonely, missing her old house and old friends. The new house was big, beautiful, and new, but it wasn't home. The children asleep, she got ready for bed. Clyde was already there reading a book.

"You look exhausted! Come and get something to drink." He coerced her over to his side of the bed and there it was, sitting on his nightstand—the green, white, and gold Ice Water pitcher full of ice and water. He smiled so big looking up at her that all her loneliness melted into nothingness. They toasted their new house with the ice water. Clyde picked her up and playfully threw her onto the bed. They both laughed out loud, Jennie putting her hand over her mouth, realizing the need to be quiet. He reached over to her bedside table and turned on her light.

"Blue light! You are so sweet to me." She felt thrilled, excited, cared for, and loved. They devoured each other in the soft blue light of their new bedroom, without forgetting the doctor's orders.

In an effort to make up for his long absences as well as to help Lilly get better, Clyde decided to take Jennie, Lena, and Lilly to Mineral Wells, near Dallas, in June, to bathe in and drink the therapeutic waters there. They left the boys behind with Grannie and took the train north.

Lena was accomplished at livening things up, especially when it came to Lilly, who easily became a silent observer of things going on around her or slipped off to sleep. Clyde adored Lena's playful heart and daring antics. She could do no wrong in his eyes. Clyde had bought a baby grand piano that Lena was learning to play. She was already becoming a frequent invitee to social engagements, and Clyde understood why. If only he could get her to pay more attention to her schoolwork and less to boys.

After checking in at the Fairfield Inn, they walked down to the Crazy Drinking Pavilion for their first taste of the miraculous water. One of the names given to the waters was Crazy Water because, the story went, a crazy woman had become sane after drinking some. Lilly took such a tiny sip that it was doubtful even a drop had made it down her throat. Lena dived right in and took a big swig, only some of which made it down her throat before she spit the rest out all over the sandy ground.

"Heaven sakes, Lena!" Jennie said. Shocked and embarrassed, she looked around to see if anyone had noticed her daughter's faux pas. Three men standing at the outdoor bar guffawed at the sight of Lena spitting the water out and then trying desperately to wipe every drop from inside her mouth with her hands and sleeves. Clyde couldn't help himself and burst out laughing as well. Jennie was red with embarrassment, and Lilly's jaw had dropped open.

Lena got up from her chair and banged her hand on the table. "That is the *worst* tastin' thing I ever put in my mouth!" she exclaimed. "I am *not* drinkin' any more of that stuff!" She stomped her foot emphatically.

"Come here, daughter," Clyde said, patting his lap for Lena to come and sit. She sat down heavily on her father's lap and looked him in the eye. "A sip at a time, a sip at a time." Jennie shot an angry look at Clyde, who smiled and shrugged his shoulders. Suddenly, Lilly began to laugh, and everyone chimed in.

One of the tourist attractions in Mineral Wells was a donkey ride through the rocky, wooded hillsides and down around Lake Mineral Wells. The rock outcrops were everywhere, making the trek seem treacherous at times, though Clyde felt sure it must be safe. Clyde went alone with the girls; Jennie thought it would be an adventure they would always remember as a special time spent alone with their father. Secretly, she also suspected that riding for hours on the back of a donkey would be very uncomfortable.

At the end of their stay, all of them said they felt really good—except Lena, who maintained that drinking all those minerals had given her a stomachache that she feared would "never ever" go away.

Lena, Clyde and Lilly, Mineral Wells, Texas 1914

In early 1911, back on Bayou Teche, the tugboat *Comet* and the steamer *Laura Sutcliffe* burned at Morgan City when a lamp exploded. Clyde owned them both and, since they were only partially insured, suffered a $20,000 loss. He had only a few boats still operating on the bayous and kept them in the back of his mind as replacements should any of the boats he was now using in Houston become disabled. Though difficult to do, he stopped himself from dwelling on the monetary loss; it was a pittance compared to what he was working on now. Never in his wildest dreams did he imagine being indebted to a bank for the amount he and his partners were indebted to Gotham National Bank for. He couldn't dwell on that, either, or he would be paralyzed.

Jennie had trouble settling into life in Houston. She found the big city intimidating. Almost everything was new—their neighborhood, their house; even downtown had buildings going up all around. The locals were pleasant and accommodating, but she missed the feeling of kinship she had with the people in Franklin, most of whom were involved in one way or another in the same businesses. Clyde fit in effortlessly wherever he went; Jennie not so much. She was more than content to stay home with the children, living through them and for them.

Although the bulk of his time was now spent in Houston, Clyde often traveled to Franklin on business. He still had the Teche Transportation Company there which had just secured the contract at Charenton for 50,000 cubic yards of shells for the Iberia, St. Mary & Eastern Railroad. On one of his trips there, he was able to finalize the purchase of the Louisiana Petroleum Company, which was disposing of all of its holdings. He paid $12,500 for it and immediately sold it off at a sizable profit to the Texas Company. He was particularly pleased with how he was able to flip this so effortlessly. The Texas Company, which would become Texaco, already had a presence in Mexico. Clyde used this opportunity to negotiate a future deal with them for the oil transportation company he would be setting up in Tampico, Mexico.

Clyde was president of the Galveston, Harrisburg & Houston Transportation Company. It was the largest firm of its kind in Texas, supplying sand, gravel, crushed rock, concrete, and brick to many of the largest projects in the state. After winning the contract for the Galveston Causeway, the firm received the contract for the concrete work on the Houston Belt & Terminal Railway Company's palatial Union Station and the large cotton warehouses of the Galveston, Harrisburg & San Antonio Railway Company at Galveston.

It was decided that Lilly would not attend school until she was better. The doctor didn't want her exposed to the normal childhood illnesses that move from child to child in a school environment. She slept a lot and had trouble eating, which kept her frail. One issue the doctor could pinpoint was arthritis, which they treated with copper wires that she wore on her wrists and ankles.

At the dinner table one evening, Jennie was, as usual, encouraging Lilly to eat. Lilly smiled up at her mother with her cherubic face, sad eyes, and soft smile.

"Lilly," said Clyde from the end of the long table, "if you eat your dinner, I will buy you a pretty bracelet downtown tomorrow. How would that be?" he asked, smiling at his precious Little Princess.

She smiled back at her father. "That would be perfect, Daddy!" She managed to eat what they considered to be all of her dinner, and Clyde returned home the next day with a simple silver bracelet bearing her initials.

At their new house on Avondale, there was a small apartment over the garage for servants that was never used. During her year out of school, Lilly turned the space into a school room, and every day she played teacher to her little brother, Will. Lilly was very organized. School started and ended at set times every morning. Will was required to sit at his "desk" during school until it was time for recess. Lilly was so diligent that by the following school year, when Will was to enter first grade at the Fannin School and Lilly to enter third grade, she had taught him everything she knew, and he, too, was ready for the third grade.

On February 12, 1912, the largest fire in the history of Houston swept through the Fifth Ward, northeast of downtown. The damage totaled more than $3 million, but luckily no one was killed. Clyde took his three sons and many of his workers to assist in the cleanup. Jesse, as usual, stuck close to his father, asking questions.

"What do these folks do now?" he asked, looking around in disbelief.

"Start over, son. They just start over. Look at all the people here helping out. If we all help, do what we can, give what we can, the people who lost everything will be able to regroup and go on."

Clyde, Jr., was ready to leave as soon as they arrived. "I don't get why we have to do this. It's not our house or our church or our school that got burned out," he sulked.

Clyde snapped his fingers loudly, long the sign that he expected their full attention. "These people and their houses and schools are part of our community. *Our* community. I suggest you thank God that we aren't the ones needing help and lend a hand so when we're the ones that need the help, others will be there to help us." Clyde was sorely disappointed with his namesake. Hadn't he raised them better than that? Hadn't he shown them time and time again through his own actions that we should always help people in need? He would have to work on his son's attitude.

On May 25, 1912, the Galveston Causeway opened to vehicular and railroad traffic. The project cost around $2 million. (Approximately $61 million in 2023.) Governor Oscar Branch Colquitt led a line of 1,500 automobiles over the new bridge to Galveston. Clyde and his entire family were in their car in the pack, hooting and hollering along with all the other riders. In Galveston, speeches were given and whistles blown, and after dark, the sky lit up with fireworks over the water. The dance at the new and sumptuous Galvez Hotel was the culmination of the grand day.

With that huge undertaking complete, Clyde was ready to head to Mexico. He promised that upon his return, the entire family would travel to Mineral Wells for a respite. This idea was met with great enthusiasm from the three boys; Lena stuck out her tongue in defiance, and Lilly smiled her precious smile.

Just as Clyde was getting everything ready for his departure, James called to tell him that Pa had just shown up at his house. Clyde didn't tell anyone where he was going as he quickly took off in the car. He arrived to find Pa asleep on the couch, dirty, smelly, and disheveled. The brothers got him in the car and drove him to the new Dr. Greenwood's Sanitarium, which advertised as being "For Nervous and Mental Disorders – Alcohol and Drug Addictions." Clyde wrote a check, and James gave his information as the contact person. They weren't sure what to tell Ma.

CHAPTER 30

THE RESCUER

1913

Spencer, their new chauffeur and houseboy, drove Clyde, Jennie, and Jesse to the boat bound for Tampico. Spencer was a very tall Black man who wore a khaki uniform and didn't speak much. Clyde was brimming with excitement. He'd never been out of the country. He'd be starting an oil transportation company on the Panuco River with offices at Tampico, where his boats would transport the oil to seagoing boats that would take the oil to ports around the world. Nothing could stop his imagination from running wild with possibilities. Jesse would be accompanying him, which only added to Jennie's malaise.

"I'm going to groom Jesse to run this company," Clyde had told Jennie a few days earlier. "He's good with Spanish, eager, and he's a good pilot already—just like his father, I might add!" Jennie did not audibly protest; if Clyde thought this was the way things should be, she had to trust his judgment. But they would be gone for weeks.

Jesse said goodbye to his mother and Clyde hugged her, his eyes bright and his smile big. Jennie reached into her pocket and then put something into Clyde's hand.

He looked at it with amazement. It was their lucky coin. "You still have it!"

"Of course I still have it. It gave us five healthy babies, brought me back from dying, but now you need it to bring you and Jesse home to me safely." Jennie had promised herself she wasn't going to cry. Her eyes damp with tears that she was able to keep from streaming down her face, she said her goodbyes and headed home with Spencer.

Clyde put their lucky coin deep down in his jacket pocket. He would have to find a better place to keep it. He and Jesse boarded the steamer for their journey to Tampico.

Jesse followed his father wherever he went. Clyde did his best to meet everyone on the boat, as he knew most of the men would be heading down to look for work in the new oil fields or to start their own companies connected to the oil business.

Tampico was a bustling tropical town three miles above the mouth of the Panuco River. Most of the buildings were painted white, and palm trees swayed in the wind. There were no skyscrapers, but there were several multistoried buildings. The extra wide sidewalks, or promenades, downtown were full of people walking and sitting, enjoying the sunshine. Some aspects of the town reminded Clyde of the French Quarter: wrought-iron railings, music emanating from inside buildings and outside on the promenades. Even the general tone and slow pace of the residents were similar. Of course, the strangest thing was to hear people everywhere speaking a language he didn't understand. After a few days, though, Jesse's Spanish had improved immensely and even Clyde felt he could understand a few words. While there, he received a telegram telling him that the *Jennie Barbour* had sunk in the Teche a few miles east of New Iberia, near Dreyfus Landing. It had struck one of the many submerged barges that littered the bayous and now rested in six feet of water.

"I was thinking I might bring the *Jennie Barbour* down here to Tampico," Clyde told Jesse. "She'll have to be retrofitted to carry oil anyway, so now that she's in need of repair, we may as well do that."

"But Dad, how are ya gonna get her down here? The Gulf will tear her up!" Jesse was always eager not only to know what was being discussed, but also to understand.

"I've already figured that out. We'll sink a barge, move the steamer on top of it, and lift the barge back up. The boat will rest on top of the barge for the trip down here." Clyde smiled at what he thought was a very clever idea.

"Wow! I want to see that!" Jesse exclaimed. "It'll be kinda like having Ma down here, only she's a boat." They both laughed heartily.

The Sternwheeler Major Black on a Barge for Trip to Tampico, Mexico

While in Tampico, Clyde decided that since they'd be working together, Jesse should call him Father instead of Dad. It sounded more professional but still familial.

Clyde set up the "Compañía de Navegación Interior, S.A." (Interior Navigation Company), which would be operating an oil transportation line on the Panuco River and in the Gulf of Mexico. He and Jesse got the lay of the land. The oil fields were about 60 miles south of Tampico and 30 miles inland from the Gulf. There were four main fields: the Tamboyoche, Isleta, Panuco, and Topila. The extra heavy oil in this region, having low gravity, could not be transported by pipeline because it would require heating stations, making it uneconomical. Instead, the crude oil was barged the 50 miles upriver to Tampico, where it was put on oil tankers by means of sea lines. This made the Panuco District particularly attractive to Clyde. Several signed contracts with oil companies that were already pumping in hand, they headed back to Houston to ship down some of his boats.

They came home to a house brimming with Barbour children, not all of whom were Clyde and Jennie's. Leona was visiting with her two children, Cora and Billy, and Mary was there with her two, James, Jr., and Lucile. They hadn't had any notice as to when the captain would be home, so when he and Jesse arrived, there was quite a clamor. Jennie had arranged to have some photos taken that day and was glad Clyde hadn't arrived earlier, which would have ruined the surprise. Jesse's dog came bounding up to his master, almost knocking him down. Clyde's children were disappointed to learn that their father hadn't brought them any gifts. While not disappointed, Jennie was nonetheless surprised. "We were working from sunup to sundown. We'll be headed back down there soon enough and next time…." He smiled, and the children shouted with delight.

That night after dinner, Lena grabbed her father's arm. "I have a surprise for you!" She led him into the parlor, where the baby grand piano stood, and had him sit down. The crowd had dwindled to immediate family only, and they filed in, found seats, and whispered to each other. Lena sat on the piano stool and clapped her hands for everyone to be quiet.

"Daddy, I have learned a new song, really new. It's from the Ziegfeld Follies and it's called 'Peg O' My Heart.'" She smiled at her audience. "Will, you be quiet now—it's my turn." She played it well, although haltingly, and her high soprano voice sang the lilting words beautifully.

"Peg o' my heart, I love you…"

"That was really beautiful! Lena, I've never heard that song. How perfect for my sweet little Irish lass!" Clyde stood up and applauded, followed by the rest of the family. Lena was blushing as she stood and curtsied to her audience. "I think I might have to start calling you Peg…no, Peggy. My wonderful Irish songbird, Peggy!" And that's how Lena got her nickname. As time passed, she became Peggy to more and more of her friends and family.

That was also how the family tradition took hold of Lena playing the piano after dinner. She was often accompanied by Clyde, Jr., on the mandolin, and Lilly, who loved to sing in her quiet, soft voice. It was Clyde's favorite time of day.

On Sunday, after church, Clyde had Spencer drive the whole family for ice cream. Lilly could always be expected to eat every bite, which was an added incentive for this treat. Clyde picked her up. "You're my Little Princess, you know!"

"Of course, I know, Daddy. And you're my Cap'm!" She smiled, pleased with her new nickname for her father.

Late that afternoon, when Will was nowhere to be found, Jennie went to her husband in his study. "Did you send Will somewhere? I can't find him."

"No. Maybe he went down the street to play," he said absently.

"I'm telling you, he's gone, and I'm worried about him."

"Okay, I'm coming. Just give me a minute to finish this up." Clyde continued with his work for a minute and then followed Jennie out of the room. "Jesse, where's Will?"

"I don't know, Father; really, I don't." Jesse wasn't looking him in the eye.

Clyde could feel something was wrong. Jennie's motherly instincts told her the same thing. She followed her husband as he walked quickly toward the kitchen calling for Spencer, who came out of the kitchen at the same time.

"Do you know where Will is? We can't find him, and Jesse claims he doesn't know where he is."

"Well, Captain Barbour, you see, I was just comin' to tell ya about the car," Spencer answered sheepishly.

"What are you talking about?"

"It's gone, and I was rememberin' that after lunch today, Will was sittin' in it playin' like he was drivin'."

"He was sitting out in the car pretending to drive?"

"Yes, sir. I told him to get up out de car and not to play in there no mo'. I went out there just now and the car, it's gone." Spencer's words sent Clyde flying out the back door, Jennie not far behind, in search of their eight-year-old. The car was indeed missing.

"Damn it," Clyde mumbled. "Has he lost his mind? Spencer, you go that way down the street and look for him. I'll walk the opposite way. Jennie, stay here in case he comes home." The men set out in opposite directions, leaving Jennie standing out in front of their house trying to breathe.

It didn't take more than five minutes for Spencer to show up driving the car, Will sitting next to him. Jennie's first reaction was to hug him and kiss him and be sure he was all right. She sent Spencer out in the car to find Clyde. They returned quickly. Clyde's eyes were dark and angry, and his jaw was tightly set. He snapped at his son to come with him and walked into his office with his youngest right behind. The whole clan gathered outside the closed office door and listened silently.

"What were you thinking? You know you're not allowed to take the car. We have rules for a reason. You could kill yourself or somebody else since you don't really know how to drive yet. That car is expensive, and we take care of the nice things that we're lucky to have! You're never going to do anything like that again. Tomorrow after school, you're going to wash the car. On Tuesday, you're going to come home and help Spencer clean the garage. And the rest of the week, you're going to come directly home from school and study in your room until dinnertime." Clyde left the office and went out to the porch to think.

Lying in their bed that night, Clyde noticed that Jennie was unusually quiet.

"Jennie, you're upset. What's wrong?" Clyde asked, laying down the newspaper he was reading.

Jennie was torn between not wanting to complain that he was absent so often and yet wanting him to take more of a role in rearing the boys. She could handle the girls.

"Clyde, Jr., has been acting up a lot lately and so has Will, and I'm worried about them. It's hard when they misbehave and you're not here. They don't listen to me like they do to you."

"They're very spoiled," Clyde began, "and it's going to take both of us to turn them around. I'm going to spend more time with the boys, and as they get older, I'm going to get them more involved in the family businesses. Jesse will be going back to Mexico with me. I'm really pleased with how he's grown up. You know, he's always been by my side, eager to learn. Eventually he's gonna run things down there. That'll give us more time to focus on the other two."

Jennie swallowed hard at the thought of their 17-year-old staying down in Mexico. "But he's so young!"

"Honey, that's what we were just talking about! I'm going to spend more time with the boys and work them into the business as they get older. Jesse's just the right age to get started. We're still figuring out his college plans. When I was his age, I was navigating the Ohio and Mississippi Rivers on a flatboat and reading whenever I got the chance. And I wasn't waiting on my drunk father to figure it all out for me. His Spanish is good, he's smart, he wants to learn, and that Black Irish look of his makes him fit right in with the natives. All he has to do is what I tell him to do. I can't be everywhere at once." Clyde was emphatic. "Jennie, I'm just getting started! I need all my sons to be ready to step up as they can so that I can do more things. They need to be ready."

Jennie looked down at the covers. "How can I even help to get them ready? I can teach them manners, but I can't teach them anything at all about business or the world."

"At this point in their lives, we just need to focus on making them good people who are honest, hard-working, responsible citizens."

Clyde was busy with his fleet, adding to it and retrofitting some boats for the oil trade. His Galveston, Harrisburg & Houston

Transportation Co. bought the steamer *Hornet*, which had been a filibustering gunboat active in Cuban waters during the Spanish-American War. Originally, it had been the pleasure boat *Alicia*, owned by J.P. Morgan, Jr. and one of the most expensive boats of her size in America. His Teche Transportation Co. leased the boat. Now, it was being overhauled into a tug to handle oil barges on the Panuco River. Clyde loved the history behind his new boat.

Imagine, he thought as he'd walked through the vessel the first time, *J.P. Morgan, Jr. and all his rich, important friends sailed on her. I wonder what kind of deals were made here?*

The *Jennie Barbour*, the *William Kyle*, and the tug *Vera* were also heading south to Tampico. Clyde also purchased the *Major Black* from the Barrett Line for his Mexican fleet.

In Houston, his company was busy adding two new stories to the Union Depot, and in Charenton, near Franklin, Louisiana, he was towing shells to make the Charenton Beach into a major recreation destination for the area.

Clyde found himself continually trying to keep news of Mexico from Jennie, knowing it would spark what he saw as an unnecessary panic in his wife. Mexico had been in the midst of a revolution for years. Having lost the Battle of Juárez, President Porfirio Díaz, who had spent seven terms in office, was ousted and exiled to France in May of 1911. Francisco León de la Barra was appointed interim president until a free and fair election could be held in November 1911. Francisco I. Madero won the election, which didn't sit well with other factions of the revolution, who saw the election as neither free nor fair.

Emiliano Zapata and his men denounced Madero and recognized Pascual Orozco, who had broken his alliance with Madero, as leader of the revolution. The United States, fearing the revolution would spill into their country, sent troops to the border. Pancho Villa, a colonel in the state militia of Chihuahua in the north, took his 400 troops and supported Madero, who then sent him and General Victoriano Huerta north to fight Orozco's rebels.

From February 9 to 19, 1913, Mexico City was the scene of a battle known as the Ten Tragic Days. The American ambassador, Henry Wilson, secretly convinced Huerta and General Bernardo Reyes to change sides and oppose Madero. They assassinated Madero along with his vice president on February 21, leaving Huerta in charge.

Clyde on Top of Derrick on Panuco River, Mexico

When Jesse and Clyde returned to Tampico that summer, Huerta was president, which pleased the businessmen and the United States, even though the other factions of the revolution were still fighting it out. There was often talk among the oil field workers about how vulnerable they all were out there in the field, given all the political unrest.

"All it takes is one Mexican peon with a match and we're done here," said Denny McMahon, who worked for the Texas Co.

Clyde agreed. "But remember, even Villa and Zapata are smart enough to know they need the taxes from this oil for their country to survive."

"Well, that may be, but I still feel better with my pistols on my hips." Denny patted his guns and smiled.

"That makes two of us," said Clyde.

At the beginning of 1914, the US was ready to denounce President Huerta and to get a constitutionalist into power. The country continued to be caught up in a civil war that showed no signs of abating. Pancho Villa killed an Englishman, William Benton, which enraged the US. The temporary American ambassador, John Lind, said that peace in Mexico was impossible. Clyde refused to accept that; Mexico had become too important to his bottom line. In the first 11 months that the *Major Black* was working out of Tampico, she moved over 3,000,000 barrels of crude oil and earned nearly $250,000 gross. And that was only one boat.

Clyde was in Houston when all hell broke loose in April 1914. Admiral Henry Mayor, the Commander of US Forces in the Gulf of Mexico, was stationed off the coast of Tampico Bay in the USS *Dolphin*. On April 9, some sailors were sent to shore to get provisions and were accidentally arrested by the locals. The situation was sorted out quickly, but still, the US expected an apology, which they received, and a 21-gun salute of support, which they did not receive. US Naval and Marine forces invaded the Port of Veracruz on Tuesday, April 21. President Woodrow Wilson had already placed an arms embargo on Huerta, having decided he was a usurper of the legitimate government and that the US would support the Constitutional Army of Venustiano Carranza.

On April 20, President Huerta's Federales had taken all the unskilled labor working in the oil fields along the Panuco River and made them soldiers, leaving everyone scrambling to keep their wells running properly. On April 21, a message was sent upriver via the launch *Echo* for everyone to evacuate as quickly as possible, as the invasion of Veracruz was underway.

"Where are we supposed to go and for how long?" one of the Texas Company's men asked.

"Don't know," he was told. "Probably just a quick trip to Tampico for safety." That's what all the men thought. In the frenzy to get out, with the expectation that the men would return quickly, most wells were left flowing. If left unchecked for long, the overflow of oil would reach the Panuco River.

The *Major Black* was moored at the docks in Tampico and ready to go upriver to collect some crude. Jesse got word of the evacuation and went into action. He and his crew cleared everything possible off the boat and readied to head to the oil fields, a barge in tow.

"We have to help get those men out of the fields and up to town," Jesse told his workers.

"I'm not going out there," said Miguel, Jesse's right-hand man. "Villa and Zapata are probably there right now shootin' everybody up! It don't matter what side they're on; none of them are gonna stand for America invading their country."

"They're not gonna do that. They need the money from these wells," Jesse answered, feeling sure of what he said, having heard his father say it.

"Then why's everybody runnin' round like the world's gonna end?"

"I can do this with you or without you, but I'm headin' upriver now! My pistol is loaded and I'm ready to go," he added, feeling more courageous than was wise.

"Okay, *mi jefe!*" Miguel replied as he readied to check depths of the river.

They sailed upriver as far as Largey's Landing to pick up the oil operators and workmen at their camps. The German battleship *Dresden* had sailed upriver to the Dutch Shell camp to protect their wells and tanks from tampering by the locals. By the time the *Major*

Black arrived at the landing to turn around, there were about 171 on board, and they picked up dozens more on the way back. Both the steamer and the barge were loaded to the guards. It was quite a motley group of mostly men who had stopped their work mid-sentence and jumped on the boat wearing all manner of trousers, overalls, and even pajamas—whatever they were wearing when the boat arrived. One man had just exited the shower and pulled on a pair of trousers and grabbed a robe. Another man was covered in crude, while another wore a suit and tie. Some had suitcases that had been hastily packed. They knew that anything of value would be stolen once they abandoned the oil fields.

Arriving at Tampico, they were told they would have to leave the country immediately on a variety of ships and boats waiting in the harbor. The Gulf Refining Company's tanker *Trinidadian* had accommodations for 20 but was prepared to take on 364; the *Cyclops* (a collier) and the *Dixie* (a tender) were there to help, alongside the US battleship *Connecticut*, the steamer *Jason*, and the Ward liner, *Esperanza*. Most would be going to Galveston, the rest to New Orleans.

"What are you talking about?" asked Mr. McMahon, the one who'd fled wearing a suit and tie. They were in the Colonial Club, where the Americans spent their off time. "We can't just leave those wells open indefinitely! A lot of those wells are flowing thousands of barrels a day with only a few days' worth of storage. Do you want the overflow to end up in the Panuco?" He was indignant as he stood facing the American consul, Clarence Miller.

"We have our orders," Miller said with some anxiety. "We won't risk American lives for crude oil, and we can't let Huerta have American hostages to use against us. They need the tax revenue from these wells; they're not stupid."

"Not stupid? They're nothing but henchmen and banditos, as far as I'm concerned," McMahon said angrily.

"Well-armed and very savvy military men is what my father says," Jesse put in.

"Captain Barbour always has a wise word to say," Miller said.

"Agreed. Where is he now?" McMahon asked.

"He's at home in Houston. I've got to get word to him that I'm okay. I hope my mother doesn't find out about this," Jesse added.

"Write down how I get in touch with him, and I'll get word to him that you're fine. You are quite the hero, having saved all those people! The captain will be very proud!" Miller said, smiling.

"I'll be going back for one more load tomorrow."

"Oh no, son, your ferrying days are over. We can't have you back out there. You need to get on the *Trinidadian* and head home. If people don't want to leave, we can't make them, and I don't want to have to explain to Captain Barbour how I let his son get massacred when I was in charge. That's just not going to happen." Miller was firm.

Jesse didn't respond, but he had ideas jumping around in his mind.

The official word had just come in that the invasion of Veracruz had begun. It wasn't long before shouting was heard in the streets. A window was broken, and the locals outside began shouting curses at the people inside. The sound of smashing windows came from outside of the club as well. Apparently, crowds were also storming the Southern and Imperial Hotels. The men were prepared for this and had rifles at the ready, but no shots were fired by either side. The German commander of the *Dresden* had told Miller earlier that he'd send in his marines if violence broke out; luckily, that proved unnecessary.

Early the next morning, Jesse sneaked out to the *Major Black* with Miguel and set off upriver again.

"If the Captain finds out I went on this rescue mission with you, I plan to tell him you held a gun to my head and forced me to do it!" Miguel told Jesse. "But I can't let you go alone."

Jesse patted him on the back hard, put a hand on each of his shoulders, and said with great enthusiasm, "Then let's get going before somebody stops us! Oh, and it's my birthday today!"

"Feliz cumpleaños. Let's hope it's not also the day you die."

There weren't many people left out there, but the majority who were, were grateful for another chance to get out. John Elsner decided to stay at the Dutch Shell camp at Panuco, as did D.H. Shine, a railroad contractor.

On the way back, with only a few dozen people aboard, Miguel talked with Jesse.

"Now it's time for you to get out of this place. I'll take care of the boats until you come back. Your family needs you, *mi hijo*. I'll see you in a few weeks."

"But…."

"No but. You take your suitcase and your coat and get on the *Trinidadian*. No more talking." Miguel looked at him kindly.

They got up to the ship after almost 700 people had boarded. Miguel shooed Jesse off the sternwheeler and onto the ship. They waved goodbye, Jesse holding his suitcase. He leaned over the side of the ship to watch Miguel pilot the boat. To his horror, it was obvious that Miguel did not have control of the sternwheeler. Jesse felt his heart sink. "Oh, no!" he said out loud. "Not the *Major Black!*" He set his suitcase down and climbed over the side.

The last anyone in Tampico saw of Jesse Barbour was him standing in the pilothouse of the sternwheeler, steering it into a berth next to a German steamer.

CHAPTER 31

THE HUNTED

April 1914

"What are you saying?" Clyde yelled into the telephone to Mr. Miller. "Yesterday, you told me he was on the *Trinidadian* heading to Galveston; today you tell me he's missing?"

Clyde was in his office when the call came. Jesse had been seen getting on the boat and then he'd been seen piloting the *Major Black*. That's all anyone seemed to know. "Where's Miguel?" No one knew that either. "I'm heading down there right now!" When he was told that no Americans were allowed back onshore, Clyde hung up. He had to think. *This can't be happening.*

Jesse was missing. Clyde wouldn't be allowed to go onshore. There was a revolution going on. All those fighting hated Americans for invading their country and, apparently, Jesse had helped hundreds of Americans escape. Clyde couldn't remember the last time he felt so helpless. Mr. Miller had promised to find out what he could, reminding Clyde that there was fighting going on, so nothing much could be done. He had also refused to take any money from Clyde for his efforts. "It's the least I can do for you, Captain, but you need to be prepared for the worst."

"I refuse to think about that. He'll get word to me somehow."

"I really don't know how he'd do that," Mr. Miller said in a flat tone. "But I pray he does."

Clyde wired the Secretary of State, William Jennings Bryan, as well as Senator Sheppard, asking for any possible help in getting Jesse home safely. Nothing seemed possible.

Now, Clyde had to tell his wife. But *what* would he tell her? He didn't know what happened. *Jennie will never forgive me if something bad happens to Jesse.*

Jennie was already fretful about their eldest son. With all the recent events, it had been impossible to keep her from hearing about the troubles in Mexico. When she'd heard that Jesse was on a boat headed for Galveston, she was elated.

Clyde called his brother James and told him what he'd just learned. "What can I do? Does Jennie know?"

"Not yet. I need you and Mary to take the children and keep them for dinner tonight. Make it be Mary's idea. I need time alone with Jennie. Will you do that?"

"Sure. That's easy. Let me know what else I can do. I'm really sorry, big brother!"

When Clyde was certain the children had been delivered to James' house, he went home. He and Jennie sat in their beautiful parlor, in their beautiful house, in their perfect neighborhood, and cried together.

They decided not to tell the other children; there was no point at this time. Life went on as normally as possible, with both parents trying hard to mask their deep-seated anxiety.

A few weeks later, when Clyde heard that some oilmen were heading back to Tampico, he went with them. Still, there seemed to be no sign of Jesse and nothing he could do to find him—assuming he was still alive. The Federales were still in control of the oil fields, but no property damage had been reported. None of this mattered to Clyde; he just wanted his son to return alive. All he could think to do was throw money at the problem. But throw it to whom? There was no person really in charge in Mexico, and the fighting showed no signs of abating.

Clyde eventually found Miguel, who had been hiding out with his family. "All I can tell you, Captain, is that when I left Jesse, he was headed to the Colonial Club to see who was left in town. Shooting started, and we all ran." Miguel was obviously distraught. "I helped him rescue those people upriver at the oil field camps; wouldn't let him do that alone. He insisted on doing it. He practically held a gun to my head to help him. He's very determined, your son."

"Determined and foolish, I'm afraid."

"There's one more thing."

"What? Tell me!" Clyde pressed, shaking Miguel by the shoulders.

"It's Pancho Villa. He heard about the young gringo rescuing all those Americans. I think he's embarrassed and angry. He spread the word that he wants Jesse dead." Miguel was quiet and still, staring at the floor.

"Dead? Are you kidding? Pancho Villa wants my son dead?" Clyde thought he might pass out.

"Yes, Captain. The Villistas are looking for him, and they know what he looks like." Miguel was quiet for a moment. "I'm sorry, Captain, sorry that I couldn't stop him. What do you want me to do?"

Clyde started to pace back and forth when suddenly he remembered something he'd read: Pancho Villa didn't drink alcohol. Even though the Mexicans liked to portray him as a macho, hard-drinking man, not drinking made him seem much more dangerous to Clyde; he was a clear-thinking monster. Clyde would rather have a drunkard after Jesse than someone with a clear head.

"I'll put my own bounty on Jesse's head, but this one will be to bring him over the border to me *alive!*"

He had flyers printed up announcing he would pay $35,000[1] for the return of his son across the border into the US, or to the consul in

---

[1] Approximately $540,000 today.

Tampico, unharmed. Clyde stared at the flyer. His son, missing, in a war-torn Mexico. *How did I let this happen?* Figuring that once Pancho Villa saw these flyers, he'd be looking for Clyde's head, Clyde prepared to return to the States. If it were discovered that Clyde was a Mason, there would be even more trouble since Catholics were not allowed to be Masons and Catholicism was the primary religion in Mexico. Miguel would hire a few men to help him, not only with the flyers, but with trying to keep track of the boats and barges. Clyde left Miguel to work through the mess and returned to Houston empty-handed.

Clyde knew he could never tell Jennie about Pancho Villa. She was delighted to hear about the reward he'd put out for Jesse's safe return. Clyde stayed in contact with every politician he knew, but he heard nothing.

It was May 1914. Their new normal was very uncomfortable. Clyde had his businesses to run, and Jennie had four other children to take care of. All they could do was try to move forward. But their missing son remained at all times in the forefront of their thoughts.

Back in 1912, dredging had begun on the Houston Ship Channel, which passed through Bolivar Roads, Galveston Bay, the San Jacinto River, and Buffalo Bayou to a turning basin just north of Houston. The objective was to transform the Port of Houston into another Manchester, England, where an inland port had been made accessible to large ships. On September 7, 1914, Clyde took his family to witness when the dredge *Texas* whistled to signal that the dredging was complete. Lilly, now nine, got a new outfit and paraded around with her parasol. Her parents were very taken with her. The official opening ceremony wasn't until November.

A war had erupted in Europe at the end of July of that year, but a war across the ocean made little difference in their lives; the construction of wharves continued along the new Houston Ship Channel, the opening of which was celebrated with a floral boat parade. Jennie attended a wedding in Franklin, and Clyde worked harder than ever.

If only Jesse would show up. As time went by, the children asked more often about their big brother. The tremendous guilt Clyde felt began to show itself in anger when he was asked about Jesse. He could hear his wife crying most nights. Although knowing she was trying to hide it, he was silent. *He must be dead,* he thought, lying in the dark. *He would have gotten word to me somehow. When do we decide he's gone forever? I won't let myself think like this; he will come back to us!*

Clyde was in his office in the First National Bank Building in Houston one day when he heard a ruckus in his reception room. He sprang up from his chair and hurried into the other room. A man was yelling something about his suit, which was torn and dirty. Clyde recognized his face but couldn't recall his name.

"What happened to you?" he asked the disheveled man.

"That daughter of yours driving down the street, that's what happened to me!" the man replied loudly.

"My daughter? Which daughter?"

"The young one; the thin one with the dark hair and pale skin, ran into me with that big front bumper and tore my suit! I'm sure there'll be bruises! What are you doing letting her drive alone downtown at her age? She could have killed me!" He continued to brush himself off and bent over to look for bruises through a hole in his trousers.

His secretary, Miss Ruth, trying hard to hide the smile on her face, put her arm around the man and offered him a seat. "I'll get you a glass of water," she said and left the office for the water fountain down the hall.

Clyde sat on the corner of Miss Ruth's desk. The man's name surfaced in his brain. "Are you sure it was my daughter, Mr. Wiseman?" he asked.

"Yes, I am. I asked her what her name was; all she said was that you are her daddy."

Miss Ruth returned with a glass of water, which Mr. Wiseman gulped down.

"Well, let me just tell you how very sorry I am. Are you sure you're not hurt anywhere else? I think you should go to a doctor; I'll pay for it."

"I don't need to go to any damn doctor, Captain. What I need is a new suit. I won't be wearing this one anymore." He looked as though he might spit to show his disgust but thought better of it.

"Of course, of course. I do hope you'll forgive my little Lilly; she's not one to do that sort of thing." He turned to Miss Ruth. "Call my tailor and let him know Mr. Wiseman will be coming there for a new suit and to bill me for it. Let him know to give my friend anything he wants." Clyde was known as a dapper dresser, so this invitation was even more appreciated. He slapped the befuddled man on the back. "Is there anything else I can do to make amends?"

"No, Captain. That will do nicely. May I suggest you have a talk with Lilly and tell her that driving downtown is for experienced drivers? She could use some more lessons in the car." Mr. Wiseman stood up, handed the empty glass to Miss Ruth, brushed himself once again, and shook Clyde's hand.

"Again, I am very sorry." Clyde escorted the man to the door and closed it behind him. He and Miss Ruth stared at each other in silence long enough to be sure their guest was down the stairs, then started laughing quietly. "Lilly? Really? I can't believe it! She's nine years old and has never done anything the least bit controversial."

"Well, she's growing up! Thank goodness she didn't really hurt him! What are you going to do with Lilly?"

"With Lilly? Nothing. Absolutely nothing. I'm so glad she's not at home in her room alone feeling poorly. I think this is progress for her!"

"A strange kind of progress," Miss Ruth said doubtfully.

"But progress nonetheless!" Clyde kissed her merrily on the cheek and returned to his office, where he was working on a new oil company in El Paso, Texas, that he and his partners had decided to name Rio Grande Oil Company.

That night at dinner, Will spoke up. "Daddy, will you tell us one of your stories from when you were a little boy?"

"Sure. All of you get ready for bed and then we'll meet in the parlor. I'll try to think of a good one that you haven't heard before."

Clyde felt loved and important and could almost forget that his eldest was lost, or worse, somewhere in Mexico.

He found Spencer. "Did you know that Lilly went driving by herself today?"

"No, sir, Captain. I saw the car was gone for a while, but I figured you had it." Jennie had never learned to drive.

As Clyde and Spencer were talking, she walked into Clyde's office.

"Lilly went for a drive downtown by herself today," Clyde told her. "She almost ran over a businessman." Jennie gasped. "He's fine, Jennie. The bumper tore his trousers. Lilly told him she was my daughter, so he came up to my office demanding a new suit!" The memory made Clyde laugh again. "It was certainly an entertaining little interlude."

"I'll go get her right now so you can give her a talkin' to."

"Wait. No, I'm not going to punish her. The poor child barely ever leaves the house. It's the most ordinary thing she's done in a long time. I'm happy she had the spunk to pull it off; our frail, sickly little Lilly!" Clyde was beaming.

"But Clyde, Will got a good talkin' to when he took the car. You have to be fair."

"But that's completely different. Will needs to be reeled in a little and Lilly needs to be encouraged to branch out into the world. I'll talk to her about it, but I have no intention of punishing her. Spencer? Will you be sure to give my little Lilly some grown-up driving lessons?"

"Yes, sir, Captain. I'll start tomorrow." Spencer left the room.

Jennie looked at Clyde uncertainly. "I know you think that's how best to handle it, but it just doesn't seem right."

"Let's just leave our Little Princess to enjoy her adventure." He kissed his wife, and together they went into the parlor. Jennie asked Lena, who now wanted to be called Peggy, to play for them. "I don't want to," Peggy responded.

"What's gotten into my little Peggy?" asked Clyde.

"Why do I always have to play the piano? Why doesn't somebody else do all the work for once!"

"But Peggy, your sister and brothers play and sing with you sometimes," Jennie reminded her.

"It's not the same thing, not at all," she pouted.

"Peggy, you're my favorite piano player and singer. We love to listen to you!" Clyde exclaimed.

"I can try to sing, Daddy," said Will. "And play my mandolin!"

Jennie looked at Clyde, wondering what his response would be.

"Well, son, that would be great! It seems that Peggy is going to break my heart, so go ahead and have your own special performance tonight."

Five minutes was the most anyone could bear of the little guy, who had yet to really learn to play his instrument and wasn't known for his singing ability. Clyde's promise to tell a story saved the evening.

"I'll tell you a story about when we all lived on the flatboat. Your mother wasn't with us yet," Clyde began.

"Oh, Daddy, I love those stories!" said Will. "And I'm really tired after all that playin' and singin'." Everyone laughed.

Clyde told them the story of the time they helped a man, who had the first steam-powered merry-go-round, head down the river with his enormous piece of equipment on their flatboat.

"When my pa told us about his plans, we all wanted to run and hide, but when Pa makes up his mind, there's no turning back. Grandpa thought he was kidding. We were quite a spectacle for the day and a half it took us to get that crazy thing on our boat. I wish I had a picture of us floating down the Mississippi River with that merry-go-round," Clyde laughed. "We got a few free rides on that thing before we had to get back on the flatboat. It was a lot of hard work followed by a lot of fun!" Clyde's smile was contagious, and soon the whole room was full of laughter and talk.

In their bed, Jennie was reading her Bible; Clyde, a business journal. He put the paper down and turned to Jennie. "I think it's time Clyde, Jr., started spending some time at my office. That boy needs to start learning about business; after all, he's 15. He almost never shows interest in anything unless it's something he's not supposed to be doing."

"I agree, but remember, he's just a boy," said Jennie quietly. "Have you heard anything about Jesse, anything at all?"

"No, nothing."

Jennie closed her Bible and prayed as she did every night for her son to be found…alive!

CHAPTER 32

THE DIVERGENCE

1914–15

The winter was unremarkable. With Jesse missing since March, it had been difficult for Jennie or Clyde to find joy in Christmas, but they rallied at New Year's to celebrate Lilly's birthday. She was now attending Mrs. Kinkaid's school, which was held in her home and seemed a good fit.

Clyde had made another trip down to Tampico; he was still deriving a lot of profit from his transportation company there and needed to keep it up and running at full capacity.

"A few times, somebody said they saw Jesse but nothing definite," said Mr. Miller. "Your reward stirred up quite a commotion when it first came out. Now that it's been so long, I don't think people pay it any attention at all. I'm sorry, Captain, I really am." Mr. Miller patted the shoulder of the seated Clyde, who had no response.

Back in Houston, Clyde and Jennie took a March stroll down their street. It hadn't been very cold that winter, but March had begun crisply, with only a few flowers blooming. It was Saturday, so the couple took the opportunity to spend some time alone outside. They walked in silence holding hands. Jennie looked around at all the beautiful houses and wondered how she had gotten there; Clyde looked around at all the beautiful houses and wondered how much grander the next neighborhood they called home would be.

"So, when do we decide that Jesse is…is…well, never coming home?" asked Jennie without looking at her husband.

He tightened his grip on her small hand. "I don't know. I really don't know."

A few days later, as Clyde sat at his outsized wooden desk in his office, Miss Ruth came running in breathless and shoved a telegram before Clyde's face.

"It's Jesse! He's alive! Praise God, he's alive!" she shouted.

Clyde grabbed the telegram and read it out loud: "I'm in Brownsville and ill. Please hurry. Love, Jesse." He clutched it to his heart, let out a massive sigh, and jumped out of his chair. He and Miss Ruth hugged each other and Clyde kissed her on the lips. His smile left his face and he looked at her with tenderness. He touched her cheek, put her hair behind her ear, and kissed her again, longer and harder. She stopped breathing, her eyes closed, and her head tilted upward.

Clyde released her. He didn't know what to say or what to do. He'd never been in this situation before. He held her at arm's length. She turned her face away.

"I'm, I'm so sorry, Ruth. I don't know why I did that." He turned and sat down heavily in his chair.

"I'm not sorry," said Ruth as she headed to the door, holding back tears. "I'll get your…I'll get Mrs. Barbour on the phone for you."

"Of course, of course. We need to find the next train to Brownsville. Who do we know down there?" Clyde was trying to move on, not knowing what to say to Ruth or what to do, still stunned by his own actions.

As he was leaving the office, he stopped in front of Ruth's desk, where she pretended to be busy working.

"Ruth. Maybe I'm not sorry, but that doesn't make it right. You're very important to me." He headed home, his mind filled with a maddening array of questions.

Jennie heard the news from Clyde and screamed loudly! She had to sit down. She started to cry, then sob, and rocked back and forth, her arms crossed on her chest. Her baby was found, and he was alive!

The next morning, they were on the first train to Brownsville, Texas. The hours were long, tedious, and seemingly endless, and the terrain gave little of a distraction in its monotony. Clickety-clack, clickety-clack, clickety-clack, clickety-clack; it went on and on. Jennie couldn't think of anything but her sick child, found after almost an entire year! Clyde had brought work to do and seemed to be distracted by it. He leaned over and kissed her cheek, his pince-nez catching the light flowing in from the large window. She smiled and laid her head on his shoulder until her neck began to ache. When she sat upright, she could feel the tension she was holding throughout her body. She stood up in their private car, stretched, and paced for a few minutes.

"You're an amazing man, Captain Barbour!" she said to her husband.

"What are you talking about?" asked Clyde.

"You. I'm talking about you. You are amazing!" She smiled at him and knelt between his bent knees. "I don't know why I'm your girl, but I'm so happy that I am!" She cupped his face in her hands and kissed him on the lips. "And you're very sexy, too!" She jumped up and sat on his lap, rumpling all his papers.

"You know just how to get my attention!" They both laughed and kissed and felt that connection that only they had. Clyde wasn't the least bit annoyed when he had to flatten out all of his papers later. It felt fabulous to feel truly happy again! Their son was alive!

Jesse was at a sanitarium in Brownsville. When his parents arrived at the train station, it was only a few minutes' ride there. They left their luggage at the front desk and were led back to his room. They didn't know what to expect. He was in a ward with four other men, and they weren't sure which one was their firstborn son. The nurse stopped at the last bed. "Here he is. He's asleep. Please don't wake him. He's really sick and needs to sleep."

They walked up to the head of the bed, one on each side. The man lying there had very dark skin and looked emaciated. Jennie was suddenly afraid someone had made a big mistake, but when she rubbed his head and he opened his eyes, they both knew it was their son.

"Oh my, Jesse, what happened to you?" asked Jennie. Jesse's lips moved but no sound came out.

"Shhh!" said Clyde. "We can talk later. We're here. Everything is going to be fine. Now go back to sleep, son." It seemed Jesse had no choice but to obey his father. Clyde turned to the nurse. "May I please speak to the doctor?"

"Yes, sir. He will be back in around half an hour," she replied.

"Fine. Could you please find two chairs for us?" he asked. She smiled and left, returning with a chair for each of them. They sat, holding hands across Jesse's chest.

"Clyde, he looks awful!" whispered Jennie. "How could we not have recognized our own son?" Tears were welling up in her eyes. *No crying. Jesse needs me strong.* She stroked his chest tenderly.

"We'll have to be patient and wait for him to want to tell us what he went through to get here. All I care about now is that he gets his strength back so he can get back to a normal life," Clyde responded.

"He looks like a Mexican!" stated Jennie, shocked at the color of his skin.

"It's that Black Irish in him. I bet it helped him," said Clyde, looking at his son's face. "Imagine if having that blood in him helped him to conceal himself!"

"That would be a miracle," said Jennie quietly. "We need to pray for him." She bowed her head and clasped her hands together, as did Clyde.

"Lord, we fall so short of what you ask of us. Please be patient with us and help us spread your glory. We ask that you particularly bless our Jesse who has somehow found his way back to us. Bless him and keep him close, Lord. We ask in your name, Amen," Clyde finished.

They didn't meet with the doctor until the following morning. "Your son is very ill and very weak. How long was he missing?"

"It's been almost a year since anyone saw him," answered Clyde.

"He's suffering from dehydration, malnutrition, and I believe he has some parasites that he picked up out in the Mexican countryside. He told me he ate whatever he could find." The doctor looked over his notes on the clipboard. "He's covered with abrasions and bruises and scars. A rancher who lives just this side of the border found him and brought him here. It's amazing he's still alive!"

Jennie's tears had many meanings—relief, fear, bewilderment, gratitude. She walked over to her son and held his hand as he slept. "Will he get better?" she asked the doctor.

"I have no reason to believe he can't recover fully from this. It's going to take a long while for him to be up and walking and enjoying things again. We've started him on liquids and we're starting very slowly to reintroduce normal food to his system. He's on some medicine to help get rid of those parasites he likely has."

"How long do you expect him to stay here?" Clyde asked.

The doctor cleared his throat and looked around and into the distance. "Two weeks; in two weeks, he can probably leave the sanitarium, but he'll still have months of therapy after that."

"Can I move him to a hospital in Houston?" Clyde looked at Jesse and guessed the answer.

"I wouldn't move him. Give him the two weeks here, and then you can move him to someplace closer to your home."

"Yes, sir. There are plenty of hospitals there; fine hospitals," Clyde said.

"I would also be looking for a place like Mineral Wells or Hot Springs, where he can take the waters and have therapy." The doctor replaced the clipboard at the foot of Jesse's bed. "If there's nothing else, I have a lot of other patients to see."

Jennie stayed in Brownsville, and Clyde returned to Houston. After 10 days, the doctor allowed her to take Jesse to Houston with the understanding that he had a long way to go before he would be well again.

Jesse and Jennie left Brownsville on a train. They hadn't talked much about his travails. He had slept most of the time, leaving Jennie frightened that he might never wake up. It had been arranged for a bed to be prepared before they boarded the train. The walk from the car to the train was almost too much for Jesse. He collapsed on the bed in their private car and fell asleep immediately with all his clothes on, his hand dangling over the side of the bed still holding his hat.

When they finally arrived in Houston, Clyde and Spencer were there with a wheelchair. Clyde boarded the train to get them. Jesse stood when his father stepped into their room. "You look a lot better, son, since the last time I saw you!" Clyde hugged him tightly. "Let's get you home! Spencer is waiting just outside the train with a wheelchair."

"I am not gettin' in some stupid wheelchair!" said Jesse.

"The hell you aren't," said Clyde, who helped him off the train and into the wheelchair.

The children were still at school when they got to the house on Avondale. Spencer and the housekeeper had moved the furniture and made the dining room into a sick room for Jesse since he wasn't able to climb the stairs. A nurse was part of the deal. She was there when they arrived and quickly took over, helping him up onto the bed.

"You rest up until the children get home," said Jennie. "We told them you've been very sick but nothing about where you've been all this time."

"Don't worry, Mama; I won't tell them anything you don't want me to. I can't wait to see everybody!"

"The doctor will be round this afternoon. I'm off to the office. I'm so happy, son, that you've made it home!" Clyde tousled Jesse's hair and left.

His siblings had been told that Jesse had gotten sick in Mexico and was home to recuperate. Jennie decided it wasn't really a lie. When they had all returned from school, Jennie took them en masse to see him.

"You'll have 10 minutes with him right now, and later, I'll let each of you see him alone. He's still really weak, so please don't ask too many questions." Jennie led them into the sickroom, which instantly became a carnival. Questions and giggles and loud exclamations filled the room. Jennie stood next to the doorway watching the spectacle of a large family welcoming back one of its own. She doubted she'd ever been happier than at that very moment.

True to her word, she hustled them all out after 10 minutes. Jesse looked happy and peaceful and ready for a rest. She kissed him on the cheek and left the room.

That night at the dinner table, the children's questions got more complicated, so the story became that Jesse had gotten lost in Mexico and had to find his way back home. Since Jesse wasn't at the dinner table, most of the questions went unanswered. Clyde and Jennie had purposefully not asked him a lot of questions, waiting for Jesse to offer up the information on his own. The children were less patient.

About a week later, the nurse was dismissed, and Jesse spent much of his day out of bed. He returned to the dinner table where his siblings were told not to ask him questions but to let him eat; he needed to eat. To fend off a barrage of questions, Clyde decided they would have family time after dinner, but instead of Peggy playing the piano, Jesse would tell his story, or as much of it as he wanted to. Clyde asked everyone not to interrupt him, but he knew that would be impossible.

"The Mexican Revolution has been going on for a while. Everybody disagrees about who should be the president and they're fighting about it. I was helping Americans get out of Tampico because our country was afraid they might get hurt in all the fighting. All of a sudden, I was in the middle of a gun battle, and I ran for my life—and I kept running. I heard that one of the generals, Pancho Villa, was there looking for the gringo—that's what they call people from our country—that helped all those Americans escape, and that was me. He was mad about it and said he was gonna find me and…well…he wanted to make me sorry that I helped all those people."

"What was he gonna do to you?" asked Clyde, Jr.

"Jesse," said Clyde, reminding him to watch his words.

"I guess he wanted to put me in jail or something." Jesse knew full well that if he'd been captured, he would have been killed. "So, I hid, and I hid, and I hid some more. I knew I couldn't go back to Tampico, so I figured I'd have to make it to the border. I didn't think it would take that long, but sometimes, I would have to hide for days, and I wasn't always sure I was heading in the right direction."

"You can always watch where the sun rises and sets," said Peggy, eager to show off her own knowledge.

"Yeah, but it can be cloudy, or you can be in a forest, or for other reasons it doesn't work so easy," Jesse answered. "I ate anything I could find; lots of berries and fruit. My skin got even browner than it was already, and my hair got long; I looked just like a Mexican!"

"You do not," said Will. "Mexicans don't have big ears like yours." Everybody laughed.

"Okay, well, one day I caught a ride on a small boat on the Conchos River. I was wearing a sombrero to keep the sun off and to disguise myself. One of the Villistas stopped the boat and got on."

"What's a valleyeters?" asked Lilly.

"Lilly, it's Villistas. That's what they call a soldier who fights for Pancho Villa. We didn't know why he got on the boat with his big gun. I had to try hard not to shake 'cause I was so scared. When the soldier got to me, he lifted up the edge of my sombrero, looked me in the eye, and went on to the next man. That's when I knew God was with me."

Clyde looked around and saw the fear on each of his children's faces. *Maybe this wasn't such a good idea.*

"I twisted up my ankle so bad I couldn't walk for almost a week. I was lucky I didn't break it. It seemed like I was always bleeding from somewhere 'cause of limbs and bushes and thorns. I bet I smelled terrible, but I never noticed."

Will snickered and Clyde gave him a severe look to make him stop.

"When I finally got to the Rio Grande, I wasn't sure I could get across; I was so worn out and sick. A few Mexican workers were headed to their day job at a ranch just across the river and they took me with them and practically carried me to the rancher's house. I was so weak; I could barely talk and I couldn't write, either. It's like a hazy dream kind of thing when I think back on it. Finally, I got out 'Clyde Barbour, Houston' and it was all over. I thank God every day that he helped me get back home to all of y'all!"

Grannie had sat perfectly still during the storytelling, almost expressionless. Her eyes were full of tears, but she remained stoic. "It's a miracle, right in front of our eyes!"

Peggy leaned forward as if to add something very important. "I am never going to Mexico!" she said resolutely and defiantly. For some reason, that broke the tension and they all laughed.

"Now Peggy, I'm sure someday you'll venture across the border to Mexico," said Clyde.

"Who's Peggy?" asked Jesse.

"That's Daddy's new nickname for Lena!" said Lilly.

"A story for another time. I think I'll take Jesse back to his room and help him get ready for bed," Jennie said, cutting the conversation off, and the two of them left the room.

It was decided that Jesse would go to Hot Springs, Arkansas, and take the waters for at least several weeks. Jennie wanted the whole family to accompany him, but Clyde had too much work and the children were in school. Jennie thought that at the very least, she should go with him.

"For Heaven's sake, Jennie, he's a man now. He may only be 18 but, after all he's been through, he's a man now. I need him back in Mexico working as soon as possible."

Jennie caught her breath, put her hand to her mouth, and looked at her husband in disbelief. "You want to send Jesse back to Mexico? After all that happened? You can't, you just can't do that to me…or to him! I don't want either of you to ever go back there again. No amount of money is worth your lives."

"You have to let him grow up. His life isn't yours to control anymore. Go with him to Arkansas, get him settled in, then come back here to your family who love you and need you," Clyde said. "He won't go back to Mexico until things settle down. I don't want anything to happen to him either."

Jennie spent several days with Jesse at Hot Springs and then took the train back to Houston. When she got on the train to return home, she cried silently for a long while. The pain of being separated from her firstborn son so soon after thinking she had lost him forever was excruciating.

Jesse was good about writing his family. He was getting stronger every day. There was one constant theme: a girl named Sylvia Glasscock, who worked at the resort. He said she was a year and a half older than he was and he was smitten. Clyde wasn't surprised by the age difference, figuring Jesse had aged years on his Mexican trek. After about a month into his sojourn at the resort, he informed his parents that he and Sylvia were to be married; he had asked her father for permission, and he had said yes.

Back in Houston, the house on Avondale was a lively place as everyone got ready for the wedding. It was a wonderful reprieve after the 12 months of waiting and praying for Jesse's return from Mexico.

"I'm so tired of hearing about Jesse and Sylvia!" Peggy said at one point. "Why is Jesse allowed to get married and I'm not?" she asked Grannie.

Peggy had been dating a man from Ohio who was living in Houston. Clyde completely disapproved of the union, partly because her suitor, Forest Lewis, was 10 years older than she was and partly because Clyde wasn't prepared to lose his favorite child. There wasn't anything unacceptable about the man, but as Clyde was climbing the ladder of financial success, he had hoped his children would marry well and help extend the dynasty he was creating. Forest Lewis did not fit that profile.

Jesse and Sylvia were married on June 17, 1915, in a small family ceremony at the Presbyterian Church, as Sylvia's parents had requested. The marriage was officiated by the minister G.W. Martin, who seemed genuinely excited to be marrying the handsome young couple. Afterward, the minister joined them for dinner at their home. Jesse, though thin, looked like himself again. He had never seemed happier, and Sylvia beamed with excitement. Peggy could barely hide her jealousy, wanting to be the bride everyone was fawning over. She was angry with her father, but Clyde wasn't concerned.

During the evening, Jennie saw Peggy talking with the minister and wondered what had been said. When Jennie asked her about it later, Peggy sighed and said she couldn't even remember what they'd discussed. Something in Jennie's gut told her Peggy was lying, but she decided she could tell Clyde about it when all the festivities had ended; no reason to bring up something potentially unpleasant at such a happy time.

Jesse and Sylvia went to Galveston for their honeymoon and returned five days later. After a welcome home luncheon, Clyde suggested a walk. When the small, animated group had made their way several blocks down the street, Clyde stopped and pointed out an empty house. He began to walk up the sidewalk.

"Clyde, where are you going?" Jennie called.

"Jesse, Sylvia, come here." Clyde turned around to the newlyweds and motioned for them to join him. "Come up here," he coaxed as he walked up the front steps.

"I thought you said nobody lives here," said Jesse.

"Well, that's about to change!" Clyde took something out of his pocket and handed it to Jesse. "Congratulations on your marriage. Your mother and I bought this house for you!" Clyde seemed more excited than Jesse, who was mostly shocked and speechless. Sylvia began to cry. "Here's the key. Go inside, son. Go on!" Clyde said.

Sylvia hugged Jennie and looked with trepidation at the beautiful house in front of them. Jesse hugged his father and patted him hard on his back. "I don't know what to say! This is…this is…perfect! How am I ever going to thank you?" Jesse asked.

"You already have; you came back to us. After all you've been through, you deserve this," Clyde answered. Jennie was happy to stand back and let her husband have this moment.

"Captain Barbour…I've never felt so blessed. Thank you so much!" Sylvia didn't know Clyde well enough to know how to approach him, so she walked up to him and kissed him on the cheek. Clyde motioned for Jennie to join them, and they shared a family hug, Jesse and Sylvia's new family.

Jesse picked up his bride and carried her over the threshold, setting her down inside and kissing her excitedly. "I proclaim this house the home of Mr. and Mrs. Jesse C. Barbour!" Everyone cheered and applauded.

And so it was that Clyde and Jennie lived at 205 Avondale while Jesse and Sylvia began their marriage at 702 Avondale.

That evening at dinner, Peggy was missing. She hadn't been seen since lunchtime. As the plates were being taken from the table and the family was settling into the parlor, the front door opened, and Peggy and Forest walked in, laughing. Clyde got up from his chair and walked to the front door.

"Peggy, where have you been?" he asked sternly, ignoring Forest. "I won't have you missing dinner without telling us first." He turned to look at Forest straight on. "Do you realize how you have disrespected Mrs. Barbour and me by keeping our daughter out without letting us know where she is?" There was no doubting Clyde was angry. Jennie had joined him at the front door.

"Mama, we want to talk to you and Daddy, alone," Peggy said.

"We are alone, right here," Clyde answered her.

"Clyde. Peggy," Jennie whispered. "Let me send the children out of the parlor, and we'll go in there."

Clyde did not want to sit down, but Jennie got him to sit in his chair and she sat on the couch closest to him. Peggy and Forest sat on the opposite couch. Forest held her hand. Clyde glared at their hands and Forest released his grasp.

"If you're here to ask for my blessing, again, to be married, the answer is still no and it isn't likely to change." Clyde didn't hide his anger.

"Captain Barbour..." Forest began.

"Remind me, Forest, how old are you? I seem to remember you're 10 years older than my Peggy." Clyde sat up straight as if to draw some power from the change in position.

"Daddy, stop it! Please!" said Peggy.

"Stop what, Peggy? Taking care of you? That'll never happen."

"It's too late, Daddy," said Peggy.

"Too late for what?"

"Captain Barbour, this afternoon Peggy and I were married by the same minister who married Jesse and Sylvia." Forest said it quickly as if to be rid of it, as if once he said it, the ordeal would be over.

Jennie could see the ire rise in Clyde as his cheeks turned redder and redder. She knew better than to say anything. She wanted to pick Peggy up in her arms and carry her upstairs away from all the anger. She had to remind herself that Peggy had brought this on herself and would have to fix it by herself.

Peggy retrieved a piece of paper from her purse, walked over, handed it to her father, and hurriedly sat back down next to Forest.

"What is this?" asked Clyde.

"Our marriage license. We're man and wife now," stated Peggy, grabbing Forest's hand for support.

"The hell you are!" Clyde growled, studying the document. "Look at it; it's not completely filled out. Looks like you couldn't prove you're 18, which of course, you're not; you're barely 17."

"But Daddy, the preacher did the ceremony and signed it, so it's official in the sight of God," Peggy replied indignantly.

"Not according to the state of Texas, it's not, and not according to me!" Clyde jumped out of his chair and stood over the couple, waving the piece of paper.

"Captain Barbour. I love your daughter. I can support her and care for her, and I will, forever. I promise!" Forest had risen.

"Support her? Look around you. This is what she's used to. Can you provide her with this?" Clyde waved his arms around the room to show Forest what he was referring to. "Do you have any idea how much the dress costs that she's wearing? More than you probably make in a month! And those shoes!" Clyde's anger was not abating.

Peggy stood up to join her husband. Jennie did the same. The four of them stood in a circle of love and anger and disappointment.

Suddenly Grannie appeared in the doorway. She stood there, at a distance, her eyes full of love. "My dear Clyde, they love each other. You do remember that feeling when you and Jennie got married, don't you? God has shone down on their marriage; who are we to undo what God has done? Forest is a fine man."

"But Mother, the marriage isn't final until this document is published by the state of Texas," said Clyde.

"The state of Texas doesn't marry couples, a preacher does; God does. My marriage to your father wasn't made through any state." Grannie kept her distance as she spoke.

"But Mother, not Peggy!" Clyde lamented. Grannie smiled at him and disappeared.

They stood in silence, the clock chiming on the mantel. "You've left me no choice. You have your marriage. Now leave my house!" He thrust the paper at Forest and pointed to the front door.

Peggy hugged her mother and Forest shook her hand. Peggy ran to her father and put her arms around him and held him tightly, but he didn't hug back. Forest tried to shake his hand, but Clyde turned away and walked upstairs.

Jennie walked to the front door with them. "It's gonna take a long time for him to forget all of this. He feels betrayed and unloved and helpless, which is an awful way for a father to feel. Pray tonight. Pray for God to bless your marriage and pray that your father can learn to forgive."

CHAPTER 33

THE MAGNATE

August 1915

Halfway through August of 1915, Galveston was hit by yet another deadly hurricane. All the work that had been done after the devastating hurricane of 1900 to elevate the entire city and build a new seawall helped lessen the damage. The storm tore through Galveston Island as a Category 4 hurricane, with a storm surge in excess of 16 feet and winds up to 135 mph, and then headed north to Houston. It left behind extensive damage to the Galveston Causeway. It was no surprise when Clyde was awarded the contract to do the repairs.

At the end of a particularly long day on the job, Clyde, still on the Galveston side, decided to have dinner with his brother, James. James was working for Clyde on the causeway and was living in a small place he kept on the island that was unharmed by the hurricane. James was happy for his rich big brother to take him to dinner. Most of the places on the water were closed due to the hurricane, but James found them a place to eat.

"Hey, Clyde, I haven't seen you on the job in a while. What were you doin' out there today?" James spoke through a mouthful of fried fish.

"It's my reputation on the line. If somebody messes up, it'll be my problem. I think it's important that my crew actually see me out there; it builds respect." Clyde was enjoying a hot bowl of seafood gumbo.

A woman approached the table smiling. "Hey, Honey!" she said to James as she leaned over and kissed him on the lips. Clyde didn't say a word.

"Hey, Annie! This is my brother, Clyde," James responded. "Join us!" James got up and pulled the chair out for Annie to sit down.

Annie was small and pretty and full of personality. They obviously knew each other very well. Clyde invited her to join them for dinner, an offer she readily accepted. *What in the world is going on?* Clyde wondered. When dinner was over, James and Annie thanked Clyde and got up to leave.

"James, I need to talk to you for a minute." Clyde smiled.

"Sure. Annie, wait for me at the door," James said and sat back down.

"Well?"

"Well, what?"

"You really don't know?" Clyde asked, flabbergasted.

"Oh, Annie! Yeah, Clyde, she's great! She's crazy about me!" James was smiling from ear to ear. "And she has Ma's name!"

"James. Have you lost your mind? Ma's name? Who the hell is she?" asked Clyde, speaking in almost a whisper.

"She's my Galveston girl! When I stay down here, we stay together. She's a lot of fun!" James answered, his smile never fading.

"What about Mary? You know, your *wife?*" Clyde said in disbelief.

"This has nothin' to do with Mary. She's at home with the children and that's the way she likes it. And I like it that way, too. Don't you go messin' in my personal business. If you don't wanna know, then forget about tonight. Now, my girl's waitin' for me. I'll see you soon, brother." James walked to the door, put his arm around Annie, and they were off, leaving behind a stunned Clyde.

All the way home, Clyde thought about this unexpected bombshell. He couldn't say that he was surprised, given that James had chased females all his life. *How am I going to tell Jennie? Should I tell Jennie? If I don't tell her and she finds out I know, then what? What is he thinking?*

Clyde's mind found its way to Ruth. *Ruth. What am I thinking? Who am I to throw stones at James?* Of course, there was a vast difference: Clyde and Ruth had grown close through their daily contact at the office and had not done the unforgivable. But could Clyde be sure that he never would? Then his thoughts moved on to Lena, his Peggy, who was now a wife. Two days after her secret marriage, Clyde had gone down to the courthouse and signed a waiver allowing the marriage to endure uncontested. He owed it to his own wife and to his mother.

Clyde didn't have to invent things to keep him busy and his mind off Peggy's marriage and James' infidelity. He was busy putting together a lease for 1,000 acres in Caracol, Mexico, that had belonged to the Tampico Fruit Company before it went bankrupt. This included a well drilled to only 2,200 feet. From what Clyde had been able to determine, they'd have to drill down to about 3,300 feet to find the oil and he had hired Harry Humble to take charge of all the drilling. The mortgage owners, Ed Williams and Associates of Tampico, were thrilled to have Clyde taking it over as his reputation was sterling. *How am I going to manage all of this?* he wondered. "Everything will fall into place," he said out loud to himself. "One step at a time."

Pa had been in the Greenwood Sanitarium since Clyde had put him there. Mentally, he was a wreck. His memory had left him, and he lived in a state of constant confusion and overwhelming lethargy that was followed at times by bouts of euphoria. He had suffered from hardening of the arteries for years. He had recently been diagnosed with gangrene, which the doctor said had probably been caused by low blood flow. It had been a few weeks since Clyde had made his monthly pilgrimage to visit his pa. He would always bring his mother with him, as he thought it better not to have her go alone. Now Pa's doctor had called Clyde and asked that he come quickly to the hospital. He rushed there by himself from his office and was ushered in to see the doctor.

"Captain Barbour," the doctor said as Clyde walked in his door. "Have a seat and I'll get right to the point. Your Pa has contracted septicemia and if we don't get control of it fast, he's not gonna survive."

"What do you mean, Doctor?"

"The hardening of his arteries led to inadequate oxygen to his feet, which caused the gangrene, but you already know that. The gangrene caused an infection that must have gotten into his blood stream and is poisoning him. If he goes into septic shock, he will die quickly. I suggest you get your ma up here to see him. There's not a lot we can do." The doctor had his nurse call Jennie so she could get Grannie to the hospital immediately.

Clyde went to see his pa. As he entered his hospital room, he was struck by the smell of something foul, like an animal that had been dead for days. Pa was lying in bed groaning, perspiration on his forehead. When Clyde looked at this man, the man who had brought him into this world and trained him in the ways of the rivers, he could find nothing left of the father he remembered.

Where is the man who taught me to catch a rope? To use the sweeps? To steer the flatboat? To hunt and catch fish? Where is the man who was always ready and willing to help a stranger? Who so graciously took Jennie on the flatboat? Who danced with Ma in the glow of the gas lanterns on the river? Where's the man who taught me how to negotiate prices and always be on the lookout for opportunities so we could make a living?

"Pa. Pa, it's Clyde. Can you hear me?" Clyde stood next to the bed and leaned over his father.

Pa's eyes opened slightly and seemed to be looking off into the distance. Pa smiled just enough for it to be perceptible, then let out what sounded like a birdcall.

"Yes, Pa, I remember that whistle. It meant 'To oars!' We moved as fast as lightning when we heard that," Clyde mused sadly. Pa moved his mouth in an effort to speak but made no sound. "Pa, you rest. Ma is coming; Ma and Jennie are on their way, Pa!" There was a fearful tone to Clyde's words.

He walked over to the window and stared out. What he saw was the Ohio River, the cliffs topped with trees, and the Mississippi River running fast and furious after heavy snows or rains up north. He could see Pa and Luke tying a skiff to the back of the flatboat to help a family who needed to get down the river faster, then his angry face as he yelled at Clyde after Jennie fell in the water. "I don't want to see his angry face," he whispered to himself.

Jennie and Ma came rushing in, Ma to Pa's bedside and Jennie to Clyde. The doctor followed them in and explained to the women what he had already told Clyde, then added, "The nurse reports that his symptoms surely show signs of septic shock. Is there anyone else that needs to see him now?"

"James, my brother, but he's in Galveston. It will take quite a while for him to get here." Clyde thought about Annie and felt angry that because of her, his brother might never see their pa alive again. *It's his own fault,* thought Clyde, but he did ask Ruth to contact his brother and tell him to get there quickly.

Clyde and Jennie stayed by the window to give Ma time alone with her dying husband—who had not been a husband for a long time. The nurse came in with three chairs.

"I think he's asleep," said Ma as they each took a seat.

"Did he say anything?" Jennie asked.

"He said my name! Annie Brumbach. Of all the things to remember...my maiden name!" Ma smiled slightly. "At least he knows who I am."

The hours seemed endless: up and down from the chairs, over to the window and back, a walk down the hall for fresh air. Clyde got them each a sandwich and even made some work-related phone calls from the doctor's office.

It was dark outside when the doctor stopped in on his way home. "It's time you went home and got some sleep. He doesn't even know you're here. I'm afraid he doesn't have much time left. Have the nurse call me if you need me. I'm sorry, Mrs. Barbour, Captain." He patted

Clyde on the back and rubbed Ma's shoulder. They sat in silence for a long time.

"I want you two to go home now," said Clyde. "Jennie, the children need you, and Ma, you need some rest. I'll stay."

"No, son. I'm the one stayin'. If your pa's gonna die tonight, I'm gonna be here to hold his hand." Ma spoke clearly, her jaw set in determination. Clyde looked at her and knew she wasn't going anywhere.

"Okay, Ma, you stay. I'll take Jennie home, sleep for a few hours, and come back. I'll see if the nurse can set up some kind of cot for you," Clyde said, happy to have something to do. He and Jennie said their goodbyes to Pa, kissed Ma, and left.

"Should we take the children to see him tomorrow, if…if…you know…he's still with us?" Jennie asked on the way home.

Clyde thought for a minute. "No, I don't think so. They never knew him well and death is ugly."

In the wee hours of February 10, 1916, James A. Barbour died with his wife, Annie Brumbach Barbour, and his two sons, James R. Barbour, and Clyde A. Barbour, by his side. The three of them accompanied his body to Jeffersonville, Indiana, where he was buried next to his father, William Barbour/Grandpa, his mother, Elizabeth Crandall Barbour/Grandma, and their son, William Cilas, who had died as a child.

After the funeral, Clyde and James returned to Houston and Ma stayed in Jeffersonville for a few months to visit with family.

The month before Pa's death, Pancho Villa and his Villistas attacked a train in Chihuahua, Mexico, and killed 17 Americans, including men who worked for American Smelting and Refining Company. President Wilson retaliated by sending an army of roughly 10,000 to El Paso, Texas, led by General John Pershing, to go in search of the desperado. The soldiers had 600 trucks, all of which needed fuel. It was a huge boon to Clyde's Rio Grande Oil Company. Clyde sent Jesse to oversee the work.

Shortly thereafter, Villa and 500 men attacked the small border town of Columbus, New Mexico, as if to taunt the United States' efforts to get rid of him. Mexico's president, Venustiano Carranza, ordered the US to remove its soldiers from his country. The back and forth between the countries continued, and on May 14, General Pershing sent his second lieutenant, George S. Patton, into his first combat, leading a detachment of US soldiers into Mexico, where Villa was said to be in San Miguelito. Three of Villa's men were killed there, including his personal bodyguard, Julio Cardenas, but not the intended target.

Jennie was beside herself at the thought of Jesse being so close to Mexico, so close to Pancho Villa, whom she now knew had wanted him dead. Jesse was nervous but didn't say so. He knew he could wear his pistol there and the thought provided some reassurance. A pregnant Sylvia was due to deliver in August, so in mid-July, Jesse made his way back to Houston for the birth and to look after affairs at the office while Clyde traveled to New York City. The Tennant-Lovegrove Co., Inc., was chartered in May 1916 and included Clyde and Jesse as investors. The company was to handle a full line of machinery for work in the oil shipping trade.

Before he could head north, Clyde made a trip to the Clooney Construction & Towing Co. near Lake Charles, Louisiana, to oversee the building of a new sternwheeler and three barges. He had named the sternwheeler the *Tamboyoche*, and it would work with the *Major Black* on the Panuco River. The three barges combined had a capacity of 50,000 barrels and their addition to the Interior Navigation Company's fleet increased the loading capacity to 125,000 barrels.

Could he keep all his plates spinning at one time?

"Everything will fall into place," he repeated aloud to no one as he surveyed his newest babies. "One step at a time." He walked alongside his new sternwheeler and felt a rush of pride. *Just another addition to my Mexican fleet.* He grinned from deep inside and said a little prayer of gratitude to God. *Now all I have to do is pay all this money back!* He laughed, then took in a deep breath. *One step at a time.* Little did he know that with the discovery of oil in Monroe, Louisiana, that year, he would be stepping into his new and very lucrative role as the King of Carbon Black, which became a pillar of Clyde's fortune.

Clyde loved going to New York City. He loved to walk down the street in the hustle and bustle of business, smelling the unfamiliar odors of cooking from different ethnicities. Having been there only a few times, he was just beginning to make some friends.

In 1910, the Singer Building was being touted as the tallest building in the world; in 1913, it became the Woolworth Building. The world's largest hotel, the McAlpin Hotel, at 34th and Broadway, had opened in 1912. It boasted 25 floors, 1,500 guest rooms, and a staff of 1,500. A Turkish bath and a small swimming pool were on the 24th floor. The 23rd was a miniature hospital. One floor was strictly for single women and women traveling alone and included a separate check-in desk and female-only staff. The 16th floor was called the Sleepy 16th; it was set aside for guests who slept during the day. Clyde decided to stay there in one of the less swanky rooms, which was nonetheless beautifully decorated with plenty of space. He spent the first evening going over his papers for his meeting with Steve Hilton at Gotham National Bank the next day.

Imagine, he thought, *I have a New York City banker!* He spoke out loud as he studied his reflection in the mirror: "Hi, I'm Captain Barbour and this is my banker from New York City, Mr. Steve Hilton." He laughed at himself and at what seemed a ridiculous notion that he was someone special. "I'm getting there," he told the reflection in the mirror. "Just watch me!"

"The president of the bank wants to meet you," Steve Hilton told him the next day as they shook hands in the Gotham National Bank. "Let's head over to his office." Clyde had prayed this would happen. Walking down the corridor, Clyde was once again struck by the beauty of the building. The vaulted ceilings suggested the interior of a cathedral, which added to an aura of reverence. *Reverence and money; I guess that's right. We do tend to idolize it. I will not let the dollar own me. I won't let it become my God*, Clyde told himself as they moved along the open expanse of this elaborately decorated house of money. He had to smile and laugh to himself. *I hope I can live up to that statement!*

The sign on the door read TIMOTHY BRYAN, PRESIDENT. He had two secretaries in his anteroom, one leaning over the desk of the other in deliberation.

"Hello, ladies!" Mr. Hilton said as they entered. "This is Captain Barbour, all the way from Houston, Texas! Captain, this is Mrs. Margaret Hill and her assistant, Miss Becky McWilliams." Clyde nodded to the ladies. "The boss is expecting us," Mr. Hilton said, smiling maybe a little too much at Becky, the younger of the two.

"I'll let him know you're here," said Becky, her voice warm and mellow. It reminded Clyde of his grandmother's voice and then he could see her smiling face light up the office. Clyde could feel his grandmother there and smell her clean skin. His emotions transitioned from missing her to pride that she was sharing this moment with him.

"Captain?" Mr. Hilton startled him out of his reverie, and he joined the moment.

Timothy Bryan stood up as they entered his inner office. He was a tall man with wide shoulders and an attractive, soft look about his face. Clyde sensed honesty in this stranger's smile and liked him immediately.

"Captain Barbour, Mr. Timothy Bryan," Mr. Hilton said. The men shook hands and Mr. Bryan motioned for them to sit down.

"Please, call me Tim. It's a pleasure to meet you. I've heard a lot about you and all of it intrigues me."

"I asked him to call me Steve a while back but have yet to hear it," Mr. Hilton told his boss with a laugh.

"Your Southern formality is a nice change from things up here," said Tim. "We could use a little more of your gentility."

"You give us too much credit, Tim. It's all we know." Clyde reached into his briefcase and pulled out a small box, which he handed to Tim, who immediately opened it and pulled out a four-leaf clover.

"My Lilly, who is 14 and quite the peacemaker, wanted me to give this to you for good luck!"

Tim was visibly surprised. "Well, that's the nicest thing. I'll have to put it in a place for safe keeping. She sounds like a wonderful girl." ·

"Delightful. Quiet, demure, pretty, and very smart. She dreams of coming to New York City with me sometime," Clyde mused. "My wife, on the other hand, is happy to stay in Houston with the children."

"By all means, bring your Lilly to see us. We'll be sure she has the time of her life!" said Tim, with Steve nodding his agreement. "Before we get down to business, Steve says you like opera."

"That's very true. New Orleans has a beautiful Opera House and we've been there several times. My older daughter has a beautiful voice and loves to entertain us with her singing. I haven't been to your Metropolitan Opera."

"I'd like to change that, Captain. Please join my wife and me tonight for dinner at Delmonico's followed by *Luna d'Estate* performed by The Great Caruso at the Metropolitan. I hope you won't mind that we've asked a friend of Mr. Caruso, an opera star from France, Opal Perrette, to join us."

"I would be honored," Clyde said, a little lost for words. He understood that this invitation was something people dreamed of.

Clyde had his tuxedo with him, as he'd hoped to go to the Met during his visit. Going as the guest of the president of Gotham National Bank raised the experience to a new level.

Mademoiselle Perrette was also staying at the McAlpin Hotel, so it was decided they would meet in the hotel bar for a cocktail before dinner. Clyde took the elevator downstairs early. Looking around, he didn't see his hosts or any women sitting alone. He felt uncomfortable not knowing the rules governing such an occasion.

Do I go into the bar and get a table or is there already one reserved? Should I sit here in the lobby and read the paper until I see them? How will I know if Miss Perrette is sitting right next to me? Clyde decided that sitting and casually reading the paper would give him something to do and make him less anxious. It was warm in the lobby although a large fan whirled above his head. The starch in his shirt combined with the perspiration around his tight-fitting collar and bow tie made him itch. The more he tried not to notice it, the more it bothered him. He looked over the top of his newspaper to be sure no one was looking, then put his index finger between his neck and his shirt for a quick scratch. His eyes caught sight of a figure standing before him, so he quickly removed his finger and felt as sheepish as if he'd been caught picking his nose. He fumbled putting down the newspaper and stood up, hat in hand.

"I must agree—it is very warm in here this evening! I don't think *mon châle* will make it onto my shoulders tonight. Sorry; my, ahhh, shawl!" Whoever she was, she was beautiful, with dark brown hair pulled back and ornamented with a comb of pearls. She looked to be in her mid-thirties. She had a French accent and her mixing languages together and her smile put him at ease. "I don't know how men wear those collars so *serré*. I would certainly have mine loose, making all my friends upset!" she laughed.

Just then, Tim and his wife walked up. "I see you two have already met!"

"Not formally," said Clyde. "We just started talking and then here you are!" Clyde shook hands with Tim and turned to introduce himself to the woman on Tim's arm. "I'm Captain Clyde Barbour," he said, then took a slight bow.

"Captain, my wife, Mrs. Nancy Bryan. And this lovely creature is Miss Opal Perrette, our favorite opera singer!" Clyde took Miss Perrette's hand and kissed it as she dipped in a small curtsy and lowered her face. She then turned to Mrs. Bryan and did the same. "Let's get into the bar and find a place to sit. I need a large glass of cold water," Tim said, pointing the way.

They sat down, each ordering cold water along with a cocktail.

"I think you men should let go your bow ties and relax," Miss Perrette said.

"That's a nice thought, my dear, but I don't believe we'd be allowed into the Met with our collars unbuttoned," said Tim, as he laughed and looked over at his wife. "They're very serious at the Met; very serious about everything!"

"As the dresses of women get *plus ample et plus courte*, you men will be left alone to suffer in the heat!" She took out her fan as she spoke and opened it up. It was bright, colorful, and looked like a tapestry. "Sorry. I mean to say…" She used her hands to mime looser and shorter.

"Looser and shorter," Mrs. Bryan added with a smile. "I am so envious of your lovely French!"

"The French Opera House in New Orleans was the first in the country," Clyde put in. "My family lived in south Louisiana for a long while. We've been there several times. It's definitely a tuxedo and evening gown affair down there as well." Clyde felt good to be able to relate to something.

"I have performed there. A beautiful place. Lovely people. So friendly! *Et* the food… *merveilleux!*" Miss Perrette said exuberantly, putting her fingertips to her lips, kissing them with a flourish and then throwing her fingers out, a few French words mixed in as usual.

Clyde found her delightful. He guessed that anyone would and did.

Delmonico's Steak House was deemed one of the best restaurants in the country and one of the oldest. The entryway was sumptuous, with marble floors, dark wood paneling, a large staircase, and mirrors. As was the style of the times, the dark carpet had a swirling pattern, and the wall was covered with a patterned wallpaper. Mr. Bryan was instantly recognized by the staff and the four were led to a table in the middle of the action.

Clyde had never been in a restaurant this fancy. Everything was immaculate. The servers spoke as if they were college graduates. With no prices on his menu, he could only imagine how much this dinner for four was going to cost the Gotham National Bank, and that got him thinking. *How is it possible that I, Captain Clyde Barbour, warrant all this attention?* Then it struck him: he did warrant it. He was already very successful. Maybe not the kind of wealth that is generational, but then he was far from finished! He sat up straighter, listened more intently, and effortlessly added to the conversation. He was ready for the Met.

At the Met, Tim led them all to the room where the elite, who purchased parterre boxes, waited, and sipped on after-dinner drinks. The room was full but not crowded and smelled to Clyde of expensive perfume. What first caught his eye was the beautiful jewelry; it hung from all the women's necks and ears and adorned their fingers and wrists. Gold and platinum, large diamonds, emeralds, and sapphires, and lots of pearls. The dresses were full of detail from intricate beadwork to lace embroidered with ribbon. Clyde wished he could capture this moment in time to revisit over and over. He would have given anything for Jennie to be there standing next to him. He could have taken her to buy a beautiful dress and some jewelry that might not have been as expensive as what he saw in the room, but would be shiny and new and delight them both. However, deep down, he could not imagine Jennie being happy in this opulent setting surrounded by people you read about in the society section of the big city newspapers. His thoughts were interrupted by Tim introducing him to someone.

"Captain Clyde Barbour, this is Mr. J.P. Morgan, Jr.," said Tim. "The captain's up here from Houston, Texas, so we're giving him a taste of our city." Clyde and Mr. Morgan shook hands. "He's a riverman and an entrepreneur. He's up here to obtain funding for a few more ships; one of them is said to be the largest and most powerful towboat ever built!"

"A riverman? Well, that's unusual these days. Oh, and my friends call me Jack." He gave Clyde the once over. The man had thick almost black eyebrows that hovered over his close-set eyes. His burly mustache hid his wide upper lip, and although not really smiling, he had a pleasant, calm look about him.

"I'm a yachtsman myself. We belong to the New York Yacht Club," said Jack, smiling at Clyde. "I'd love to hear more about these ships of yours."

"Well, I grew up on the Ohio and Mississippi Rivers. Most of my business is in water transportation. I think you'll be very surprised to hear that your former yacht, *Alicia*, has been retrofitted to serve as a tug to handle oil barges for my company on the Panuco River in Mexico; I now own her. I need more boats to add to my line down there. I own a company, or I guess two by now, in Mexico."

"My *Alicia* is in Mexico? I gave her to the government to be used in Cuba. I loved that boat! What a coincidence. So, you're a riverboat captain then. You'll have to come out to the yacht club! Your work in Mexico must have been more than a little dicey these last few years. And here's my lovely wife, Mrs. Jane Morgan," said Jack with a lilt in his voice. "My dear," he said as he held his wife's hand, "this is Captain Clyde Barbour of Houston, Texas. A riverboat captain, no less! And he now owns the *Alicia*!"

Mrs. Morgan held out her hand and Clyde kissed it and bowed to her. "It is an honor to make your acquaintance." She raised her left eyebrow as if to say, "Look but don't touch!" Her ivory skin, golden hair pulled up on her head, and her sheer silvery dress were striking. She was holding a fan and quickly opened it to fan herself.

"Thank you, Captain. You and my husband have something in common." She smiled ever so slightly at Clyde. "Jack, look over there; it's Edith Vanderbilt! She must have just returned from Biltmore. Captain Barbour," she added as she turned to face him, "it's been a pleasure to meet you." She was off across the room. Clyde thought the abruptness a little odd.

Her husband smiled, "Captain, I look forward to talking to you again." He nodded to the two men and took off after his wife.

Clyde watched as Miss Opal Perrette made the rounds in the reception room. It seemed everyone wanted to talk to her, to tell her their tale, to fawn over her. He'd been told of her career but hadn't fully realized her celebrity. She saw him looking at her and winked. Clyde smiled back. She excused herself from her present company and joined Clyde.

"You're very popular," said Clyde, smiling. "How did I get so lucky to be your escort tonight? You must have had many other options."

"Well, yes, that is true, but Mr. Bryan asked first, and I do get so bored with the same people tout le temps!" She took Clyde's hand and said coyly, "And you, you are a very interesting man, Captain!" Clyde found himself unsure, once again, as to how to respond. Her frankness continued to surprise, amaze, and delight him.

"Not nearly as interesting as you, Mademoiselle!" She laughed, opened her fan, and attempted to cool them off. "By the way, that's about the only French word I know. I don't want you to get the wrong idea."

"I have many wrong ideas...." Her voice trailed off as she spotted someone else she knew. "Come with me. You should meet maybe the wealthiest man in New York City." They walked to where a couple was talking quietly together. "Bonsoir! Mr. and Mrs. Whitney! I want you to meet my new friend, and a friend of Tim Bryan as well. Henry and Gertrude Whitney, please meet Captain Clyde Barbour from Houston, Texas!" Her introduction was so enthusiastic, Clyde felt it draw out the couple's smiles.

"Captain Barbour, Henry Whitney." The men shook hands. "I don't suppose you served in our Navy? My father was secretary of the Navy back in the '80s."

"No, sir. I'm a riverboat captain and have been since I was 20 years old. I grew up on the Ohio and Mississippi Rivers. My main business now is water transportation." Clyde wished desperately that he had something noteworthy to say to this man of high finance. "Most recently, I've been transporting oil on the Panuco River in Mexico." He hoped that sounded interesting.

"Fascinating! Truly fascinating! I'd love to sit down and hear some of your stories." The chimes rang, announcing it was time to be seated. Opal—as Clyde found himself privately referring to Miss Perrette—had been talking to Mrs. Whitney, and Henry turned to them. "I apologize; this is my lovely wife, Gertrude Whitney." He took his wife's hand and squeezed it.

Clyde took her other hand and kissed the back of it, bowing as he did. "It's a pleasure, Mrs. Whitney."

"This is Captain Clyde Barbour," Opal added. "I'm his escort tonight!" She put her arm through Clyde's and smiled at him.

"It's a pleasure, Captain Barbour. You're bound to have a delightful evening alongside our favorite chanteuse!" Mrs. Whitney took her husband's arm, and everyone headed into the theatre.

Chanteuse, thought Clyde. *I wonder what that means? Who can I ask?*

"It means singer, you know. Chanteuse. It means singer," Opal whispered in his ear. He had to stop himself from laughing at the timing.

As awed as he was meeting these titans of industry, Clyde was equally awed by the tenor voice of Enrico Caruso after the gold damask curtains had opened.

After the opera, the Bryans dropped Clyde and Opal off at their hotel.

"I would ask you upstairs, but I'm on the women-only floor." Opal frowned.

"I'm surprised that you'd be on that floor," said Clyde.

"Something new. Like I said, I like new!" Opal smiled her coy smile, which sent Clyde over the moon.

Clyde, unsure how to respond to this French woman's advances, if they were that, offered an alternative. "How about dinner tomorrow night? We could just stay here in the hotel and eat."

"*Très bien!* That would be nice. 7:30?" Opal got right to the point, as always.

"7:30 at the bar. How do you say 'good night' in French?" Clyde asked.

"*Bonne nuit.* That's how we say it!" she said teasingly.

"Bun newie, Opal. See you tomorrow evening!" Clyde kissed her hand, then didn't protest as she put her hands on his shoulders and kissed him on both cheeks. Then she was gone!

He sent a telegram to Jennie, telling her of his escapades that evening, leaving out the part about Opal Perrette. He asked himself why he felt the need to leave that out. *She wouldn't understand,* he told himself, pretending to believe that was the reason.

Clyde and Opal had dinner two more times before she left for Paris, and on the day of her departure, they had early morning coffee.

"You look beautiful, as always," said Clyde as he kissed her hand.

"And you, Captain, so handsome and so intelligent!" Her smile captivated him as always.

"Again, I beg you, please call me Clyde."

"Yes, I will call you Clyde, *mais* you must promise to write to me, you know, *une lettre de temps en temps*." Opal's head was hanging down and she lifted only her eyes to meet his in a seductive way. "From time to time." She smiled demurely, and he was lost in her.

When they said goodbye with a hug and kisses on each cheek, Opal held his neck in her hands. "This is how we kiss in France." She slowly and gently put her lips to his and kissed him deeply. He returned the kiss, and when she finally pulled away, his entire body ached for her. He longed to take hours reveling in her being, absorbing her essence. And then she was gone once more.

Clyde dedicated an entire day to visiting the recently opened New York City Library. He'd been told that the library housed more than a million books and that they could find any book you were looking for in as little as six minutes, a timeframe heretofore unheard of. He allowed himself two hours to look at whatever he wanted, meaning ships and rivers and even some poetry mixed in. The remainder of the day he spent on business research, especially on a gas by-product called carbon black. Interest in this substance had resurfaced as automobiles were becoming more abundant and one of the uses for carbon black was in the production of tires. Clyde was already immersed in the oil business, so it seemed a smart path for him to investigate. He loved that part of his work.

CHAPTER 34

THE AFFAIR

1916–1917

Clyde arrived home just in time for the birth of his first grandchild, born to Jesse and Sylvia on August 6, 1916. It was a boy and they named him Clyde Arthur Barbour III, thrilling everyone.

Then on September 2, Peggy and Forest had their first child, a boy, and they named him Clyde Edward. It was also the day Jennie had planned a belated birthday party for Clyde.

"My 42nd birthday and I am blessed with two baby grandsons! And I still have a 10-year-old boy of my own!" Clyde laughed heartily and tousled Will's hair; he had been looking very left out.

The following month, the *Fuel Oil Journal* mentioned his becoming a grandfather in double measure:

"Foxy Grandpa Has It Cinched

Capt. C.A. Barbour of the Interior Navigation Co. has the unique distinction of having been tagged grandpa twice almost simultaneously. On August 6 C.A. Barbour III was born to Mr. and Mrs. Jesse C. Barbour, and on Sept. 2 a son was born to Mr. and Mrs. F.E. Lewis of Houston, Mrs. Lewis being the daughter of Capt. Barbour. He'll have to increase his towing capacity!"

Clyde and Jennie found themselves amused at the mention, and he was delighted that he had attained such stature that people were expected to know who was being written about.

September also found Clyde once again at the Clooney Construction Company, supervising the loading of the *Tamboyoche* aboard one of his new barges, Barge 112. They would both be towed down to Tampico by the tank steamer *Topila* in October. The *Tamboyoche* was said to be the most powerful and largest towboat ever built in the South, with 1,700 horsepower. Clyde would accompany his newest boats to Mexico.

The United States declared war on Germany on April 6, 1917. In June, the Selective Service Act was passed, requiring men between 21 and 30 to register for potential military service. Clyde encouraged Clyde, Jr., to enlist in the summer of 1917, as soon as he turned 18. Jesse and Forest, Peggy's husband, were both exempted, being married men with a child under the age of 12. It wasn't certain how long that deferment would stay in place if the war became a long engagement.

"Daddy," said Clyde, Jr., one day when Clyde returned from work. "I'm going in the Navy!" he announced proudly.

"Well, of course you're going in the Navy; the water is part of your heritage. I'm proud of you, son. Congratulations!" Clyde shook his son's hand and smacked him hard on the back.

Jennie was sitting across the room in her chair looking as if she'd seen a ghost. She and Clyde had talked endlessly about this. Jennie would protest and Clyde's heart would ache, but he wasn't going to let this incredible learning and maturing opportunity pass their son by. It was the right thing to do; it was the patriotic thing to do.

All the young men were excited about the opportunity to shoot guns and cannons and ride on ships across the ocean. Only the elderly could remember the horrors of the Civil War and the toll it had taken on the young men of the time. The Spanish-American War in 1898 had lasted only 10 weeks, ending in the Treaty of Paris that same year, and did nothing to dampen the enthusiasm of young men looking for an adventure.

Clyde, Jr., was sent to Coasters Harbor Island in Newport, Rhode Island, where there had been a Naval training center since 1883. New recruits were required to be segregated for 21 days as a quarantine against disease, which could spread rapidly in such tight quarters. By the time his quarantine was over, Jennie, Lilly, and Will had moved into the Ocean Hotel in Newport, where they would spend the summer to be close to Clyde, Jr., during his training. Clyde didn't put up much of a fuss. The ocean breezes would be good for Lilly, and it was a necessary concession for him to make for his anxiety-ridden wife.

The night before Jennie left, Clyde walked into their bedroom and locked the door. It made her start laughing.

"What's so funny?" asked a confused Clyde.

"I don't know, it just seems funny. Funny 'cause I know what that means. Funny because we're hiding like children doing something bad. Funny because I'm excited to make love with you!" Jennie had been sitting on the bed. She stood up and began unbuttoning her gown.

"Let me help you with that," Clyde offered as he walked over to where she was standing. He helped her remove all of her clothes and then stepped back to look at her in the soft light of the blue lightbulb. "How can you still be so beautiful? Grandmothers are not supposed to look this good." Clyde smiled as he held her hand at arm's length so he could take her all in. Still clothed in his trousers and shirt, he helped her onto their bed and they reveled in their oneness.

She sat up looking dazed. "Darling, you make this grandmother feel like a newlywed again! I just wish...."

Before she could continue, Clyde kissed her on her lips. "We have each other. We have our own kind of lovemaking. We're okay."

As they lay next to each other, they were each caught up in their own private thoughts. Jennie wanted to tell him that she would understand if he found sex somewhere else. *And it would be just sex,* she thought. *He wouldn't make love to anyone else; he couldn't! Who am I kidding? It would kill me.*

Clyde's thoughts were running parallel to his wife's. *How can I love Jennie so completely, yet still have desires for other women? I'm a horrible husband.* They cuddled and Jennie used all of her wiles to make her man as happy as was possible under the circumstances. They fell asleep in each other's arms, exhausted.

Jennie and her two youngest children took the train to Rhode Island. They stayed at the Ocean Hotel with its majestic Victorian architecture. The cobblestone driveway was bordered by a short stone fence that led to the front entrance. The hotel was a grand yellow building fronted by a large portico with white two-story Corinthian columns reached by a wide set of front steps. To either side were smaller one-story porticos and, of course, the ocean. A widow's walk topped off the front of the hotel.

Off to one side were several dozen bicycles.

"Mommy, look!" shouted an excited Lilly. "Bicycles! We can all three go for rides!"

"That will be a lot of fun!" Jennie smiled, feeling happier about her decision to come here for the summer.

They had a two-bedroom suite that included a kitchen. Lilly and Will would share a bedroom, a fact neither of them appreciated. Jennie had left Grannie and Josephine in Houston to help with the two grandbabies and found a woman in Newport to cook. They could hire a car if they needed transportation. Clyde would be traveling back and forth to Mexico and Louisiana and wherever else his business took him and would do his best to see them but couldn't promise.

"If I end up going up to New York City, I'll definitely come visit you," Clyde had told Jennie. This could be their longest separation since they were married all those years ago.

It took only a few days for Jennie to settle into life on Rhode Island. Life with just the two youngest children was a breeze compared to having all five and running a large household. Clyde, Jr., visited nearly every weekend and often brought another Navy recruit with him named Andrew, who had been attending Washington and Lee University in Virginia. Lilly, now 15 years old, had her first big crush on Andrew. Jennie cringed watching Lilly so awkwardly try to insinuate herself in with the two young men. At Lilly's age, Jennie's father had already promised her in marriage for the first time. She could remember being paraded like a prized heifer. The memory made her shudder. Then she relived in her mind her own awkward days with Clyde when she first stepped onto the flatboat, and her body yearned for him now.

Mexico, with all its problems, was very good to Clyde. His Interior Navigation Company was doing most of the towing on the Panuco River. Every day, he towed approximately 14,400 barrels for the East Coast Oil Company and two locations for the Mexican Gulf Oil Company, all ending up in or around Tampico. The Texas Company was towing approximately 4,500 barrels a day on the Panuco River to Tampico. It was good to be king.

The newest Constitution of Mexico in 1917 stated that Mexico had the right to expropriate any natural resources deemed vital to the nation. Clyde lived each day knowing if that were to happen, it would destroy his most significant income stream. *I won't let myself think about that. I have to know it's not going to happen; I won't let it happen. Fear can kill the best-made plans. I will not fear!* Clyde had to counsel himself often.

January 1918 was plagued with shipwrecks along the Panuco River and Clyde's Interior Navigation Company was not exempted. On January 29, Clyde, on the *Paciencia*, had called for an early dinner. He, Capt. Charles Hamilton, and a few of the crew were eating in the dining room and galley when the boilers exploded. A piece of the boiler was blown through the dining room wall and barely missed Clyde. The boat quickly sank in 25 feet of water. Three Mexican workers died in the explosion. Roughly $100,000 worth of damage was done to the boat. Clyde was shaken; it had been a very close call. Memories of the accident that killed Luke and almost killed him and

Pa flooded his mind. It was later discovered that the explosion had been caused by a fire that started in the crude oil and spread to the boiler. He could never let Jennie find out about this near miss. The next day when he was thinking more clearly, he remembered that he'd been offered $110,000 for the steamer the week before. Now he'd be paying $100,000 to have her fixed!

In the spring of 1918, Lilly was visited by a woman from Miss Mason's School in Tarrytown, New York. The school had come highly recommended by Tim Bryan when Clyde had asked about a finishing school for Lilly. Clyde was not surprised when she was accepted into the school; Lilly had always been a good student and was well-mannered. She loved clothes and Clyde enjoyed dressing up his Little Princess. What did surprise him was the cost and the fact that Lilly seemed so ready to leave her mother behind in Texas. She would begin her schooling there in September.

Their third grandchild was born on June 9, 1918, to Jesse and Sylvia, who welcomed their second son, Jesse, Jr., into the family. Clyde, who was gone as usual those days, sent a telegram and an impressive bouquet of flowers to mark the occasion and even called on the phone.

Jennie was always flabbergasted at how easily women seemed to deliver babies. Sylvia was up and about in two weeks, already enjoying their new precious bundle. Their house was full of visitors who brought their own children along, making it a fun and noisy home.

It was a difficult adjustment for Clyde. As the number of his own children at home dwindled, he began to love and appreciate the quieter environment. The evenings that had once been filled with piano-playing and singing and storytelling were now frequently times of solitude for Clyde when he could work without interruption, which so rarely was the case at his office in the First National Bank Building downtown.

"Everybody wants something," he said to Ruth. "Even my own children. Will wants a car; can you imagine? He's 13 years old and he's asking for a car. Lilly rarely asks for anything. Do you think it could be because he's a male?"

"If I dare say so, Captain, I think it's because he's spoiled." Ruth was one of the few who would talk this way to Clyde.

"Well, that's probably true, but not every son can be like your Michael—quiet, smart, dedicated."

"I think that not having a father has made him more responsible," Ruth added, remembering the awful accident that killed her husband when Michael was still an infant. "I have news about him. He was just accepted into Seminary School! He is so excited! That's all he's ever wanted to do." She was smiling and her eyes were moist at the same time.

"When does he leave?" asked Clyde, genuinely interested. Michael had begun to feel almost like one of his own.

"We have to wait and see if he gets a scholarship. You wouldn't believe how expensive it is!"

"That's nonsense; I'll give you the money."

"What? Oh, no, Clyde. I couldn't let you do that but thank you," Ruth said, stumbling over her words.

"Ruth, I'm happy to help a wonderful young man study to be a priest. It would be an honor!" Clyde rose from his chair and walked over to her. He put a hand on each of her shoulders and looked her square in the eyes. Her moist eyes were leaking tears now.

"No. I won't let you. I can't let you." Ruth removed his hands and walked back into the front room. "It would feel all wrong." Ruth was weeping now.

"Why are you crying? What's wrong?"

"You're such a kind man. You're such a wonderful person. Why didn't I find you first?"

Without giving it a second thought, Clyde locked the office door. He grabbed Ruth's hand and took her into his office, locking that door behind them as well. He picked her up and sat her on his desk. She was looking down, still crying and rubbing her eyes. Clyde took his handkerchief out of his pocket and began to wipe her eyes with it. When she did finally look at him, he could see that the pain ran deep into her soul, her brows furrowed in distress. She was trying desperately to stop crying, to steady herself, her emotions. She watched this man almost every day as he went about his business and his life. The fleeting kisses and hugs they had shared thus far only made her want him more.

"But you did find me; I'm here, right here. I'll always be here for you, Ruth. I will!" he said quietly. He lifted her chin with his fingers, kissed her lightly all over her face, then reached her mouth, where he slowly and gently separated her lips and tasted her. He found himself so excited he had to hold back. He wanted to tear her clothes off and devour every inch, but he didn't. Instead, he began slowly and lovingly to undress her.

He stood over her, his palms resting on his desk. He studied her, first with his eyes and then with his fingertips. She closed her lips tightly as if to stop any noise from escaping. He took off his shirt and tie and pulled her to him, her breasts warm against his chest. He smelled her hair and behind her ear and down the side of her neck. She smelled of the new Carnation perfume he had given her for her birthday. He carried her to the couch, took off the rest of his clothes, and lay down on top of her. When he finally let go, trembling overtook his entire body until he collapsed on top of her in a daze. Neither of them spoke. Clyde moved over and they sat silently next to each other on the couch.

Ruth stood up and quickly dressed herself, muttering about being behind in her work. Clyde heard nothing as he pulled on his pants and sat back down on the couch. His ecstasy quickly turned to agony as he realized the seriousness of what he had just done and the potentially devastating ramifications. *Jennie would be devastated if she found out that I've done the unforgivable, and reputations would be destroyed; Ruth would be labeled a homewrecker and I would be deemed a philanderer. I love Ruth; I can never let that happen to her. But I could never love anyone the way that I love my Jennie.*

The next day, Clyde called the Seminary School where Michael had been accepted and gave an anonymous scholarship that was to go to Michael. The president of the school agreed to keep Clyde's involvement a secret. Michael would be going to Seminary.

Jesse, Sylvia, and their two sons all boarded a boat for Tampico the first week of August. Clyde needed him down there running the office. Clyde had chosen and purchased a beautiful two-story house for them with large screened-in porches. He also hired a housekeeper who would help with the children and do the cooking. Sylvia kept reassuring her father-in-law that she was quite a good cook, but Clyde insisted. He still felt the need to repay Jesse for all the hardships he'd endured during his perilous journey home through a hostile Mexico. He had been amazed and proud of his eldest son's heroics. *Maybe there's still hope for the other two boys.*

Jesse wasn't concerned about the storm they said was brewing in the Gulf, but they left a few days early just to be safe. It had already begun to rain in Houston. Jennie was at home fretting about her little family traveling in the rain, which became a hurricane that hit just east of the Texas/Louisiana border. They didn't hear from Jesse for four very long days. Jennie couldn't sleep and Clyde was worried as well, but he knew that as a man, it was Jesse's responsibility to go out in the world and make a life for his family.

When a phone call did come through, it was the weekend, and they were both at home.

"Mother?" Jesse asked. "Is that you?"

"Jesse, oh Jesse, is it really you?" Jennie asked.

"Yes. Yes. We've finally made it to Tampico. But listen, Mother. Can you hear me?"

"I can hear you fine. Here's your father." Jennie gave the receiver to Clyde.

"Jesse? Are all of you all right? Did you make it safely?" Clyde was to the point.

"Sort of. The baby, Jesse, Jr., is very ill." Jesse sounded scared.

"What do you mean? What happened?"

"Well, the water was so rough we couldn't warm up any food and ended up eating raw fish. I'm not joking," said Jesse, obviously distraught.

"How did Jesse, Jr., get sick?"

"Seasick, of course; everybody was seasick. I don't know. Maybe, somehow, something bad from that raw fish got into Sylvia's breast milk. I don't know."

Jennie was in the background, trying to think. "Tell them to get the baby back to Houston quickly so he can get better!"

"Jesse?" Clyde asked. "Do you think you should get him back here to see a doctor?"

"No, I'd be afraid he wouldn't even make it there."

"Listen to me, Jesse. Go directly to Clarence Miller. Do you remember him? He's the American consul there. Tell him to find you a doctor. Immediately!" Once again, Clyde felt responsible for something awful happening to his eldest son. *What if they lose the baby?* he thought and then was comforted by the fact that he'd told Jesse to wait out the storm, but he wouldn't be swayed.

Jesse wasn't surprised to find that the lovely house his father had bought for them was fully furnished and ready to be lived in, and the housekeeper was waiting with food already cooking on the stove. The American doctor was located, and a nurse was installed in the nursery to stay with the newborn. It took three weeks for the baby to regain the lost weight and begin to smile and coo once again. Sylvia swore she would never again take a baby on a boat.

At the beginning of September 1918, Clyde was back in Lake Charles, Louisiana, at the Clooney Construction yards to check on his latest build, which he had every reason to believe would be the largest seagoing oil barge ever built. Any man would feel a great sense of pride at such an accomplishment; the *biggest*. It was all just perfect!

Someone could look at me and say I'm a small man, but I know that's only true of my height, not my stature! He laughed to himself at his play on words. One look at this new vessel of his and he felt at least a foot taller.

The hurricane had wreaked havoc in that part of Louisiana, the eastern edge of a hurricane always being the wet side. The high winds and large amounts of rain had some devastating effects.

"There's nothing else out there that can carry 25,000 barrels," Mr. Clooney told him. "And if everything goes like it's supposed to, you'll be able to pump it all the way to empty in only 12 hours! You'll be happy to know, Captain, that your new barge only has about $400 worth of damage from that hurricane. Now, the rest of the wood to finish the job…well, I hate to tell ya, but it caught fire and burned to nothin'." The man pointed over to a heap of ashes.

"You're telling me that you have no extra lumber anywhere that we can use to finish my job?"

"That's what I'm sayin'. Ya know the government ain't letting nobody have wood for anything right now; they need it for the war."

"Yes, and they need oil for the war, and that's what my barge will bring them," said Clyde confidently. He knew immediately what that meant; a trip to Washington, D.C., to convince the War Industries Committee that it was in the interest of the war to get this barge completed so they would make it a priority. In the end, the committee agreed.

As soon as he got back to Houston, it was time to take Lilly up to her new finishing school in New York State. Jesse and Sylvia's baby was beginning to thrive, and Clyde, Jr., was off on a Navy ship somewhere. Jennie slept poorly every night now, worrying about one child or another.

Clyde and Jennie sat on the back porch, fans whirring above their heads and taking the temperature down a few degrees. The gardenias planted next to the porch were giving off their heavenly fragrance, which wafted through the warm early evening breeze.

"I've been thinking," Jennie began, hesitantly, shifting in her wicker chair. "I hope you won't be upset if I don't go with you to take Lilly to school."

"What are you talking about? Why don't you want to go? We'll stay in New York City for a few days, see the opera, and then take her up. You've never been there!" Clyde felt his back stiffen and his defenses go up. "Who's going to chaperone Lilly? What do you have to do that's so important that you can't go with me to take our daughter to school?"

Clyde's voice had an edge to it that was unfamiliar to Jennie. She'd heard that edge many times—used with their sons, with a business associate, but never with her. It took her back to a time long ago when that kind of tone came out of a man she was close to: her father. It instantly took her breath away. She couldn't respond.

Clyde heard her gasp and his head turned quickly to see what was wrong. "Jennie? Oh, Jennie...." He hung his head in shame. He reached over to hold her hand, which she allowed but didn't turn her head back to face him. "We have got to talk about this," he said after what seemed like a long silence. "I want you with me. There's a whole world out there we've never seen. I want to see it all. I want to experience all of it, and I want you by my side. We can do that now and still be very comfortable wherever we visit. Where would you like to go? Where can I take you that would make you happy? You know, that's all I really want to do—make you happy."

Jennie turned to face him and saw the longing in his eyes. She felt she could see through to his soul, the soul that had pulled her in as a young woman and had never let her go. She touched his face and smiled softly.

"Look how far you've brought us! Who would have thought this would even be possible? You've continued on with your wonderful journey and will continue on, fast and rocky and exciting for you. I'm not made to be that way. You've known that for a long time. I love watching you climb the ladder of success; I'm so proud because it means so much to you! But Clyde, I'm not ready to climb up that ladder; I don't fit in up there."

"Of course, you don't fit in up there; you haven't tried to fit in! I wouldn't either if I hadn't worked hard to figure it all out. You can do it. I know that you can if you'll only try! Let me help you!" Clyde squeezed her hand tightly. "Look what we've accomplished together already. We can do anything!" Clyde was smiling at her with hope in his eyes.

"Don't make me, please don't make me. Love me enough to let me be where I'm happy and content. I always want you to be my husband, standing at my side, protecting me and loving me. Nothing could ever untangle the life you and I have made. I promise to go to New York with you, just not this time; please understand!"

Clyde shook his head and dropped it back, staring up at the fans. "Of course, I'm not going to force you to do anything you don't want to do. I'll try really hard to understand the way you feel. It seems like you already understand how I feel. Just promise me you'll never leave me; I couldn't bear it!" Even though he'd known it all along, this moment in time gave him the stark realization that no matter how much he had hoped she would someday change her mind, this was how things would be moving forward.

"How could I ever leave you? God has connected our souls for a lifetime; I'm sure of that!" Jennie had tears in her eyes and felt shaky as she spoke, and at the same time she was relieved that they had finally confronted the elephant in the room. She also feared what this could mean for their relationship.

The next morning at breakfast, she approached Clyde as he was getting ready to head to his office downtown. "I know who can chaperone Lilly! Ruth! You hired Alice to be Ruth's assistant, right?" she asked.

"Well, yes, but she hasn't been there very long yet."

"Nowadays, you can talk on the telephone every day if you need to. Ruth will be there with you to assist with all your business dealings while you're out of town and she can take care of Lilly! I think it's a great idea!"

Clyde was so taken aback that he wasn't sure how to respond. "That's…well…that's an idea. I'll have to give it some thought and ask Ruth, of course."

"I feel so much better! See, I can solve some of your problems!" She kissed Clyde goodbye and went to find Lilly.

Clyde didn't know what to make of Jennie's idea. Did she suspect something? Was it a coincidence? He really wasn't sure, but it did make a lot of sense, in spite of the fact that he and Ruth had gotten too involved.

It was a dream come true for Ruth. Not only would she get to travel with the man she loved, but she would also be seeing and doing things she'd never imagined.

It was arranged, so Clyde, Lilly, and Ruth said goodbye to Jennie at the train station and set off on their adventure.

As Tim Bryan had promised, Lilly was treated like a princess. They went to the opera and had many dinners out at fine restaurants, a different young man of suitable age and lineage accompanying them almost every evening as Lilly's escort. It was like a coming-out party for Clyde's little debutante. Lilly and Ruth spent days shopping and sightseeing, guided by Mr. Bryan's wife, Nancy.

Clyde wasn't sure what was appropriate where Ruth was concerned, and he was aware that there were very strict rules surrounding propriety up here. Should she go with them everywhere? Should she not go along when Tim arranged an escort for Lilly? What about at the opera? He decided to broach the subject with his oldest friend in that big city, Steve Hilton, and to gauge his reaction.

"Although I have my secretary, Ruth, accompanying me as Lilly's chaperone, I'll also be including her in some of our social activities. She's thrilled to finally get out of Texas for the first time and going to New York City was unimaginable for her. It's a pleasure for me to be able to give her this opportunity. She'll fit in just fine. Just let me know if there's an occasion when that might not be appropriate."

Hilton closed his door. "I'd say you're in an enviable situation. You're a novelty up here; a Southern riverboat captain who's on fire in the business community. I say you can pretty much make up your own rules and as long as you act as if they're okay, others will go along with you," he said, a slight smile on his face.

Clyde wondered, *Have I been too obvious with Ruth? Have people picked up on our relationship?*

"Whatever you do or don't do with your secretary will only add to your intrigue in this city." Steve left it at that.

So, Clyde took Ruth along most evenings but not all. He loved being able to take her to the Met and to see her face when the gold damask curtains opened. He also decided he would drive alone with Lilly to take her to her new school in Tarrytown-on-Hudson, New York.

Tim Bryan lent Clyde his chauffeur and limousine to make the trip up to Tarrytown. Clyde and Lilly sat in the back holding hands. Clyde felt proud riding in this expensive car sitting next to his Little Princess. Lilly had unknowingly done a great job of filling the void that Peggy's marriage had left. She was very sweet, loyal, smart, and demure but still a little fragile. She'd been too young to remember when their lives weren't comfortable. She naturally fit into this life of leisure that made her mother so uncomfortable. She had been at ease dining in the fine New York City restaurants and attending the opera. He was so proud that she was his daughter to adore and spoil.

"Daddy, I'm so excited! And I love all my new clothes! Thank you, Daddy." She kissed his cheek and all he could think about was that Jennie chose not to be there. How could she pass up being part of this special moment in Lilly's life? What else was she going to miss?

"I know you'll make me proud. Your mother needs to hear from you, often. If it's allowed, we'll send you back down for Thanksgiving; Christmas for sure."

Miss Mason's School for Girls, otherwise known as The Castle, had been teaching girls since 1893, when Miss C.E. Mason opened the doors of this impressive stone castle edifice. It was very well respected around the country and close enough to New York City that Clyde would be able to see her every time he came up to the big city on business.

The school certainly lived up to its reputation. The first thing they saw as they started up the curved driveway was a two-story stone building with large windows adjacent to a large stone crenellated castle. Two narrow towers held the portico and at the end was a large circular protrusion. It looked like the perfect place for Lilly's new adventure. Clyde felt comfortable leaving her there and felt it was the right place for her.

Back in the big city, Clyde had a private meeting with Tim Bryan at lunch.

"I'm organizing a new company, a whole new venture for me," Clyde announced proudly.

"I'm not surprised, of course. When aren't you off on a new project?" Tim laughed.

"I'm setting up a Delaware Corporation to manufacture carbon black. The plant will be in the Monroe, Louisiana, oil fields. I seem to have a head start on this one. It's bound to be a winner!" Clyde spoke confidently.

"I have no doubt, Captain, that if you're involved in it, it will be a success!"

Clyde and Ruth had two nights alone in the city before they had to head back to Houston. The first night they walked around the corner to a café for dinner. The second night, they stayed in and ordered room service. Ruth wanted to relax in the tub. When she was settled in the warm water, Clyde joined her in the bathroom, shirtless, kneeling by the side of the tub. He got a washcloth, lathered it up nicely, and leaned over the side of the tub to bathe her. He started with her fingers, hands, and arms, then moved to her toes, her feet, and her legs. He put the washcloth down and used his hands to clean the rest of her. He helped her out of the tub and used the large towel to dry her body. She was shaking with pleasure and anticipation. She giggled when he rather clumsily picked her up and took her into his bed where they spent the night in pleasure.

CHAPTER 35

THE DALLIANCE

November 11, 1918, marked the end of the war. Celebrations erupted all over. Champagne toastings were held, but only in private since Prohibition had begun that year. It made no difference to Clyde, as he had ended his drinking days that night in Franklin when he was horsewhipped. He had watched his father, his brother, and so many others succumb to the enticement of alcohol only to pay a steep price for its influence. He felt the need to be in top form at all times. He served alcohol at his house, was happy to drink a toast on special occasions, and didn't mind the company of those who imbibed, but he was otherwise content to pass it by. Jennie enjoyed wine, so Clyde bought her some beautiful green crystal stemware with engraved sterling around the lip in New York City when he had gone there to deliver Lilly to her school.

"They're so beautiful! I've never seen glasses with sterling there. The color is like an emerald!" Jennie exclaimed, holding one up to the light.

"In all my days of sellin' on the flatboat, I never did see anythin' so pretty!" Grannie said as she examined one herself.

"I think you'll be needing a bigger china cabinet," said Clyde, grinning from ear to ear that his purchase was so well received. He loved bringing gifts, and especially the reactions.

Opal Perrette had been writing to Clyde once or twice a month for the past year and a half since they met, and he replied, though less often. The letters were mailed to his office and Ruth, seeing them as personal, never opened them. Instead, she would make a point of bringing the letter, with its embellished handwriting on the envelope, separately from any other correspondence. It didn't escape Clyde that when Ruth delivered them to him on the requisite silver tray, she would be wearing a forced smile and look him directly in the eyes. He didn't feel the need to explain anything to her. His feelings for Ruth were very special but were between them; his love for his wife was between husband and wife; his infatuation with Opal was just that. They hadn't been in the same city at the same time since they first met. They were both working to change that.

When Clyde returned to Houston from New York City, he held a meeting with potential partners in his carbon-black venture. There was a lot of paperwork involved in getting it incorporated. His close friends C.L. Kerr and Robert Randle were there, along with J.H. Alexander, R.R. Beaman, W.A. Windsor, W.H. Lovegrove, and several others. Obviously, it would be incorporated in Delaware and Clyde would be the president. The chief objective of the company would be to manufacture gas and carbon black. They decided they would need about $1 million in capital stock. The name was very important to Clyde, less so to his fellow investors.

"What do you think about this? United Oil & Natural Gas Products Corporation. It gives us plenty of room to expand the scope of the company. It sounds solid and important to me," Clyde said seriously.

"Sounds fine to me," Mr. Kerr said. "It's a bit long, though."

"I like it. Long and solid, like the captain said," Mr. Lovegrove commented.

"Let's go raise some money," said Clyde, smiling as he stood up, and everyone shook hands, feeling excited at the prospect of a totally new adventure.

Alone in his office, Clyde turned his mind to the money end of the venture. It was a balancing act at which he was particularly adept.

He realized that he could leverage himself right into the ground if he wasn't careful. He had so many different companies, each its own little microcosm with its own personality and its own issues. He tried to treat each of them as equally important and his employees as worthy human beings.

"What makes sense at this moment is to liquidate something to make some cash available. The only place I can see doing that is in Mexico. I can sell the steamer *Tamboyoche*; that leaves me with the *Major Black*, and also sell the *Paciencia* and some barges…my new barge can take over a lot of that load. What about selling the dry dock in Tampico?" He was talking to himself out loud. "I won't sell the company's charter, and I'll continue towing on the Panuco. There's still a lot of money to be made down there!"

When all was said and done, Clyde accumulated almost $500,000 by selling those assets. He was particularly pleased that he was able to make money on the sale of some of his equipment and yet continue to do his work on the Panuco, making even more.

The Panuco Oil District was producing 90,000,000 barrels a year. Most of the output was from a small number of gusher-type wells within an area less than 25 miles long and 2 miles wide. Though very closely spaced, the wells varied greatly in their output and depth. It continued to be a home run for Clyde's Interior Navigation Company.

Clyde began paying Jesse $20,000 a year to be in charge of that company, but still had to travel there frequently—four times in 1918 and five times in 1919. Now that he was starting the carbon black company, he would have to let Jesse take over the reins of the Tampico operation almost completely. With the assassination of Zapata in April of 1919 and the retiring of Pancho Villa that summer, Mexico seemed, at least temporarily, a less dangerous place to live and work.

In 1919, the United Oil & Natural Gas Products Corp. was organized in Monroe, Louisiana, with offices in Houston and New York City. The company leased 2,000 acres in Ouachita and Morehouse Parishes, with another 30 acres in fee. His life would now be consumed with carbon black, and he'd be spending a lot of time in

Monroe. He would eventually be taking Clyde, Jr., with him there to learn and work.

The Port of Houston was five to six hours by boat from Galveston Island on the Gulf of Mexico. The big boats could get to the Port of Galveston easily, particularly after that channel was deepened to 25 feet in 1897, but getting goods from Galveston to other parts of the country was difficult. The Port of Houston was connected by an increasing number of railroads that traveled to faraway places, but getting from Galveston to Houston by boat meant a long journey on a windy, often-shallow Buffalo Bayou. Although the federal government had agreed to deepen the channel up to Houston in 1900, it wasn't until three years after the hurricane in 1900 that the work actually began on dredging a channel across Galveston Bay, 150 feet wide but only 18.5 feet deep. By 1908, with the work still not complete, Mayor Horace Rice of Houston went to Washington, D.C., to see Houston Congressman Tom Ball with the Houston Plan. The plan would dredge the channel up to Houston at a depth of 25 feet, which first required creation of the Houston County Ship Channel Navigation District. The unique part of the plan was that locals would fund approximately half the cost of the project, or $1,250,000, by buying bonds. Seeing the absolute necessity of this project for Houston's growth, a local entrepreneur, Jesse H. Jones, took it upon himself to sell the bonds. It was the first federal project to have a local matching component to it. The money was raised, and the job commenced in 1912 and was completed in 1914. It was in 1919 that the first shipment of cotton left Houston for a foreign port on the *Merry Mount*. Within 10 years, Houston became the leading cotton port in the United States.

Since traveling to Galveston to help after the hurricane of 1900, Clyde had been fascinated with the inherent problem of sea access so inconveniently located. When he helped construct the causeway, he understood that it wasn't a solution. He had gone up and down the Ship Channel many times and knew its shortcomings. With more and more railroads coming into Houston, the possibilities were endless.

Railroads were the only logical means of transporting the enormous amounts of goods from these boats. Their unloading point needed to be closer to the Gulf of Mexico but still protected from future hurricanes. Clyde worked on this equation for years.

The summer brought Lilly home from school. Although she was the same sweet and docile child that had left home only nine months before, she seemed more confident and was full of new things to discuss. Clyde was ecstatic at his Little Princess turning into a fine young lady. Jennie felt distant from her, as if Lilly were learning a foreign language in which Jennie was not well versed.

At the end of 1919, Clyde, Jr., returned home from the Navy to a special celebration at home. Although he had seen no combat, he was full of harrowing tales of his year away. Lilly came back down for Christmas and the whole family was there to celebrate, including Jesse and Sylvia and their two children. With so many people there, the wrapped gifts seemed to be everywhere. In the midst of the din, Clyde sneaked away. When Jennie noticed he was no longer there, she knew just where to find him. She went quietly into his study where he was at his desk reading papers with the door closed.

"Clyde, you have your whole family here. You are the head of this family. Please come back and be with us!" Jennie went over, swirled his desk chair around, and sat in his lap.

"You certainly know how to get a man's attention!" he replied, hugging her and kissing her neck. "The noise gets to be too much for me; I can't think. It has nothing to do with how I feel about all those wonderful people out there; I just needed to clear my head. You know, my work doesn't stop just because it's Christmas Day."

She kissed his forehead and looked at him closely. "I don't know what to do," she admitted.

"Yes, you do. Do what you're so good at. Go out there and enjoy every one of them. I'll join you in a bit." Clyde patted her on her bottom, dismissing her. Jennie laughed and left feeling loved; what else did she need?

Christmas Dinner was held down the street at Jesse and Sylvia's house so the cooks would have room to work. The weather was particularly pleasant that day and the meal was served in the backyard with all the glamour of the dining room. The green crystal glasses were a wonderful addition to the tablescape.

When dinner was finished and everyone was enjoying dessert, Clyde stood up, as was common, to say a few words as the patriarch.

"I look around this table, and I'm so proud to see the family that has sprung up from your mother and me. God has certainly blessed us, and let's not ever forget that. Being a family is very important to me. We are all related by blood. You know the saying, 'Blood is thicker than water.' Never forget that. Never turn your back on your family, and never forget who you are and where you come from. Our good fortune needs to be shared. In Luke 12:48 it says, 'For unto whomsoever much is given, of him shall be much required.' Take time to love each other. One day I'll be gone, and I expect each one of you to work tirelessly to make sure your mother is comfortable and well taken care of, as she has done all these years for all of us. I love each and every one of you. One more thing; I have a final present for your mother here." Clyde reached inside his jacket pocket and produced a tiny box tied with a bow. "Merry Christmas. My life would be nothing without you." He handed the box to Jennie, who quickly opened it and found a house key inside. All the children knew what that meant.

"A new house? Why?"

"It's bigger and more beautiful. It's not far from here, down on Montrose. It has lovely columns on a rounded front entryway, and it's made of brick! And the backyard, it's beautiful. I can't wait to show you." Jennie stood up to hug and kiss her sweet husband. All the family hooped and hollered, standing up and toasting the newest Barbour home, at 3602 Montrose Boulevard. The street was known for being where many of the Houston elite had their mansions.

"Daddy?" asked Lilly when the table had quieted. "Is that where you hid my big Christmas present that you told me about?"

"Yes, it is. Whoever wants to go, let's pile in the cars and head over there. Spencer, Mrs. Barbour and I will go with you. Come on, Will and Lilly, hop in with us. Will, did you hear me? Come on," said Clyde to his youngest, shaking his head in wonder at Will's lack of engagement.

The house was grand. Three stories high and made entirely of brick, with semicircular brick stairs leading up to the semicircular front porch with two Corinthian columns on either side. On the ground level were three windows with green-and-white-striped awnings. The second level had windows with shutters and there were three dormers in the roof. On the right was a driveway and a columned porte cochere almost as stately as the front entryway.

3602 Montrose Boulevard, Houston, Texas 1920

"I'm gonna need some fancier clothes just to live in this fine house!" Jennie said, smiling at Clyde and holding his hand.

"Look over there." Clyde pointed to a place in the curb where a parking space had been carved out. "Mayor Holcombe's housewarming gift: a parking space right in front of our house!" Clyde was obviously very impressed.

Lilly was very patient, wondering in each new room they toured if she would find her present. Clyde noticed and said out loud, "I think we should go see the backyard so Lilly can finally have her last present. Come on!" He took Lilly's hand and led them outside. She was giggly with anticipation, which made Clyde's heart sing. Lying on the grass was a dog.

"Oh, Daddy, is that my present? Is that my Russian wolfhound? Can it be?" Lilly ran to the white dog, which got up and started dancing with her around the yard. "It's just what I wanted! My very own Russian wolfhound to walk along the beautiful street. Oh, but instead of Avondale Street, we'll be strolling down Montrose Boulevard together; that's even better!"

"I crown him 'Vargo!'" Lilly announced to many cheers. She looked over to see Spencer holding a large garment box. "What's that?" she asked.

"What else did you want?" Jennie prompted. "A coat..." she began before Lilly finished her sentence.

"A coat to wear while I walk her down the boulevard!" She ripped open the box and immediately put on the fur coat that nearly swallowed her thin physique.

"Lilly, is it too big?" asked Jennie.

"Oh, no Mother. That's the fashion!" Lilly modeled the coat for everyone and then stood next to her new best friend, Vargo, for everyone to admire. Lilly was all about fashion now. After the end of the war, women began to become more emancipated. Strict codes of conduct were being lifted. Wearing makeup was more widely accepted but smoking less so.

"I want a dog, too!" shouted Will. "Why can't I have a dog?"

"First, you learn to behave, then you get special gifts," answered Clyde, as he watched Will lower his head and kick the ground in frustration, mumbling to himself.

Back inside, everyone wandered through the house. Peggy called from the kitchen. "Mother, come here!"

Jennie found her way into the kitchen followed by Clyde.

"Look what's here already!" Peggy pointed to the old green, white, and gold Ice Water pitcher, which held a beautiful bouquet of yellow roses. "Father never forgets!"

Jennie walked up and felt the cool roses on her cheeks and lips. She smelled them and enveloped them with her hands. "The Ice Water pitcher never looked so beautiful!" she said, smiling with moist eyes. Clyde took Jennie into his arms and, to the delight of the family, gave her a long kiss.

April 1920 found Clyde in Pittsburgh buying another steamer to use in Tampico, where there seemed to be no end to the oil coming up out of the ground. The steamer was named *Cruiser* and belonged to the Pittsburgh Coal Company, which was owned by the Mellon family. Clyde had also been interested in mining for a long time. He had traveled to Pittsburgh to see what he could learn from this company that was eager to partner with him. Clyde wasn't sure he'd be partnering with anyone, but used buying the steamer as an entrée into this new world.

His mind being the sponge for knowledge it had always been, Clyde was in his element. He was treated with great respect, all his questions and ideas being seriously listened to. He felt proud and important, and left ready to conquer the world.

At Christmas, Lilly had spoken privately with her mother and father.

"Señorita Le Ross, you know, my Spanish teacher at school? Well, she wants to take a few of us to Europe this summer; just a few girls, and her grown son will go, too. We have to have a man with us, after all. Flo is going!" Lilly's new friend from school, Flora Gonzales, had been adopted by her uncle, Mr. Grunewald of the Grunewald Hotel in New Orleans, when her parents passed away. She was a frequent visitor to the Barbour home. Flora and Clyde, Jr., had shared an immediate attraction to each other.

Lilly pulled out a legal-size sheet of paper on which was typed an itinerary.

Clyde looked it over carefully. "Paris, Montreux, Brussels, Amsterdam, Edinburgh, London. Quite a trip!" he said. "Has Señorita

Le Ross talked about all the damage done in some of these places during the war?"

"Yes, Daddy, she thinks it will be an eye-opener for us to see what the aftermath of war really looks like." Lilly's excitement was evident. "Don't you think that's true? Señorita says there's nothing better than studying a place you've really seen!"

"That's true enough. So, you leave on the *Mauritania* and return on the *Kroonland*; both good ships. The *Mauritania* is the fastest ship afloat; gets to Europe in five days!" Clyde turned to talk to Jennie.

"But Lilly, dear, how is it gonna feel being out in the middle of the ocean on a ship? What if the seas are rough? Once you're on, you're stuck!" Jennie couldn't imagine letting her precious Lilly go off on such an adventure without at least someone from the family going along.

"Oh, Mother, Daddy says the water is part of our heritage! Daddy's always going on big ships down to Mexico where those crazy Mexican desperados are waiting to shoot people! This is nothing like that."

"It costs $1,825 per person for the two months?" Clyde asked.

"Yes, Daddy. I know it's a lot of money but—"

"I'm not concerned about the money. I think it would be wonderful to have you be the first person in our family to visit Europe. I'll be going over there soon myself, with your mother, of course!" Clyde smiled and patted Jennie's knee. Jennie sat quietly, a panicked look on her face.

"Really?" Lilly squealed. "Really?"

"Yes, really."

Lilly jumped up and went over to shower her father in kisses, then sat on her mother's lap. "I can't believe it! I have to tell Flo and Señorita! You're the bee's knees!"

"I'm the what?" asked Clyde with a chuckle.

"The bee's knees! You're the best!" said Lilly.

"Lots of postcards; I'm expecting lots of postcards from Europe," added Clyde.

So, on July 1, Lilly, Flo, Jake, and Señorita Le Ross left New York onboard the Cunard Line's S.S. *Mauritania*, headed for Cherbourg.

It took a few weeks for Lilly's postcards to begin trickling in from Europe. With a drawing of the ship on the front, the first one said: "Quiet 4th day out and 4th of July still no word from you. Attended church services. Slept all afternoon. Getting used to the rocking of the ship. Señorita Le Ross's birthday. Dressed up for dinner and toasted everyone and everything. Danced on top deck to sax and mandolin."

A week or so later came the second one: "Queer little train with compartments for six through beautiful Normandy with houses made of stone with thatched roofs. Swiss cheese and charged water. Poppies. 'In Flanders Fields, the poppies grow.'"

And another: "I'm delighted with Paris! Lovely room at the Continental. A real 'bain' fixed by a real French maid. French pastry and thick chocolate. Rainy and chilly. For change we get stamps instead of coins because silver is so scarce. Wonderful works of art at the Louvre. Bonne nuit."

Finally, one came that they knew was inevitable. "First evidence of war zone; trees killed by frequent gas attacks. Passed through villages where the ruins of former homes is heartbreaking. Lunch at Saissons which is almost completely destroyed and next door the Cathedral that's now only a shell."

Clyde and Jennie were tearful as they read the next, which was written on a small note card from the Continental Hotel. "Walked through battlefields, remains of French soldier's clothes and equipment. Picked up some souvenirs. Passed a bride en route to marriage in a shell-torn church. French, English, and German cemeteries on each side of the road. Tour of the Cathedral at Reims, where the rain is coming through gaping holes in the roof, gives one an idea of devastated France never to be forgotten. Four years for another crop of grapes to grow for the making of champagne. Bodies are being found in the fields every day approaching Chateau-Thierry. Mail from you finally."

The family was over for dinner when the next postcard came. "These French people have terrible table manners. Took the Bernese Overland train through the beautiful Alps. More mail at Cook's. Took boat on Lake Lucerne then up funicular to the Rigi. Swiss Independence Day with fireworks and dear little boats with lanterns on the lake. Eleven-hour train ride to Brussels. All like Brussels immensely, seems so much like Paris. Rain." Everyone laughed.

As fate would have it, Opal would be leaving New York City for London at the same time as Lilly would be arriving in New York from her trip abroad. Clyde had arranged to meet Lilly and Flo and take them back to Houston. When Clyde, Jr., wanted to be there to meet Flo when she disembarked, Clyde was torn. There was no good reason to say no, but it was going to interfere greatly with his plans.

"Jennie, are you sure you don't want to go with me to New York to meet Lilly and Flo?" Clyde had asked his wife at the end of July. "We can go to the opera!"

"You know I don't want to go," she responded demurely. "It's so hot on the trains in the summer; it's miserable!"

After Jennie's expected refusal to accompany him, Clyde made plans with Opal. He arranged for his son to arrive in New York several days after him, allowing him time alone with Opal, and then all of them would take the train back down to Houston together.

"I'm having Clyde, Jr., meet me up in New York City after I've had time to conduct some of my business," Clyde told Jennie.

"I think that's a great idea. He needs to learn the business," she replied.

"I've set up two appointments for the day before the boat arrives that have to do with my carbon black business, so he'll be there for those," Clyde responded. "I'm including him in every opportunity I think is appropriate. We've been working together at the office. I'm planning to send him to Monroe in October to be number two in charge of those gas fields and the carbon black plant. You know that he's always been a very slow learner; it's almost as if he doesn't want to learn. It's the damnedest thing I've ever seen." Clyde shook his head.

"Clyde, not everyone has the smarts you have," Jennie said, defending their son.

"I know that, but my blood runs through his veins. Wouldn't you think that would be enough?"

"And then sometimes I think you leave Will out. He's 14 years old now! Have you thought about taking him with you?" Jennie asked.

Clyde laughed. "Jennie, you can't be serious. The boy can't even sit still for an entire meal, and he can't seem to get through an entire day without getting punished for some bad behavior. He is not ready. We have to keep working on him; we don't want him turning out like James." That was that.

Clyde stayed at the McAlpin in New York; he purposefully wanted to stay where he and Opal had met and last enjoyed each other's company. He booked a suite with two bedrooms. When asked, Opal suggested they eat at the hotel the first night as she would be arriving late. Clyde laughed when he caught himself in intense preparation for his "date." "There's no fool like an old fool!" he said out loud.

He was unaware that Opal had been escorted into the suite and into her room while he was showering and dressing. He walked out into the sitting room, and when he saw her purse on the coffee table, his mind went into overdrive. He called the restaurant downstairs.

"Yes, good evening. This is Captain Barbour. My guest and I would like to eat dinner here in my suite." Before Opal officially showed herself, a table had been set up with a white linen tablecloth, a bottle of white Graves was chilling in a silver bucket, and menus were waiting.

Opal opened the door to her bedroom and sauntered out in her perfectly French way. She was immaculately dressed in a short, sleeveless beaded dress with a top of see-through chiffon decorated with a double scallop of pale sequins. The waist was covered in large gold sequin daisies with black beaded eyes, and at the hem hung a curtain of nude-colored fringe.

Clyde realized he was staring, really staring, at this vision of beauty. He walked up to her, took her hand, and stood at arm's length, taking her all in. "*Bon soir, Mademoiselle.*" He kissed the back of her hand. She turned her head to the side and looked coyly at him.

"Your French, *Monsieur*, it is *beaucoup mieux*," Opal replied.

"And you look gorgeous! How can I keep you in here all to myself when you look so lovely? New York City deserves to see the famous Opal Perrette in all her splendor!" Clyde took her other hand and pulled her to him to kiss. "I would enjoy some more lessons in French kissing, please!"

Their bodies pressed against each other sent a bolt of lightning down Clyde's entire body. Her tongue was thin and warm and inquisitive in his mouth. He breathed in the scent of her perfume; he could smell the soap she had used to bathe her body and the shampoo she had used on her hair. The large vase of mixed flowers sent out its own aroma. When their lips separated, he looked at her and saw her eyes still closed and her head tilted back, relishing the moment.

"*Mais, non,* New York City cannot have me tonight; I belong only to The Captain!" she stated defiantly.

"I would love nothing better than to have you all to myself. Come sit down and let me pour you a glass of wine." Clyde pulled back her chair and she lithely sat down. Just as she was getting settled, there was a knock on the door. Clyde answered it and let two waiters in.

"I ordered a few appetizers to eat while we decide on dinner." One of the waiters was carrying a large silver tray, which he put on the table.

"*Madame. Monsieur.* Here we have some smoked salmon, seared foie gras with pear, and a small venison terrine." He pointed to a white bisque terrine with a deer head with antlers on top. The other waiter was opening the chilled white wine.

"*Madame?*" He offered to pour her a glass.

"If you please, it is *Mademoiselle!*" she told the waiter who had addressed her. "Graves. Of course. I'd love some. How did you remember?" She seemed surprised.

"I make it my business to remember things," said Clyde, smiling. He motioned to the waiter to pour him a glass. "So, what shall we toast to?" he asked his beautiful dinner companion.

"Many more dinners *comme ceci!* An encore to be sure!" They clinked their glasses, and each took a sip. That was the only sip of wine Clyde had all evening.

When the table had been cleared away and the waiters had left, Clyde and Opal settled onto the couch next to each other. Opal took off her shoes and lifted her legs up to rest on top of Clyde's thighs. He began to rub her feet and her calves.

"Mmm. That feels very nice," she said quietly, closing her eyes.

"Is it true that Russian men enjoy kissing the feet of their lovers?" Clyde asked, toying with her toes.

"*Mais, oui!* That is what I do hear. *Pourquoi?* Do you like to kiss my toes?" she asked, giggling.

"I'd like to kiss every part of your beautiful body," Clyde admitted, kissing her neck softly.

"Oh, *mon Dieu!* Where to start?" She smiled and pulled him down to her to entangle their mouths again. Clyde lay on top of her. Opal tried to switch places with him, wanting to be on top, and Clyde ended up on the floor. They laughed loud and long. Clyde stood up, grabbed her hands, and pulled her up to standing. He led her to his bedroom.

It felt extravagant to Clyde to leave the bedroom door open, not to worry about the outside world. He was here, completely here, with this beautiful woman who was like a dream, whose very voice sounded seductive. He unhooked her dress at the neckline and pulled it down slowly over both her shoulders and down to her waist and pulled her to him, their bodies pressed tightly together. They made love passionately until dawn.

Their time together flitted by. They both had business to attend to during the day, but spent every unfilled hour together, eating all three dinners in their suite. He learned a few French words and was smitten not only by her beauty but also by her dry French wit, which kept him laughing. She left for London the morning of the day Clyde, Jr., was to arrive. As they said, "*Au revoir!*" Clyde gave her a small box tied with a ribbon.

"Oh, *mon Dieu!* What is this?" She was grinning from ear to ear, rapidly untying the bow and finding the treasure inside. "It is an opal pin!" she inhaled excitedly. "*C'est magnifique!* So beautiful!" She rubbed her finger over the silver filigree and the stone, and he pinned it on her jacket.

"A fire opal! To remind you of our passion." He reached back into his jacket pocket and pulled out a lapel pin with a small fire opal on the end and put it on his jacket. "And to remind me of the beautiful, fiery French woman who graces my path and lights up my soul!" He kissed her once on each cheek.

"Ah, yes, that is how we French kiss our friends, but not how I want to kiss my lover." Opal pulled him to her, wrapped her arms around him tightly, and they kissed endlessly.

Because it took so long for the mail to reach Houston, Lilly had returned home before the rest of her postcards arrived. When Lilly, Flo, Jake, and Señorita Le Ross disembarked in New York, Clyde and Clyde, Jr., were there to meet them and escort them home.

"Daddy! Daddy!" Lilly waved furiously as she ran toward her father.

Clyde hugged her tight. "I almost didn't recognize you," he teased. "Quite the cosmopolitan!" He noticed a young man walking up under the weight of an excess of baggage.

"Daddy, this is Eddie Eagan. Eddie, this is my father, Captain Barbour!" Lilly was excited to at last be able to introduce her newfound crush.

"Captain. It's a pleasure to meet you. Lilly has told me all about you." Eddie put down the bags and the men shook hands.

Clyde stood up taller and gave Eddie a long and intimidating once-over.

"Daddy?" said Lilly, embarrassed.

"Mr. Eagan. So, you met my daughter onboard the *Kroonland?*"

"Yes, sir. She's a very precious lady and a lot of fun!" Eddie put on his best smile.

"Indeed, Mr. Eagan, she is that and much, much more." Clyde let go of his hand.

"Daddy? Eddie just won an Olympic gold medal in Antwerp in the light heavyweight boxing competition! Isn't that grand?" Lilly's infatuation was obvious.

"Congratulations, son! Imagine, the Americans beating the British at boxing!" Clyde was at least momentarily impressed.

"Show him your medal," said Lilly. Eddie had it on under his clothes and pulled it up to show. Clyde, Jr., was all over the young man and they talked for several minutes.

"I hate to break up this farewell, but we have a train to catch for Houston. Once again, congratulations, Mr. Eagan, and thank you, Señorita Le Ross, for taking such good care of my Little Princess!" Clyde was eager to get going.

Eddie gave Lilly a kiss on the cheek, whispered in her ear, and said, "I'm gonna dust out of here. It's been a pleasure."

When Eddie was out of hearing range, Clyde asked the young people, "What does that mean?" The three of them laughed and informed him it was slang for "to leave." "Why didn't he just say that then? You would think he'd want to make a good impression." Clyde was unusually sulky. *Who is this young man wanting to spend time with my daughter? He may have won an Olympic gold medal, but that doesn't make him good enough for my Lilly. What are his intentions?*

On their first night on the train, they were in the dining car when, after coffee had been served, Clyde, Jr., sprang from his seat and got down on one knee. "Flora Gonzales, I have loved you since the day I met you. I'm miserable every time we're apart. Will you please marry me and never leave me like this again?" He took out a velvet ring box and opened it. A diamond sparkled in the lamplight and twinkled off the crystal.

"Oh, yes, I will marry you!" said Flo, perhaps a little too loudly; maybe a little too fast.

Back Row: Clyde, Jr. and Jesse
Front Row: Will and Captain Barbour

With the Grunewalds already coming to Houston, the couple decided to get married right away. So, on September 18, 1920, the wedding took place in the backyard of the new house on Montrose. Lilly was delighted that her best friend was now part of her family, but she couldn't understand what Flo saw in her irritating brother.

In December, Lilly came home again from Tarrytown for Christmas. To her great delight and surprise, her parents presented her with a car, a Locomobile. Clyde, Jr., and Flora were already living in Monroe but came down to Houston for the holidays. Lilly was full of stories about Eddie Eagan, who had visited her in Tarrytown that fall. Clyde simply rolled his eyes, sure that there was no way that at her school she would be allowed to be without a proper chaperone. *Over my dead body.*

"Daddy, Eddie said..." Lilly started.

"I can't stand to hear any more about Eddie Eagan. Please!"

"Why don't you ever like anybody I date?"

"That is not true!"

"I think it *is* true," said Jennie, smiling. "You haven't liked any of her boyfriends."

"Well...no wonder. She's a very special young lady. I've told you, Lilly, that young men may be interested in you because they see dollar signs. You have to be aware of that fact," Clyde stressed. "You know this."

"So I can never believe that a man loves me for who I am?" Lilly asked. "What kind of life is that?" She began to cry.

Jennie walked over to Lilly and hugged her. "Of course not, Lilly." She looked to her husband to say something.

"Lilly," Clyde began, "that's not what I meant. We just have to be extra careful, and I don't want you taken advantage of."

CHAPTER 36

THE CADET

1921
Jennie finally agreed to go with her husband down to Tampico to visit Jesse, Sylvia, and the two grandsons. They traveled at the beginning of April, planning to stay four or five weeks. Despite her reticence, Jennie enjoyed the sea breezes and the rocking motion of the ship. Her thick auburn hair piled high up on her head, she stood at the bow with Clyde and soaked it all in. Errant strands of her hair blew out from time to time, and Clyde made a game of tucking them back in.

"You have some escapees!" he teased.

"And more coming, I'll bet," answered Jennie, who was soaking up this much-needed attention. She got even more that night when they cuddled in bed, enjoying each other's bodies to the once-familiar rocking of a boat on the water. "I feel like a newlywed again! Remember the bed you made for us to sleep in after we got married?"

"Of course, I remember. I put a lot of love into that bed, and on top of it!" Clyde said and they both laughed. They were together, they were alone, and they were happy.

They stayed up late that night sharing stories of their life together on the flatboat and on the bayous. They laughed a lot and then when they talked about Luke, they cried.

Jennie loved Tampico! It was, of course, a boat town, so it had a familiar vibe. Jennie loved Jesse and Sylvia's big two-story house with expansive screened-in porches. They had a maid, a cook, a chauffeur, and a nanny. Jennie whispered to Clyde that she thought it was a little much, to which Clyde replied that he was just glad that they all seemed so happy.

Jesse accompanied his parents on a ride up the Panuco on the *Cruiser*. Clyde was content to sit back and let their son be the tour guide. Everyone was happy to see the captain again and to meet Mrs. Barbour. When a worker mentioned Clyde's near miss when the *Panciencia*'s boiler exploded, Jennie turned white, staring at her husband. Clyde smiled, his teeth clenched, guilt written all over his face. He patted Jennie's shoulder and rushed to another topic of conversation.

Clyde and Jesse were rarely seen at the house except to eat and to sleep. Jennie gave the nanny some time off, preferring to care for her grandchildren on her own. She particularly loved rocking and singing them to sleep. One late evening, Clyde walked quietly up the stairs and listened as she sang to Jesse, Jr.:

> "The stork has brought a baby brother
> into my house today.
> And I am crying for my mother
> 'cause she can't come out and play.
> Oh, the chicks have strayed into the garden,
> and my cap has flown away.
> So please kind man do help me find it
> 'cause I'm all alone today."

Clyde's heart was beating so hard he thought it would jump out of his chest. He closed his damp eyes as he listened from outside the nursery door and was flooded with memories of their own babies and the horrors of those deliveries, and throughout, the song he loved so much kept playing in his head.

As Clyde and Jennie were settling in for the night, Jennie was brushing her hair, getting ready for bed. "You seem extra tired tonight, sweetie. Did something happen today?" she asked.

"Something in Monroe," was all Clyde said.

"Please tell me Clyde, Jr., isn't in trouble again."

"No, no. I had to give the order to kill a wildgasser on Gutherie Farm. The boys said it was spouting gas and mud and water 100 feet high. That well cost us $25,000 and was putting out 11,000,000 cubic feet a day; that's a lot of oil." Clyde shook his head. "Once it's killed, I'm going to drill another well right next to it."

As was frequently the case, Jennie would not understand the intricacies of her husband's shop talk but could generally glean some idea of what was taking place.

"Seems like you have an answer to your problem," added Jennie.

"Yes, you're right. It's an expensive answer, but still an answer, I guess." Clyde walked across the room to where Jennie was brushing her hair, took the brush from her hand, and began to brush it himself. Jennie's eyes closed as she luxuriated in this show of tenderness that she adored.

"After all these years, I still love when you brush my hair!" Jennie opened her eyes, twisted her head around, and kissed her lover on the cheek. "Just like my mother used to do, only better!"

"I know, I know," he replied, his love a bright light shining in his eyes.

By 1921, Clyde's United Oil & Natural Gas Products Corp. was the largest carbon black company in the world. The discovery of oil at the Long Beach Oil Field in Signal Hill, California, which would become the world's most productive oil field, was made by a much less impressive gusher than the one in Monroe. Clyde's attention turned to California.

On October 13, Theodore Grunewald was born to Clyde, Jr., and Flora in New Orleans. He was named for the guardian who had raised her.

Shortly thereafter, Clyde received a telegram from Lilly, who was back at school in Tarrytown-on-Hudson.

"Daddy. Going to West Point. Need a dress. Found one on Fifth Avenue. Only $300.[2] Please may I buy it?"

Clyde answered, "Yes. Go to my bank and get the money. I'll call them. Have fun."

"You're the best, Daddy. I love you." Lilly didn't ask for much, so it made Clyde feel extra happy to do this for her.

In early November, a letter came from Lilly. In it, she told about her weekend at West Point.

"It's the most magical place, sitting up high on the cliffs of the Hudson River. All the buildings are old and made of stone. The cadets dress in their uniforms all the time and look dreadfully handsome! We stayed at the only hotel there on the grounds, Hotel Thayer. My date was a dreamy young man named Thomas J. Holmes. He's from Chicago, where his father is a judge. I think he was smitten with me; I really do! And everyone loved my dress! I felt like your Little Princess in it. Tommy Holmes asked me to please come back for another weekend as his date. I'm thrilled!"

"Another boy. Of course," said Clyde.

"Yes," said Jennie, "another boy you can pretend not to like." She smiled at him.

"You have to agree that she has yet to find a suitable partner. Maybe I need to ask around in New York City and see what eligible bachelors are up there." Clyde tapped his foot as he thought.

"New York City? But Clyde, that's way too far away from us. What's wrong with a boy from here in Texas, or better still, Houston?" Jennie was not going to let her Lilly marry far away from home and live forever at a distance if she could help it. "I want those grandbabies close by. We don't even know how Lilly will do having a family and having to do all the things that come with that. She may need our help."

---

[2] $4,700 today.

Later that month, a pregnant Sylvia sailed back to Houston from Tampico to deliver her child. She traveled with her two sons and the nanny. Jesse followed a few weeks later, and they all settled into their old house on Avondale. They had a baby girl they named Sylvia Lucile on December 22, 1921, just in time for Christmas, Lilly's nineteenth birthday, and New Year's Eve.

The next year, Houston began replacing its old wooden bridges with steel and concrete. It wasn't a big contract for him, but Clyde liked to be involved in projects around his hometown to keep his name in the minds of the local business community. He had James and Milt take charge of this project. He didn't see much of either of them anymore. Clyde was busy and on the move, making money.

"Hi, little brother," said Clyde, as he clapped James on the back.

"Woah, there, brother," replied James, laughing.

"Be careful with the lover man; the women want him from New York to Galveston! Never seen anythin' like it!" Milt shook his head, laughing.

"You can't talk; you leave a trail of them everywhere you go," said James in an effort to normalize his behavior.

"Where ya been?" Clyde asked his brother, dismissing their chatter.

"Been spendin' lots of time up in Kentucky the last year or two. Had some business up there," replied James matter-of-factly.

"Business? Is that what you call it?" Milt laughed.

Clyde ignored Milt, who seemed a little tipsy, as did James. "What's going on in Kentucky?" he asked.

"Well, ya see, I was up there workin' on the river doin' this and that. Met a nice woman named Sarah and we hit it off. That's all. No big deal," said James, trying unsuccessfully to downplay his story.

"I thought you were stuck on your Miss Annie in Galveston?" said Clyde sarcastically.

"She's still my Galveston girl, for sure. Now for a little fun in Kentucky!" James and Milt laughed heartily and shook hands.

"Here's to all the women in America!" The two pretended to toast with imaginary glasses. "And I learned everything I know from my cousin, Milt!"

"Aw, ain't nothin'," Milt replied.

"That's just wonderful, James. Let's not forget you're married with two beautiful children in Franklin! What's gotten into you?" Clyde's stern expression and tone said it all.

"You need to stop talkin' about things you don't understand. Mary's happy as can be home with our babies and then happy as can be when I come home after a long trip out workin'. My Annie does what she pleases and gets all excited when I'm around, which suits us both. Now Sarah, she's just the prettiest thing! And our baby girl looks just like her!" James' words trailed off.

Clyde was flabbergasted. James had always been extremely good-looking and had any woman he wanted. *Did he say he has two wives? How is that even possible? Poor Mary, and their children! Does she even know? Is he never going to grow up?* Then it hit him: he was doing some of the same things. *But it's different,* he tried to tell himself. *It's different—Jennie and I love each other unconditionally and that will never change,* he told himself. But it all sounded hollow suddenly as thoughts crowded his mind. *Ruth only has me, no other man,* he told himself. *I help her, I care for her, I love her, and Opal is still just an infatuation.* But his righteous indignation and rationalizations still sounded hollow. He tried to think of something to reassure himself, to ease his emotional pain and resolve his cognitive dissonance.

"Does Mary know?" he asked James.

"Now why would I go and do that?" laughed James. "I'm takin' good care of 'em, don't you worry. So, big brother, you're gonna tell me you never thought about sex with any woman 'cept Jennie? Really?"

"Yeah, Clyde, how about that?" asked Milt.

"All I can say is that Jennie will never have to worry about how much I love and cherish her," Clyde answered, ready to move on to another subject.

"Yeah, sure, Clyde," James slurred, and the subject was closed.

Peggy's husband, Forest Lewis, did a good job selling Fords in Houston. He was passionate about it, which Clyde appreciated and wanted to encourage. He had some oil rigs pumping out in California and was intrigued with the new business of making movies. After much research, he decided to open a car dealership in Hollywood that could provide Peggy and Forest with a better lifestyle and set things up for a new place for the family to visit.

"Captain," Forest replied after he was presented with the proposition, "why are you so sure that this is a good idea?"

"Forest, that's what I do; I balance risk and reward. If it doesn't interest you, please tell me now." Clyde was a little irritated with his son-in-law, but the last thing he wanted was an unhappy employee, much less an unhappy Peggy. The amount of oil coming out of the ground in California was astounding. They were having trouble keeping the price stable, but Clyde figured that was a short-term problem he was willing to wait out.

Forest was willing to give it a try. It was decided, or Clyde decided, that it would be a Ford dealership. Peggy, Forest, and little Clyde Edward waved goodbye from the train window, Peggy unable to stop the tears flowing down her cheeks. Jennie promised herself that she wouldn't let Peggy see her cry. Jesse hadn't seen her cry when she first saw him in the hospital. She didn't cry at either of her son's weddings or when Jesse and Sylvia sailed away to Mexico. She felt it her duty to support her children's decisions and not to lament her own loss in those situations. However, when the train was out of sight, Jennie rested her head on Clyde's shoulder and shed a few tears.

Lilly was anxious for her parents to meet her new beau, Tommy Holmes. Finally, on one of Clyde's trips to New York City that spring, he invited Tommy to join Lilly and several of her girlfriends from school for lunch at the Warwick Hotel. Clyde wanted the opportunity to give him the once-over in a group setting; he felt he'd be able to find out more about him that way.

Clyde met the girls' limousine at the entrance to the hotel. Lilly popped out of the car dressed in high style from head to toe, talking all the while to her friends, who were giggling as they exited the car.

"Daddy! It's so good to see you!" Lilly hugged her father and kissed his cheek. "I know you remember my friends Jinty Moore and Millie Bateman." The girls shook hands with Clyde, and he was very pleased at the company Lilly was keeping. "Tommy should be here any minute! I'm so excited for you to meet him!"

"You're going to really like him, Captain Barbour. He's so handsome and smart and fun," said Jinty with a glint in her eye.

"I'm sure he is," Clyde said as he led the pack into the hotel and to the restaurant.

They had scarcely been seated when a tall, dashing cadet in uniform approached the table.

"Tommy! Tommy!" the girls sang in unison.

The cadet, back straight and arms at his side, walked up to Clyde and introduced himself.

"Good afternoon, Captain Barbour. I am Thomas Jefferson Holmes, Jr." He stood with perfect posture next to Clyde, who rose to shake his hand. "It's a great honor to meet you, sir, and to be invited to have luncheon with you and these lovely ladies." He smiled at Lilly, who blushed and lowered her head.

"Have a seat, son. I've heard a lot about you," Clyde said.

After food had been ordered and polite conversation had begun, Clyde dived right in.

"So, Mr. Holmes, where are you from?"

"Chicago, sir. My parents still live there." Tommy seemed at ease during this questioning, which impressed Clyde.

"And what does your father do?"

"Well, sir, my father is a lawyer. He served as the president of the Bar Association in Chicago, and he's a judge." The answer rolled easily off of his tongue.

Nice pedigree, Clyde thought. *Attractive. Intelligent. Respectful. So far, so good. If only I had had that kind of upbringing.*

For dessert, they shared a cake that was a specialty of the restaurant. It received high praise from everyone. Lilly played her role as the Little Princess when she asked her father if he would ask the chef for the cake recipe. "Josephine could make it for us this summer," said Lilly, delighted with her idea. Her girlfriends chimed in as well. It didn't take long for the recipe to show up in an envelope marked "Warwick Hotel."

"That was a wonderful idea, Lilly. I'll give it to you to hold onto, so I don't lose it in all my business papers." He handed her the envelope. What he didn't tell anyone was that the bill included a $25 charge for the recipe.

Tommy made a great impression on Clyde, who found himself surprised that he had finally met a male who was dating his precious Lilly of whom he approved, at least so far. From then on, whenever Clyde visited New York City on business, he rented a suite of rooms so there would be a parlor for Lilly and Tommy to use for visiting.

The 1920 Imperial Session of the Shriners had been held in Portland. Clyde hadn't had the time to make it all the way out there, but some of his friends and colleagues did make the trip. Clyde had voted "Yes" in absentia to the idea of opening the first Shriner's Hospital for Crippled Children, which would be in Shreveport, Louisiana, and would be specifically for pediatric orthopedic care. The ribbon-cutting took place in May 1922 and Jennie agreed to go with him. She was excited when Clyde insisted she buy a new outfit for the occasion. He really wanted Ma to go with them, but Grannie had become very heavy and could not get around easily. Clyde had tried to get her to the Mayo Clinic, thinking she might be suffering from thyroid problems, but she flatly refused.

Clyde came bounding in the front door in early May carrying a small shopping bag with a big smile across his face. "Jennie! Jennie!"

he called. Will was the only child left at home and was nowhere to be found. Josephine was busy banging pots around in the kitchen.

"Clyde?" Grannie called from the living room. "Is everything okay?"

Clyde walked to where she was sitting. "Yes, Ma. I bought something for Jennie, and I can't wait for her to see it. It's for the ribbon-cutting ceremony!" Clyde turned to see Jennie walking into the room. "Come sit down over here. I have something for you!" Jennie gladly did as she was told and wondered at the excitement she saw in her husband's face. "It's for you to wear to the ceremony in Shreveport." He handed her the small bag and stood watching as she took out the small box and opened it. Inside was a lovely broach inlaid with diamonds surrounded by delicate silver filigree. "It will sparkle everywhere when you wear it on your new black lace evening gown!"

"It's perfect, Clyde! I love it!" Jennie stood up to kiss her smiling husband. "What made you think…."

"I saw it in the window at the jewelry store and just had to buy it for my bride!" Clyde made a slight bow. "Beautiful diamonds for a beautiful lady!"

They took the train to Shreveport. Everyone rejoiced at the wonderful weather. Wearing her black lace gown and new diamond broach to the gala, Jennie felt like a princess.

Will had just graduated from high school when the family took off for Lilly's graduation ceremony. In truth, Will had barely squeaked through to get his diploma with the aid of a daily tutor. Clyde didn't like seeing Will's resemblance to his own brother, James. Will was very handsome, smooth, and charming. He'd never seen a rule he didn't want to break, and he was obsessed with the opposite sex. Having just finished school, he wasn't the least bit interested in a long trek from Houston to New York City.

"Son, you've never been to New York City," Clyde said at dinner when Will began to whine about the trip. "It will be a good introduction to more of our great country. Traveling imbues your spirit with the sense of adventure, appreciation, and perspective that you need. You'll see." Clyde watched as Will's sour demeanor turned to disdain. When Will opened his mouth to speak, Clyde cut him off. "Continue your pouting in your own room so we can enjoy our dinner."

"But Dad, I'm hungry! And besides, I wasn't gonna say anything bad," he protested.

"Then take your plate and your bad mood into the kitchen and eat in there." Will didn't move an inch. Clyde wiped his mouth with his white linen napkin and made as if to stand, which got Will moving, and he did as his father had ordered.

"Clyde," Jennie started, "Will is just—"

"Just what? Lazy? Insolent? Self-centered?"

"Clyde, stop it," said Grannie quietly. Jennie put her hands in her lap and stared down, and although he said nothing, it was obvious Clyde was seething. The regulator clock ticked off the seconds as the three sat in silence at the table.

"I'm sorry," Jennie said, so quietly it was difficult to hear her. "I know I haven't done a good job rearing the boys. Even Peggy wouldn't listen." Tears welled in her eyes as she shook her head, determined not to cry.

"Jennie, no, Jennie. It's not you. Please stop." Clyde grabbed her hand and squeezed it. "No one on this earth could have been a better, kinder mother. They were lucky to have you. I'm afraid they get their bad traits from my side of the family."

"Why in the world does one of you have to be to blame for what nature and God created?" Grannie demanded. "We love 'em and guide 'em and we try to help 'em, but they have their own way to go. Your brother, James, still does me in, and your pa, well, you know that story. We just love them the best we know how." She stood up from the table and walked around to kiss each of the parents, who were lost in thought, Clyde wondering what his mother would say if she knew what James was up to, much less himself.

For reasons that evaded Clyde, Jennie had agreed, without protest, to accompany him to Lilly's graduation in the spring of 1923. She even seemed excited at the prospect. Clyde wondered if it was because Will was going with them, which meant none of the children would be at home. Whatever the reason, he was happy to finally play tour guide for his wife.

A few weeks later, Will, Jennie, and Clyde arrived at the train station in Houston, the Union Depot that Clyde had helped build, for the first leg of their summertime journey. Their train car looked brand-new and bigger than the others from the outside, and once they stepped inside, Will and Jennie looked at each other questioningly.

"Welcome to our new train car!" said Clyde as he opened his arms wide to welcome them aboard.

"*Ours?* Our very own?" asked Will, taking it all in as he turned in a circle.

"Yes, it is!"

"It's beautiful! I had no idea!" said Jennie as she walked around touching all the beautiful fabric and furnishings.

"Follow me," said Clyde, taking Jennie's hand. Down a short hall was a small kitchen and a bathroom. "And this is where everyone sleeps on those long trips, like out to California where we'll no doubt be visiting Peggy. It sleeps six easily, more if we need to, and at the very end, our bedroom and private bath!" Clyde was enjoying the reaction to his latest surprise. "I'm hoping this will get Grannie out of Houston, and going to New York City will be a lot more pleasant for me."

Will was overjoyed. "Can I get to the rest of the train from here?"

"Yes, you can. But Will, remember, this is our private car; I won't have it turned into a party room."

"Of course, Daddy!" responded Will, but his sheepish look hinted at the potential antics playing around in his head.

Neither Jennie nor Will had ever seen anything like New York City. Jennie was content to absorb it all from the inside out, preferring not to linger too much in the crowds but rather to sit on the sidewalk and watch the horde pass by. On the other hand, Will wanted to wander around aimlessly, go into every skyscraper and ride the elevator to the top. Steve Hilton had arranged for a young man to play tour guide for Will, so everyone was able to experience the bustling city in whatever way he or she wanted.

When they first entered their suite, a large, wrapped gift box was waiting on the sofa. Clyde took Jennie by the hand and led her to it. Inside the box, she found a garment that looked like a painting on fabric with fur trim. She pulled it out and stood with her mouth agape as she donned the fabulous opera coat. The collar was a four-inch band of fur, and fur also outlined the ends of the oversized sleeves. The coat was lined with bright pink velvet, and the exterior was an Art Deco-inspired collage of flowers of orange, pink, green, gray, and black on top of which was an array of large, embroidered flowers and leaves stitched with silver thread. A thin horizontal tag at the neckline read "Made in Paris."

"Clyde! It's…well…it's beautiful, only more than beautiful! I've never seen anything like it!" Jennie danced around like a girl in her first evening dress. "I don't need to wear any jewelry with this on!"

"Whatever makes you comfortable. You look lovely!" Clyde went over and hugged his wife, and then examined the opera coat again closely.

"Do I get a present?" asked Will.

"Your present? I brought you to New York City in a private train car to stay in a suite at the McAlpin Hotel. That's not enough?" asked Clyde, angry at Will's sense of entitlement.

"Oh sure, right, of course. I wasn't thinking, Daddy. Sorry." Will did a fairly convincing job at looking contrite. "It's beautiful, Mama! And so are you!" He smiled and went up to kiss his mother and get some of her special brand of attention.

A trip to the opera had been planned for all of them. Will wanted nothing to do with such an outing and tried everything he could think of to stay behind at the hotel. It didn't work. Halfway through the second act, Will excused himself to go to the restroom. At some point, Clyde realized that Will had been gone far too long. He excused himself and went in search of his son.

He found Will in the Green Room, engrossed in a conversation with several of the bartenders and waitresses who were cleaning up and readying for the next wave of the society elite.

"What are you doing here?" Clyde asked his son. The service people quickly disappeared. "You come back out there with me right this minute and learn how to sit still, listen, and learn." He wanted to pull out his belt and whip him right there; whip out all the obstinance; whip out all the years of laziness and lies. But it was too late for that. He felt his face redden with anger.

Just then, Tim Bryan walked into the room.

"A little difference of opinion? Happens all the time at my house." He walked up to Clyde. "Listen, I have to leave early. How about I take Will back to your hotel and have him looked after until you get back?"

Clyde took a deep breath. "No reason to ruin everyone's evening because of one…Tim, that would be perfect. Thank you!" Clyde slapped Tim on the back. "And you, son, stay in the suite until we return."

"Yes, sir!" Will was so glad to escape the confines of the opera that he would have been willing to do just about anything else.

When they had gone, Clyde stood for a moment and decided that letting Will leave with Tim was the best and the least embarrassing of his options. Clyde would deal with him later.

They took the limo up to Miss Mason's School, The Castle, Tarrytown-on-Hudson, as Lilly's school was officially called. The Castle and grounds were even lovelier than Clyde remembered, having been dressed up for the special occasion. It stood there stately, reserved, and refined, opening its doors to the small group of privileged girls and young ladies fortunate enough to be able to cross its threshold over the last 27 years.

The senior class girls had been secreted away preparing for the ceremony. After much pomp and circumstance, the 22 young ladies walked out, one at a time, each wearing her own version of a solid white dress with white stockings and white shoes with straps, each carrying a matching bouquet of roses and greenery with ribbons and vines hanging down. Lilly had added a thin piece of lace to her bateau neckline and was the first to walk down the path because she had been voted school president that year.

Jennie and Clyde held hands, smiling at each other with pride and disbelief that they had somehow created such a lovely, educated, and confident young lady.

It was a long but wonderful afternoon filled with speeches, plays, poetry readings, singing, and much more. It was 5:30 p.m. when the four of them climbed into the back of the limousine and headed for New York City.

Lilly and Will sat facing their parents. From the small wooden cabinet between the siblings, which had held liquor and crystal glasses before Prohibition, Clyde pulled a small light blue box with a white ribbon tied into a bow on top.

"Your mother and I have a graduation gift for you," Clyde said, smiling.

He could just barely make out what Will muttered under his breath: "Guess everyone but me gets a present these days." Clyde chose to ignore him.

Lilly cried out, "A Tiffany box! Oh, my word!"

Inside the box was a large diamond ring with sapphires setting the diamond off from the platinum band. Lilly's jaw dropped but she quickly remembered her manners and closed it shut. She was speechless.

"The diamond came from Mexico. The setting was made specifically to fit that diamond." Clyde reached out his hand and patted Lilly's knee. "We couldn't be prouder of our Little Princess."

"We love you so much, Lilly! You're so beautiful and so smart!" Jennie added with a smile.

"I adore it!" said Lilly, holding her hand at arm's length to look at the ring on her finger. "I've never seen anything more beautiful in all my life!" she exclaimed. "Thank you, thank you forever and always!" She made her way over to her parents, sat between them, and hugged them both.

CHAPTER 37

THE EXPANSION

Fall 1922

In September, Lilly was back at The Castle to do some post-graduate work—and to pay visits to West Point.

In the September 25, 1922 issue of *The Oil Weekly* magazine, one article was titled, "Large Tract of Columbian Acreage Is Purchased in Fee by Houston Operator." Clyde had purchased 1,250,000 acres with two rigs already in place, planning to drill for oil. In addition, there were "300,000 acres of virgin timber which is estimated to contain 7,000,000,000 feet of marketable lumber." The property was approximately 90 miles long and 30 miles wide. "It is the largest tract privately owned in fee in that country." It was nearly the size of the state of Delaware. Clyde would be spending even more time away from home.

Clyde had already decided that he would buy a house in Los Angeles. Not only were Peggy and her family out there permanently now, but he saw it as a good investment. It occurred to him that the sea breezes would be good for all of them, especially in the hot and humid Houston summertime. He set Peggy on the hunt for a house and eventually bought a large two-story white house with a California look that nevertheless had beautiful columns up under the front entryway that both Clyde and Jennie loved. The address was 533 Lorraine Boulevard in Old Windsor Square. He hired a decorator to fix up the interior in the trendiest 1920s style, with dark wood floors and staircase complemented by light walls and ceilings with wide, plain molding. In the living room, small rugs were strewn haphazardly around on top of the carpeting, as was at least one lavishly decorated floor pillow. Every detail was chosen with Clyde's input. Jennie wasn't really interested in that sort of thing but shared Clyde's excitement as the work went on.

Clyde on Front Porch of Residence in Los Angeles,
California on Lorraine Boulevard, Windsor Square

Most of the family went out to Los Angeles for Christmas 1922. Peggy and Forest enjoyed playing tour guide. Clyde and Will visited Southern California University. Will was ecstatic when he was accepted; not only would he be very far from his parents, but he also found the girls in California quite attractive and flirtatious.

"So, Will, what are you interested in studying at college?" Clyde asked before their tour.

"Rocks. I'm interested in rocks!" Will answered without hesitation.

"Let's see. I think the best option for you, enjoying rocks as you do, would be a geologist, or maybe even a miner," Clyde said. "They search rock formations for oil and minerals and ore."

"No, Dad, I don't mean that kind of thing. I want to study rocks and go out and find things buried in them; you know, like treasure hunting!" Will became animated just talking about it.

"A treasure hunter? Hmm. I don't think that's going to give you the income you need to support a family." Clyde wanted to roll his eyes but was determined to deal with Will on his own level.

"But I don't have a family," Will replied.

"Not yet, thank God, but you're going to want one eventually. A man has to be prepared." Clyde could feel that Will was slipping away in his thoughts.

"Were you prepared when you and Mama got married?" Will asked, knowing the answer.

"Things were different back then," Clyde began.

"You always say that, but I don't think so," Will replied defiantly.

Clyde was tired of this topic. "What I can tell you is that I worked all day, every day, all year round. I used my mind, and I used my body until it ached, all to support my family and so that my children wouldn't have to endure all those hardships. I also did all of this so that you could build your life from a starting point I couldn't have imagined at your age. I certainly didn't do all this so that you could be a spoiled, rich loafer who just wants to play all day. I still work endlessly, but in a much different way. That's what a man does. He provides for his family and does his best to put them in a position that will help them be successful. Maybe your way of thinking about the world is an unintended consequence of me being gone so much." Clyde stood up and walked outside to the porch.

Clyde was planning his first trip to Europe. He was going to visit his Anchor Chemical Company offices in Manchester, England, and go in search of more opportunities in carbon black throughout

Europe. He planned the trip to coincide with Lilly's summer vacation. When he approached Jennie about joining him, he was met with the same flat "No."

"But I'll have to have a chaperone for Lilly; I'll be busy with work," he insisted.

"I know, I know," Jennie answered. "But I have to get Will ready to go off to school this fall."

"Certainly, there can't be that much to do," Clyde protested. "After all, he'll be living with Peggy's family. What's there to do other than buy him some clothes?" The conversation took on its usual tone.

"But sweetie, there's much more to it! Besides, you know how I hate to travel!" She was, as always, groping for the right words. "I'll have to take him out there, after all."

"This is very different. We're talking about going to Europe! It will be a life-changing experience; one that I want to share with my wife. Imagine seeing all the beautiful treasures at the Louvre and the statues in Italy and even Versailles!"

"Please don't be angry with me. I never want to disappoint you! I just...I just...want to stay home. Please!" Jennie reached over to Clyde and held his hand. "Take Ruth! She can keep you up to date on your business and chaperone Lilly. What an amazing opportunity you'll be giving her, a widow and all!"

"I'll never understand why you don't want to travel with me. You could have been with me at the World's Fair and in New York City when I was first introduced into high society there." Clyde was on a roll.

"I'm not high society and I don't want to be. You know I just don't care about that sort of stuff. That used to be one of the things you loved about me so much. What happened to that? Why am I not enough the way I am?" Jennie was feeling a mixture of sadness, anger, and shame. It wasn't like her to feel angry, especially at her husband. She felt displaced. She left the room quickly and closeted herself in their bedroom.

Clyde was exasperated. *Doesn't she understand that traveling would only help her feel more at ease around people who have the kind of money we do now? Does her simple nature bother me? Am I embarrassed by her lack of knowledge? Does any of this make me love her any less?* These thoughts chased one another around and around in his head, making him feel sad and lonely. He sat down and rubbed his head with his hands, trying to massage it all into a nice, comprehensible whole.

A little while later, they were getting ready for bed. Clyde knew he needed to end the silence between them that was eating him up. There was only one thing he could do, regardless of how he felt, so he did it.

"Jennie, come sit next to me." Clyde sat down and patted the mattress next to him. She obeyed, her eyes moist with tears. "I'll try really hard to accept your unwillingness to travel with me. Nothing matters more to me than you. We couldn't have made it this far if we didn't love each other, and if I didn't know, no matter where I am, that you're at home supporting me. That gives me a lot of comfort. I couldn't do what I do without you. I'll be happy to have Lilly go with me; she's always a delight." He kissed his wife and slid under the covers. But there was no lovemaking that night; no bodies moving in sync, no moans of ecstasy. They fell asleep in each other's arms and slept with their bodies in constant contact and woke to another day full of possibilities for Clyde.

Clyde, Lilly, and Ruth boarded the S.S. *Majestic* on June 23, 1923, for the six-day journey to Southampton, England. Lilly had been up and down Fifth Avenue buying clothes for her trip and her ebullience was infectious. Shoes, hats, dresses, stockings…. Her schoolmates and teachers had warned her to leave room in her trunks for the clothes and trinkets she would want to buy in Paris and London. They were led to their staterooms, D136 and D138, Lilly and Ruth sharing a room. Lilly was welcomed by four dozen red roses from her brother Jesse and Sylvia.

The first night, the moon on the water captivated Lilly. She wrote in her diary, "The moonlit ocean is perfect—like a fairyland, so wondrously like silver in the moonlight. One is happy and sad, lonely and glad, all together. Beautiful Atlantic."

They spent the days writing, eating, talking, and sitting on their deck chairs. Clyde spent a lot of time alone working, but always found time to spend with Lilly. He loved the idea of this unprecedented amount of time to have with his Little Princess, who wasn't little anymore.

Clyde was known for having the largest carbon black manufacturing plant in the world, in Monroe, Louisiana, where the oil fields were. Some of this was sold to Europe. He had an office in Manchester, England, and he had managers there who came to his office in New York City for meetings. Clyde made sure to entertain them lavishly. Now it was their turn to reciprocate.

When they reached Southampton, a business associate of Clyde's, Mr. Taylor, came aboard to help them move quickly through passport control and customs. Another associate, Mr. Hewlett, had sent his car, a lovely Daimler limousine, for them to use throughout their time abroad. They were driven into London with Mr. Taylor to the Savoy Hotel by their driver, whose name was Judge and who was part of the package deal.

Their suite was lovely and beautifully appointed. The Savoy would serve as their base for their trip; they would leave luggage and packages there while they traveled around and then retrieve everything on their way back to the States.

On their first full day in London, they were taken to the races at Sandown, and after lunch, to the horse show at Olympia. The Taylors and the Hewletts took them to the *Midnight Follies* at the Metropole for supper and dancing. Though they arrived back at the hotel around 1:00 a.m. exhausted, Lilly was full of excitement at what lay ahead.

The following day, July 1, Lilly was grateful that her father needed to spend the day talking business with men from his Anchor Chemical

Company in Manchester. The Manchester Ship Channel, dredged in the 1890s, had transformed Manchester from a landlocked city into a major port. Clyde planned to spend a great deal of time studying it and talking to those involved in its upkeep.

The ladies spent their time shopping, especially at Harrods. There was a trip to Hampton Court and several trips to the theatre, including a performance of *Music Box Review,* and a lavish dinner every night.

"Daddy," Lilly said one afternoon, "I don't think I can possibly eat another thing!" Her tiny appetite had definitely grown since she'd been traveling with her father.

"I tell you what, try this. Just take two bites of all the first courses and save your appetite for the main course. And dessert, of course!" Clyde laughed.

That was how most of their days were spent: shopping, a visit to a local tourist attraction, dining, and going to the theatre. Evenings never ended before midnight, often later. Lilly loved it; Clyde found it exhausting. "Thank God I don't drink," he said to himself in the mirror while getting ready for bed one night.

At the Houses of Parliament, Mr. Flannigan, a Member of Parliament, gave them an insider's tour of the House of Commons and the House of Lords, both of which were in session.

Clyde joined the ladies for a tour of the Tower of London, followed that evening by a trip to the theatre and finally to the Savoy for dinner and dancing.

Lilly was called on by Walter Horridge, whose parents were friends with the Taylors. They thought Walter would be a pleasant companion for Lilly. Unbeknownst to her, here in Europe she was looked upon as an American heiress at the perfect age for marriage. Clyde knew this would be the case and was cautious; he felt Walter an appropriate companion, but he wasn't going to accept anything else. Walter was frequently around before they left for the Continent.

Lilly enjoyed his company, especially when it gave her the opportunity to ride in his very sporty convertible Sizaire! One evening, Walter surprised Lilly with a beautiful antique silver candlestick.

They traveled to a very misty and rainy Glasgow and on to Edinburgh, where on an unusually lovely summer day, the king and queen were visiting. One morning, sitting at a window in their hotel, they saw a horseman in scarlet livery followed by the royal couple as they drove into Edinburgh from Holyrood Palace in an open carriage drawn by a pair of greys.

"Oh, Daddy, how very elegant! We are very privileged people indeed!" Lilly exclaimed.

They spent several days at the Hewletts' spacious country home in Northenden, just outside of Manchester. It was a brooding red-brick mansion with a wide driveway leading to the front entrance whose only decoration was a set of Doric columns on either side of the porch. The back of the mansion was much more attractive, with its rolling gardens and a paddock off in the distance.

The dining room table sat 20 and all the seats were occupied the next evening. Clyde was overwhelmed by the intricately decorated sterling and the shining Waterford crystal glasses. There were flower arrangements all along the center of the table and what Clyde felt sure were Irish linen napkins with a large monogram.

After the guests had all departed, Clyde, Lilly, Ruth, and the Hewletts retired to the smoker for some cognac. Their two young children, Donald and Margaret, who hadn't been seen all day, appeared to say good night. They were precious in their white lace and fine cotton batiste pajamas.

"I will never hide my children away all day," Lilly whispered to Ruth.

A few days later they were off to spend the weekend at the Horridge's summer home, named Plas Llanfairpwll, on the isle of Anglesey in northern Wales. Lilly was happy to be in the Sizaire with Walter while the others traveled along in the Daimler. They stopped several times to see local landmarks and then for tea at the Waterloo Hotel, where they were served on the lovely lawn under the trees. They crossed the bridge to Anglesey and on to their estate, where Walter and Lilly walked through the woods and to the farm where black-and-white cattle grazed.

The estate was truly grand. The house of gray stone would have looked like a castle if only it had had a turret. Over the front door was a sign indicating that the house had been built in 1620. Clyde was amazed. Servants were everywhere. Every morning, they were awakened by a servant with a tray of tea for them to enjoy in their beds. In the rear of the mansion were lovely gardens and an area referred to as The Park.

There was a gong downstairs that the butler would ring whenever something important was about to happen, like dinner. That night their beautiful oval dining table was adorned with an overflowing low flower arrangement in the center. Radiating from the center were lovely pastel ribbons at least 4 inches wide that flowed over the edges of the table.

Upon their departure, Walter gave them all sweet peas, peaches, and magazines to keep them busy on their trip.

On July 23, Clyde, Lilly, and Ruth boarded the *Normania* for the trip to France. Unfortunately, their cabin had bunk beds. Ruth and Lilly tossed a coin and Lilly won. She chose the lower bunk. They got in the Daimler, which was theirs to use touring around the continent, the next morning, reaching Paris early in the evening.

They stayed at the Continental, where Lilly had stayed with Señorita Le Ross. Suite 31. Lilly was excited to discover mail waiting for them. She was quite smitten with her West Pointer, Thomas Jefferson Holmes, Jr., or Tommy. He wrote her long letters every few days espousing his love for her and telling her how miserable he was without her:

"I have a feeling that all is right with the world. I do not now feel conceited in saying I am sure of Lilly's love and Lilly must know how truly and deeply I love her. Oh dearest, I am so sure that all is well in our dear dream world."

Clyde, having met Tommy in New York City, was fond of him, or as fond as he could be of any of Lilly's suitors. Tall, handsome, smart, a West Pointer, from an apparently prestigious family. However, Clyde would do his due diligence in looking more deeply into this young man's character. What he didn't know was that the pair were already in love. Clyde didn't have to worry about some young man with a title trying to win over his daughter.

Sightseeing all over Paris in the Daimler was Lilly's idea of perfection. "Isn't this just grand!" she said to her father. Judge smiled from ear to ear and was sure to tell his employer what had been said when he returned to England.

It was even more perfect to drive up to the Palace of Versailles in the beautiful Daimler. Lilly had been there with Señorita but was nevertheless once again awed by the beauty and the grandeur.

Clyde found himself literally speechless at times inside the palace. He found the Hall of Mirrors indescribable. The tapestries particularly interested him. He remembered seeing the Gobelins at the World's Fair. He wanted so much to touch them; to go right up to them and see them up close. *I could spend days in here,* he thought, *maybe weeks!*

That night at dinner, when it was time for dessert, Clyde's mind was still on the beautiful tapestries he had seen. "*Garçon,* please bring us some tapestries for dessert." Everyone laughed. It took Clyde a moment to realize he'd said tapestries instead of pastries. It became one of the jokes from the trip that would be retold for years.

When it came time to move on to Spain and Switzerland, Clyde made an executive decision. "I'm going to send Judge and the Daimler back to the Hewletts. It doesn't feel right to keep them any longer."

"But Daddy, it's so wonderful to ride around in such high style!" Lilly complained.

"We have enough high style with you and Ruth! We'll be just fine."

Thus, on July 30, they traveled in a sleeping car to Madrid, where they stayed at Hotel Roma. There, *mantones* (beautifully handmade and hand-embroidered squares of silk worn as shawls) were all the rage. Their first day there, Lilly chose an antique black with beige embroidery and long black fringe for 1,100 *pesadas* and Clyde picked one out for Jennie. Ruth, of course, had to have one as well, which Clyde secretly paid her back for later.

The express train took them to Barcelona.

"Lilly, I'm not well at all this morning," Clyde told his daughter just two days into their stay.

"Daddy, you don't look well. Please, don't get up," said Lilly as Clyde attempted to get out of his bed.

"I've already called for the hotel doctor," Ruth said. "He should be here soon."

"What is it?" Lilly asked.

"I'm just tired," Clyde offered. "We've been going full speed since we left New York."

"But Daddy, you always go full speed."

The doctor came. Luckily, he had an American nurse who also served as interpreter. The doctor's orders were for Clyde to stay in bed for three days, after which the doctor would return. Their plans for Marseilles and Nice were cancelled, and they'd be going directly to Paris on August 10.

Lilly was frightened. She couldn't remember ever seeing her father ill. She spent a great deal of time sitting next to his bed writing letters. It suddenly began to haunt her, the idea of a world without her father in it. *That's not possible. We would all be lost without him!* She thought and prayed and decided that God wouldn't do that; he couldn't do that!

With the "all clear" from the doctor, they headed for the train station and were almost late for their train. The driver was taken down a notch by Clyde, who had had enough of Barcelona. It was so unlike Clyde that Lilly didn't know how to react. She and Ruth were both quiet and followed along behind him quickly.

"What an awful day," Lilly said. "It's miserably hot and this train is so uncomfortable!"

It didn't help that they reached the frontier at 1:00 a.m. and were required to show their passports and show customs everything they had purchased, which was a considerable collection. An old lady examined their things but asked for only two of their bags to be opened.

"That's the first nice thing to happen in days," said an uncharacteristically grumpy Clyde, who was ready to get off the train.

Back in Paris at the Continental Hotel on August 10, Clyde met his ladies at the suite for tea. After that, he worked almost every day and Lilly shopped almost every day. Both were content.

Clyde was interested in looking at the Gobelin tapestries that had so captivated him at the World's Fair and at some Louis XIV furniture, for which he relied on Monsieur Henri Woog. Although he took the time to do both of these things, he found nothing that made him ready to put down the amount of money it would take to purchase something. He could wait but was happy to order two tapestry handbags at Gobelin for Lilly, one black-and-white to go with her *mantone*. Later, when he and Lilly went to a jeweler in Place Vendome, he found a beautiful diamond-and-sapphire bracelet with square stones around the entire bracelet and bought it for Jennie.

Lilly was fascinated with a women's shop called Paul Caret she had heard about. At dinner on the night she first went to this salon, she was full of stories about her visit.

"Daddy, I went to Paul Caret today. You won't believe what happened!" she began, Clyde smiling at her obvious excitement. "First of all, you don't try on any of the clothes."

"How do you know if it'll fit?"

"Wait, Daddy, I'll tell you. A Russian princess named Madame Helene waited on us. We sat on a beautiful settee and drank tea while we watched the models come strolling by in all the different outfits so you could see the fall line and see if you liked anything. It was so... well...civilized!"

That sent everyone at the table into laughter. "The French really know how to be civilized, in some respects, that's for sure!" Clyde said, smiling. "This is probably a silly question, but did you see anything you liked?"

Lilly's smile broadened. "Yes, sir, I certainly did. You know how I've been looking everywhere for an outfit to wear walking Vargo?" she asked.

"Of course, dear, everyone with a snow-white Russian wolfhound needs the right clothes to wear walking down Montrose Boulevard in Houston!" Clyde teased her good-naturedly and she took it happily. "After all, your fur coat is usually a little warm for Houston." He wondered about the unintended consequences of the way they had raised Lilly.

"Well, there was one model who wore a black-and-white dress, sort of a satiny fabric, with white collar and cuffs; I think it would be absolutely perfect! And the fabric is lightweight for our Houston heat." She seemed pleased with her find.

"If you like it, I'm sure it's perfect. Please go back and buy it," Clyde said.

"Oh Daddy, thank you so much! Here's the thing, since there are no try-ons, you have three fittings and it's made just to fit you and nobody else! Can you imagine?"

"Sounds like this outfit will be something you enjoy before you ever wear it, as well as when it's complete!"

At bedtime, Lilly thanked her father again for allowing her to purchase the dress.

"Lilly, my precious Lilly," started Clyde, cupping her face with his hands and looking lovingly into her eyes. "You ask for so little. But I want you to do something else, too." Lilly looked at him questioningly. "Get a few more outfits. I want you to feel great when you walk the streets of New York City in your new finery. I know you'll take good care of them." He kissed her forehead, and she hugged his neck tightly.

"You're the most wonderful father in the whole world!" Before their trip was over, Lilly had made three wonderful choices of outfits at Paul Caret.

Their next stop was Lucerne, Switzerland. As soon as they checked into the Grand Hotel National and stepped out onto the balcony, they were in love with the city. The blue lake was picturesque—the sailboats with their white sails beckoning, the chalets on the high hillsides, and the cattle grazing on the slopes. "How do those poor creatures hold on and eat at the same time?" Lilly wondered out loud. "Poor dears!" Everyone laughed.

There was a contingent of Americans there, some of whom they already knew. Lilly enjoyed some nights out without the "grown-ups" and Clyde enjoyed the nights here and there when he and Ruth could be alone, or almost alone. One such opportunity came in Lucerne when Lilly's group went to the casino and then out to dinner. She informed her friends that she was there with "Clyde Barbour's luck," so they should be prepared for her to win.

"We're alone!" Ruth whispered, as if saying it out loud might change the status. She walked over to Clyde, put her arms around his neck, and kissed him. When she stopped and put her arms down to step back, he put his arms around her waist and held her close, smiling. The main door out into the hall locked from the inside; they could feel safe from instant intrusions and would be prepared for an unexpected knock on the door from Lilly, who they expected would be gone for hours. They wouldn't test fate with an all-out session of lovemaking, but instead would enjoy those smaller pleasures.

In Clyde's bedroom, Ruth dropped back onto the featherbed as if to make a snow angel, her body becoming enveloped by the comforter. Clyde laughed and sat down next to her and leaned over to smell her hair.

"Lilly and I had perfume shampoos yesterday!" Ruth said.

"Beautiful smell. Definitely worth every penny!" He kissed her hair and lay down next to her in the cushy comfort.

"You learn a lot about somebody when you travel with them," Ruth said thoughtfully.

"Yes, you do. Such as?"

"Well, so many things. You brush your teeth two times every day. Oh, and you like to have your picture taken," Ruth began.

Clyde laughed again. "Very interesting observations! Very insightful! I sound a little vain...." He tickled her and she feigned trying to escape, dragged down by the comforter. "And you are uncomfortable in vehicles."

"Only when they're going down the wrong side of the road! Or when I can't see land anywhere! Or when the train cars look so old,

I'm afraid they're going to fall apart underneath us!" Ruth hurried through her defenses. "But I simply love it!"

"I see, I see!" said a smiling Clyde.

They caressed, they touched, they kissed, they delighted each other, and then it was time to reenter the real world.

On their last night in Lucerne, the traveling friends had a grand seven-course dinner together at their hotel; the Barbours, Ruth, the Roses, and the Martins. Lilly kept the menu and had all the guests at the table sign the back to remember.

They took the train back to Paris and the Continental Hotel. Clyde and Ruth had the opportunity to visit the Eiffel Tower alone one afternoon and then were off to *Les Ambassadeurs* for a quiet dinner together. Although he knew the likelihood was high that they would run into people they knew there, he didn't feel the need for a cover; Ruth was Lilly's companion, and everyone knew that. He was also aware that the Europeans didn't look down upon that sort of thing anyway; they felt that a man of great wealth was expected to have his dalliances.

About a week after they returned to Paris, Lilly noticed that Clyde and Mrs. Rose had been gone for hours shopping. Her 21st birthday was in four months, and she had her heart set on a string of pearls. That night, after the opera, they were enjoying their usual sandwiches and milk in the suite with Mr. and Mrs. Rose. Clyde went into his room and came out with a beautiful, long, rectangular box.

"Lilly, Mrs. Rose and I spent all afternoon shopping at Tiffany's and Cartier looking for the perfect gift for your upcoming monumental birthday. Here it is, just for you! I hope you will love them and pass them on to your own little princess one day. Happy Birthday, Lilly Lucile!" He handed the box to Lilly and watched as she opened it to find a beautiful strand of pearls.

Lilly stood up and gasped, almost spilling the pearls, then hugging her father around the neck as hard as she could.

"How beautiful! I will wear them every day! Oh, Daddy, Lilly is the most fortunate girl in the whole world!" She kissed him and turned around for him to clasp them in the back. She put her hand on top of her new necklace to feel their coolness, then walked up to the mirror and preened.

Clyde was eager to see Amsterdam. He was intrigued by the idea of canals used as roads throughout the city, not unlike the bayous in Louisiana. But he was even more excited to see Rotterdam and its port. He had read that the distance from Rotterdam to the North Sea had been 18 miles up until the end of 1896, and because it was shallow and irregular, it often took steamers several days to traverse. They had decided to dredge a new 14-mile channel from Vlaardingen to the North Sea, going right through the Hook of Holland. It was completed in 1896 and had a depth of 27 feet, which gave steamers a trip to Rotterdam of only two hours instead of several days.

Since 1906, they had been busy building an even larger harbor called the Waal Harbor, which would consist of 800 acres and would double the size of the existing harbor.

Clyde went off to meet Mr. Taylor and Mr. Hewlett at the train station in Rotterdam while the women went on a trip to Volendam. The men had a meeting with the harbormaster. They were taken to his office by a young Dutchman who was all smiles.

"Captain Barbour, this is Meneer Tony de Groot," said their tour guide in perfect but heavily accented English.

"I have heard very much about you; you are a man of many visions!" the harbormaster said.

"Thank you, Meneer de Groot." Clyde was trying his best to incorporate the guttural Dutch pronunciation into his words. "What you're doing here with the new Waal Harbor excites me! I've read that you've already shortened the trip for the steamers from the North Sea to Rotterdam and now you plan to double its size."

"Ja, that will be the case. With the channel already dredged, we are now working to make the harbor bigger, with many more quays and warehouse facilities. In the past, the custom was for a merchant to store his goods in his own house. I don't think that will work anymore, do you?" The men laughed.

"We have a similar problem in Houston, Texas. To get a steamer from the Gulf of Mexico to the Port of Houston takes five to six hours. I'm looking to cut that in half," Clyde stated boldly.

"Then we should go on a tour of this place! My assistant will drive us around for a better look." Meneer de Groot led the men out to the vehicle. No interpreter was needed; Clyde had learned that the Dutch pride themselves on being proficient in many languages, their country being so small and their language not being prevalent.

As they were driven around, Clyde loved looking at all the steamers and the dredging and the loading and unloading of ships. It was in his blood. With the sound of the mud as it was pulled up out of the water and the smell of freshly dug sludge, if he closed his eyes, he could have been in most any port in the world. The ruckus of the stevedores sounded no different in Dutch, or whatever language they were speaking. It wasn't the singing he so loved on the Mississippi River, but it had a rhythm all its own.

This was exactly what Clyde had in mind for Houston, a landing spot for large oceangoing vessels that was only a few hours from the Gulf of Mexico. It would change the fabric of Houston forever.

When he returned to the Hotel Victoria in Amsterdam, the cacophony coming from their suite was concerning. Clyde moved quickly to open the door and enter. He found Lilly, Ruth, and Mrs. Taylor all talking at once.

"Oh, Daddy, I'm so glad to see you! We've had an awful time, just awful," Lilly told him.

"What in the world? Are you hurt?"

"Oh, no Clyde, we're not hurt," said Mrs. Taylor, "just frustrated."

"Well, that's good to hear," said a relieved Clyde. "From the sounds I heard down the hall, I wasn't sure. So, what awful thing happened to you ladies?"

"Well, Daddy, we went to Volendam, a really quaint little town, then took a boat tour. We're riding along just outside of Mannikendam when *Boom!*—we run into a sandbar, shoving us all over the place. I ended up almost in the lap of some poor old man! The captain said we were stuck on the sandbar," explained an animated Lilly.

"Stuck on a sandbar outside of Mannikendam?" Clyde couldn't help but chuckle. "Were you stuck hard and fast, as we used to call it?"

"I'm not sure what that means but I would say yes," said Ruth. "We were stuck there for over an hour! So, when we reached Leiden, we had to motor back to Amsterdam."

"You're lucky you weren't stuck longer. When I was a boy, we'd get stuck on a sandbar in the middle of the river and be there for days! Did I ever tell you the story of when your mother, Papa Jim, Grannie, and I were stuck on a sandbar and danced on top of the flatboat to Grandpa's music?" Clyde asked.

"Yes, Daddy, you have," said Lilly, unwilling to compare the two events or diminish her own distress.

That evening, Clyde, Mr. Taylor, and Mr. Hewlett went to dinner together to talk business. The three ladies dined at a small place on Dam Straat. The evening ended with the ladies having to run in the rain, which started Lilly laughing and quickly infected the other two women, who laughed with her.

It happened to be Jubilee Week in the Netherlands, Queen Wilhelmina celebrating her 25th anniversary as queen. With a great deal of patience, they were able to get tickets to the viewing stand opposite Town Hall and see the queen and Princess Julianna drive up in grand Dutch style. The Royals entered Town Hall and came out on a balcony that was draped in red velvet. Everyone sang the national anthem and the bell towers in the town all rang out.

"I have now seen two real queens. I am one lucky Lilly!" she said to her father when he came to kiss her good night.

They took the train back to Paris and, back at the Continental, Suite 35, Lilly was collecting all the parcels of things she had purchased. They took their last big tour, this time of the battlegrounds from the war.

Outside of Belleau Wood, 2,264 little white crosses represented the dead Americans whose bodies had been found. They were still finding bodies in the "woods" that, after the battles, were no longer woods. They saw the town of Bligny, which had been completely destroyed, not one wall left standing intact. The towns were in ruins. There were separate cemeteries for the Germans, Americans, and French. By stark contrast, the cellars of the Clicquot winery were miraculously unharmed. The army had kept the Germans too busy fighting to mess with the winery. Outside, though, the scene simply got worse. Trenches, shell holes, and lots of barbed wire entangled. They were all speechless after the tour.

Mr. Woog saw them off at the train station. They took the boat to Dover, and then the train to London, where they checked into the Savoy for the last time.

Mrs. Taylor had arranged for Lilly to have lunch at the Bath Club with another eligible bachelor, Dr. Harry. Lilly found him "very dear" and enjoyed his "cute little motorcar," but she was not impressed with him.

While packing for the trip home, Lilly received a phone call from Walter Horridge. They enjoyed lunch together and didn't return until 3:00 p.m. Still, he, too, failed to make an impression. Only Tommy occupied her thoughts as she filled her trunks full of the trinkets, dolls, fans, and clothes she had purchased on her trip.

Mr. Hewlett, Mr. and Mrs. Taylor, and Walter accompanied them on the train to Southampton. They came onboard the S.S. *Berengaria* for lunch and waved farewell on the dock until they could be seen no longer.

As they sailed, Lilly wrote in her diary, "Who knows, maybe in the far away future we may fly there often for holidays!"

CHAPTER 38

THE BRIBE

Fall 1923

As soon as they returned to the United States, Clyde headed to Monroe. He and the officers and some stockholders of his United Oil & Natural Gas Products Company had started a new company, which they called Consolidated Carbon Company. The now-operational factory included 120 burning houses with a capacity of 12 million cubic feet of gas per day. They also put in a gas plant. The company owned 1,000 acres of rich gas lands and a number of wells that were already on the land. The first carbon black plant in Texas had just opened and Clyde was going to make sure he kept up, which included traveling to northern Texas to see the set up and buy some stock.

Their house in Hollywood was decorated for Christmas when the Barbours began to arrive for their second holiday season there. Clyde, Jennie, Grannie, Lilly, Jesse and Sylvia, Clyde, Jr., and Flora, and all their progeny descended on the house on Lorraine Boulevard.

"What a difference," Jesse said as they walked in the front door. "Having the train car changes everything!"

Grannie agreed. "After that trip here last Christmas, I promised myself I wasn't gonna do that again!"

"Well then, it's a good thing we have it, since I'm not leaving you behind for Christmas!" replied Clyde, who went over and hugged his mother, whose girth had continued to expand.

The day after Christmas, Forest approached Clyde. "Captain? We need to sit down with Will for a private talk." Clyde looked over Forest's shoulder and saw Will waiting, head hung low, pretending to pick at something on his hand.

"Let's go into my office." Clyde led the way and, instead of sitting behind his walnut desk, took a seat in one of the overstuffed chairs, motioning to his son-in-law and son to take the remaining seats. "So, what's going on?" Clyde was ready to get to the point of what he figured was going to be an unpleasant conversation.

"Well, sir, Will...he got himself into some trouble at school. I tried to get him out of it, but they weren't interested. They won't have him back. Sorry, Captain." Forest couldn't make himself look Clyde in the eye.

"Will, did you get kicked out of college?" asked Clyde, his face growing red and his breathing shallow.

"It goes like this..." Will began and then stopped. "You know, I don't know what I did that made them so angry!" he said adamantly, slapping his fist on his knee.

"You're not answering my question," said Clyde, his jaw tight.

"It was no big thing," Will kept on.

"Obviously, it was a very big thing, or you wouldn't have gotten expelled! Now what was it?"

Suddenly Lilly appeared. "Why are you so angry, Daddy?"

"Your little brother just got expelled from college. I'm waiting to hear why," answered Clyde abruptly.

"Well, Daddy, you know Will has a mischievous side to him. That's one of the reasons people like him so much; he's fun! I'm sure he was just having trouble fitting in with the other students who are mostly from California." Lilly was trying to soften the blow.

"Lilly, you have been Will's protector since he was a little boy. I think it's time you let him grow up and learn to deal with me, just me." Clyde was trying to be calm with her. "Please leave us alone, Lilly.

Thank you for your help." Lilly left his office almost in tears as she appreciated that something awful must have happened.

"Forest," Clyde continued, "you can leave the room, too. This is not your problem."

"But Captain, he's been living with us; I feel responsible!" Forest answered.

"I know my son well enough to know that whatever trouble he got into was of his own making. I certainly don't hold you or Peggy responsible." Clyde meant what he was saying.

"Yes, sir, but I'm still sorry," added Forest as he left the room.

Clyde stood up and started to pace. He shook his head and mumbled to himself before speaking out. "I'm waiting to hear from *you* what happened." Clyde walked over to where Will was sitting and stood over him. Will's expression lacked any sense of foreboding and even seemed to be trying to hide a grin. Clyde was frightened by his own thoughts.

"Dad, it's no big deal. I just couldn't stay away from the beach and all those pretty babes out in the sun. So, I missed a few classes. No big deal. And so I flunked all my classes, that's all. And some of the stupid teachers were out to get me, you know? I swear they hated me. Then they got all angry when I told them what I thought of them. I swear that's all, Dad. It's no big deal."

It took all Clyde had not to slap him. "You have to get a college degree and that's final!"

"Okay, Dad, I got it, but can't I please stay out here in California? I love it out here!"

"No!" Clyde yelled. "You'll go back with us on the train. And don't you ever embarrass our family again! Do you like the way you live? Do you like having everything you need provided to you by my hard work? You'd better figure out how to make a living or your lifestyle could take an unpleasant detour. You need to get yourself together and start acting like an adult." Clyde stalked out of the room and called out to Spencer who had come with them on the train from Houston. Spencer was there immediately.

"Yes, sir?" he said to his boss.

"I need to go out for a drive. Now." Clyde didn't want to see anyone, even his precious Jennie, so the two men drove around Los Angeles and up into the hills. Clyde tried not to think about anything. He breathed in the air and filled his eyes with the pretty scenery, so different from where he lived in Houston. After some time had passed, he began to pray.

> "May you see God's light on the path ahead
> When the road you walk is dark.
> May you always hear,
> Even in your hour of sorrow,
> The gentle singing of the lark.
> When times are hard may hardness
> Never turn your heart to stone,
> May you always remember
> When the shadows fall—
> You do not walk alone."

He hadn't realized he was speaking the words out loud. Spencer spoke up. "What's that you sayin' back there, Captain?"

"It's an old Irish prayer. My grandma taught it to me," answered Clyde, only half listening.

"Mighty pretty, mighty pretty," Spencer answered before going back to his solitary driving.

The spell broken, Clyde was able to think more clearly. He felt that too much analysis was counterproductive; he needed to learn from the past and move on. He needed to get back into his flow and minimize the distractions. It was both a blessing and a curse that every bank he walked into was eager to lend him money. He had to always be mindful not to overextend himself the way he had seen so many others do, even on the river. His entrepreneurial thinking churned up new ideas constantly. And now that he'd opened the door to Europe and all it had to offer, Clyde saw no end to what he could achieve. *But for what? Why do I continue to drive myself so hard? My family is more than taken care of. Who am I doing all this for? Who am I trying to impress? Jennie? I truly believe she'd be happy even if we were still living on a sternwheeler. My ma? No. My pa? Gone. Grandpa and Grandma? Gone. My brother James is a nightmare; so is Will. Clyde, Jr., would just as soon not work. Why doesn't he get that good feeling from working hard and accomplishing things? Thank God for Jesse, who's always just one step behind me. And my daughters, of course. And my grandchildren. I suppose that's why you keep striving for more; you want to have a legacy to hand down to the new generations that are coming along. Maybe I do it just to prove to myself that I can. Or maybe it's just some kind of internal drive that's part of my nature. Or maybe it's a little of all of those things. I guess it really doesn't matter why; it's just who I am.*

When Clyde arrived at the house, it was strangely quiet. He walked from room to room not finding anyone. "Jennie?" he called out. He heard her coming in from the back porch. He found his first smile in hours and hugged his wife for a long while.

"Are you okay?" she asked, looking him squarely in the face.

"I am now!" He smiled and gave her a kiss. "Where is everybody?"

"I sent them out, every last one of them! They won't be home until dinnertime. It's just you and me and the servants. Oh, and Grannie, who's hiding." She smiled at him, took his hand, and led him to the back porch where the table was set for tea. "Josephine made some great cookies, and she's making the tea now, so we can relax out here." She handed him a light lap robe. "It's nice and chilly; the weather is perfect out here!" She tugged on her shawl to pull it closer to her. Nothing more needed to be said. They reveled in the quiet and then were equally happy when the troops returned with all the stories of their adventures.

Back in Houston on Saturday, April 12, 1924, Clyde finally came out of his home office at around 5:00 p.m. He had started the Barbour Coal Company based in Colorado and was talking to his counterparts in the US. He saw Jennie walking toward him in a beautiful long blue evening gown.

"I was coming to get you. We have to leave soon!" She was smiling and looked lovely, adorned with beautiful earrings he had bought her. "It's the museum opening tonight!" She took Clyde by the hand and led him to their bedroom. "You haven't got much time to get dressed. I laid out your tuxedo for you." When they entered their room, he began to quickly get dressed.

William Hogg got the momentum going to make an edifice to house the museum's collection, which was growing quickly. It was to be called the Museum of Fine Arts Houston. Jesse H. Jones, R.S. Sterling, W.W. Fondren, K.E. Womach, Mr. M.D. Anderson, an 18-year-old Howard R. Hughes, Jr., and J.M. West were a few of the well-known Houston businessmen, along with Clyde, who had each given $5,000 for the building. William Watkin, who was the architect, and James Chillman, the first director of the museum, were both Rice University professors.

This was the night of the official opening. Jennie seemed excited about going, which pleased Clyde tremendously.

"I've lost some weight!" she said proudly, putting her hands on her hips and twisting from side to side. "The seamstress had to take my dress in! I even got my hair fixed today; just like you like it!" Jennie had been blessed with an abundance of hair, so much so that she would often call it a curse. Her soft, light eyes lied, seeming to reflect a lifetime without cares.

"I can see that! You look wonderful, and better yet, happy!" Clyde said.

"I think my bad tooth helped me not eat! Now that the pain is gone from that, I feel brand-new!" Jennie said.

The Neoclassical building was exactly what the couple were always drawn to.

"It reminds me a bit of Oaklawn Manor," said Clyde as they walked up to the building. "That place still haunts me. I want it to be ours."

"Well, you always told me that someday it would be ours. I believe it!"

The night was spectacular, spent rubbing shoulders with the who's who of Houston, most of whom Clyde already knew. He was particularly intrigued by the young Howard Hughes, Jr., whose mind seemed to work much like Clyde's, all kinds of ideas rolling around up there. He reminded Clyde of himself as an 18-year-old, only with virtually endless wealth supporting him.

Later that month, Clyde was back in New York City. Tommy Holmes had sent him a note asking to meet with him privately the next time he was in the city. He had the cadet meet him in his suite.

"Captain Barbour, thank you for seeing me. I'll try not to take up much of your time," Tommy said politely and waited to be invited to be seated.

Clyde motioned for him to sit down. "How's school going?" he asked, trying to get the conversation going.

"Fine, sir, but it's tough! They work us from the time we wake up to the time we go to sleep. I'm sure this training will benefit me later, sir." Tommy seemed nervous, even perspiring in the nice spring temperature.

"And what are you studying?" Clyde continued.

"Mechanical engineering, sir."

"That's a wise choice. You can use that in many areas of the workforce."

"Yes, sir! It's very interesting." Tommy readjusted his sitting position.

"What's on your mind today, Cadet Holmes?" Clyde was ready to move along.

"Well, sir, you have been very good to me, letting me see Lilly, and I really appreciate it." Clyde smiled at the young man and let the silence deepen, watching Tommy squirm. "I just can't imagine my life without Lilly in it. She means everything to me. I love her and I'm requesting your permission to ask her to marry me, sir."

Clyde feigned surprise. He had been expecting this and had already conducted a thorough investigation of the young man's family in Chicago and his record at West Point. From all outward appearances, he was an impressive young man. He had an excellent pedigree and he seemed to have all the attributes Clyde would require in a husband for his Little Princess, including the most important of all, that he would be able to take good care of her. Clearly, Tommy truly loved Lilly and she loved him. He felt Tommy would be a good husband for her.

Clyde cleared his throat. "So, tell me about your plans for yourself and my Lilly once you leave West Point."

"I plan to be in the Field Artillery, sir. I love horses. I'll be graduating this spring and stationed in San Antonio initially," Tommy stated. "We could be married any time after that."

"Interesting! Mrs. Barbour has always loved horseback riding; you have something in common! Tell me about the Field Artillery." Clyde continued with his questioning, purposefully making the straight-backed Cadet squirm just enough.

"Well, sir, we've been doing a lot of work to make our artillery better. We go in first, before the Infantry, with the firepower. We're starting to incorporate the caterpillar tractors, but they just aren't as reliable as our horses. And we're using the French 75 guns that have a much smaller recoil, so we don't have to aim the guns again after each firing." Tommy was obviously caught up in the subject.

"Very impressive; very impressive, indeed." Clyde finally stood, causing Tommy to jump up from his chair and stand bolt upright at attention facing his potential father-in-law. Clyde held out his hand to shake Tommy's. "Yes. You have my permission to ask my daughter to marry you. You'll have to be gentle with her; she's always been quite delicate. But she'll make you a wonderful wife." There were tears in both men's eyes.

"Thank you, Captain, thank you. Really. I don't know what to say. I'm so happy!" They shook hands heartily until they were both smiling and laughing.

A month later, Tommy went to Tarrytown-on-Hudson and proposed to a delighted Lilly in the gardens at the school underneath a huge tree. She said, "Yes!"

He presented her with a miniature of his West Point ring, which he had had made at Tiffany's, the diamond coming from Tommy's mother. "I'll never take it off!" she cried. And she never did.

Clyde and Jennie were able to witness the majesty of West Point firsthand when they accompanied Lilly to Tommy's graduation on June 12, 1924. The party of three took a boat there so they could arrive on the Hudson River side of the Point. West Point was on a picturesque promontory on the west side of the river. Surrounded on both sides by wooded slopes, the large stone buildings stood out like a fortress with several large towers. They could see many buildings set close together like a medieval town. Others arrived by boat as well, so they were quickly drawn into the excitement of the day.

Tommy's parents and younger sister were there from Chicago. Clyde had taken the train up to meet the father, Judge Thomas Holmes, and his wife, Nellie, soon after the proposal and he found them to be as represented and delightful. Neither Lilly nor Jennie had met them.

It was approaching twilight when the three of them left the Thayer Hotel on the property and walked up the walk to see the campus up close. The large gray stone buildings radiated strength and stability; they looked impenetrable, solid, and old. The grounds were spotless. Men and young men alike walked about in their perfectly pressed uniforms, their backs arrow straight, their shoulders pulled back, every movement seemingly in concert. It was a formidable sight, all taken in at once.

Could anyone possibly walk these grounds and not feel that the lives of their family and countrymen were in good hands, the leaders of our armies coming from such a place as this? Clyde thought.

At the graduation ceremony, the families sat together to celebrate their cadet. There were 405 new officers that day and a crowd of about 3,000. The Plain, as it was known (or the Parade Grounds), was awash in white uniforms with gold buttons and highly polished belt buckles. The sight was breathtaking. Immaculate order and precise execution accompanied everything that transpired that day. Even Clyde and Lilly, who had seen spectacular displays of ritual in

Europe the summer before, were stunned into silence. And there sat Thomas Jefferson Holmes, Jr., in the midst of it all, the most handsome of cadets.

After the graduation weekend, the Barbours returned to New York City and the Holmes went home to Chicago. Clyde was off to Europe soon, so Jennie and Lilly took the train car back down to Houston. A few weeks later, they traveled back out to Hollywood, where Tommy joined them for a six-week vacation before going to Fort Sam Houston in San Antonio, Texas. The young couple would be married in December.

That summer, Clyde traveled back to Europe, this time by himself. His tour took him to England, France, Italy, Germany, and Switzerland. Although it was an intense business trip, he found time to do some shopping for antiques to adorn his home in Houston. And then there was Oaklawn; no one knew he was already looking into buying it with the expectation of restoring it to its former splendor. It would need a lot of furnishings.

Clyde and Opal had seen each other only three times since they first met. Clyde was able to schedule this trip to Europe to overlap with some of Opal's engagements overseas. He felt that in England and Paris he was the most likely to run into people that he knew. They decided to meet in Berlin and in Baden-Baden, Germany, where they could bathe in the special waters the town had long been known for. In Baden-Baden, Opal suggested the Hotel Stephanie, owned by the Brenner family. It just happened to be the most expensive hotel in the city, known for hosting royalty and the elite from around the world in grand fashion.

The hotel was a large, stately stone building with 200 sumptuous rooms. It faced the Lichtentaler Allee, a well-known promenade and arboretum; one and a half miles long, the grassy promenade sat on the west bank of the Oos River that led to the Lichtentaler Abbey. Lime trees lined the path to the "Shepherd's Cottage," and red and purple rhododendrons bloomed everywhere. Among the many varieties of trees and plants, one could always find a bench for somber reflection. Charming bridges added to the idyllic feeling of a fairy tale.

They shared a two-bedroom suite, in case it should matter, which in Europe, it did not. They looked out upon the Allee and were mesmerized even at a distance. Clyde put his arms around Opal's waist, and they gazed as one.

"What is that beautiful park?" Clyde asked.

"*C'est très célèbre!*" Opal answered, as if surprised that he had never heard of it before.

"And that means…."

"Famous. Very famous!" she replied in her thick French accent. "We must go there, *demain*, after a long breakfast in bed!" She turned to face Clyde, her sly, enticing grin riling him up once again.

When the bellboys had finished placing their trunks in their respective bedrooms, they asked in German, "*Darf ich deine koffer jetzt auspacken?*"

Opal responded in French, "*Non, merci, plus tard.*" It was expected that the bellboys would understand her French.

"I hope you're not selling off my firstborn child!" laughed Clyde who, of course, understood none of it.

"Relax, *mon chéri!* I asked that they unpack our trunks later." Her grin returned. He reached for her hand and led her to an oversized chair, where he sat down, then pulled her onto his lap. She petted him all over his head, neck, and shoulders, and finally kissed him softly.

Clyde allowed himself to be perfectly still during her prelude. He could smell the perfume in her hair and feel her silken skin on his head, neck, and his stubbly face, spellbound in the totality of her attention. He opened his eyes, rubbed her shoulders, and spoke. "How about a bath. We should take a bath together after traveling."

"*Oui! Bonne idée!* That is a very good idea!" Opal got up and walked toward their bathroom.

"Wait. We need champagne. And candles!" said Clyde, moving to the phone to arrange their playtime.

Before too long, they were standing in the bathroom in their underclothes, Opal in her very lacy, very sexy French lingerie and Clyde in his very American white boxers. Clyde snickered. "What's a beautiful, sexy woman like you doing with such a bland American man?"

"*Mais, non, mon chéri,* your American body *me captiver* et your American mind is *très sexy!*"

Clyde removed his underwear and then took his time removing her few remaining garments, until they stood together, naked, enraptured by the endless possibilities offered by a bottle of champagne in a silver ice bucket, two beautiful crystal flutes, and a large bathtub full of warm water surrounded by twinkling candles.

After three full days of luxuriating in Baden-Baden, Opal was able to accompany Clyde to Berlin. At an art gallery there, he fell in love with several paintings. He had intended to purchase one for the living room at his home on Montrose, but in the end, decided on two.

Clyde and Opal said goodbye under the Brandenburg Gate. They had never spent so long a period of time together. Opal was off to enrapture audiences with her lovely voice, and Clyde was off to make some new business investments and relationships, and to strengthen old ones.

On his final day abroad, Clyde was at the Savoy Hotel in London when he received a telegram from Jennie. Will had been expelled, again, from college. After much trepidation and a long conversation with the Taylors, who expressed how very important it was for Will to get a diploma and help in Clyde's affairs, he knew what he had to do.

After his ship arrived in New York City, he spent several days there working tirelessly to catch up on all the details he'd missed. All he wanted to do was head south to his home and sleep in his own bed. Instead, he took the train car out west, where he had been able to get an appointment with the president of the university where Judge Holmes had gone to school. The following day, he was early for his appointment.

"Captain Barbour? I'm Scott Adams. It's a pleasure to meet you. I have read a lot about you and wish I could talk you into teaching a class in business at my graduate school." They both chuckled.

"Maybe one day," Clyde replied. "It would be an honor." He shifted in his chair, wondering how best to approach the subject. "I'm here to see if perhaps you and I could come to a business agreement."

"I'm intrigued! Please go on," answered Mr. Adams, smiling eagerly.

"Well, I have a son who has been a bit of a challenge scholastically; he has a good mind, but he's a bit of a free spirit," Clyde began slowly. "Obviously, to be part of the family businesses, he has got to get a college degree. I don't have time for loafers. He's interested in geology." Mr. Adams sat quietly, listening intently. "Unfortunately for him and me, he has managed to get expelled from two colleges; he spent one semester at each. He's really very intelligent and engaging, but I think he just needs an extra firm hand on him to get down to business, and I can't be that person."

"You're correct, Captain; depending on the child, at his age, a parent can be the worst disciplinarian. Have you employed tutors?"

"Oh, yes sir. The first time it happened he was out in Los Angeles and said he couldn't stay away from the beaches and all those girls in bathing suits. I thought moving him would be a simple fix. Now I know that's not true." Clyde looked down briefly before looking back up into the president's eyes, trying not to plead.

"Please tell me what it is you think I can do to help," Mr. Adams said kindly.

Clyde debated whether to stand; he would have more of a presence; show more dominance. *No, not this time,* he thought. "I'd like to offer you a deal that would benefit us both greatly." Clyde began feeling nervous, not a common feeling for him. He even felt sweat around his collar. "It would be my honor to pay for the costs of constructing a new building on your campus; name it what you like. All I ask for in exchange is that you accept my son into your university." As soon as the words left his mouth, he was ashamed. He wanted to take it all back and run out the door.

"Well, my goodness," said Mr. Adams thoughtfully. "That would be highly irregular. We have a very rigorous acceptance process that involves lots of other people. It would set a terrible precedent. But God knows the university is always in need of capital assistance. Of course, there are few families who could afford such an outlay of money. I'll take your offer under advisement, and we'll get back to you shortly."

Clyde was silent. He wasn't sure what to say. Could he take back what he said and restore his dignity with this man? He would look weak; he couldn't allow himself to do that. When he learned a few days later that the answer was no, Clyde was actually relieved.

Lilly and Tommy were married on December 20, 1924, at Christ Church Cathedral in Houston. The night before, a terrible ice storm—an anomaly that far south—had crippled parts of the city. Electricity was down in many areas, as was running water. The rehearsal dinner at River Oaks Country Club was unreachable due to the icy streets. Many guests were staying at the Rice Hotel downtown, while others stayed with the bride's family and at other friends' houses. The Montrose house had electricity but no water, so guests had to be shuttled, carefully on the icy streets, to the hotel to shower.

Tommy was extremely ill. The doctors finally decided his recent sinus surgery had led to an infection. He was kept in bed until the last possible minute, and then he dressed in his uniform and did his best to stand up straight. A nurse stood close by throughout the ceremony just in case.

Lilly's wedding gown was made of cream-colored satin. It was long-waisted and went down to mid-calf, as was the style. It was adorned with pearls at the neckline and below the waistline. She had asked for a pearl headpiece to resemble Juliet's in the famous play and her veil puddled on the floor. She carried a trailing bouquet of lilies of the valley, baby orchids, and stephanotis, accented with the green of Bells of Ireland. A dozen cream silk ribbons attached to her bouquet hung down to her knees and were knotted every so often. The bridesmaids wore pastel colors and carried bouquets of pastel roses, the two flower girls carrying baskets of the same flower petals. The groomsmen were all dressed in their uniforms complete with their swords, which added even more spectacle to the already spectacular.

Clyde helped his Little Princess into the limousine, and they rode to the church together, holding hands. Clyde had given a lot of thought to what he would say to Lilly as they drove to her wedding.

"Look at you! You look like an angel!" he began. "Our little angel. I really believe you've found a prince in Tommy; if I didn't feel that way, I couldn't let you marry him. He will be a good husband. God knows you'll be a perfect wife with your peaceful ways and sweet personality. Just stay the way you are, and you will have a wonderful life." Clyde had tears in his eyes. He kissed his daughter's hand and smiled at her. "Just be sure to take care of yourself. You've always been a little fragile, but as long as you respect that about yourself and take care of yourself, I know God will watch over you and help you be strong."

"Oh, Daddy, I'm the luckiest girl in the whole wide world! Thank you." Lilly leaned her head onto her father's shoulder and closed her eyes.

There was still no electricity at the church. The church staff had run around in search of candles, which now shimmered in every window in the church as well as down the aisle and on the altar. It looked like a church set in a wonderland! Lilly and Clyde walked down the aisle to a waiting Tommy. Clyde kissed his daughter goodbye, shook Tommy's hand, and sat down in the front aisle next to Jennie.

The candlelit ceremony was magical. The church wasn't as full as expected due to the ice storm. The minister pronounced them husband and wife, and just as Lilly and Tommy turned to face the congregation, the lights flickered back on. The guests thought it was so beautifully planned; the couple knew it was God's work.

The reception was at their house on Montrose. The guests signed the wedding book sitting on the Louis XIV desk that had just arrived from Paris. Clyde and Jennie presented the newlyweds with a new Packard Roadster, which the couple drove to San Antonio. They lived in the Officer's Quarters at Fort Sam Houston, Tommy being a second lieutenant in the Field Artillery.

CHAPTER 39

THE MANOR

January 1925

Clyde had been working for quite a while to merge carbon black companies in Louisiana and surrounding states. The strong demand for carbon black stimulated overproduction to such a degree that the government put quotas in place regulating how much natural gas could be used in the production of carbon black, concerned that there wouldn't be enough left to use in making gasoline.

"As I see it, we can either join together and keep us all afloat, or the smaller players are going to go out of business," Clyde told a meeting of the presidents of all these companies.

"That's all great and everything, Captain, but Southern Carbon Company won't have anything to do with this merger," said one of Clyde's compatriots. Southern was one of the largest of the companies in the area at that time.

"I know that. We'll have to do it without them; it'll still work," Clyde assured him.

And so it was decided that 15 companies would consolidate under the name of United Carbon Company, with Clyde as president. He transferred $1,224,000 from his United Oil and Natural Gas Products Corp. into the new company, which filed its charter in Delaware in 1925. Clyde's Consolidated Carbon Company also became part of the merger. United Carbon Company, at the outset, was worth $2.5 million in Ouachita and Morehouse Parishes alone.

C.L. Kerr had been a good friend of Clyde's for years. He was district sales manager for Gulf Refining Company in Houston and was on several boards with Clyde, including acting as secretary/treasurer for United Oil & Natural Gas Products Corp. Both men had been at the merger meeting in New York City. The prior day, at a meeting at Gotham National Bank, Mr. Kerr had accepted a position on the bank's Board of Directors, a position Clyde already held. The two men traveled back to Houston together in Clyde's train car.

"What's happening in the coal business?" Charles asked Clyde as the men relaxed after dinner.

"The Barbour Coal Company is up and going in Walsenburg, Colorado. I'm the chairman there, and also at Alamo Coal Company," Clyde answered. "I've put a lot of money into them."

"Alamo's a big company!" Charles sounded impressed. He laughed for a second before going on. "How do you keep all those balls in the air?"

Clyde grinned. "I use excellent people, like you, to help me along. I greatly mitigate my risk by diversifying my interests; you know, a little of this and a little of that. I really love learning new things, always have. It's like floating down a new river trying to read its own subtle language of hazards hidden and unhidden. One bad move and you're swimming!" The men were quiet for a moment.

"I've heard the conditions are awful for the miners," said Charles.

"You wouldn't believe it. I don't know how the men stand it. I'm trying to do something about that, but the resistance to any change is met with such hostility from other companies that it's almost frightening!" Clyde shuddered as his mind went to the mines he'd visited recently.

"Money corrupts," said Charles. "No doubt about it!"

"The only people making money, and a lot of it, are the business owners and the coal operators, of course, not the miners. There's plenty to go around. We could build some basic decent housing for the miners and still make a fortune, as well as giving them a place to live and making the mines safer." Clyde shook his head.

"Not many are as generous as you, Captain," Charles replied. "Tell me what's happening along the Houston Ship Channel. I know that's your other new baby!"

Clyde laughed. "You're right about that! The channel has finally been dredged to 30 feet and they've widened it. Terminals are being built at the turning basin."

"I read that soon there's going to be 45 industries located on the main channel. That must make you happy."

"Definitely! What did they say the expected capital investment's going to be? Was it $100 million?"

"Or more," said Charles. "Add a daily payroll of around $30,000 and you're open for business! Is it really possible? $30,000 a day? That doesn't sound right."

"I know. Seems impossible. I've been buying up land along the ship channel near Morgans Point to dredge my own channel closer to the Gulf of Mexico. Oh, and I'm planning a residential area next to it called Shore Acres, basically in LaPorte."

"Why residential?" Charles asked.

Clyde stood up and walked over to look out the window at the endless scenery passing, mile after mile of America. "Workers," he said. "This project is going to require hundreds of workers, both during construction and after, everything from men to pilot the vessels to longshoremen to empty the contents. They'll need a place to live—a decent place to live—and a community to be part of. I'm building lives out there, not just jobs." He looked straight at Charles.

"Watch out, here comes Clyde the Benevolent; they'll eat you alive with that attitude," said Charles, whose face became hard and serious.

"It's not a matter of benevolence, it's just good business. We want to hire the best and keep them. Charles, you know me, this is who I am."

Clyde and Jennie arrived back in Houston on the same day. She had spent a few days with Lilly and Tommy at the base in San Antonio.

It seemed strangely quiet in the house. Josephine served them dinner on the back porch.

"Tell me about our Little Princess," said Clyde. "Is she happy?"

"Oh, Clyde, she's so happy! They have a little place in the Officer's Quarters, which really isn't much of an Officer's Quarters at all. You know, the Army is low on money since the war, so they're using an old medical building for housing. They have three little rooms all in a row. Remember how Tommy painted it before the wedding and got that infection?" Jennie asked.

"Right. It sounds a little sparse."

"I suppose, but when you think about our first home on the flatboat…. Tom only makes $125 a month," Jennie added.

Clyde laughed. "True. I'm glad she's happy. I have to go to Franklin in a few days. How about going with me?"

"Oh, I would love that. Franklin still kind of feels like home, you know?" she replied.

"Yes, I agree. It's a special place," Clyde mused. "It's having a real hard time now. The cane crop has failed twice, so you know nobody has any money. They have to find a new kind of cane to grow. Some of the planters have put in rice."

"That's awful! Oh, Clyde, that's terrible!" Jennie shook her head.

"I've been working on something. I'm trying to buy Oaklawn Manor, along with some of the land. I'm not interested in having any crops, you know, but I want the land." Clyde's tone had changed to exuberant. "Let's go see what we can do!"

In Franklin, Clyde and Jennie went out to Oaklawn to walk around. Approaching it from the road instead of from Bayou Teche, it wasn't as impressive, its gray tones not inviting. The columns were intact, and the exterior walls were still standing. To the left was an attached colonnaded two-story wing, much shorter than the main house. There appeared to be little, if any, glass left in the windows and any remaining shutters were badly battered. An old wooden cistern sat next to the main house and there were steps leading up to the main back entrance.

"Look at those trees!" said Clyde, breaking the silence. "Some of those live oaks must be hundreds of years old!"

Oaklawn Manor Before Restoration, 1924, Porte Cochère

The couple walked up to the nearest oak and Clyde examined it carefully. Jennie smiled and shook her head. *This house is falling apart and what does he notice? Oak trees!*

They walked up to what had been the back terrace and climbed the steps. Clyde pulled open one side of the door, the other side opening up on its own.

"Did I tell you that Oaklawn was built in 1837 by a man named Alexander Porter? His family emigrated from Ireland when he was young. He was a lawyer and US senator."

"I guess it's the Irish blood in this place that kept you coming back. Oh my," said Jennie, "it's enormous!"

They stepped across the wooden threshold and onto the wide cypress plank floors in the main hall. The floors seemed to be mostly intact, so they took a few more steps inside, testing the floor with each step.

"Clyde, are you sure it's safe?"

"Yes, I think so, but I'll go in ahead of you just to be sure," Clyde replied, moving over to be in front of her. "What's that smell?" It wasn't an unpleasant smell but the smell of age. "It sort of reminds me of being on the *Jennie Barbour* sailing down Bayou Teche; you know, wet wood, vegetation."

"Musty," Jennie said. "Kind of musty, like an old person's house, where no one ever leaves the place. But it's not a bad smell. I'd say the smell is the least of our worries!"

Clyde walked ahead to the center of the large hall. The ceilings were 15 feet high! He could see what he supposed to be rat holes in the floor as well as rain damage from broken doors and windows. Cobwebs made thick with old dust hung in most every corner.

"I don't see any cows or smell any manure!" They both laughed, remembering Peggy's fear of the cow house.

"They probably shooed them out before we got here." Clyde took advantage of this vantage point to get a look at the layout. "Well, it's a typical plantation layout; a great hall from front door to back door with two large rooms on either side." Between the two rooms on the right was a smaller hallway with stairs leading upstairs and a door, a miniature of the front door, out to the porte cochère. "Jennie, come here. Look at these inside walls. They must be 16 inches thick." The walls showed as much brick as plaster.

Jennie walked over with trepidation and examined the wall between the front room and the side hallway. "I guess these walls could hold up most anything."

"Come here." He took her hand and led her into the front room. It was a large room with two full-length French doors along the front—or what had been French doors—two windows along the side, and a large fireplace. "The ceilings must be at least 15 feet tall! And look out the front!" Clyde sounded like a little boy on Christmas morning.

Jennie turned to look out through the broken glass and saw Bayou Teche in the distance. A sternwheeler was passing by and blew its whistle for some obstacle they couldn't see. "Did you plan that?" a smiling Jennie asked.

"No, I promise, I didn't plan it!" Clyde sounded so sincere, yet Jennie still had her doubts.

"That makes it almost feel like home in here," Jennie said quietly.

Clyde turned and walked back to the staircase with the dark wood railing. "Come on, let's go upstairs!"

"I don't know about that, Clyde. I think I'm fine staying down here. You go up and scout it all out for us."

"Okay, scaredy cat!" Clyde teased. "I'm off on the adventure of a lifetime, alone. Wish me luck!"

"Surely a captain with your experience will be fine going upstairs alone," Jennie teased back. "However, if I see any critters down here you *will* hear me scream!"

"That sounds fair." Clyde slowly ascended the staircase that made a U-turn at the landing and kept going up. "It's identical up here; same hall with the two doors, same four rooms, and another staircase. I heard in town that Henry Clay used to stay here when Alexander Porter lived here. Apparently, Clay slept in the front bedroom on the opposite side of the hall."

"My Kentucky hero? He stayed here? Amazing." Jennie could hear him walking tentatively around on the second floor. "Anything interesting?" she called up the stairwell.

"Just more dust and rats' holes and water damage. The cobwebs look like they could trap a man! I'm going up to the top floor." Jennie wanted to dissuade him but knew it couldn't be done. "Looks like a dormitory and maybe a ballroom? Not sure. I'm coming back down now." When he got back to the first floor, he saw Jennie walking out the front door. "Hey, wait for me!"

They stood together on the wide front porch looking at the bayou. Ancient oaks were scattered on either side of the house. The fence they had seen all those years ago around the front steps was still there, in part. Jennie walked up to one of the massive white columns and rubbed it with her hand. "It makes me feel so small!" she said, looking up to the top. She wrapped her arms around it, her fingers not coming within two feet of touching. "I can't even reach around it!"

Clyde walked to the next column and did the same. His fingers didn't touch either. "I feel just the opposite," he said. "We're going to own this beautiful, solid, 100-year-old piece of history. That makes me feel part of something bigger than myself; something that will go on for another 100 years or more!"

Jennie walked over to the steps and sat down. She looked back at the neglected mansion, over to the old oak trees hung with moss, and out to the bayou they both loved so much. He had promised her this house when they were a young couple whose family was not yet complete. From time to time, over the years, she had imagined living here with their family. The children would have all this space to play and grow. They would have horses to ride and chickens and a cow or two. It would have been similar to how Jennie had grown up. But now, in 1925, all their children were gone. Clyde was gone as often as not. It began to look like a large, lonely house.

"It's so big, Clyde! It's gonna be awfully lonely way out here with just your mother here with me," said Jennie. "What'll we do out here?"

Clyde sat down next to his wife and put his arm around her shoulder. "Jennie, my sweet, I have no plans to lock you and Ma away out here. There's our house in Houston, our house in Los Angeles, and the house in Tampico. I'm even looking at a place in New Jersey. You can go wherever you want, whenever you want. So, you see, you're not stuck. And once we have this place done over, it will be such a showplace that we'll have to turn down people who want to spend time with us out here. Think about how the grandchildren are going to love it here! This house will be brimming with family and guests!"

Jennie looked her husband in the eyes. "I can see it; I can see all of it! The picture you paint is exactly what I want. But are you sure this beautiful, derelict old thing can be made into the place you want so much?"

"I absolutely believe it. I can see it in my mind. It will be perfect! And you will be its queen." He kissed her, stood, and helped her up. He waved his hand in front of them from side to side. "This is all ours, yours and mine, forever! We'll grow old here together!"

Clyde was off to Europe again. With the purchase of Oaklawn Manor assured, not only did he conduct his usual business but also spent time buying beautiful furnishings and antiques for Oaklawn. He was able to purchase his most prized possession to date: two Gobelin tapestries from the 17th century that had hung in Versailles. He remembered with joy the first time he had seen such a tapestry at the World's Fair in 1904. *It only took 21 years to be able to buy them,* he mused, *but I knew eventually they'd be mine.* He was surprised to feel a heartstring or two being pulled with the desire to return back to that time—that time when life was still tender and oh so much simpler. *But was it really?* Clyde remembered his silent striving to provide for his family, the unending work to help alleviate that worry. Or was it easier now, with plenty of money to fall back on, which also meant plenty of money to lose with one wrong move? *One time doesn't have to be better than the other,* he decided; *it's just different. Life presents you with a constant stream of complications and you can let them overwhelm you or embrace them and try to turn them into opportunities.*

While in Paris, Clyde received a telegram from Lilly. She was pregnant and expecting in February of the following year. Clyde cabled back, "I'm thrilled! Love to all three of you. Daddy."

The US Military was greatly downsized. There was a feeling that there would be no more big wars. The Army was being shrunk down to 200,000 on active duty and the Navy was being shut down and many ships mothballed. Tommy would soon be out of a job with a pregnant Lilly. Jennie was very upset.

"We've got to do something to help them," she told Clyde. "Poor Tommy, after all his work at West Point. What will he do?" She looked up at her husband with the sad eyes of a worried mother.

Clyde asked Tommy and Lilly to come to Houston for the weekend. The women enjoyed shopping for the baby and even had a baby shower for Lilly. Clyde and Tommy spent hours together in the study. Clyde had made a sizable investment in some coal mines in Colorado. It was decided that Clyde would pay to have Tommy attend the Colorado School of Mines for one year to get his master's degree in mining and take over running the coal business. Clyde was even more impressed with Tommy when he was told that both his mother and sister had graduated from college; it was unheard of for a woman to have a college degree.

"Tom," as Clyde now called him, "I don't know if it's a fortune or a misfortune for the Army to be downsized so soon after your enlistment. I'll take it as a good omen!" The two men shook hands on the deal.

The school was in Golden, Colorado, at the foot of the gorgeous Rocky Mountain range. They found a cute little house to rent at 1222 16th Street. Jennie promised Lilly that she would come up there with a baby nurse before the delivery, which helped to ease both women's anxiety about the frail Lilly delivering a baby. Jennie didn't let on about her added anxiety knowing what she had been through in childbirth.

CHAPTER 40

THE REVIVIFICATION

The restoration of Oaklawn Manor began in September 1925. Clyde hired Marvin Morris, Sr., as the architect and put Buddy Lauden, who moved into the old house by the gate, in charge of electricity and plumbing on the rebuild. Clyde knew there were no jobs to be had in Franklin and that gave him a willing and eager force of workers for this monumental project. Not only would they be rebuilding the manor house, but they would also be adding a swimming pool, a nine-hole golf course (the first private pool and golf course in the South), and a six-furlong (three-quarter mile) racetrack.

Clyde had told Marvin and Buddy to put the word out in Franklin on a Sunday that they needed laborers, and lots of them, to start the next day. The project would be a real boon to Franklin, as it would keep a lot of men busy for quite some time with good pay.

He still had two sternwheelers working the bayous, so he got a ride on one to the manor house, where he had to jump to the shore. *I've still got it,* he thought with a smile. As he collected himself and began to walk toward the manor, he saw people already milling about. He had seen a few pirogues and now he saw mules, wagons, and horses. There must have been 50 men there already, and a stream of them coming down the bumpy road from town.

"Oh, my God!" Clyde said as he came across Marvin. "Looks like we're going to have the manpower we need!" Buddy Lauden had begun organizing the hoard. Clyde walked up to him. "Okay, let's get after it!" Clyde couldn't have been happier to get his dream project underway and to be able to provide these neighbors with work.

"If a man makes it out here and he's willing to put in a full-day's work for a full-day's pay, put him to work. There's more than enough to do out here to keep them all busy."

Clyde stayed for three days. At the end of the third day, someone slapped him on the back. He turned around to see a very smiley James. "Hey, little brother!"

"I hear you're hiring," said James. "Gotta place for me?"

Clyde laughed. "Yes, as long as you can stay out of trouble. Talk to Buddy over there and see what you can do to help. That would be a good place to start." They walked over to a makeshift bench and sat down. "Where have you been?"

"You know me, here and there. Work's a little hard to find these days. But hey, I have another little girl! Isn't that something? We call her Betty." He looked like a very proud father.

"Where is she?" Clyde asked.

"She's in San Antonio with her mother, Sarah. We need to bring the girls over to Houston to see y'all," James said. "You know how much I love children. I've been busy!"

"Sounds like it. Are you and Sarah married, by any chance?"

"Oh, yes, we have the papers and everything." James smiled.

"Good. Good," Clyde replied, not knowing quite how to approach this news. "Are you still married to Annie?"

"Galveston Annie? We were never married, Clyde. Nope. Never married." James rolled a cigarette and lit it up.

"What about Mary?"

"That's a long story. I'll catch ya up on all that later," James replied, "and you can catch me up on what's happening with you and Jennie and the kids."

"How's your drinking?" He looked questioningly at his little brother.

"Dry as a bone, brother, dry, dry, dry!"

"Good thing. I won't have any drinking on this job site. As long as you behave, I'm happy to have you here. Don't embarrass me. And another thing—stay away from the local women, please. I don't want any unnecessary complications. Hear me?"

"Cross my heart and hope to die!" James answered, making a cross on his chest and trying to stifle a snicker.

Clyde shook his head, hugged his brother, and went to speak to Marvin. "My brother, James, is here to work. Do not give him any slack. If he shows up here drunk, let him go. If he's not pulling his weight, let him go."

"Yes, sir, Cap'm!" Marvin answered.

Clyde had trouble staying away from the rebuild. He'd hired Marvin Morris because of his knowledge of plantation manor houses and everything they were expected to contain, plus he truly loved that style of architecture. Clyde wanted everything, down to the last detail, to be precisely as it would have been when it was built in 1837. Clyde even designed a table for the formal dining room. It had a curved wrought-iron base and a bronze and off-white marble top. He designed two extensions for larger groups, which would be used as side tables when not needed.

In early December, he spent a few days there looking everything over again. He went looking for James but couldn't find him.

"Buddy? When's the last time you saw my brother James around here?" he inquired.

"Been a couple a days. He showed up here drunk one morning, and I sent him away and told him to go dry out before he comes back and never to come here drunk again." Buddy kept his voice quiet, not wanting to start spreading any rumors.

"I was afraid of that. Do you have any idea where he's staying around here?"

"No idea. If I hear anything, I'll let ya know."

"Thanks, Buddy."

He went off in search of James but got distracted by a dozen different things before he remembered where he was headed, and suddenly, there was James talking to Marvin. Clyde caught his attention and the brothers met halfway.

"Hey, big brother! Where ya been? Ain't it lookin' great around here?" He pointed to the manor house.

"It's getting there. Now tell me why the hell you showed up here drunk the other day?"

"Well, you ain't gonna believe this. Sarah, you know, my sweet wife and mother of my two beautiful daughters? She off and divorced me! Just like that! Said I'm a no good drunk and I can't keep my pants on. What is she thinkin'?" James was shaking his head in disbelief. "I treated her just the way I've always treated women and they've all been fine with how I am. It's a disgrace! People in San Antonio are laughin' at me. And she don't want me to spend time with our girls! Now Clyde, whatever else I am, I love my children." It was true, James the womanizer also happened to love children, particularly his own. "You've got to talk to her, Clyde, please!" James seemed truly distraught.

"I don't even know her, and besides, sounds like she's got you pegged. But I can't believe she's allowed to keep you away from your children. You need to go ask somebody at the courthouse about that. But if you keep getting drunk, no one's gonna want you around those girls, and no one's going to be able to help you until you decide your children are more important than liquor. It's about growing up. It's about being responsible for your family, or families, or whatever!" Clyde was trying hard not to make a scene in front of all these workers. "Look, Ma would be so grateful to see you, and Jennie will be happy to have you with us." Clyde stared at his brother, waiting for a response.

"Are you gonna help me or not?" James demanded.

"I'm trying to, but I have a million things to do here. Go back to San Antonio and see what you can find out. And listen, no need for you to be alone on Christmas; come spend it with us in Houston. Just don't show up drunk, ya hear?" Clyde wasn't sure why he was extending the offer. Did it come from a sense of guilt? Was he just being a sucker? After all, it was his little brother.

"Thanks, big brother. I can't wait to see that big, fancy place of yours in Houston and all the family."

Clyde turned and walked off.

James called after him, "Thanks! I'll be there! Unless Buddy won't give me Christmas off," he snickered.

The day before Christmas 1925, Clyde was working in his office at home. Jennie was making last-minute touches to the decorations while Grannie was napping. Will was home and listening to the radio. Leona and her family were expected at any moment. Jennie looked out the front window and saw James approaching carrying a toddler. She rushed into Clyde's office.

"Clyde, uh, James is coming up the walk and he has a toddler with him," she said, not smiling.

Clyde got up and accompanied Jennie to the front door where James was standing on the stoop holding a toddler, who looked to be a girl. He put her down and began taking off their coats and hats with Spencer's help.

"James! So you took me up on my offer! That's great! And who is this precious child?"

"That's Betty, remember? I told you about her," said James, a huge smile on his face. "Betty? This is your Aunt Jennie and Uncle Clyde!" The child moved to stand behind one of James' legs and held tight.

Jennie looked at Clyde questioningly, but Clyde just shook his head. He saw the sizable frame of his mother coming toward them. "James? Is that really you? James?"

"Yes, Ma, it's me! And this is your granddaughter, Betty!" James picked up the little girl who refused to look at any of these grown-up strangers. "She's shy at first, but give her a few minutes and she'll warm up." He kissed his daughter and then his mother and gave her a big hug.

"Come in! Come in!" said Jennie, not yet sure what to think about this unexpected addition to their Christmas. "Spencer, please have Josephine make some coffee for James. And what would you like, precious?" Jennie reached out for Betty, who wasn't budging. "We have some cookies and some warm milk to warm you up; what do you say?" She reached out again for her niece.

"It's okay, Betty, this is your Aunt Jennie!" With a little coaxing, Betty ended up holding Jennie's hand and they headed to the kitchen.

"Uncle James! Wow! This is great!" Will had appeared and they shook hands excitedly. "Come on in. I'm listening to the radio."

Clyde was perplexed. Why did James have his daughter? What had he done this time? He had to get James alone. He walked to the kitchen, too anxious to be aware of the wonderful smells wafting through the hallway. He walked through the swinging door and saw the three women attending to Betty, who was busy stuffing a cookie into her little mouth.

"Josephine, would you please take Betty and her snack," Clyde smiled and patted the child on the head, "into the other room?"

"Yes, Cap'm." They left together, smiling and laughing.

Clyde sat down at the table with his wife and mother. "I think we may have a problem." He got their attention instantly.

"What is it, honey?" asked Grannie.

"I talked to James a few weeks ago at Oaklawn. He said that his latest wife, Sarah, had divorced him and wouldn't let him see their daughters."

"I know they have two daughters. I don't know Sarah," said Jennie. "So how did he get Betty?"

"Clyde, you don't think he, you know, he took her in secret, do you?" Grannie's voice was quivering.

"Who knows, Ma. He's done some crazy things." Clyde thought for a moment. "He doesn't sound drunk."

"Thank goodness," said Jennie. "If he drove her all the way from San Antonio and was drunk…." Jennie had no more words but sucked in her breath.

"Son, go get James. I think we need to talk to him together." Grannie's voice was stern.

"No, Ma. You let me deal with him; leave the women out of it." His voice was low and determined.

"No, Clyde. I don't want you goin' off half-cocked. This is serious. He'll listen better to me," Grannie said, equally as determined. "Go on. Get him." Clyde obeyed. He returned quickly with the ever-smiling James.

"Isn't she the cutest thing?" James asked them all.

"She is one cute little girl," Grannie said. "Where's her ma?"

"She's back in San Antonio. It was a long drive all the way here." James wiped his brow as if wiping away perspiration.

"I'm surprised she let her baby go, it being Christmas Eve and all." Grannie smiled at him.

"Yeah, James, and you told me she wasn't letting you see your children," Clyde added. Grannie looked at Clyde with a scowl.

"Funny thing, that. I did what you said, Clyde. I went to the courthouse, and they said there's nothin' I can do. He said to try being extra nice to Sarah and maybe she'll change her mind." James walked over to take an empty chair. Clyde remained standing.

"So did you change her mind?" Clyde asked bluntly.

"Shhh," said Grannie. "James, honey, does Sarah know where Betty is?"

"Oh yes, she knows. She wasn't so happy about it." James was smiling.

"What the hell, James? What did you do?" Clyde demanded, almost yelling as he paced.

"Clyde, hush," said Grannie sternly. "James, tell me exactly what happened," she said softly.

"Okay, well, this is how it went. When I got to our house, or her house now, I guess, I walked inside."

"Did you knock first?" asked Grannie.

"No. I'm not knocking on my own damn front door!" James' demeanor began to change. "Sarah walks out of the kitchen with Betty on her hip. When Sarah saw me standing there, she starts yellin' at me, like I'm some kind a robber or somethin'. I told her I just wanted to take the girls with me to spend Christmas here with y'all. She said there was no way in the world she would let that happen. So, I held out my hands to Betty and asked her to come see me. Sarah grabbed her real tight. She's the one made Betty cry, not me!" His eyes narrowed as he got angrier. "So, I just took her! I got her out of Sarah's arms, ran to my car, and started driving here. I picked up everything she needs to be happy and here we are. She didn't cry for very long; she loves her daddy!" James' smile was returning.

The kitchen was silent. They were all dumbfounded. Surprisingly, Jennie was the first to speak up.

"James. You need to call Sarah right now. She must be worried sick!" Jennie was close to tears imagining what the poor woman must be going through.

"She knows I took her. What's the big deal?"

"The big deal is that you told me you're not allowed to see your girls unless Sarah says it's okay." Clyde was somewhere between disbelief and anger. "That would mean that you have just kidnapped your own child!"

"A man can't kidnap his own daughter," James insisted. "That's crazy!"

"No, James, it's not crazy. You need to call Sarah right now. The police are probably looking for you!" Clyde gritted his teeth. "I'm going to call our chief of police right now and get him to call San Antonio."

"Wait a minute, big brother. Why are ya makin' such a big deal about this?"

"You can bet Sarah called the police the minute you left and they're looking for you. The best thing we can do now is try to minimize how much trouble you're in."

He left the room and hurried to his office. He was able to get the chief of police on the phone quickly. After an embarrassing few minutes of explaining to the chief what had happened, he was told to sit tight and keep James there while the chief called the San Antonio Police. Clyde returned to the kitchen to be sure his brother didn't try to leave. He found him on the floor in the living room, Betty sitting on his lap clapping her hands and trying to sing. The rest of the family was in there as well. It looked like a Christmas Eve in any house on any street in America—a family smiling, laughing, singing. He was sorry to ruin it, especially for poor Betty, who seemed to be having a great time.

Jennie was sitting away from the group, a look of despair on her face. He saw her effort at smiling.

James stood up and picked up his daughter. "I think maybe it's time we go on outta here," he said. "We have a bunch of people to see, don't we?" He smiled at Betty and pinched her cheek.

"But you said you were staying for a few days," Will objected. "We haven't even had any time to talk!"

Clyde, expecting a scene, left and stood by the front door to block James' exit. He looked out the side lights and saw three police cars in front of his house. As he stepped outside, the chief walked up to him.

"Captain! We don't want to ruin Christmas Eve, but I have to take your brother and his daughter back to San Antonio. I've called the chief over there, so he's probably calling Mrs. Barbour right now to let her know where her daughter is."

"Thank the Lord," said Clyde. "That poor woman. Can you take them back together, so the child doesn't have to be scared on that long drive home?"

"I'll be happy to. We'll put them in one of our cars together for the ride." The chief looked over Clyde's shoulder at James, who was just exiting the front door holding Betty in his arms.

"Well, look here, the police have come to wish us Merry Christmas!" said James, jostling his baby daughter on his hip.

"James, the police are going to drive you and Betty back to San Antonio together," Clyde said. "They're going to take her back to her mother so they can spend Christmas together and then take you back to their office where you'll most likely be spending Christmas with them! I'll get your car back to you." Once again, the sarcasm was thick. "No need to bother Betty with all this grown-up stuff!" He ruffled her hair and kissed her forehead. He wondered how much of this she would even remember at 19 months old.

Jennie brought everyone out to say goodbye to the poor little girl whose crazy father had taken her on a very long joyride. She handed the policeman a bag of food for the trip.

The next month, Clyde was off to Europe again. In addition to his usual business, he was on the lookout for chandeliers and marble fireplaces for Oaklawn. They would have to be perfect. He found himself spending more mental energy on acquiring the things for his new home than on his business. When he got back to Houston at the end of January, Jennie was packing to go to Colorado to be on hand to help Lilly before and after delivery, which was expected to be the end of February.

Amidst the usual frenzy of packing for Jennie to be out of town for an extended period of time, he found his wife in the parlor folding clothes. In his most romantic style, he took the blouse out of her hand, threw it on the sofa, leaned her over his arm, and kissed her. She was too full of giggles to respond.

"*Bonjour,* wife!" He smiled at her, still holding her hand. "What a mess!" He laughed as he looked around.

"No surprise to you after all these years of marriage," Jennie responded, returning to her folding. "Spencer is supposed to tell Josephine you're here, and she'll make us a snack and some coffee."

"I'll go change clothes." Clyde went upstairs, ready to rid himself of the dusty suit he was wearing. When he returned downstairs, he found Josephine heading down the hall with a silver tray full of treats. "Hello, Josephine! That looks delicious! How are things?"

"Cold, Cap'm. Been colder than I likes. Mrs. Barbour showed me a photo of where Lilly is livin' up in Colorado, snow everywhere. I hope I never has to go there!" She shivered just thinking about it. They got to the dining room, where Jennie was waiting. Clyde took his place at the head of the table, sat back, and watched the cook spread their nibbles out on beautiful small matching plates and silver dishes.

"I remember your mother telling me that she thought food always tastes better on pretty plates! I wonder why she's not down here with us?" Jennie asked.

"I saw her upstairs and she's content to stay up there until dinnertime. I know these stairs are getting hard for her to maneuver."

"What's she going to do at Oaklawn? Those stairs go on forever!"

"I've been thinking about that. When I'm out there next, I'm going to talk to Marvin about some kind of a lift for her." Clyde reached out to hold Jennie's hand. "I'm sorry we don't have much time together before you go to Colorado."

"Me, too, but I'm anxious to get to Lilly. Oh, Clyde, I pray she hasn't got that bleeding problem I had. She's already so tiny. I don't know if her body could take it! I did find a nurse to go with me up there to be her private nurse; wonderful woman; very experienced." Jennie's face had taken on a somber, thoughtful look.

"If something goes wrong, I'll be there right away. We can bring her back here, if we need to, where we know the doctors." It was Clyde's attempt to allay some of his wife's fears.

They sat in silence for a minute until Clyde decided to liven the conversation. "You won't believe the things I found for Oaklawn on my trip! Amazing things! Rare finds!" His voice became more excited with every word. "I bought three marble fireplaces and mantels in Italy. When I say the library, do you know which room I'm talking about?" he asked.

"Yes, the room to the left when you come in the front door. The room on the other side of the hall will be the drawing room, with the dining room next to it."

"Right. Well, for the library, I found a beautiful pastel chandelier of hand-blown Venetian glass that's being made for us now. They're made on a little island called Murano; that's close to Venice." Jennie did as she always did when he talked about his foreign travels—she shook her head and smiled. It wasn't a fake smile. Whenever he returned from these long trips, he was full of wonderful stories that animated his face. Jennie loved that he found such pleasure in his life, a life generally spent taking care of everyone but himself. However, it hurt her to her core that her fear had stopped her from being by his side and sharing that part of his world.

"For the drawing room and dining room, since you see them both at the same time, I found a twin set of hand-blown Baccarat crystal chandeliers," Clyde went on. "It's hard to describe them. It's such a difficult technique that they don't do it anymore. The chains that loop around the chandelier are made from crystal links hand-blown one into another, like this." He tried to show her by making a circle with his thumb and index finger, doing the same with the other hand and lacing them together. "So, see, you actually blow one circular link, then blow the next one through the center of the first one, and on and on. There are no wires holding them together!"

Jennie looked quizzically at Clyde, trying to match her fingers to his. "Oh, I see. You blow one through the middle of the other! That must take a lifetime! No wonder you can't find anybody to do that tedious work anymore. Now everything has to be new and modern, and machine made." Jennie shook her head and frowned her disapproval. "What about the fireplaces?"

"The fireplace for the library is extraordinary. It's black marble with gold veins running through it. It's from the Italian Alps, but there's only enough of that marble left to make trophy stands and small things like that. The mantel is solid black Belgian marble they call Belgian Black, which they told me is the rarest of all the marbles. So, of course, when I found another fireplace made of the same Belgian Black marble with a matching mantel, I had to buy it for the dining room."

"Clyde, you must be spending a fortune!"

Clyde held her hand and kissed it. "Jennie, I promise I'll never spend money that we don't have. Oaklawn is going to be one of the finest country homes in the US. And when I'm finished with it, I'm going to endow it with enough money so that it will always stay the beautiful home it's going to become." He smiled lovingly at his wife.

"What does endow mean?" she asked.

"It means that I'll put aside enough money so that whoever in the family is living here will have plenty of money to take care of it properly."

"That would be a wonderful feeling as we get older, Clyde, knowing that we always have such a beautiful place to live."

"But wait, I'm not finished. The fireplace and mantel for the drawing room is a white Carrara marble. Wait until you hear this story! It has a beautiful design of flowers on it. So, to give it perfect symmetry, a right-handed sculptor worked on the right side and a left-handed sculptor worked on the left side! Isn't that crazy?"

Jennie really wasn't sure about that last bit, the right-handed and left-handed sculptors, but it sounded beautiful. "Imagine, every room will have its own story!"

In 1926, it was a cold beginning of the year by Louisiana standards. On any given day, there were about 350 men working on Oaklawn Manor. They did their best to stay warm.

"Better than workin' in the heat of summertime!" said Buddy, as he rubbed his gloved hands together over a fire set off a distance from the construction.

By the beginning of February, it took very little imagination to see that a beautiful estate was emerging from the dried out, dusty, weather-worn old mansion. Whenever Clyde made his way there, he and Marvin spoke for hours. It was difficult for Clyde to conduct any business out there with no phone services or electricity. It was an easy, though expensive, decision to have both cables run all the way out to Oaklawn from town.

Clyde was at his desk in his downtown office in Houston when Ruth rushed in.

"Clyde, the phone, the phone's for you. It's Mr. Morris." She stood in the doorway waiting for him to pick up the receiver, fidgeting with her hands.

"Hello, Marvin. How are things over there?" Clyde asked nonchalantly.

"Captain Barbour, there's been an accident."

"What happened? Did someone get hurt?" Clyde felt his entire body stiffen and heard a quiver in his voice.

"No, Captain, no one is hurt badly," he offered quickly.

"Thank God," Clyde said. "Thank God." His grasp on the receiver slackened as his body relaxed. "So, what happened?"

"Well," Marvin began, "it's been really cold out here, you know?"

"Yes, I know, Marvin. Get to the point." Clyde was, as always, busy with his work and didn't like being interrupted in the midst of it.

"One of the workers was keeping warm with a fire inside a little sugar kettle."

"You're telling me you let them have fires in that dried out wooden mess of a house?" asked Clyde, his voice not disguising his anger.

"No, no. There was only one, but you see, I didn't know it was there." Marvin's voice trailed off.

"How is that possible?" Clyde was growing angrier.

"He was working on the third floor; I didn't know it was there."

Clyde took his glasses off and set them down on his desk. "How extensive is the damage?"

"It went up like a bonfire, so fast there was nothing we could do but watch it burn." Marvin cleared his throat before continuing. "Apparently, sparks began to pop out of the kettle onto the old cypress wood floors while everyone was eating lunch. When the floors caught, there was an explosion; it was so dry! In a few minutes all the floors puffed away, and flames came out of the old French doors where the balcony is. All the wood burned to pieces. Of course, the old brick in the walls and columns are still there. Nothing could bring them down." Marvin tried to lighten his voice and interject some positivity.

Clyde was stunned into silence. *I hope I'm dreaming. Please, somebody wake me up from this nightmare! My Oaklawn, what have they done to my Oaklawn?*

Marvin ended the silence. "So how do you want me to proceed?"

"I don't even know yet," said Clyde. "This is a damn disaster! You need to figure out how much more it's going to cost us. I'll be out there tomorrow to work on a new budget." Clyde's mind was reeling. He put his head in his hands, his elbows on his desk. He wanted to lash out at somebody or something; to hurl something across the room and listen to it break to pieces. He wanted to fire everyone on the project. He wanted to be at Oaklawn right then. Maybe, just maybe, he even wanted to cry, but didn't.

That night, alone at his home on Montrose with only his mother to keep him company, he told her the horrible story. She seemed stunned. "I'm so sorry, son. Are you gonna tell Jennie?" she asked.

"No, Ma, I'm not going to bother Jennie. It will only make her worry. Let's keep it to ourselves for now," he answered. They sat in silence for a long while.

"Now Clyde, I don't know nothin' 'bout your big wheeling and dealings, but I was just thinkin'." Ma looked at him intently. "Remember when we was poor? You broke somethin' and it took a good while to get it fixed up and ready again. It didn't matter 'cause you had no other choice; you had no money to buy a new one. Now this big ole house was a big mess," she continued.

"A gigantic mess now," replied Clyde.

"You're blessed to have the money to build it up again. Maybe it'll end up being easier and faster than it would have been. Get it all shiny and new. I was just thinkin'." Ma got quiet.

"Ma, you know what?" answered Clyde. "You just might be right. Of course, we've lost most of the old parts, some of which can't be replaced. We have plenty of photographs to show us what it looked like on the outside. I'm going to go get in bed and think it through in the quiet. You are amazing, Ma. I love you!" He got up, hugged and kissed his mother, and told her good night. He was up most of the night thinking, renovating his ideas, coming to terms with the change in circumstances, and massaging it into his strong opinions of what it was to look like when it was complete.

The next day, Clyde took his train car to Franklin. He thought he had readied himself for what he was going to see, but he was wrong. Nothing resembled the manor house he had loved for 25 years. It was more like an ancient ruin bereft of any life-giving force, but Clyde refused to let himself think like that. Instead, he enlivened the mass of saddened workers who felt certain that their jobs would now cease to exist.

Oaklawn Manor After the Fire

"So, men, there's been quite a setback but we're going to get back to work. Under no circumstances is anyone to start any kind of fire without asking Buddy first. We're going to build Oaklawn back and it's going to look even more beautiful than I planned."

On February 27, at St. Luke's Hospital in Denver, with Jennie holding one hand and Tom the other, and with the help of Dr. Harry Seymour, Lilly delivered a beautiful baby girl with no complications! They named her Lucile DeVoe after Lilly and after Tom's sister, DeVoe, who had died along with her husband in the flu epidemic of 1917. Jennie's eyes welled up with tears when she saw her Little Princess breastfeeding her newborn child. That night, Jennie got on her knees and prayed in deepest gratitude to God for helping this latest grandchild and mother breeze through their delivery.

A telegram arrived from Clyde wishing them well, not mentioning the trials he was going through in Franklin. That could wait until Jennie's return from Colorado.

CHAPTER 41

THE AMBASSADOR

Spring 1926

The fire at Oaklawn continually at the forefront of his mind, Clyde did his best not to wander too far from Franklin while the rebuild went on. In May, he did make a trip to Colorado to visit his Barbour Coal Company mining interests and his newest granddaughter. He took Tom and a few of Tom's classmates to visit and have a look around the mine.

Back in Houston afterward, he confided in his wife. "I have to tell you, Jennie, I don't like going down in those mines. It makes me feel like I can't breathe, like I might get lost and never find my way out again." He shuddered and grimaced.

"I know I'll never go down in one of those. Poor Tommy will have to do a lot of that! People do die down in there you know." They were both silent.

The rebuild of Oaklawn was completed in September. Clyde had been there for two weeks, making sure everything was as he had ordered. He had planted over one hundred 12-year-old oaks and had tree surgeons come in to help the older, ailing trees. One of the tree surgeons told Clyde that many of these great oaks were there when Columbus discovered America. A few of the older branches were chained together in preparation for the hurricanes that were an inevitability on the Gulf Coast. One thousand rose bushes were planted in the formal garden, which had been designed by a French architect to look like Versailles. Clyde's good friend, Charles Kerr, had purchased, in Italy, an original Carrara marble statue of Psyche, the Goddess of Soul, which was delivered the week before; it was his housewarming gift to Clyde and it occupied an honored position overlooking the rose garden. There was an azalea given to Clyde by Prescott Foster, son of the governor, which was said to have been at the old Foster place, Dixie Plantation, along Bayou Teche for 150 years. There was even a steam-heated greenhouse, or conservatory, just for Jennie.

On August 25, a hurricane came ashore at Houma, Louisiana, about 45 miles east/southeast of Franklin, with highest sustained winds of 115 mph. It brought with it nearly 10 inches of rain but weakened rapidly once it got onshore. With the Open House scheduled for Labor Day, there was a mad dash to ready the grounds—again. Clyde had a large fallen cedar tree sawn up to make into a log cabin for the grandchildren to play in.

"A hurricane twelve days before our Open House. What next, a flood?" Clyde asked Jennie, who was helping to get the interior ready for guests.

"Clyde, look around us; look how beautiful it is in here. The hurricane didn't bother the house one little bit!" Jennie was smiling at her husband.

Marvin added, "Captain, under this one-inch-thick marble flooring, there's four inches of reinforced concrete sitting over two layers of wide cypress planks running in different directions. And don't forget how thick the walls are. Oaklawn will be fine, even if it does flood." He turned to walk away, then added, "Except maybe for the wine cellar in your 'smoker!'" He smiled and walked away.

The night before the weekend guests arrived, with all the hustle and bustle of preparations behind them, Jennie found Clyde sitting on the step at the bottom of the beautiful marble staircase. She could tell he was deep in thought.

"What are you thinking about?" she asked, sitting next to him and putting her hand on his knee.

"I guess I'm trying to take it all in," he said, looking around. "Up until now, Oaklawn has been a dream and then it became just another project to complete on time. It was an intricate puzzle with logical steps checked off one at a time, and now…it's complete. Not only is it complete, but it's ours to live in and love and take care of after waiting 25 years to make it our own. I'm sitting here looking around and remembering where all these beautiful things came from, knowing that we chose them, and still I can't believe that it's ours—really ours! How did this happen?" Clyde took his wife's hand in his and looked at her, searching her eyes.

"Know what I remember?" she asked. "I remember all the hours, days, and months of you working all the time. How about all the time you spent away from us in Europe and Mexico with never a thought about yourself? You're the one who chose most of these beautiful things and you should feel proud."

"You know, Jennie, I wanted to do this for a lot of reasons. I did it for the Louisiana that I love so much and the people of Franklin who took us in as their own and helped us get ahead; they have so little to look to for inspiration these days. I wanted all of our family to have a place to come for celebrations and just to rest." He stood up and pulled her up after him. "But mainly and most importantly, I did it for you, as I promised I would. I couldn't love you more and we definitely wouldn't be standing in this beautiful mansion of our own if you hadn't been able to do so much without me. Come here." He led her up to their second-story bedroom, onto which had been added a bathroom. He switched on the beautiful crystal chandelier in which he had placed blue lightbulbs. "I want you to always have your beloved blue moonlight!" he said. He grabbed her and kissed her long and hard.

"Clyde, Clyde," she almost cried. "I thank God every day that you wanted me. I still don't know why. I've never been able to keep up with you or talk like you or know what to do all the time like you. You're a sophisticated businessman, but I'm still that little girl who ran away to your flatboat." The dim light played tricks on the tears that ran down her cheeks. "I don't know what to do with all those fancy people coming to stay tomorrow."

Clyde wiped the tears from under her eyes with his thumbs. "Come here, my darling Jennie." He led her into their new bathroom and pointed to the green, white, and gold Ice Water pitcher that had followed them everywhere on their adventures. "Sip some water." Jennie stroked the pitcher as if it were a kitten and smiled at her husband. "We're both living this wonderful life because God blessed me with abilities to create things that help others and I feel it's my responsibility to do so."

Jennie sighed. "I'm so lucky to have such a good man as my husband! Come on," she said, smiling and pushing him toward their bed. "It's time for bed!" He laughed as he pretended to be pushed onto their bed, the blue moonlight shining above.

Oaklawn Manor Open House, Part of the Crowd

The official Open House was held on Labor Day, September 6, 1926. People, primarily men, had arrived in fine private automobiles and private train cars all the way from New York City down to Houston and beyond. There were as many plus fours as there were long pants, all worn with a white shirt and brimmed straw hat. Bow ties were sported even more than the traditional tie. It was quite a gathering of who's who. Clyde, Jr., and Flora were down from the Monroe carbon black plants that he was still managing.

The entire population of St. Mary's Parish was invited. People of all races dined under the huge oak trees on long tables filled with delicious food. In an effort to control crowding inside the manor house, only overnight guests, of whom there were 40, were invited inside that weekend. When the guests opened the large front doors with the double crosses said to keep out ghosts, they stepped over a doorsill made of a single massive beam of cedar and onto the marble floor with its checkered pattern.

When asked about the flooring, Clyde explained that since the original cedar floors had burned in the fire, he had found this marble, which had been used in the original St. Charles Hotel in New Orleans and had been in a salvage yard since the hotel went up in flames in 1851. "I had Captain Gotreaux bring the heavy cargo on one of my steamships from New Orleans up the bayou. Slow going, took him five days!"

The Oaklawn Golf Course had nine holes. There was a tournament that weekend, which Clyde participated in even though he hadn't had enough leisure time in his life to become a good golfer. The first tee was set on a patch of grass to the side of the sprawling back terrace made of flagstone that had once been used as ballast on ships.

Only a few children swam in the 60-foot swimming pool that sat among the oaks with its two white Greek Colonial-style bath houses, one on each side. It looked like something out of a movie! It was Jesse and Sylvia, who had brought their family all the way from Tampico for the big event, who started the swimming trend with their children.

Jennie teased Clyde about giving him an elaborate stag party. She secreted herself as much as she could get away with but found herself slightly more at ease with the gentlemen after they'd been guests for two days.

On Monday afternoon, during the festivities, Man, now a father himself, came up to Clyde and tapped him on the back. "Hey, Clyde Barbour! This here's my second son; name's Clyde." Man was beaming as Clyde's name rolled slowly off his tongue.

"Clyde? You named him Clyde?" he asked, looking truly surprised.

"Sure did! My first boy's named Luke for my daddy and now we got Clyde. I figure we's finished!" A big grin covered his dark face. Clyde put out his arms to take his namesake from Man, but the child wouldn't let go of his father. "Go on, boy," he coaxed to no avail.

Clyde thought about Luke. It had been a long time since he'd felt those particular heartstrings sing out in pain. "I'm honored, Man, really, I am! He's a fine-looking boy!" Clyde tried to tickle the baby, who resisted but giggled anyway.

"Luke over there," Man pointed to his son across the way with his mother and a little girl, "he wants to know if'n he can dance up there on that big stage, he and his friends. What do ya think about that, Clyde Barbour?"

"Well, yeah, I sure don't mind if they want to show off their dancing skills! I'm sure everybody would like to see it. Come on." He walked up onto the terrace where guests were drinking iced tea and talking. He found the reluctant Jennie and told her what he was planning. He also found Will, who was there from the University of Chicago, where he'd managed to stay enrolled. Clyde asked Will, always the party boy, to help get the whole thing started, which he did gladly. He was able to carve out a circle in the middle of the crowd of over 100 people, then led half a dozen young children out into the middle where they stood waiting for the music to begin. Will started playing the harmonica and Luke, Jr., led the way, starting to dance with abandon. Soon others joined in the dance, while the guests clapped and tapped their feet in a chorus of human gaiety.

Oaklawn Manor Open House,
Clyde and Houston Mayor Holcombe Shaking Hands

A week later, at the Colorado School of Mines, Tom and his classmates were taking a class put on by the US Bureau of Mines called Mine Safety. It was a mandatory class. They went to an abandoned mine nearby and donned the safety masks that were required to protect them from the dust and underground gases. They went down with their picks, shovels, and wheelbarrows and started to work. Shortly thereafter, Tom gagged and fell over. It took four men to get the tall Tom out of the mine and into the fresh air. He wasn't breathing. The men from the Bureau of Mines were well trained for just such an emergency and were able to do some on-the-job-training of the students as they worked on Tom, who came to, coughing and spitting. A valve had malfunctioned in his mask. Tom debated not telling Lilly;

why worry her about such an unlikely occurrence? The decision was made for him when the school doctor insisted on driving him home to tell Lilly how to best care for him overnight. Lilly sent a telegram to her parents in Houston. She wanted her father to tell Tom to quit school and find something else to do. Clyde said it wasn't his place. Tom was not willing to quit.

On September 20, 1926, the Miami Hurricane, which had moved along the Gulf Coast all the way to Louisiana, came ashore near Pensacola, Florida, with 24 hours of storms along the central Gulf Coast. Oaklawn was fine but it seemed to shake something in Clyde.

I don't like this; I don't like this at all. What if something happened to Tom down there? Would it be my fault? I asked him to study mining. Every day I send men down into those mines. They have families who love them and depend on them. There's no way to be sure the miners will be safe underground. Clyde tossed and turned in his sleep.

In the middle of the night, he woke up screaming. Jennie sat up and reached over to touch her husband. He was covered in sweat, his eyes bulging.

"Oh Lord! Oh Lord! Oh Lord!" Clyde whispered as he looked at Jennie in fear and gripped her with both his hands. "Tom and Lilly and the baby were stuck in a mine!"

"Clyde, shh, shh. It's okay. It was just a dream." She stroked his head and helped him lie back down. "Let me get you some water." She went into the bathroom and returned with a cup.

"It was so real! How awful." He sipped the water and put it down. *What am I supposed to do?* he asked God.

It was easy for him to find a reason to make a trip to New Orleans. He had to see his palm reader, had to get some insight. The last time he'd felt so driven to visit her was 20 years before, when Jennie was going to deliver their last child, Will.

Clyde walked into her storefront on Royal Street and, seeing no one, sat down on the small couch in the front. He could hear the muted sound of the voices of palm readers deep in translation. The strong smell of incense seemed to help him relax and he closed his eyes and looked inward. He saw himself reading, high on top of the flatboat. He felt the chilling wind on his cheeks and bare hands as he tied the knots to secure the boat. He could smell the combined sweat of him and Luke and Pa as they worked down in the hold and the sound of Ma humming in the kitchen as she cooked.

"Captain?" Clyde heard her before he felt her presence.

"Yes. Hello! I'm afraid I've been daydreaming." Clyde smiled as he stood up.

"Do not apologize; I'm glad you are so comfortable in my parlor. Come with me, Captain, and we will discover together." She led the way behind the curtain, where they each took their place on either side of the table. "You look very disturbed. I see fear in your eyes, the fear of knowing. I believe you already know what you need to do, so why have you come to me?"

"Everyone thinks I'm so sure of everything; if they only knew."

She took his hand and began to look it over, rubbing her finger along the creases in his palms. She mumbled quietly to herself, then reached back for her crystal ball and put it on the table between them. "It's very dark in there. I can't see anything. There's a man, a tall man. I feel that he's part of your family. He's down very deep in the earth in the dark with only a small light to guide him. It is not safe down there; not safe for anyone!"

Clyde sat back in his chair, perspiration on his forehead, dismay in his eyes. "There's a fortune to be made down in those mines. I've just started up that business. Tom's getting his master's degree; what the hell do I tell him?" Clyde spoke out loud, hoping for a different answer, but nothing came. He thanked her, paid her, and stepped out into the daylight. "That's it," he told himself, "I'm selling that business. There are lots of other ways to make money."

Back in Houston, a new opportunity presented itself to him immediately. He agreed to a meeting with a young but well-seasoned and well-respected real estate operator from New Jersey named Leon Edgar Todd. He was looking for a backer in a new residential community he wanted to build just outside of Philadelphia, a weekend and summer retreat. Surely there would be a place for Tom there.

They met in Clyde's office. After the obligatory Southern welcome that Clyde gave this and every other guest, Mr. Todd pulled out maps and photographs to show Clyde.

"It's called Ballinger's Mills, 1,300 acres of wild pineland jungle with brackish streams and swamp. It's being offered for $3 an acre," Mr. Todd began. "Some of it is old cranberry bogs."

"How far is it from Philadelphia?" Clyde asked as he looked over the documents.

"About 30 miles; it's perfect!"

So Clyde met Mr. Todd in Philadelphia, where they headed out together to the tract. Once there, they got into a small boat and went around the lakes and then trudged through the pine forest in an old truck and on foot. He was mesmerized by the untamed, even primordial look of the place.

"I feel like I'm exploring land never before seen by mankind," he told Mr. Todd.

"There are still a few Piney Woods people living way back up in the woods. They'll be displaced." Mr. Todd thought that was the end of that conversation.

"Displaced? That's not right. We can't displace people who have lived in this wilderness all their lives!" Clyde protested. "We'll have to figure out a place for them."

"Honestly, Captain Barbour, that's going to cost money we don't have."

"Well then, we'll just have to find the funds somewhere, or I'm not in."

The $4 million deal was done. Clyde called his new company Medford Lakes Development Company, as the community would be called Medford-Lakes-in-the-Pines. He talked with Tom, told him about selling all his interests in mining, and asked if when he graduated a few months down the road, he would be willing to bring Lilly and their daughter, DeVoe, to New Jersey to head up the development.

"Your engineering degree will come in handy," he assured Tom. "First we'll have to lay out the roads and dredge the lakes." After the shock of getting a master's degree only to be told it was no longer relevant, Tom felt he had no choice. Lilly refused to let her husband go back into mining and who would be so foolish as to say no to an enterprise with Captain Barbour? So, Tom moved his little family into a pretty two-story house in Merchantville, New Jersey, only 15 minutes from the development.

Tom paid the piney woods people to help clear the land and promised them a place to live when it was all finished. Only one of these men knew how to sign his name and to read.

Mr. Todd and Tom had a difference of opinion over what type of housing would be used within the development. Clyde wanted to use prefabricated houses such as those being sold through Sears and many others. He knew they could make a good profit on them by manufacturing the houses themselves. Mr. Todd had always envisioned the place with log houses to blend in with the environment. He won that argument when he agreed to pay the Piney Woods people to get the logs for the houses. Tom designed the houses, and experts in notching and fitting logs put them up. In the end, the community consisted of 300 rustic cedar log cabins, each with a large fireplace for heat during the winter. They were all built around the natural and man-made lakes that now were part of Medford-Lakes-in-the-Pines. It was a small, picturesque, and unique spot.

The massive Mississippi River flood of 1927 began in mid-April when the first levees were breached in Illinois after what had been torrential rainstorms. People in Franklin said it rained all the way up to Canada. The waters didn't subside until August. There were 637,000 people forced to relocate, many into quickly constructed camps, and 23,000 square miles of land was submerged to 30 feet. More than 250 people perished. The property damage in today's dollars would be in the billions. It was one of the most destructive floods in history. The following year, the new Governor of Louisiana, Huey Long, passed the Flood Control Act of 1928, the first long-term flood management program.

The water from the Teche reached back into the gardens of Oaklawn, where it was deep enough to row a skiff, but none of the buildings were affected. Clyde remembered his comment after the hurricane just before the Open House about a flood coming next. He hoped he hadn't jinxed his home.

Some of the homeless were stranded on what became islands accessible only by boat. Miles and miles of tents were pitched. Clyde, who felt the need to keep some sternwheelers on the Teche, sent two of them to the worst-hit area to help. In Franklin and elsewhere, all available men went out to build local levees and fill sandbags. Many of the townspeople were out of their homes for weeks, so Clyde helped feed them. It was a scene reminiscent of the 1900 hurricane in Galveston.

Clyde, Jr., and Flora were still living in Monroe, Louisiana, with their baby, Theo, where he was overseeing the carbon black business. With all the oil and gas discoveries there, it had become another boomtown, attracting both the finest and the worst in society. There were lavish parties in the homes of the wealthy and Shreveport, Louisiana, was able to satisfy the needs of the city slickers. Being one of the wealthy, Clyde, Jr., and his family lived a lavish lifestyle in this small town of oil rigs.

Clyde had been working on a new and improved process to extract carbon black from the natural gas in order to get more carbon black out of a given quantity of gas. The new process yielded two or more pounds of carbon black per 1,000 cubic feet of natural gas, about double the current yield. It would revolutionize the industry and avoid the price increases that would have resulted from the reduction of supply. Clyde, Jr., had been working with him on it and finally they were awarded the patent under the name of Clyde, Jr.

"But Dad," said Clyde, Jr., "you're the one that figured it out."

"You helped me, didn't you? Weren't you there working alongside me? And you're my carbon black man. It should be yours. No more said. We'll keep this to ourselves." Clyde patted his son on the shoulder and smiled. "I'm happy when my family is taken care of. My purpose is to help you as my son, and I don't need it. It should help your career."

They formed the New Process Carbon Black Company, Inc., with a capitalization of $625,000. They were required to have the state Conservation department test the process to be sure it worked properly before it would be given a permit. Theodore Grunewald, Clyde, Jr.'s father-in-law, was also part of this new venture. The test would be supervised by Professor C.S. Williamson of Tulane University.

After much wrangling with the other carbon black companies in the area, the test was done; it demonstrated that 2.17 pounds of carbon black could be made from every 1,000 cubic feet of gas, rather than the one pound that was the current standard. The permit was granted in early June of 1927. The test results proved that Clyde had been able to figure out how to double the carbon black yield.

Also in June, Clyde and Ruth set out for Europe again. It was the second time she had accompanied him, the first without Lilly to chaperone. It was extremely helpful on the business side of things to have her there; it made the return to the office in Houston almost seamless. Of course, there was the added benefit of an unprecedented amount of time alone, just the two of them. Clyde bought a copy of a sculpture in the Vatican Museum in Rome—"The Dancing Faun"—which he planned to install by the conservatory at Oaklawn.

On July 7, the Texas Legislature authorized the Port of Houston Authority to act as an autonomous government entity. This gave it the authority to appoint a self-governing body that could pass laws and levy taxes, as well as make informed, unforced decisions, independent of the U.S. government. This opened the door for Houston to become the second busiest port in the nation and tenth-largest in the world. Captain Barbour was instrumental in making it happen.

Underneath the pleasantries of familial interactions, Tom couldn't shake the feeling of having been promised a prize he would never be receiving after all his hard work at the Colorado School of Mines. Lilly was pregnant with their second child and didn't want to be stranded in New Jersey, away from her family. They both felt that a life in southern California, where the weather was always pleasant and where there would be family around, was what they wanted.

Tom talked with Clyde, who also felt bad about the mining debacle. He wanted Tom to be happy and engaged in his work, so he asked a friend who had an office in a large investment company in Los Angeles to take Tom on and teach him the ropes selling bonds. Everyone was happy. Tom and Lilly rented a house in Hollywood and were barely settled in when their baby boy, Thomas Jefferson Holmes III, arrived on September 2.

Back at Oaklawn, Marvin Morris, the architect, had returned and asked Clyde if there wasn't something else he wanted.

The Barbour Mausoleum, Franklin Cemetery, Franklin, Louisiana

"Let me think, Marvin. One thing I really want is a family mausoleum. How about talking to the folks in town about buying a piece of the land in the cemetery for a Barbour mausoleum? Look into it and let me know what you find out." Clyde saw a look of relief on Marvin's face; times were getting hard all over the country and people needed work.

"One other thing; the grounds on the other side of the rose garden need something. I don't really want a whole building, but someplace covered where we could have coffee and be outside. I've decided to call that part of the land The Park. My English colleague, Mr. Hewlett, uses that name for a piece of his property in Angelsey in Northern Wales. It was a lovely spot." Clyde smiled at the memory of him and Lilly being there a few years earlier. Marvin designed a miniature facade of the manor house, brick steps and all, which seemed to complete The Park.

In November, Clyde wrote to his two daughters out in California, offering to give them his house at 533 Lorraine Blvd. to sell; they could each buy a small house with the money. Although the letters were typically businesslike, the salutation "My dear daughters" and the closing of "With love to all, affectionately, 'Daddy'" showed the depth of his feelings. He was a businessman, but also a loving father.

Tim Bryan, the president of Gotham National Bank, called one day. He had become a close friend after all the time he and Clyde had spent together doing business deals and attending events.

"Hi, Captain! Ready for Christmas?" he asked jovially.

"We're getting close. Decorating Oaklawn is quite an undertaking. All the children are coming with the grandchildren, so it'll be a raucous occasion to be sure!" Clyde laughed.

"At least you have plenty of space. Have you found a closet you can hide in if need be?" Tim teased.

"Well, let's see. The wine cellar is dark, confined, and cold. And there's the butter house, which is also chilly and doesn't remind me of being down in a coal mine. The conservatory is another idea; it's at least slightly warm and I can hide behind a rhododendron or something." Both men laughed. "What's the real reason you called? Need a vacation down South?"

"Not far off. Paul Claudel, the Ambassador of France to the U.S. is heading South. He has a keen interest in Louisiana's French heritage, and he'd also like to see Oaklawn. The ambassador is quite the luminary—a well-known poet, writer, and he's even written some plays and operas. He was nominated for the Nobel Prize in Literature last year. What do you think? He'd be coming in a week or so and just stay a few days."

"Of course. It would be an honor! Wonder what he'll think of my miniature, very miniature, Versailles on the bayou?"

"Be careful that he doesn't try to take some of those fine French antiques back home with him!"

Clyde immediately called Opal to tell her about the ambassador's visit because he knew she would be excited. He told her that Tim Bryan said he has a keen interest in Louisiana's French heritage and that he wanted to see Oaklawn. She told Clyde the ambassador was an old friend, as they ran in the same circles, and said that she had no doubt her friend would be delighted to have her accompany him, if that would please Clyde. The prospect of the ambassador coming to Oaklawn accompanied by Opal raised the level of anticipation for Clyde. The local newspaper reported that the town of Franklin would be putting together a reception for the visiting dignitary at the new Boy Scouts' auditorium, which had recently been expanded to hold more than 500.

Clyde found Jennie in the kitchen and told her about the ambassador coming. "I don't know the details yet, but I can't imagine he'd come alone."

Opal called Clyde back right away to tell him that she would be accompanying her old friend to Oaklawn. The following day, Clyde gave Jennie the details, adding, "The ambassador is bringing a friend with him; she's a well-known opera singer that I met a couple of times in New York City; she's such a fixture in the New York City society scene that you can hardly go to a party without running into her."

"Let's sit down right now and make some plans," Jennie said. "Tell me more about the singer."

"She's very French and very outgoing. She's a famous entertainer and she plays the part perfectly."

They arrived late Saturday morning, December 3, 1927, and stayed until Monday morning. Jennie had them stay up on the second floor. The ambassador slept in what they referred to as the Henry Clay bedroom. It had been restored to be just as it was when Clay visited the manor in the 1840s. Opal was in the other bedroom at the front of the house, across from Clyde and Jennie's room. Both visitors' rooms had views of the Teche. Jennie had thought it fun to set the two up for a possible late-night rendezvous on the balcony.

After they had freshened up, a tour was in order. In the library, the Louis XIV desk, known to have been used by Napoleon at one of his palaces, was a highlight. When they stopped in front of the Aubusson tapestry that hung in the hallway, the ambassador's eyes widened. It was a depiction of La Petite Trianon and part of the gardens at Versailles that dated back to the 17th century.

"*Ouah!*" said the ambassador. "How did you get this tapestry?"

"One of my contacts in Paris. He said it was from the 17th century and that it had actually hung in Versailles! Isn't that amazing? A beautiful tapestry that once hung in a royal palace now hangs in my home," Clyde said proudly.

The ambassador addressed Opal in French. "*Ce riche Américain, sait-il que ce qu'il a fait est enterdit? Personne n'est authorisé à faire sortir de notre pays une antiquité Francaise d'une telle valeur!*" ("This rich American, does he know that what he has done is forbidden? No one is allowed to take out of our country a French antiquity of such value!")

Opal replied, "*Je ne sais pas. Je doute que quelqu'un lui ait dit. Ils savaient qu'il avait de l'argent et ne se souciaient pas de règles.*" ("I don't know. I doubt anyone told him. The person knew that he has a lot of money and didn't care about the rules.")

"*Celle-ci doit retourner en France!*" ("These must be returned to France!")

"*Je ne sais pas quoi vous dire,*" Opal said, shaking her head. ("I don't know what you're talking about.")

"If what you two are bickering about has something to do with me, I would appreciate it if you'd do it in English," Clyde said.

The ambassador addressed Clyde. "Captain, do you know that this tapestry, as well as that desk, should never have left France? These types of valuable antiques are to be kept in our country." He spoke politely, without judgment and with a smile on his face. There was a moment of silence as Jennie and Clyde took in the news.

"No," Clyde began slowly, "I wasn't aware of that. Well, they have a beautiful home right here now." He smiled back.

"The French government feels strongly about these French treasures; they must be returned to their rightful home." The ambassador's smile seemed more forced now.

"Frankly, I'm surprised at your country's position on this, given its long history of pillaging much of the Western world. I must say, however, that I thoroughly enjoyed seeing the spoils of that effort firsthand while visiting the Louvre. *Merci,* but I'll just keep them here." Clyde wasn't about to give up this prized possessions.

Jennie intervened, trying to distract from the awkward moment. She pointed into the dining room. "Come see something my husband designed himself!" They followed her into the room and she continued. "This dining table and the two side tables were designed by Clyde! He used this beautiful Pyrenees marble from the old Grunewald Hotel in New Orleans. We loved the color! He designed the wrought-iron base and had it made in New Orleans."

The moment had passed. Nothing else was mentioned about the "black market" antiques that weekend. However, the matter was discussed at length at the French Embassy back in D.C., as well as in Paris.

Opal was beautifully dressed every minute of the day. Jennie even commented to Clyde that she'd never seen a woman dressed in such finery.

"French women are just that way," he told her. "And of course, she's a star."

"I would hate to have to dress like that all the time."

Clyde found it unsettling to have Opal sleeping just across the hallway as he lay next to Jennie, her arm slung across Clyde's waist. Her soft, warm breathing fell onto his back in warm iteration. A part of him, the male animalistic part of him, wanted to cross the hall and mount the voluptuous creature sleeping there. He could visualize her curves and crevices, feel her impossibly soft skin, smell the perfume in her hair. He gently took Jennie's hand in his and let the rational side remind him of what he already knew; everything was right in the world just the way it was, right at that moment.

When deciding how to entertain their French guests that Saturday night, they knew they couldn't compete with the many lavish balls their guests had attended, so they chose to downplay the festivities and hold a dance in the barn. The barn at Oaklawn, like everything else there, was visually appealing. It was used primarily to house the various pieces of equipment required for keeping the grounds immaculate and the place running smoothly. It had been emptied of just about everything and decorated for an elegant but casual dinner. Clyde had asked Opal if she would like to sing at the party, and she happily agreed; it was decided that she would sing an aria accompanied by a local who had studied classical piano in New York City.

The sun was going down as Jennie, Opal, Clyde, and Paul Claudel walked over to the barn, the women in lively conversation. Clyde and Paul sported plus fours and casual shirts. The moss that hung from the massive oak trees cast soft and somewhat eerie shadows all around, the glorious manor house getting ready for sleep behind them. Jazz music emanated from the barn they could see in the distance.

Cars were parked in the field: Locomobile, Packard, Duesenberg, and Willy's Overland, among others.

"There are a lot of cars here," said Paul, pointing.

"It helped when the government passed a Federal Highway Act that built lots of new roads and improved many of the existing ones. Cars are everywhere now!" Clyde told Paul. "Do you like jazz? Some of the students from our university in Baton Rouge came out here to play for us."

"I love it!" replied Opal. "It's *très* fun and makes me want to dance!" She took Jennie's hand and pretended to be dancing with her. Jennie began to laugh.

"*M'accordez-vous cette danse, Mademoiselle Perette?*" Paul asked.

"*Mais oui, merci!*" answered Opal, and they began to waltz.

"Madame Barbour?" Clyde said to Jennie, "May I have this dance?"

"*Oui,*" answered a shy Jennie who nonetheless waltzed with her husband alongside the glamorous French pair.

"What is that song?" Paul asked Opal.

"It's a waltz called 'Charmaine.' *C'est très mignon!*" she replied.

As they walked into the barn, people were milling around, some dancing and some seated at the tables. The long wooden tables were covered in white tablecloths that helped brighten up the interior. Centerpieces ran the length of the tables and were a mixture of greenery, moss, and red ribbon, interspersed with hurricane globes protecting red candles. Four chandeliers hanging from rafters were laced with greenery and red ribbons.

The band played on a stage at one end of the room. A large Christmas tree was on stage as well, covered in red and green balls and silver tinsel.

They served local food but French wine and champagne. Clyde took his obligatory sip of the Veuve Clicquot when toasting his guests and then put down the glass. He knew the laws of Prohibition didn't apply on his property; being friends with all the local police made it so. He didn't take advantage of this relationship, adding alcohol to the menu only on special occasions.

After a dessert of bread pudding, Clyde walked over to Opal, who was sitting at a table with the Governor of Louisiana and escorted her to the stage.

"Friends, we have a special treat for you this evening. Some of you have already had the pleasure of meeting Mademoiselle Opal Perrette, who is visiting Oaklawn from France. She is a world-renowned opera singer who has sung in the most prestigious opera houses in the world, including our own Metropolitan Opera House in New York City. She is here with the French Ambassador to the United States, Monsieur Paul Claudel, both of whom we are privileged to host here in Franklin. Mademoiselle Perrette will sing an aria for us from the opera *Gianni Schicchi* by Giacomo Puccini. The song is titled, and I apologize for my terrible accent, 'O Mio Babbino Caro,' or 'Oh My Dear Father,' in English. I leave the rest to you, Miss Perrette."

Although she wasn't dressed in her usual finery, Opal's cerulean-blue silk dress, overlaid with sheer gauze embellished with gold and black lace appliqués, was hauntingly beautiful.

"*Bonsoir!* I am in love with your *Louisianne* and your people who are *très gentil*, I mean very kind. *Ici*, at Oaklawn, you have one of the most magnificent *maisons*...I mean homes, I have ever seen! Take good care of her. I say *merci* to Captain and Mrs. Barbour who have been the most wonderful hosts. I hope you will enjoy this beautiful *chanson* about love and torment." After the polite applause, she began to sing.

"O mio babbino caro..."

Her beautiful, strong voice rose and seemed to fill the surrounding countryside with the powerful, pleading emotion of Puccini's lyrics. There was a stunned silence when the last note died away. Moments later, the diners sprang to their feet, applauding loudly. The mayor of Franklin presented Opal with a beautiful bouquet of flowers, which she graciously accepted as she curtsied and smiled and calls of "Encore!" reverberated throughout the barn.

"An encore? You will like an encore? Let me see." Opal appeared to be thinking of what to follow with. "I have it! Something new, a Gershwin from the musical *Oh, Kay!* It is such a lovely *chanson*. It is 'Someone to Watch Over Me.'" She walked over to the pianist to relay her wishes, then stood back in front of the adoring crowd as the piano began and she followed in song.

"There's a somebody
I'm longin' to see...
Someone to watch over me."

The guests leapt from their chairs clapping and whistling. Clyde stepped onto the stage and whispered in her ear. "You are amazing!" He took her hand and led her off the stage and into the crowd, who had become instant fans that evening.

The barn dance was an enormous success and became a regular happening at Oaklawn, although there were no opera singers in the years that followed.

Sunday, after brunch, the guests took time for themselves. The ambassador enjoyed doing some work seated at the Napoleon desk. Jennie was in the kitchen talking to the help and left Clyde and Opal alone to go out for a walk. The old brick walkway was difficult for her to maneuver in her fancy shoes. Her wobbles made them both laugh as Clyde was forced to reach out to steady her frequently.

Once inside the conservatory, Opal walked up to him and stood only inches away, staring into his eyes. Clyde looked over both of his shoulders before speaking. "You dazzled everyone at dinner, but I knew you would. It's very difficult to have you here and not be with you."

Opal moved forward to kiss his neck lightly. "This place, it is *très, très belle mon Capitaine!* I can feel the...how do you call it...*esprit, non*, spirit. I can feel the spirit of this place." She looked around her, reached out, and touched the flowers. "I can see why you love it here. Your house is like a *musée*, a museum that is alive." She ended with the usual French flare in her voice.

"I like the way you said that. A living museum!" Clyde held both her hands. "I love Oaklawn like my child."

"*Oui*, I can see. And *je t'aimes aussi!* Please, just one kiss for your French mistress." She looked at Clyde with love and lust and caring as she pulled herself into him and placed her lips softly then roughly onto his and they melted into each other. She was the first to pull away. "And now we must return." She rubbed a spot of lipstick off of Clyde's cheek, smiled, then led the way back to the manor house.

The two guests left on Monday. That evening, Jennie and Clyde were sharing a meal alone in the back dining room off the kitchen. They would be off to Houston the next day and would return to Oaklawn for Christmas with the entire family.

"Miss Perrette is so beautiful!" Jennie said with a sigh. "And her voice!"

"Yes, she is. Everyone seems to adore her."

"No wonder. She was very kind to me. I like her. It seems like you two know each other pretty well."

"As I said, our paths have crossed in different places." Clyde was beginning to sense something deeper in her words. "I'm sure she would find me a bore."

"I don't think anyone could find Captain Barbour a bore! In fact, I could feel she has a soft spot for you, the way she looked at you and listened to everything you said."

"I think she has to pay more attention because, you know, English isn't her first language. You're sounding a little jealous. Am I right?" he asked, trying to lighten the mood.

"Not really. I mean, there's part of me that would like to be that elegant, but most of me is happy just the way I am."

"And I wouldn't want you to be any other way either." Clyde reached out and squeezed her hand.

Jennie wasn't finished. "I would think almost any man would want her; it would be only natural."

"Let's not talk about that. I love you; I've always loved you. Do you doubt that?"

"No, never doubted it. Never will doubt it, Clyde. My life would have been nothing without you. You're my hero! That isn't going to change." Jennie looked deeply into Clyde's eyes and saw his love for her and his tumult.

The moment ended when a servant came in to clear off the table.

"Jennie, I have a bit more work to do before I come upstairs. I'll see you in a while." He stood up, leaned over to kiss his wife on the cheek, and left the room. He went into the library and sat at Napoleon's desk where his papers were laid out. His mind was racing along with his heart. *What does she know? How long has she known? Did she see us kissing today?* He couldn't work. Jennie was the reason for everything. No woman in the world could replace her. *What am I doing?* He sat in agony, an agony that he knew was self-inflicted. When he saw his wife start up the stairs for their bedroom, he packed his papers away into his briefcase and climbed the stairs himself.

When they were both settled in bed, Clyde turned to his wife.

"I want you to know that I could never love a woman the way I love you. We belong together. I don't love you any less because we can't have intercourse. You have always pleased me in other ways. I don't want you to worry that I would ever or could ever leave you, not for any woman, anywhere. I'll love you until the day I die, Jennie Hobbs Barbour!" They kissed and fell asleep in each other's arms.

The Christmas of 1927 was the kind of family Christmas they hadn't had in years. Jennie, Clyde, Grannie, five children, and all the grandchildren; four servants in the kitchen, a chauffeur, a butler, a nursemaid for the youngsters, and 18 men working full-time on the grounds and house. Oaklawn was alive as it had not been since Alexander Porter lived there. The very tall and full Christmas tree in the front room was surrounded by piles of gifts.

As always, Clyde worked during the holidays, not all day but many hours every day. He would close the doors into the library to minimize the endless noise. Lilly's oldest child, DeVoe, now almost two years old, appeared at his door, smiling, and he motioned to her to come in. He sat her up on his lap and pointed out the pretty things in the room. She particularly liked the pastel crystal chandelier.

Suddenly, a few of the grandsons went running down the hall and out through the back screen door, which made a very loud *bang* as it closed on its own.

"Do not slam the screen door!" he yelled after them. DeVoe, caught unawares by the loud noise and the yelling, began to cry. Clyde lowered his voice and told her it was the boys that were in trouble, not her; that he loved her, and she was fine. He held her close, patting her back and talking quietly into her ear. As he held her tight, he was suddenly overcome with the knowing that this was his Little Princess's little princess. He thought about all the times Lilly had been sick and frail, but was always smiling. He loved this little girl and would always protect her!

The Entire Barbour Family at Oaklawn Manor Around 1927
Clyde and Jennie are in the rocking chairs.
Back Row: Peggy (Lena) and Forest Lewis; Sylvia and Jesse Barbour; Emilie and Will Barbour; Flora and Clyde Barbour, Jr.; Lilly and Tom Holmes. Annie Barbour, Clyde's mother, is between Emilie and Will.

CHAPTER 42

THE CUT

January 1928

Clyde was particularly excited to finally be able to concentrate on making his mark on the maritime industry in Houston. He had spent a great deal of time researching the Houston Ship Channel and meandering around the various bayous and other waterways that intersect it. Sailing from the Gulf of Mexico to the Port of Houston and the turning basin was a 50-mile trip that took five to six hours, with many bends and a narrow channel at some points. Clyde was planning a marine terminal as big as the Port of Houston but located only 25 miles, or two and a half to three hours, from the Gulf of Mexico. That would shorten the trip by more than half with no winding channel to maneuver.

He had been buying up land around Morgans Point near the spot where Buffalo Bayou and the San Jacinto River meet Galveston Bay. He had purchased 1,435 acres so far. He was very familiar with this part of the waterway, as his Colorado Gravel Company had used sand from the sandbars located near there to make the concrete for the Galveston Causeway and other large projects nearby. This had ended in a lawsuit filed by a landowner just upstream who declared that removal of those sandbars would lead to saltwater from Galveston Bay finding its way onto his property. On his last trip to New York City, Tim Bryan had introduced Clyde to Colonel Perry, the president of Standard Dredging

Co. His company had done extensive dredging in the major ports of the U.S.. The three met in a conference room at the bank.

"Colonel Perry, Captain Barbour!" Tim announced. The men shook hands, smiling. Clyde liked him immediately.

Colonel Perry began. "Captain, I found your proposal intriguing! It's very ambitious and I don't see much on the downside."

"Thank you, Colonel. I really don't see how we could lose on this. As you can see," Clyde pointed to the map laid out on the table, "the side channel will be about two miles long, then another three miles of dock and wharf space." Clyde moved his finger along the map. "Here, at the end, is the turning basin. My thought is to put the dredge material on the north side of the channel to build it up." Clyde took a deep breath and realized that, in his excitement, he was talking too fast. "Sorry," he laughed.

"Your enthusiasm is contagious!" said Colonel Perry, smiling. "So, you've planned for dredging down to 30 feet. Will you be responsible for maintaining that depth?"

"The Houston Ship Channel was dredged to 30 feet three years ago, so, yes. The Corps of Engineers will keep our new channel dredged to 12 feet below mean low tide," Clyde answered, reveling in the birth of this new enterprise that he had no doubt would forever alter the landscape of the Port of Houston. "I've agreed to spend $1,000,000 but I know it'll exceed that. With any luck, my banker," Clyde cast a sly look at Tim Bryan, who responded with a smile, "will float me any extra cash I need over that amount!"

"You have all the land purchased?" asked the colonel.

"I've leased all submerged lands within 2,900 feet west of Morgans Point from the Navigation District. I have one holdout on purchasing the land, a Dr. Usener, who has about four acres on the water just in from the Point that he wants to charge me an exorbitant amount of money to purchase. The submerged lands in front of his property were originally part of what I leased and they're telling me that was a mistake. We're in court over it now." Clyde's frustration was evident.

"Only one lawsuit? I'd say you've done a great job if that's all!" the colonel responded.

"Riparian rights are killing me," bemoaned Clyde, which elicited a laugh from the other two men. "If you think that's funny, the port also deeded me a cemetery by accident. I know better than to mess with the spirits." They all had a good laugh, but little did they know that Clyde was being serious.

Colonel Perry was intent on the map once again. "I see the railroads over there."

"Right. In '24, the port formed the PTRA—the Port Terminal Railroad Association—so that any lines that are interested can have access to places farther south than the existing port. It's always been my goal to make it easier for the big ships to dock and easier for the railroads to meet the ships and get their cargo. I've finally got all the pieces in a row!"

"I say let's get started!" said the colonel enthusiastically.

In June, the dredging began. Clyde was doing the work under a new company name: the San Jacinto Dock & Terminal Company.

Clyde (left front), Jesse (with cigar) and an Unknown Gentleman watching the start of the dredging at Barbours Cut.
(Could it be Benjamin Casey Allin III, the First General Manager of the Port Authority or perhaps Colonel Perry of Standard Dredging?)

"Just imagine the possibilities this opens up!" said Clyde as he watched. "I've been working toward this day for 20 years!"

"Congratulations, Father, congratulations!" said Jesse as he stood with his hand on his father's shoulder, watching.

In the latest Houston Chamber of Commerce brochure, Clyde's work was mentioned. "A group of far-seeing financiers have secured possession, and entered into contracts with the Port Commission to build a harbor and turning basin much larger than the Port of Houston. Work has begun and initial expenditure of $1 million has been pledged." The port officials praised Clyde's foresightedness.

On September 25, the *Houston Press* newspaper said: "The past few months have seen the beginning of a port project that has been hailed as the greatest single step forward ever taken by any port, and one that eventually, it is estimated, will cost in the neighborhood of $15 million. CAB & Asso. are dredging a side channel at Morgans Point, near the mouth of the waterway and, when this is completed, will begin work on the installation of more than three miles of modern wharves. The channel and docks are being built on some of the lands deeded the Navigation District by the state a year or so ago and leased by the builders from the Port Commission." A lot was expected of Captain Clyde Arthur Barbour.

Clyde traveled back to Tampico on November 16 to check on his companies down there, where Jesse and Sylvia were still living with their children. Jennie stayed behind at Oaklawn with her sister, Leona.

Christmas at Oaklawn was quieter that year but just as lovely. Clyde had an etching done of the manor house and sent it out as their Christmas card. It was Clyde who felt the need for a dog out at Oaklawn. "Von," a German Shepherd, was the first of many.

In April 1929, Clyde received a telegram from someone in Corpus Christi, Texas. It had arrived at his offices in Houston, where he was hard at work on his ever-growing portfolio of companies and interests. Ruth brought it into him on the silver tray. She had opened it, as she did all his correspondence that wasn't personal, and the news was grave.

"Clyde," she said as she entered the room, "you need to see this right away."

He looked at her, saw the strain on her face, and jumped from his chair to get the telegram. It read:

I REGRET TO TELL YOU THAT YOUR BROTHER JAMES HAS DIED HE DIED OF CIRRHOSIS PLEASE INFORM AS TO WHAT WE SHOULD DO WITH HIS REMAINS

Clyde sat down heavily in his chair. *James is dead. I didn't even know where he was! His poor wife...I mean wives...I don't even know. Drank himself to death. If only I could have reached him on some level. Did I really try? Maybe it wouldn't have even mattered.*

Ruth snapped him out of his reverie. "Clyde, how do you want to respond?" She stood next to him, her hand on his shoulder. He reached for her hand and squeezed it.

"Jeffersonville. He would want to be buried in Jeffersonville next to Pa and Grandpa and Grandma and the baby, William Cilas. Please make the arrangements, Ruth; I can't bear it. Whatever it costs. I'll go up there for the funeral with my mother and whoever else wants to go. I need to go home and tell Ma. It's going to break her heart." It sounded odd to his own ears to call her Ma; she'd been Grannie for so long now. But to him and James she would always be Ma.

Clyde, Jennie, and Grannie took the train car to Jeffersonville, Indiana, to bury James. Grannie's smiles were strained, and Clyde seemed to have lost a spark. Although the place held lifelong memories for Clyde, there was no joy in being there. Some of the older people who remembered the family came to the funeral, as did a few retired workers from Howard Shipyards. Afterward, they quickly returned to Oaklawn to rest; Clyde could now work from there easily.

He had continued to have a tumultuous relationship with Leon Todd at Medford Lakes, New Jersey. Clyde had lost interest in the project and was happy when Mr. Todd agreed to buy him out. *More money for my port project*, he thought. He had also sold off about a thousand acres of undeveloped gas land on Glendora Plantation in Monroe, Louisiana, but he continued to be heavily invested in carbon black.

Jennie loved being at Oaklawn, as long as Clyde was there. It was big and lonely without him. Grannie was living there with her, and they spent most of their time there instead of in Houston, where they still had a home. The two women were sitting outside under the arbor drinking iced tea.

"Grannie, do you enjoy being out here at Oaklawn?" Jennie asked.

"Yes, I do. It's beautiful and quiet. You know, I'm in my last years of life and there's no place I'd rather live out my years than here." Grannie smiled and patted Jennie on the knee. "What about you?"

"I've never even seen a place as beautiful as Oaklawn. Living here seems almost like a dream. I just wish my children were closer; I miss them a lot!"

"But they all live in different places now. There's nowhere to live that would be close to all of them. At least at Oaklawn, they have their parents to visit as well as lots of fun things to do." Grannie sipped her iced tea.

The next day Jennie heard from her little sister, Leona. Her husband—and Clyde's cousin—Milt, had disappeared. Leona's oldest child, Cora, was living with her own family in Monroe, working in the carbon black company. Leona didn't want to intrude on them. Jennie immediately sent word for Leona to bring all her things to Oaklawn, where she was welcome to live as long as she wanted.

When Clyde heard the news, he was furious. "What is wrong with the men in this family? Pa was always disappearing from us until he finally stayed gone for years. James had wives we probably don't even know about; maybe he was married to more than one at a time. Then he drinks himself to death. Now Milt is gone, who knows where? What is it? I swear I'm embarrassed to say I'm related to these men. Please assure Leona that she is part of our family and will always be taken care of."

So, Leona moved in, which delighted Jennie to no end. The first thing she said to her little sister was, "I told you, all those years ago, in the middle of the night, that I would come back for you and always take care of you. Now, we can be together forever!" They cried and held each other.

Another problem had been plaguing Clyde's work near the Houston Ship Channel. The Texas Secretary of State, Jane Y. McCallum, had been refusing to receive and file the charter for Barbour Terminals, Inc., of Houston.

"What is she saying?" Tim Bryan asked Clyde over the phone.

"That 99 years is too long a lease and that the new Navigation District doesn't have the right to give me this lease at all! It's more complicated than that really and I'm losing my mind!" an exhausted Clyde declared. "What does she think? That the Navigation District is going to do all the needed upgrades to make this into a world-class port? That it will magically come up with the millions and millions of dollars it's going to take?"

"Surely the law is on your side."

"You would think so. I've filed an application for mandamus; now I wait," Clyde told him.

Shortly thereafter, the mandamus was awarded, and the company became official.

In early June, Clyde was thrilled to get a letter from Lilly, who wanted to invest some of her money from the sale of the house on Lorraine Blvd. in Los Angeles. She and Tom were tired of living way out in California and didn't want to put that money into a home there. She wanted to either lend Peggy's husband, Forest, money for his automobile business or to buy an interest in it. Her father didn't like that idea at all. He wrote:

"We have, as you know, the corner of Texas and Austin Streets, which cost us $225,000. We will take $25,000 of the money which you have and give you a first mortgage on this property at 6% for three years. This is considerably better than you can get out of most other things, and it is absolutely safe."

As was common when writing to his loved ones about business, he signed it, "With love and best wishes, Affectionately, C.A. Barbour" instead of the usual "Your Daddy."

Luckily, the Barbours were at Oaklawn for Memorial Day that year. Downtown Houston flooded, with the gauge at Buffalo Bayou reading 43.5 feet, the second-highest stream gauge reading on record at that time; property damage was estimated at $1.4 million. Both Buffalo Bayou and White Oak Bayou came out of their banks. Fortunately for the Barbours, their latest house in Houston, at 2120 Southmore Avenue, was largely untouched.

That was also the month the Dow Jones index reached an all-time high of 381. In the years of 1923 through 1928, the stock market had enjoyed approximately 20% growth each year. This made investing in the market an attractive proposition for even those making a modest income, especially as it had become much easier to get bank credit and loans, and buying on margin was too good to pass up. Unemployment was low and the booming auto industry helped prop up the economy. President Herbert Hoover was inaugurated in January 1929. The Hoover bull market, when stocks soared to unheard-of heights, lasted for about six months, peaking on September 3.

Investors were ecstatic; they seemed to think there was no end to their good fortune. However, Clyde was uneasy about it. Although his investment in the stock market was only a small portion of his overall wealth, he didn't want to be outsmarted by the overly optimistic attitude of most investors. He had already divested himself of his interests in Medford Lakes and those acres of undeveloped gas lands in Monroe.

"I don't like it. The stock market is too high," Clyde told Charles Kerr in his Houston office, tapping his foot nervously. "I've divested myself of some of my holdings and plan to put that money towards my port project. One thing I do know is that the country has to have ports to do business; that kind of growth is necessary regardless."

"And then you own companies in several different countries," Charles observed. "Certainly, that will help minimize any downturn. But why are you talking about downturns at this point? I'm still keen on investing in your project." Charles got up to leave.

"I've bet on you every time, Captain! I'll give serious consideration to what you just said. Maybe it really is too good to be true."

Stocks began to decline on October 18. On October 24, better known as Black Thursday, 13 million shares were traded. After a brief rebound, on Black Tuesday, October 29, 16 million shares were traded, leaving thousands of investors broke as the Dow closed that day at 230, down almost 40% from the September 3 high of 381.

Although he wasn't heavily invested in stocks, Clyde felt the impact of the market crash. All the misery surrounding him took the wind out of his sails. He retreated to Oaklawn, where he spent hours alone in the gardens. He wandered to the end of The Park and had coffee on the patio. He sat in the midst of his beautiful roses and thought. He walked down Cedar Walk and inhaled the lovely scent. He walked among his mighty live oaks, reaching up to feel the moss that offered itself up so easily. He invited friends over to play golf and for dinner, but none of it eased his mind. And he wasn't feeling well. All his trips over the years to Mineral Wells and Abita Springs to bathe in and drink the healing waters seemed to have been a waste of time. The doctor said it was his kidneys again.

"Your poor kidneys are still trying to digest that awful Mississippi River water you drank as a boy!" Jennie teased.

Clyde actually smiled. "Probably so. I have a new medicine to try. We'll see if that helps." But it didn't.

"Do you remember the mansion where we had lunch in Greenville where Dr. Worthington lived?"

"Of course, I remember. Her name was Darla, and she was determined that you were going to be hers! I had never seen anything like that place." Jenny smiled at her recollection.

"Standing in that beautiful house, I decided that I was going to live like that one day. I imagined it over and over again, my own mansion full of beautiful furniture and paintings. Now here it is, so much grander than I even imagined," Clyde said, looking around the hallway.

"I'm just glad it's me standing here with you and not Darla!"

"Me, too." They both laughed.

On New Year's Day 1930, Jennie arranged for all the family who were there to eat under the arbor at the end of the rose garden. A table was set up with Jennie's favorite china as well as the silver service Clyde had given her with the initials "O.M." on top of each other for Oaklawn Manor. It was chilly but not cold and the sun shone on them. Tucker served them boiled cabbage, black-eyed peas, and cornbread with butter.

"Thank you, Tucker. It looks like you've covered all the bases for our prosperous New Year! Be sure everyone gets some," Clyde said.

Tucker, who was a very dark-skinned Black man, had an endearing smile and was known to be the best-paid cook in Franklin. He would tell his friends he was the luckiest cook in the world to work for the Barbours, who truly cared about him and treated him with respect and dignity, as they were known to do with everyone they encountered.

Lilly and Tom were tired of living in Los Angeles so far away from their families. The stock market crash had left Tom's father, Judge Holmes, with a loss of $100,000.[3] It was devastating. Lilly and Tom decided they would move to Chicago and help Judge Holmes in his lubricating business, The Swain Company. Tom headed straight to Chicago, while Lilly and the children went to Oaklawn for a long visit.

"Mother, why is Daddy so quiet these days? Is it the crash? Are we going to be all right?" Lilly asked.

"He's not feeling good and of course he's worried about money. He said we're going to be fine, but it will be hard to find money to invest in his projects. He's putting everything he can into his port project to keep it going. That has always been one of his dreams, you know, to make Houston the biggest port in the country." Jennie smiled at her daughter. "He's getting older and he's tired; I can see it in him and feel it."

"Can't the boys help?" Lilly asked.

---

[3] $1.7 million in 2023.

"Jesse's already working hard in Tampico, and we need him there. Clyde, Jr., and your father had a quarrel, so they won't be working together for a while. And Will is still in college." Jennie spoke matter-of-factly.

"Clyde, Jr., and Daddy? What happened? It's the first I've heard of it." Lilly looked mortified.

"Well, they had an argument about how to run things in Monroe. Your father gave him the choice of doing things the way he wanted them done or leaving." Jennie's eyes were tearful. "It broke my heart!"

"Clyde, Jr., left? Moved away? Where did he go?"

"I think he's in California. He won't even talk to me."

"Mother, why didn't you tell me? That's awful!" Lilly held her mother's hand. "Maybe I can talk to him."

"I think you should leave it alone for now. He said he's tired of having his father looking over his shoulder all the time; he wants to be on his own." Jennie sighed.

Not wanting to upset her mother anymore, Lilly let it go. She could work on that later.

It took all of Clyde's faculties and more smarts than he knew he had to keep the businesses that were left from failing. His focus remained on the port, where what he had named Barbours Cut had been dredged. He recognized that as a lifeline for future sustainable income. There were now nine oil refineries operating along the Houston Ship Channel and the Port of Houston was now ranked third in the United States for foreign export.

Clyde was ecstatic that his name would be forever a part of the Port of Houston. *Half the travel time from the Gulf of Mexico to offload ships; just think about how much time and money the shorter route will save, and those kinds of savings ripple through the entire economy.*

Jennie's only question was why there was no apostrophe in "Barbours Cut." Clyde explained that it was the maritime naming convention.

And there was still carbon black. He needed to travel to Europe to be sure things were being properly handled in the dire financial situation most of the world found itself in. Travel was the last thing he wanted to do. The trip seemed more than he could take on in his present state of health, but he had no choice.

He decided to wait and tell Jennie about the trip after the big Mother's Day party they were planning at Oaklawn on Sunday, May 11. There would be 19 couples. This wasn't going to be just another Mother's Day. Clyde had decided to have a gathering of loved ones because he needed it and so did they. They all needed something to look forward to. He wanted to express his gratitude, knowing he wouldn't have made it so far without the help and cooperation of others. He also knew they needed to stick together to make it through, and he wanted all of them to feel there was hope in the midst of the darkness they were surrounded by.

That Sunday, the guests arrived in the morning, stayed for lunch, and then spent most of the afternoon enjoying the many activities at Oaklawn. There was, of course, a golf game, and a few people floated around in the pool. At one point, Clyde gathered them all for a trip down Bayou Teche on a sternwheeler.

Luncheon was beautifully served *en plein aire*, beneath the oak trees. The white linen tablecloths fluttered in the soft breezes. The tables were set with the formal Oaklawn Manor china and silver flatware. The Baccarat crystal glasses reflected prisms on the table and the rose centerpieces, all picked from the garden, added a velvety softness to the tablescape.

Once bread pudding had been served for dessert, Clyde stood up to address his guests.

"What a perfect day for a picnic! Thank you for coming to celebrate all our mothers, especially my own mother and my Jennie, who's been the most wonderful mother to our children. On days like this, we celebrate things that are truly meaningful to us as a family, as a community, and as a nation. Even though we're suffering through these extremely trying times since the market crash, we're here together, able to enjoy this beautiful day. I want to toast to all of you; that the good fortune, hard work, and the grace of God that have gotten us this far will continue to grace us. We must also pray for all of those whose lives have been altered for the worse; I know all of us will do everything we can to help lighten their load. And lastly, I want to say 'Welcome!' to my latest grandchild, John David Barbour, born to my eldest son, Jesse, and his wife, Sylvia." Everyone clapped and Clyde sat down to enjoy his dessert.

The gathering seemed to touch everyone there. Both Jennie and Clyde felt it deep down inside. It was not a feeling of triumph or relief at having dodged as big a bullet as they had, but rather a sense of warmth, understanding, and belonging. Clyde had a photograph taken in the front of Oaklawn Manor with the signatures of the men who attended at the bottom of the page. Directly underneath the photograph was printed:

A TOKEN OF MY APPRECIATION OF YOUR VISIT
TO OAKLAWN MANOR, MOTHER'S DAY,
SUNDAY, MAY THE ELEVENTH,
NINETEEN HUNDRED AND THIRTY

CORDIALLY YOURS

It was such a memorable occasion that the story of that day was passed down by word of mouth for generations within the Barbour family.

The next month, Clyde was working at his office in Houston. The volume of mail had increased substantially every day since the market crash; letters from people needing loans, or jobs, or wanting to sell what was left of their businesses. It was all bad news; nothing inspiring or exciting crossed his desk. *If only I could shake this feeling of foreboding,* he thought. *I have created a sizable fortune for my family; I have to sustain it somehow. I can do this. I want to do this. I must do this.*

The next envelope he came to bore the return address "Columbia Sugar Company," which was part of the old Columbia Plantation just up the road from Oaklawn. Clyde opened it and read the letter from John Caffery, whose family had owned Columbia for a long time.

It was a full-page letter proposing the details for how they would work together in the upcoming harvest season. There was nothing special or unusual about the letter except its banality. It was simply basic market forces at work, allocating resources and negotiating to find an agreeable price and striking a deal. A smile cracked Clyde's serious demeanor. It was just so ordinary, so everyday. It was a tiny reminder that even with the world falling under the spell of the Great Depression, so much would still go on the way it always had. He felt a calm that had been evading him. He would relish that feeling for as long as he could.

Jennie Barbour Standing Under the Arbor in the Rose Garden, Oaklawn Manor.

CHAPTER 43

THE CONTRADICTIONS

J ennie kept trying to talk Clyde out of going to Europe. His answer was, of course, to invite her to go with him. That had never worked before, and it didn't work this time. Clyde had long ago given up hope of Jennie joining him on his trips overseas, so he wasn't surprised.

"Jennie, my sweet, I have some kidney problems; it's not dire. The doctors in Europe are as well trained as any we have in our country. If something happens, I'll be well taken care of. Now stop worrying." Clyde kissed her on her forehead.

"Even if I went with you, I wouldn't know what to do if you got sick in some faraway country," Jennie protested. "I know! Take a nurse with you, one that speaks some of those languages. I would feel much happier knowing somebody was there who could really help." She was smiling and excited about her latest idea.

Clyde was silent for a minute, then shook his head. "If that will put your mind at ease, I'll see what I can do. I'll call some people in New York."

Clyde was a master at hiding his medical issues from his wife. They were sporadic and involved a myriad of symptoms, making it difficult for him to take them seriously. The problem was that they were becoming more frequent. He felt tired a lot of the time and had difficulty getting a good night's rest, which would then affect his focus.

Nausea came and went, but that could have many causes. When he passed a kidney stone, the doctor wasn't surprised. Clyde was a good patient, if a secretive one, and followed the doctor's orders.

He traveled with his nurse, Miss Appleby. She was from Germany and had learned the European languages in school growing up. Now 50 years old, she had worked as a private nurse for 20 years. Clyde promised her plenty of free time, and with a trip to Germany on their itinerary, she was thrilled. They sailed to Southampton, where they landed on July 22, 1930, and were met by the Hewletts. Being accustomed to working with people of means, Miss Appleby kept herself out of sight much of the time. Clyde was full of stories and photos of his beloved Oaklawn, which Mr. Hewlett had already visited. The others were in awe, with Mr. Hewlett there to back up the stories with his personal knowledge.

For the first time, Clyde did his best to hurry his trip. He had a sense of foreboding that he couldn't shake. Fatigue and nausea were haunting him. Miss Appleby did a good job of getting him to eat the right foods, take his medicine, and get some exercise, and he very much appreciated the cooler temperatures.

After a quick trip to Manchester to visit Clyde's offices there, they sailed to Calais on July 26. They took the train to Paris, which held so many fond memories of being there with Lilly. He missed her soft, smiling face and good nature, not to mention the adoration he couldn't help but feel that she had for him. *I pray that she's happy,* he thought. He met with his employees there before they were off to Germany on July 30, where Miss Appleby visited her family. Clyde let her stay there while he traveled on to Italy to visit his other office and to see Opal.

They met in Milan at the end of July. It had been a year since their paths had crossed in New York. A lot had happened since then. Clyde was sitting in the parlor of their suite reading the paper when Opal made her unmistakable dramatic entrance followed by several trunks being carried by the porters. Clyde pointed the way to her room for her luggage, tipped the porters, and locked the door behind them when they left. He turned to see Opal, her hat sitting on the coffee table, hands on her hips, smiling like the Cheshire Cat. He walked over to her, placed his hand under her chin, and lifted her face for a long, luxurious kiss.

"You look like a beautiful, sexy temptress who has a whole list of things she has planned!" Clyde smiled and grabbed her, holding her close.

"*Mais, oui*, Monsieur, I have many good ideas!" she teased. "But you look so tired, *mon amour*." She looked into his eyes and rubbed his shoulder. "We should relax, *non?*" She led him to the couch, where they sat close together, holding hands.

"I ordered coffee to be sent up as soon as you arrived. I know how much you love your coffee." There was a knock, and Clyde went to the door where the waiter was standing with a tray of coffee and accoutrements which were put on the coffee table. The two sat together enjoying their tête-à-tête as usual. He had noticed a large diamond ring on her finger but waited for her to bring it up.

"…and I surprised." She stopped talking to fix another cup of coffee. "I think you see *ma bague*, I mean my ring. Isn't it beautiful?" She held her hand out, displaying a large square-cut diamond surrounded by smaller round ones.

"Yes, *c'est magnifique!*" answered Clyde in his thick American French accent, making Opal laugh. "Should I ask who gave it to you?"

"Of course. I am to be married next year! Isn't that excellent?" She moved her hand around to better display her new prize.

"I had no idea. It's wonderful! You deserve some man's full attention. I'm very happy for you!" Clyde answered sincerely. He took both her hands in his and kissed them. "I really am!"

"*Oui*, I can see in your eyes. He is not so clever a man as you, but I love him, and he wants to give me the world. I think it's time," she stated emphatically.

"Shall we toast your marriage then?" Clyde raised his coffee cup and they clicked their cups together, laughing heartily, and drank to her happiness.

After their coffee, Clyde felt unsure as to how to proceed. Did her engagement end their tryst? Should he grab her hand and lead her into his bedroom? He decided to wait and let her take the lead.

"I should first like to have a bath; will you join me?" she asked coyly.

"Absolutely!" he added with fervor. His fatigue did not stop him from being the generous, unselfish lover she knew him to be, and her engagement did not stop her from giving him her all.

They spent two nights together in Milan before Clyde needed to get to Florence. Opal was on her way to Rome for a performance and traveled with him for a two-night stay in *Firenze.* He loved the old Italian style of painting and had been in touch with an art gallery at Piazza Pitti, 21–22, which the lovers visited together. Clyde bought five paintings and gilt frames to hang in Oaklawn for a total of 1,665 Italian lira.

"Your shop is fabulous!" Clyde declared to the owner as the three of them ate dinner together that evening. "Oaklawn is the perfect place to show off these Italian treasures!" Clyde showed the man photos of Oaklawn only after he had purchased the paintings, feeling the prices might otherwise be inflated.

"I have never seen such a home in America," he said, "furnished with such taste and beauty!" Clyde felt the swell of pride.

The day they parted, Opal was wearing the opal pin he had given her. He noticed and was sure to put on his opal lapel pin as well. They drove together to the train station, where they were to board separate trains. He rubbed her pin and put her hand on his opal. The ride there was quiet. Clyde wondered if they'd ever be together again; he wanted very much to know that they would be.

"My dear Opal," Clyde said as he took her hands in his, "I hope you know that I wish you every happiness in your marriage, and I'll understand if that means we won't see each other again." He kissed her hands and looked into her eyes.

"Oh, *mon Dieu*, Clyde. He will have his own *amants* as we French do. You and me, we will always be!" Opal released her hands and placed them on Clyde's cheeks. She kissed him and turned to walk away.

"You and me will always be; it rhymes like a poem! I will have to write it down." Clyde tipped his hat to her and she was gone.

Miss Appleby met Clyde in Lyon, France, on his way to Cherbourg to catch the boat there on August 13.

"Captain Barbour, I can see that you have missed several of your pills. I hope you were more careful with the foods you ate than you were with remembering to take your medicine. And your feet look swollen." She was fussing around him, making him feel at once cared for and scolded. "I will not take my eyes off you for the rest of our trip!" And she didn't.

A few weeks after his return, Clyde was surprised to hear that his friend, Will Hogg of Houston, had died in Europe while on vacation with his sister. They were members of many of the same clubs and had worked together on the Houston Museum of Fine Arts. His family had a beautiful mansion on Buffalo Bayou in Houston named Bayou Bend where Jennie and Clyde had been guests many times. He was a year younger than Clyde and seemed such a robust character that it was difficult to imagine he was gone. It hit Clyde hard, took his breath away. When he saw Jennie later, she asked if he'd heard the news.

"Yes, I have. It's unbelievable, really."

"Oh, Clyde, if that had been you...I can't think about it!" She hugged her husband tightly, her eyes filling with tears.

"Well, it wasn't me, I'm right here! Imagine all they had to figure out to get his body back to Houston. I wonder when the funeral will be?"

There were many honorary pallbearers at the funeral, and Clyde was proud to be one of them.

In December of 1930, United Carbons announced year-end net earnings of $1,314,000. There were now 31 carbon black plants in Texas, of which Clyde had a large share. These Texas plants produced 210,878,000 pounds, or 75%, of the U.S. output. That, added to his other carbon black holdings, helped him to keep his title as the King of Carbon Black around the world.

On January 12, 1931, their longtime friend Eugene Pharr died.

"He was only sick for three days before he died," Jennie told Clyde over the phone. He was in Houston. "Jesse and Sylvia are here and are going to pay their respects for us. I feel awful!" She was sniffling into the telephone.

"Good, I'm glad they're at Oaklawn. I can't get there for the funeral." Clyde's heart sank as he thought of one of his oldest friends, who had taught him so much. "I'll have Ruth send flowers."

"No, don't do that. I'd like to do that from here. Such a sad day."

When Clyde got off the phone, he called for Ruth to come in. "Close the door, please," he said.

"Ruth, please sit down with me. I've thought and thought about this, and after the news of my good friend's sudden death, I feel I need to start conducting all my business from Oaklawn. I'm so fatigued all the time; I can't keep up. I'm going to build an airstrip across the bayou, so if I have to go somewhere, I can fly, which will be so much easier for me." He looked over at Ruth whose face was blank, her eyes searching. "Ruth. I'm not leaving you. I hope you'll accept my offer to continue to run this office and to come to Oaklawn several days a week to help me with my business from there. Or maybe one week here and one week there to mitigate some of the travel." Ruth remained silent. "Ruth? Are you all right?"

She took in a deep breath and let it out slowly. She looked away from him as she gathered her thoughts. "Clyde, of course. Of course, I'll do whatever you need me to do. I owe you everything!" Her hollow look turned into a tortured grimace as tears began to fall down her cheeks.

Clyde stood up and went over to where she was sitting on the other side of the large desk. He pulled her up to standing and held her in his arms, rocking back and forth. He took his handkerchief out of his pocket and wiped her cheeks with it. "Ruth, my dear Ruth. We've been together a long time. Even my family doesn't know all the things about me and my business that you know. You've been instrumental in my success; you know that, don't you?" he asked, looking into her eyes. "I want you to know that I have put a fund of $50,000[4] in your name. It's yours to do with what you want. I want you to have this in reserve, so you won't have to worry about money." He walked to the other side of the desk and took out an envelope with her name on it and handed it to her. "Here it is."

Ruth watched as he handed her the envelope. She saw her name on it. She couldn't move. "No, Clyde, I won't take it. What we have shared has nothing to do with money. Your generosity is unequaled, but no." She tried to give the envelope back to Clyde, who wouldn't take it.

"Surely you don't think this is some sort of payment for all that you shared with me! That's not what it is; you know that. It's because I love you that I want you to have this. If you like, think of it as a bonus given to my most trusted adviser. I won't let you say no." He walked to the door and locked it, walked back to her and, taking her hand, led her to the couch. "Come lie with me." They lay down together with nothing between them, not even air. He felt the pounding of her heart and heard her sniffles. Tears came to his eyes as well. This was not the time for making love. They kissed long and hard until a knock broke their trance.

"Just a minute," Clyde called. They stood up and helped each other transition back to reality. "I want you to go downstairs to the bank right now and make an account with that money." He kissed her quickly and went to sit down in the chair at his desk.

Ruth smiled at him, folded the envelope, and put it into her pocket. "Thank you so much. It means the world to me, as do you." She walked to answer the door.

The winter was long, wet, and dreary. What began as Clyde's afternoon nap slowly turned into half the day spent in bed. Jennie had hired Miss Appleby to stay at Oaklawn to care for Clyde, although he felt that was quite unnecessary. The blooming roses that spring gave a temporary lift to Clyde's spirits. Miss Appleby would have him walk

---

[4] Approximately $870,000 in 2023.

to the arbor every day to try to ease the swelling in his legs and ankles. By the end of April, that had become too far for him to walk.

Clyde knew what was happening to him. He'd had very frank conversations with his doctor. "We will do everything possible; you know that, Captain, but there's nothing we can do to stop the progression of your kidney disease. Your swelling is the excess fluid your kidneys can't handle. If too much fluid collects around your heart, well, that will pretty much be that."

After that conversation, Clyde sat at Napoleon's desk in the library and started making plans. He would divest himself of some of his holdings so there would be plenty of cash in reserve. He would have to be sure Jennie was taken care of...always. On May 1, it was announced that his Carbons Consolidated had been sold to the Carbon Black Production Corp., which was a subsidiary of Appalachian Gas Company of New York. He did the same thing with his New Process Carbon Black Company; he received $200,000 for that piece.

Next, he wrote a goodbye letter to Opal, tears in his eyes. He enclosed a check.

Mon amour,

I'm sitting at Napoleon's desk in my library at Oaklawn, looking at the tapestry hanging on the wall. It reminds me of you and all our happy times together. I see your flirtatious smile and grow warm all over. Thank you for being a beautiful light in my life. The doctor tells me I won't be around much longer. I wanted to be sure you know how much our time together has meant to me. Please take this token of my love and hide it away for a rainy day. When you think of me, be sure to smile and imagine me smiling back!

Je t'aime, Clyde

By the beginning of June, Clyde was spending an hour or so at his desk working, the rest of the day spent in bed. He was working to endow Oaklawn with $1,000,000[5] in government bonds to provide funds for its perpetual upkeep. He had Jennie taken care of, now he

---

[5] Approximately $17.5 million in 2023.

wanted to do the same for his beloved Oaklawn. It was while he was working on this at his desk that he collapsed back into the chair and was taken upstairs to his sickroom. He fell asleep right away and awoke to Jennie sitting next to him.

"That's strange. One minute I was working at my desk and the next minute I wake up in my bed. Miss Appleby, please bring me all that paperwork from my desk. I have to finish that." His voice was strained but clear.

"I don't think you'll be doing any more work today," the nurse answered sternly. Clyde had learned that arguing with her was a waste of his time.

"Okay, okay," Clyde answered, irritated. "Then how about a nice glass of wine?" They all laughed.

For the next two weeks, Jennie spent most of her days sitting with Clyde. He became less and less responsive. Then, on an ordinary day, in an ordinary month, Clyde had a heart attack and was unresponsive. Jennie called all the children to come to Oaklawn at once. It was the middle of June.

OAKLAWN MANOR, FRANKLIN, LA.

Oaklawn Manor Postcard

CHAPTER 44

THE ENDING

When Lilly and her children finally made it to Oaklawn from Chicago, she ran up the stairs and stopped at the entrance to the room where her father was lying. She clung to her mother, who met her at the doorway. The two cried together.

"Now Lilly, we have to stop crying. We don't know if he can hear us." Jennie took her daughter's hand and led her into the front bedroom.

Clyde was lying propped up on his side and seemed fast asleep. Lilly touched his shoulder and said, "Hi, Daddy. I'm finally here! I'm so glad to see you!" Her voice trembled as she spoke. "The children are here, too. They'll be up to see you later." Clyde opened his eyes as if responding to the presence of his Little Princess but did not look at her or say even one word. Jennie motioned for Lilly to sit in the chair next to the bed. Once seated, she looked up at her mother, not knowing what to do.

"Just talk to him. Rub his back. All that matters is that you're here next to him." Jennie did a good job of putting on a shaky smile. "And I need you here more than he does!" She left Lilly in the room, Miss Appleby reading in the corner next to the windows.

The light shone through the windows, brightening up the sickroom. Jennie had drawn the glass curtains back before leaving the room. Two sets of French doors leading onto the small front balcony with its wrought-iron balustrade stood directly across from his bed. Clyde's beloved live oak trees spread their branches in every direction and a patch of blue was barely visible above the trees. A white cloud or two lingered in the distance.

To the right of his bed were two tall windows with a light-gray marble mantelpiece between them. Lilly gazed up at the crystal chandelier as it caught a glimmer of sunshine and sparkled brilliantly.

Clyde's eye had also caught the glimmer and his mind dredged up a memory of Lilly's wedding. *Oh Lilly, how I will miss your sparkling eyes and the way you look at someone you love! Why can't I speak and move?* As he lay there, his thoughts often went back to his flatboat days. Sometimes he thought about all his trips to Europe, and other times he couldn't stop thinking about all his businesses and what was going to become of them. Even in light of his great success, he was achingly disappointed. What had happened to his sons? Jesse was the only one who listened to him and followed his advice, working side by side. Clyde, Jr., was lazy, and Will seemed to live in his own world where nothing was serious.

Who is going to run the family businesses? I don't think even Jesse can do it all by himself. It's taking all I have to run it in this environment. How did I let this happen? Clyde was distraught. *What's going to happen to Jennie and our children and Ma, without me? I should have spent more time at home and taken more time off. I could have made less money and been there for my family and raised my sons to follow in my footsteps and build on what I've created; as it is, there's no one to take over. I started with nothing and created all of this; my sons started with everything and take all of this for granted. Think how far they could go from here if they only had the desire, like Tommy.*

Despite all of Pa's faults, at least he taught us everything we needed to be successful in the world he brought us into. I didn't do that for my boys. He did me a favor being so hard on me. It prepared me for this life. But then Pa spent just as much time with James as he did me, and we turned out to be so different; maybe spending more time with my boys wouldn't really have helped much at all. Maybe there's only so much someone can do to change a person's true nature.

How can Jennie be such a wonderful wife and mother, yet be so afraid of life outside our family? What happened to my free-spirited Jennie Hobbs, who was brave enough to defy her father and run away from home? Did her true nature change? Was it something I did or something I didn't do? If she hadn't been so afraid to travel with me, and if Jennie and I had been able to continue to have a full sex life, then maybe I wouldn't have been with Opal? But that wouldn't have stopped me from straying with Ruth. Does Jennie know I did the unforgivable? It's all my fault. I'm just a weak man. Was it my ego that led me down that path, too big for my own britches? Is it possible that in some ways I was even worse than James? I wasn't even true to the one person I love more than anything, Jennie, my sweet Jennie.

It's like Luke told me—there's more than one way to be a slave. I've been a slave to my ambition and my ego. Jennie's a slave to her fears. Clyde, Jr., and Will are slaves to wealth and privilege. Pa and James were slaves to alcohol. We think we have free will, but in reality, we're all slaves to something. Maybe that's part of the true nature of all of us.

Every morning, Lilly went out to the rose garden, cut a fresh rose, and pinned it on her dress. She would stand at her father's side, lean over, and put the rose up to his nose and rub the soft petals on his cheek. "It's from your garden, Daddy! Isn't it lovely?" Every day she got no response. But one day, when she walked into the sickroom, she could just barely hear him say to his wife, "I love you, Jennie; you have always been by my side." Lilly turned around and went outside to cry. Those were the last words Clyde ever spoke.

Peggy arrived with her son not long after Lilly. Jennie had hired a woman they called Nursie to take care of the children. She was a godsend for the two sisters, relieving them of the need to be concerned with their offspring at such a time. Lilly and Peggy differed on whether their children should see their grandfather on his sickbed. Eventually, they each came, one at a time for a brief moment. They were told he was very sick and sleeping.

Clyde's German Shepherd, Von, was on the front porch one day and began howling. No one could get him to stop. Only Jesse, who had always had a dog since they lived in Franklin as children, could sometimes calm the dog and quiet him. Jesse and Sylvia had come up from Tampico, Mexico. There was no sign of Clyde, Jr.

Days later when Clyde, Jr., did arrive, Jesse got his brothers together in the smoker to discuss how to move forward with the businesses and how to be sure their mother was taken care of without the captain to guide them through this new reality.

Because it was the end of June, Lilly and Peggy were on the back sleeping porch hoping to catch a breeze as they tried to sleep. Clyde had been in a coma for about two weeks. Sometime after 11 p.m., Lilly awoke to the sound of soft singing coming from the garden. She shook her sister.

"Peggy, listen. Do you hear the singing?" Lilly asked her slumbering sister.

"Yes, I hear it. What is it?" she asked as she began to wake up. "It sounds like hymns."

"I don't know. The colored people certainly wouldn't be out at night in the garden," Lilly responded. "Oh no, oh no, oh no, Peggy. It's Daddy. It has to be Daddy. He's gone!" The sisters held tightly to each other and sobbed. Walking inside to the sickroom would only confirm what they were already afraid of. Then the loud sobs of their mother reached their ears, and they ran to her.

The nurse was leaving the room as they entered. Jennie was shaking and sobbing as she leaned over him, her chest resting on his. "He's gone," she sobbed. "He's gone." The sisters went to the other side of the bed to touch their father and comfort their mother.

The doctor walked in and stood next to Jennie. "There are no words that are right to say at this moment; none that will make you feel any better, but the truth is, Captain Barbour was the most remarkable man most of us have ever met. He will be remembered for his kindness and generosity for a very long time. I'm very sorry, Mrs. Barbour." He patted Jennie's back, then pulled her back to sit in the chair. "What can I do for you?" he asked Jennie.

Jennie sat blankly, tears flowing down her cheeks in torrents. "I just need a few minutes alone with my husband, please," she managed to say in words that were almost inaudible.

"Of course. Ladies? Let's leave them alone. Come with me." The doctor gathered the sisters and walked out of the room with them, closing the door behind.

Jennie sat in stupefied silence. She couldn't move her neck or even see. She forgot who she was, where she was, why she was. She finally looked out the window and into the darkness. *I don't want to look down,* she thought. *If I don't look, it isn't true, not yet.* But she did look down upon her lover, husband, best friend, and lifelong companion and saw his eyes closed so lightly. She ran her hands over his cheeks and forehead and smoothed his hair flat. She felt completely empty and emotionless. She got onto the bed and lay next to him, draping her leg and arm across his solid body. She nestled her face in his shoulder. She smelled his essence on his neck and kissed it. *I won't move from this spot,* she thought. *I will stay here with him forever.* She closed her eyes and lay perfectly still, her back to the closed door.

Jennie's mind went to memories of their sitting on top of the flatboat, Clyde reading to her. There was Grandpa playing his fiddle on top of the lopsided boat. She saw the explosion that killed Luke and then saw his son, Man, as a child who didn't want to leave his dying mother. There was the transition to life on the sternwheelers, which had seemed so luxurious after the confines of the flatboat. She saw the Little Yellow House in Franklin on Iberia Street and their five children she so cherished and almost gave her life for during childbirth. Their beautiful houses in Houston that made her feel like a queen. She would gladly have traded all their worldly possessions for more time with Clyde, who was away so often on business. *And now that Oaklawn is finally ours, now what? What happens now? I don't know what to do!* She started crying again, but this time more softly, although her body convulsed with emotion.

The doctor quietly opened the door and walked in, followed by Jesse. Jesse's face was covered with tears, the flow of which increased when he saw his mother lying there next to his deceased father. The doctor spoke. "Jennie? It's time to go. Jesse's here with me. We're going to take you into your bedroom to rest. I'll take care of the captain."

Jennie didn't move.

"Mother. Come with me. You need some rest. There's a lot we have to do." Jesse was trying so very hard to stop crying.

"I can't. I just can't leave him," she responded. She heard someone else enter her room.

"Mrs. Barbour? The captain is already with our Lord; he's no longer here. It is only his body that's left on this earth." She could tell it was their preacher, Reverend James McCormack. "He will always be with you, no matter where you are." He put his hand on her shoulder and prayed.

"Eternal rest grant unto them, O Lord, and let perpetual light shine upon them. May the souls of all the faithful departed, through the mercy of God, rest in peace."

He was able to get her to her feet, and Jesse held her up as she kissed Clyde one last time on his now-cold lips.

"I love you, Clyde Arthur Barbour; I always have, and I always will. I hope I'll be with you in Heaven soon, my sweetheart." Jesse held her around her waist and led her out of the bedroom. As she walked through the doorway, she looked back one last time.

Clyde's body was laid in an open casket in the downstairs hallway. People from all over the country and even Europe came to pay their respects. The people walked in the front door, passed the casket, and then exited through the back door. Most of those people shed tears as they looked around at the beauty he had created in Oaklawn, only to die so soon afterward. The people of Franklin felt that Captain Barbour had saved a monument in Oaklawn Manor, as he had their whole town, which he had helped to keep alive during these desperate times, fulfilling his lifelong dream of owning it.

When it was time to close the casket, the preacher was there with Jennie, as were all the Barbour children and Clyde's mother, Grannie. They each took a turn saying goodbye to their father, Jennie being the last. They all backed away, leaving Jennie, Grannie, and Reverend McCormack still standing by the casket. Grannie was holding Jennie's hand tightly until Jennie extricated her hand to touch what was left of her husband one last time. *He's so cold and so stiff,* she thought, *and it doesn't really look like him. I know it's not really him, but still I can't let go!* The preacher took her hands from Clyde's body and held them in his, after which he said a brief prayer. He kept her hands in his and held them tightly as the top of the casket was lowered. Jennie nearly fainted.

About an hour later, Jennie had recovered somewhat, and they proceeded to the cemetery in town where the Barbour mausoleum already stood, empty, waiting to receive its namesake. Little had Clyde known when he had Mr. Morris build the mausoleum that he would be the first occupant. The casket was in the hearse and several large black cars behind it carried the Barbour family members. All the young ones were left at home. The cortège started off at Oaklawn Manor and began the six-mile drive to the Methodist Church in town. As soon as they turned onto the main road, they saw people lining the side of the road to pay tribute to the man they had come to know as Captain Clyde.

"Look!" said Lilly, who was seated in the car with her mother. "Look at all the people!" As they made their way slowly down Irish Bend Road, there were people all along the way, many of them plantation people, many of them people who had worked putting Oaklawn back together. It continued all the way to the church.

As numb as Jennie was, her heart skipped with the realization, the knowledge, that her husband would be remembered for his kindness and compassion. That would mean everything to her Clyde.

The church was filled to capacity, overflowing outside. Oaklawn was overwhelmed with floral arrangements that had arrived from all over. The church was full of them as well. Afterward, when they arrived at the bright-white marble mausoleum, even more flowers were waiting, so many that they had to be placed at quite a distance to leave room for the mourners. All the members of the Franklin Masonic Lodge, of which Clyde had long been a member, attended, as did many of his fellow Shriners from Houston. Jennie was so thankful for the chair in which she could sit and not have to rely on her legs to hold her up. Their three sons, two sons-in-law, and Mr. Kerr were the pallbearers with honorary pallbearer, their banker, F.M. Law.

Jennie sat looking around at the people. The words being spoken had no meaning for her but were soft and comforting, like a lullaby that pacifies the infant who understands not one word. She noticed an almost sickening scent of flowers coming from the hundreds, probably thousands of flowers surrounding them, basking in the hot sun. She was finally brave enough to look over at the mausoleum and saw Clyde's casket sitting inside the edifice. Having laid eyes on it, she could scarcely look away. *Where will the casket go? Where will he rest?* She hadn't thought to ask anyone and knew nothing herself about such burial places. She looked up and stared at the name engraved into the marble over the doorway, BARBOUR. She noticed a four-leaf clover on either side of the letters; she hadn't realized they were there. The luck of the Irish. He had certainly been lucky at most everything in his life, except for his health.

When the service was over and people began to leave, Jennie sat tight. None of the entreaties to get her back into the car were even acknowledged. She held her ground silently, obviously not ready to leave the gravesite. Lilly and Jesse stayed with her, walking up to the casket with her and then stepping away to give her some privacy. They pretended not to hear her talking to their father as she rubbed the casket. "Please don't leave me! Please come to me tonight so I know you're with me. Please Clyde, please!" She took one of the roses from the arrangement on top of the casket, turned around, and headed to the car.

As they drove back to Oaklawn, Jennie's head was filled with important questions that needed to be addressed, but by whom? *What happens now? How will I get any money? How will I take care of Oaklawn? Who's in charge? Where do I start?* She had no idea of all the pieces that made up their lives or even where to begin.

When Jennie woke up the next morning, she had no desire, no reason to get up. She cried silently, holding her head in her hands. She rolled over onto her side and looked at her bedside table. She blinked several times, rubbed her eyes, and looked again. The night before she had placed the green and white Ice Water pitcher on her bedside table. It was such a simple reminder of all the wonderful homes he had provided for her. She saw it again, sitting right next to the pitcher—a coin; no, it was *their* coin, the one they had traded back and forth throughout their lives. Jennie was certain it hadn't been there the night before. She hadn't seen it in years. She sat up in bed. She stared at it again, then picked it up to make sure it was real. She looked all around the room, half expecting Clyde to come out from hiding.

"How did it get here?" she asked out loud. She held it in her hands, rubbing it, then held it to her cheeks and smelled it. She kissed it over and over and began to cry again, but this time with an understanding that Clyde really was still there, just as he had promised. She vowed never to tell anyone about this.

Jennie got dressed and insisted on being driven to the mausoleum. When she arrived, she saw the marble front on the uppermost drawer to the left, behind which she had been told was Clyde's casket. She had to stretch up high so she could stroke the marble cover. She talked to him as if he were sitting there in front of her and even smiled at one point as if he'd said something amusing. She assured him that she'd received the coin, drawing it out of her pocket and holding it up to the front of the marble drawer behind which his casket now rested. When she was ready, she walked to the car and was driven back to Oaklawn. She made her special pilgrimage every day for months and thereafter several times a week. People in Franklin became accustomed to seeing her there, talking to Clyde, and felt deep sorrow and love for her. They, too, missed the captain.

THE END

Captain Clyde Arthur Barbour Enjoying his Favorite
Resting Spot at Oaklawn Manor 1930

ABOUT THE AUTHOR

I was born in New Orleans, Louisiana. When I was nine years old, I moved with my family to Europe, where my father worked in the oil industry. We spent five wonderful years there. It was the old Europe, where every country had its distinct character. I learned French and gained an appreciation for people from very different cultures. I have traveled extensively throughout my life, which I have found to be a great help to me in my writing.

My first memory of writing for my own enjoyment was when I was 10 and living in The Hague, and I've been at it ever since. I was fortunate to have English teachers my entire academic career who encouraged my writing. In my home, you will find many boxes filled with my old journals, poems, short stories, and more.

After graduating from college, I moved to Washington, D.C. to work on Capitol Hill and at the White House in the Office of Communications where I helped formulate ways to explain to the American public the intricacies of a new expansive project. My entrepreneurial mindset led me to try my hand in several areas before settling into the garment industry where I designed and sold fashionable maternity clothes in a market with few choices, under my own label, Nancy Potter, Houston.

I have a son who was born with a rare genetic skin disease called Epidermolysis Bullosa (often referred to as E.B.). A defect in his keratin gene caused him to lose nearly half of his skin while being born and then to produce hundreds of blisters every day, which had to be lanced and bandaged over the course of many years. He could scarcely be touched, as the slightest contact could tear off his skin. He even had blisters in his mouth, which necessitated having a feeding tube inserted into his stomach when he was just a few days old; he lived with the feeding tube for four years. He required 24-hour care, which I provided. Out of his many years of pain, I learned to marvel at the least little thing he could accomplish, and to have great compassion for those with special needs. To aid in raising awareness and funds for research into this dreadful disease, I put on the first-ever major fundraisers for E.B. in the 1990s at what was then The Ritz-Carlton Hotel in Houston, Texas, and I continue to work to bring awareness to the disease. Please consider helping at www.debra.org. At 31 years old, my son is doing well!

My debut novel, *Barbours Cut*, is based on the life of my great-grandfather, Captain Clyde A. Barbour, whose exceptional rags-to-riches life continues to be an inspiration to all who know of him. Born in 1874, he was instrumental in the development of Houston, especially the Houston Ship Channel, a portion of which bears his name today, Barbours Cut, that includes Barbours Terminal.

The process of writing this novel began in 1985, when I recorded interviews that I conducted with my maternal grandparents; my grandmother was Captain Barbour's daughter, Lilly. Lilly's story is the basis of my next novel, which I have already begun to write.

My home is brimming with memorabilia pertaining to *Barbours Cut*, some of which dates back to the late 1800s. This memorabilia was indispensable to me in writing this novel, as it greatly helped me bring the scenes and the characters to life.

Publishing *Barbours Cut* after all these years has brought me great joy, and it is my wish that you enjoy reading this entertaining and inspirational rags-to-riches story beginning on a flatboat on the Mississippi River and ending in boardrooms across the U.S. and abroad.

Please consider donating to debra of America today!

debra of America

What is debra of America?

Because the cost of doing nothing is too great. This axiom defines debra of America's mission and directs all that we do. We are dedicated to improving the quality of life for those living with **EB**. To achieve our mission, we do two things in parallel: we provide free programs and services to the **EB** Community in the US and fund the most innovative research directed at symptom relief and a systemic cure.

In 2022 alone, our largest program, the Wound Care Distribution Program, sent over **$1 Million worth of specialized bandages**. *That translates to over 108,000 pieces of wound care sent to families across the US.* Our research funding identified the genetic basis of **EB** and supports the science, which is at the forefront of gene and stem cell therapy, RNA repair, protein replacement, and inhibition of squamous cell carcinoma.

debra of America

debra of America | www.debra.org
P: 212-868-1573 x102 **Toll-Free:** 833-debraUS
We fight "the worst disease you've never heard of"

SPENCER'S STORY

WHAT IS EB?

My son was born with Epidermolysis Bullosa, or **EB**, which is a rare connective tissue disorder with many genetic and symptomatic variations. A defect in his keratin gene caused him to lose nearly half of his skin while being born and then to produce hundreds of blisters every day, which had to be lanced and bandaged over the course of many years. He could scarcely be touched, as the slightest contact could tear off his skin. He even had blisters in his mouth, which necessitated having a feeding tube inserted into his stomach when he was just a few days old; he lived with the feeding tube for 4 years. He required 24-hour care, which I provided for 3 years. Spencer is now 31, but with all his developmental delays, he is still learning to live independently.

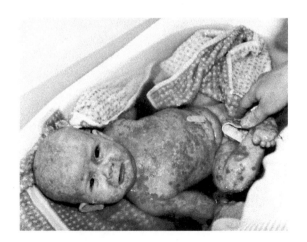